Immortal Illusion

LOST ROYALS OF TRANSYLVANIA

BOOK 1

IMMORTAL
ILLUSION

ALEXA WHITEWOLF

Immortal Illusion
A Lost Royals of Transylvania **novel**

by Alexa Whitewolf
Copyright ©2021 Alexa Whitewolf

Cover design by Y. Nikolova at **Ammonia Book Covers**

ISBN: 978-1-989384-14-5

Editing and formatting by Luna Imprints Author Services
Second Edition

This is a work of fiction.

Names, characters, places, and incidents either are the product of the author's imagination or fictitiously, and any resemblance to actual persons, living or dead, business establishments, events, or locales is entirely coincidental.

10 9 8 7 6 5 4 3 2

ROGUES EXTENDED UNIVERSE— READING ORDER

Author's Note & Acknowledgements

Well, it finally happened. If I was hesitant to write about werewolves way back in 2018 when I started the *Moonlight Rogues* series, I was even more hesitant to write about vampires. I mean, what else could I possibly say that hasn't been said?

And then, the dreams started. And I realized I did, in fact, have a lot to say. So yes, yes, you can have your jokes: a Romanian writer finally writing Romanian vampires. I'm all for a good laugh. But read, enjoy, and please consider dropping a review at the end!

As always, a huge thanks goes to my family. This series was going to be tough from the beginning, but I didn't expect to be consumed day and night (I mean, a girl's gotta sleep, right?). But I was, am, and will be until its finalization! All in good fun... Still, I wouldn't be able to write these words if hubby wasn't feeding me and keeping me from crashing.

Huge thanks also to my beta, Siobhan, for her awesome comments that fleshed this story into its better version. Extra thanks to Annemarie for the last-minute proofread that saved my butt!

And a massive, massive thank you to Y. Nikolova at Ammonia Book Covers whose cover design for this entire series has had me crying tears of joy!

And I'll forever be indebted to you, the reader, for taking a chance and reading this.

Happy readings,
Alexa

GLOSSARY

A few quick things!

Da/nu – yes/no

Frate/sora – brother/sister

Mulțumesc – thank you

Țuică – a freaking fantastic Romanian drink that you should never, ever drink unsupervised!

Scuze – sorry

Draga mea – my darling

Inima mea – my heart

Creatures

Vampir/vampiri— (I loved to use the Romanian spelling here) vampire / vampires

Vârcolac/vârcolaci—Romanian werewolf/werewolves (Note: vrykolakas are the *undead* version)

Stafii—ghosts...of a sort

Don't worry, I won't fill the pages with Romanian dialogue haha – but these vampires insisted on being bilingual!

Chapter 1

Nicolae

Tick. Tock. Tick. Tock.

The damn clock pendulum swings back and forth, forth and back, as annoying as ever. Perched on a wall facing the leather armchair I'm sitting in, it should be inconspicuous. Faded brown wood; a long, oblong shape. Within it, the hands of the clock move incessantly.

Despite the intense aggravation the sound provokes in me, I keep staring at it while sipping from my smooth, red wine. And staring. And staring.

After all, I have all the time in the world, don't I?

A bitter laugh escapes me, and I lift my glass to take yet another deep swallow. The wine's slightly cherry, slightly woodsy taste trickles down my throat. It's about the only thing I can taste—in the way humans understand it.

Vampiri, at least the ones as old as me, from a lineage as dark as mine, are incapable of sustaining themselves on regular human food. Fresh blood, taken from a living, breathing victim? That's the truest elixir of life for us.

Which is why we have to be careful, so as not to give away our existence. Humans have lived this long without being aware of us, and, well, now would be the worst time to actually come out of the shadows. And I'm not just saying that because of the rise of technology and humans' obsession with technological advancements.

My five siblings and I... Well, if you can call them siblings. I guess I should start from the beginning, right?

Centuries ago, we were each chosen by the vampir ruler of these Carpathian lands. He was a great lord, a feared lord, but he was also our father. Some know him as Vlad Țepeș, others as the Demon of Hell. His name—our family name, our crest name, our entire bloodline name—Dracul, means, literally, *the devil*. And he was one, make no mistake about it. He was ruthless and brooding and...lost. But he was our sire, our master, our mentor, and above all? Our only family.

I'm still not sure exactly why he picked me, turning me into what I am now. Over the centuries, I thought long and hard about it, finding no answers. Perhaps he saw something of himself in me, maybe in all of us.

We're an odd bunch, one could say. Some of us look alike, enough to pass as real siblings. For the most part, we have too many differences that set us apart, too many things that humans find disconcerting.

What I *can* tell you is, Father's choice? This new life? It led to me losing whatever humanity I ever had. And I gained siblings, da, but we haven't been a true family for a long, long time. We sure as hell know how to stab each other in the back, though.

"Drinking again, Nico?"

And there goes my peace and quiet. With deliberately slow movements, I place the tall, crystal glass on the ebony table and stand from the armchair, facing my sister.

"Elizabeta."

She looks as perfect as if she'd stepped out of the cover of a human model magazine. Once upon a time, she turned heads in her sweeping gowns, and had men wrapped around her little finger. She was filled with the joy of life...

She still is, in a sense, although that joy has been warped to something much more sinister. And she can still turn heads, even in faded jeans and off-the-shoulder tops... Except for the nasty scar on her right cheekbone, currently hidden by waves of tumbling auburn locks. Its jagged edges have long since healed, and all that remains is an angry, red line from her cheekbone to her jaw, almost contouring that part of her face.

A cold smile graces her coral lips. She knows when I use her full name, it's because I'm annoyed. Not that she cares, really. Liza's anything but a people pleaser.

In a completely sweet voice, she says, "Come hunt with us?"

"Nu, thank you."

A sigh escapes me, and I move past her. All I wanted was some peace and quiet, yet here I am, interrupted yet again. What's a centuries-old vampir got to do to find some blasted peace in this castle? It's big enough for all six of us—or at least it should be.

Maybe we should've bought two.

"You've become a bore, Nicolae!"

I roll my eyes at her childish shout but don't give in to the bait. "Haven't we all?"

Believe me, immortality isn't all it's been made out to be. I should know—I've been a vampir for the better part of five hundred years.

Despite my lie to Elizabeta, I don't go to my quarters. Bedroom? What is the right term, these days?

In the odd times I've indulged in human shows and movies out of pure boredom, I've had to laugh at how simplistic they make their vampiri. According to them, immortality is nothing more than a big party, with a chance to fix everything wrong in one's life and find one's true purpose—and true love.

Fucking lies. All of them.

Immortality isn't a chance to fix mistakes—it's a chance to make them. Over and over and over and over again. Ad nauseum. Humans weren't made to live forever, our brains cannot comprehend the true nature of *eternity*.

Or maybe others do. Maybe it's just mine that's so...so...

Ugh. I wish I'd taken that wine glass with me. Drinking doesn't affect me in the same way it does humans, but it sure numbs the constant thoughts for a few hours. Or until I get a fresh new supply of blood in me.

As I wander the hallways, my eyes take in the dusty portraits in some parts, and barren frames in others. What's left of the carpet I'm stepping on should be burned, as it lies in tatters. Parts of this, we've been able to salvage and return to its former glory. Mainly thanks to Violeta and her good contacts. But it's all a sham, an illusion.

To think how far we've fallen. Half a millennium ago, we were living the great life. A castle with luxuries, opulence, the best of the best. Then again, Father was alive then. He was protecting us. He never warned us of the other clans of vampiri ready to chop off our heads. He never warned what would happen after he disappeared. And he certainly never ensured we'd be provided for.

That bit? We had to do it ourselves.

Then again, Vlad Țepeș was not a regular father.

My thoughts linger on him, on the memories with him. How he'd take us—those of us he'd already turned back in those early years—on hunts of Ottoman packs left on our lands. How we'd all enjoy the sweet, sweet blood of our unwilling preys. And how we'd return home, hailed as heroes.

What possessed him to choose us six, out of anyone else?

Me with my inability to connect. Alexandru with his sensitivity to humans—a joke, now, given he only uses it to sharpen his skills at hunting them. Vlad, the younger of us, with his brilliant mind. Mirabela, the oldest, with her motherly skills—one could say she's lost those, over the years. But she gained many others. Elizabeta—Liza—our crazy sister. And Violeta, easily the best of all of us. She's the light to our darkness, the hope to our despair.

I'll never understand what Father saw in us.

Then again, I'll never understand why he took his own life, either.

On another sigh, I wander the halls some more and exit through a lesser-known passage. The grass outside feels cold against my bare toes. I didn't bother today with a full-on attire. Mirabela's taken the last of our money, our gold, and replenished the castle as best she could. Replenished our closets with human clothes, too. I simply can't make myself wear them just yet.

The jeans on my hips feel tight; the odd, stretchy material of the shirts scratches my skin. Perhaps it's because I'm older than the rest of them, but it will take me a moment to get used to it. Odd, given I care about nothing these days.

I turn my face to the sky, the stars and the blanket of darkness covering us. The air is cool, crisp. We're nearing the end of fall, and soon enough it'll be winter once again. I like winter. I like the purity, so at odds with my own. And the quiet...

As I release a deep breath—one I don't need, but force myself to take—I turn around, taking in our home. Dark towers reach for the sky. Arched windows reflect the light of the moon. Beyond the original wall is a courtyard, surrounded by a fortress keep.

Mirabela found this new home for us, when the last one was burned by a clan of unsettled vampiri.

Though we're supposed to be their princes, their rulers, they still rebel against us. They think our father's death made us weak. They aren't wrong... we did lose our army. And our ability to sire a new one. But are *still* their princes, dammit.

In the end, the decision to run was not mine—I was out-voted by my siblings. Not that I cared enough to voice my opinion, either.

So here I stand, facing my new home, trying to connect together all the pieces that make me, *me*. Centuries have gone by, and I don't remember what I used to be like as a human. Sometimes, in vague nights, I get taken by dreams I believe are memories. They remind me of feelings, emotions, that there's something more out there— something I'm better off without.

So I shove it all down, focus on the useless beyond, the boredom of my current existence, and hope that someday soon, the monotony will be broken. Who knows, I may get lucky sooner rather than later, if those vampiri find us again.

I tear my gaze from the cold walls of this new fortress, instead letting it wander over the ground. For thousands of years, this was one of Vlad the Impaler's lesser-known hangouts. At the bottom of the castle hill there is a village, fully operational and filled with humans. Food for us, according to half of my siblings. The others, well, they feel bad for the weak creatures.

I couldn't care less.

These days, I doubt whether I care for anything, period.

Dismissing the blanket of darkness, I turn to the woods. Their wide expanse is alluring. Their thickness could drown me, allowing me a much-needed respite. The treasure they hide could feed me, and allow me to forget.

I *could* technically join Liza and Alex—it must be he who joined her; Vlad wouldn't hunt this close to the full moon. Not because he turns into a wolf, but let's just say he's not his regular self, either.

Da... We've all got secrets, that's for sure.

"Nico!"

I snap to at Mirabela's annoyed tone. When I turn, she's emerged behind me. Almost too close, given how her flowing raven hair smacks me in the face. She always does have an uncanny way of knowing where I am.

"What is it?"

"Why didn't you join in the hunt?" she asks. "You could've made sure Liza and Alex at least use the time productively and eliminate some problems."

She's always been the quickest of us to adapt. Ironic, since she's the oldest in human years and the one most set in her ways. But as far as human speech and fitting in? Mira could give lessons, especially with how quickly she learned to modulate her new speech pattern and forego the olden.

I took much longer.

A snort escapes me. "Eliminate problems? You must mean create some. Let's be honest, they're no one's saviors, those two."

Her eyes narrow on me, her lips a flat line. "Don't take that tone with me." Her expression becomes pinched, once more reminding me that if vampir immortality was not a thing, she would be my senior. Why Father chose to turn her when she was already in her late-thirties, I'll never understand.

"I didn't realize I had." I step closer. "Just because you're the oldest of us doesn't mean I have to bow down to you. You know I was chosen first."

"Da, and you never let me forget it. The precious *first* of us, the treasure of Father's eyes. If only you'd act with half the responsibility that title comes along with."

Mirabela never did like my casual laissez-faire attitude, even when I wasn't dealing with all the shit that made me shut down. One could say it's always been a point of contention between us—who's the head of this family, and all.

Her eyes flash from blue to red and she moves on me. We're the same height, but I outweigh her thin frame. Even with her vampir strength, she'd be no match for me. Not that she seems to care tonight, as the stark blue in her eyes, so similar to mine, turns to burgundy—a tell-tale sign she's more aggravated than she's letting on.

"Is that how you want to play it tonight?"

I roll my eyes. "Retract your cat claws, sister dear. What is it you want?"

Her jaw clenches, as do her fists. One would think immortality would teach us to better control our impulses. Ha. *Ha!* Joke's on us.

"The muroni must be dealt with, once and for all."

Muroni... Lesser vampiri, nearly rabid; prey to insatiable blood-lust and unable to live or pretend to live as humans. If ever our existence becomes known to humans, it'll be because of their idiocy.

And a nest of them near our new castle? Only bodes trouble. If humans start disappearing all too often, and some of them come to investigate, it'll be us the blame is laid on. That...and muroni are plain disgusting, period. They're the scum of our race.

Once upon a time, I would've cared enough to clean out the new territory we've emerged in. These days? Not so much. Which is probably why my reaction to Mirabela is little more than a shrug. "Not my concern."

I try to head past her, but she blocks me, swift as ever. While we've learned to watch ourselves around humans, we don't bother hiding our ability to move at vampir speed while with each other.

"It should be," she hisses. "Or else I will make it."

Violeta drawls, "Could we all get along, for once?"

I glance over Mira's shoulder at her, sighing. Out of all of us, Violeta makes the most effort. She's able to pass as a human like the best of actresses. The mild makeup helps, as does the fact she's naturally cheerful. With her short bob of black hair, she could be Mira's little sister.

She's also the only one who's been able to reach me these last centuries, probably on account of our history of growing up together.

If she's our hope, then surely, I'm our despair.

I stuff the thought aside and grin at her. "You know how hard that is."

Mirabela scoffs and moves out of my way. "Make yourselves useful and head out in the morning, when the muroni least expect it. I don't like having a nest so close to us."

"It's not the first time, Mira," Violeta says and winks at me. "They multiply like pests, turning humans left and right."

"And one of these days, those humans will clue in that they're not the apex predator. We don't need more of that hassle, not so close to the last one."

That sobers Violeta up, at least enough to turn her pleading gaze to me. "Come track them down with me?"

Gritting my teeth, I offer her a single nod, then leave, trying to control my rage. I've done such a great job that unfortunately when it does come out, it tends to tear everything in its path.

Dawn comes soon enough, and I follow Violeta into the woods. Sunlight doesn't hurt us, given how old we are, but it sure kills the muroni. Though we look down on these lesser beings, I'm not stupid enough to underestimate them.

Neither are Vi and Alex, following in my footsteps.

Though he hunted just last night, he didn't want to miss out on more killing. And to think this guy was training to be a doctor centuries ago... His skill with knives is great, but not to save lives.

I try to jerk my thoughts back to the "mission" at hand. We

moved fast originally, but we slow down now. My siblings are quiet. Too quiet, almost, the closer we get to the ravine and the caves it hosts.

Violeta, behind me, makes some weird noise. I turn to her. "What is it?"

She shakes her head. "Nothing. Let's keep going."

"Let's." Alex grins. He runs a hand through his short blond hair and wiggles his fingers. "I'm in the mood for some murder."

The caves are nearer. Muroni cannot survive in the sun, the humans did get that part right. What they didn't get right is the *why* of the matter. Once upon a time, muroni used to be like us, able to walk in the sun. But abuse of their powers, and constant killing, took a toll on their souls until Darkness itself consumed them. As beings of pure Darkness, they cannot stand Light—metaphorical or literal. Hence our advantage. Though sunlight weakens us, making us move slower if we're in it for prolonged durations, the muroni hide in caves. Ideal hunting grounds for us, one could say.

The problem is by allowing Darkness to consume them, muroni have also given in to the additional powers they get as a result. They can blend with shadows in a heartbeat and, unlike us, they can still shapeshift into their bat forms. Coupled with their unpredictable nature, is it really surprising we've chosen to hunt down and destroy each nest we find? Survival of the fittest, and all.

"Watch yourselves," I whisper to my siblings. I say whisper, but no human ear could have picked up my words, quiet as they are.

We enter the cave, bare feet. Disgusting as it is, we didn't want the crunch of our shoes on something to give our presence away.

Not that it seems to have worked...

Movement to my side alerts me and I grip the muroni by the

neck when he tries to launch himself upon me. My eyes pick up everything in the darkness—the matted, oily hair. The sickly yellow skin. The protruding fangs—we keep ours retracted unless ready to feed. Muroni don't have such qualms. They *want* humans to know what they are.

One of his hands tries to swipe at me with long, mud-caked fingernails. The monster growls. My nails dig into his throat and, soon, I've decapitated him.

Already, I hear Alex's soft sighs of triumph, and know he's killed a few more in the time it took me to take care of this one. Of course, he has. When I think of the man he was as a human, the doctor who wished to help humans, I shake my head. Immortality changes everyone. The good ones, even more so.

I move to another muroni, striding into the depths of the cave. And a third.

Blood gushes over my hands. I hate the mess, but we cannot take any chances that these monsters will heal in darkness.

Lost in the fight, I don't immediately notice Violeta's having issues. It's only as a muroni gurgles his last breath under my attack that I catch her muttered curse. By the time I turn around, she's crowded in by a trio. On a normal hunt, she never would have allowed this to happen. I flag her mistake to discuss later and instead move behind the muroni, gutting them one by one.

When I face Violeta, blood dripping from my hands, she sends me a quick, grateful smile. A moment later, she sways and drops to the ground.

I rush to her, and check her for injuries—no smell of blood, nor anyone else's touch on her. What the hell is going on?

Picking her up in my arms, I seek out Alex. His blonde hair is matted with blood, and his blue eyes seem to gleam with feral intent. I don't think there's a single inch of him that's not covered in blood.

He frowns at me, while one-handedly holding another muroni. A few more stir in the shadows behind him—less than half a dozen. "What's going on?" he asks.

"Not sure. I'll bring her back home. Can you finish up here? Decapitation and burning, Alex. No fucking around."

The glint in his eyes is part madness, part glee. "Gladly."

Chapter 2

Tassa

"Hand me the mint tincture, would you, Tassa?"

I tear my gaze from the distant castle and look through my father's satchel. Once I identify the amber bottle, I hand it over and he puts a few drops in the child's water. While the poor sucker drinks the bitter mixture to help his stomach—and promptly bursts into tears—my gaze is drawn again to the massive gothic structure.

I can't see it fully from the living room window. Though it's perched on a hill outside the village, there are acres and acres of forest that surround it, at times making it play hide and see with whoever's looking upon it. Right now, all I can catch sight of are two grand towers, sweeping, arched windows, dark brick with vines all over... it's about all I can tell from this far under it.

And why it's catching my attention, over and over, I can't tell.

"*Nataşa!*"

Oops. Dad only calls me by my full name instead of my moniker—Tassa—when I'm getting on his last nerve. I jump and follow him, whispering my goodbyes to his patients and exiting their home.

In a village like this, Dad still prefers to be old school and visit his patients directly. One could say the twenty-first century hasn't quite arrived here, in the depth of the Carpathians. We still like to meet up at the local pub every Friday, bake things for each other, and basically nosy up in each other's business. It's a tight-knit community, one I'm lucky to be a part of.

Of course, it also means everyone knows when something goes wrong. Which is why, even as I follow my dad down the street, I avoid the pitying glances that come my way.

We're heading to the other side, walking because he doesn't want to pollute the air. And besides, our old Volkswagen car wouldn't even be able to make the trip. A better dinosaur there has never been.

I shouldn't complain. The walking keeps me in shape, and I need that since I've been overtly curvy from a young age. Insert mental sigh.

"Why were you staring at the Ţepeş castle?" Dad asks from ahead of me.

Shit. I'd hoped he hadn't seen me...

"I wasn't."

Dad—Doctor Ion Mureş to everyone else—slows down his step to keep in time with me. "Don't lie to me, Nataşa. I saw you." The fact he's called me *twice* by my full name means he's really annoyed. Oops. He glances over to said castle only, unlike me, there's a hint of fear in the tightening of the skin around his eyes. "You know the rumors about that place."

In a village like this, ghost stories predominate. Too much so. And for the better part of my childhood, the castle has been home to some creature or another. First it was vârcolaci—our werewolves. Then it was vrykolakas—same werewolves, but the undead version. Then it was stafii—ghosts that could possess the sinners, rumored to stick around because of a deep connection with a loved one... And so on. No one can figure out where these rumors pop up from, but they do and in a spot like this, they spread like wildfire.

The last two years, it's been rumored to be home to—what else— vampires. Or vampiri, as we call them here. Those rumors increased these last few weeks.

Thanks to the popularization of said legends, the local kids keep trying to play pranks on each other—or so I hear whenever I wander to the local pub. My lonesome nature never had me make friends easily and, well, when surrounded by this seclusion? They end up leaving, anyway.

I push aside thoughts of the glamorous lives my old friends are living in the capital or mainstream Europe, and snort. "Come on, Dad. As if that old crap still exists. It's old wives' tales!"

He stops walking and turns to face me. Is it just me, or has his expression grown much paler?

"Never say that!" he hisses, grabbing my arm. "Do not discount the tales of old, they hold more truth than you understand."

I wince at his tightening grip. To say I've never seen him this riled up over some old legends would be correct. So in an effort to pacify him—because what else am I going to do with my only living relative in these parts?—I nod. "All right, all right. *Scuze.*"

He says nothing to my apology, but he does let me go and resumes walking as if nothing happened. There's a new tension in his shoulders, though. And as I follow him to the next few appointments, my gaze becomes more and more inexplicably drawn to the castle, like the proverbial forbidden fruit.

"You're quiet," Dad says as we eat dinner.

I nod, my nose practically in my bowl of perișoare. It's a local soup delicacy, meatballs and vegetables in a soup, and more often than not fills my stomach enough so I don't give in to the carbs craving I always get.

My loosening clothing tells me I've lost weight these last few months, and it's enough of a mental push to keep going at it. Not because I'm so desperate to show my body off to some hunk—rather, I long for the days when I'll be comfortable in my body once again.

Dad's sigh draws my attention, not fooled in the least. "Will you please eat the rest of your soup?"

"I'm eating."

My mumble must not be very convincing, as he clears his throat, demanding silently that I look at him. "I know you're still wary about your weight, darling, but as a doctor even I have to admit you're starting to worry me. You've lost a lot, in too little time."

I shrug. He's a family doctor, not a nutritionist, but I keep the barb to myself. "So? It means I'm closer to my goal weight."

"And what is that, exactly?" He frowns, looking me up and down. "Your clothes have long passed the baggy stage, Tassa. Please. One guy isn't worth all this."

I scowl at him. "How many times do I have to tell you? It wasn't a stupid breakup that caused all this."

"Then was it the fact Petru up and left the country?"

"No!" I slam my hand on the table, wincing at the sting of the hard wood. "I may dislike him for cheating and using my body as the excuse to do so, but Dad, I'm doing this for me. To feel good in my own body and stop second guessing myself."

"And when will enough be enough?"

"Soon," I mutter.

He sighs, not fooled in the least. But like always, he's a pro at changing the subject. "I'm sorry. For earlier, my outburst."

I glance up, surprised. "It's not the outburst that bugs me, Dad, but why it happened. Do you seriously believe all that crap and legends?"

He holds my gaze for a moment, indecision in every wrinkled line of his features. For a sixty-two-year-old, he's still very fit, unlike most men his age I see at the pub. With his white hair swept in a low ponytail, his warm brown eyes and easy smile, my dad could have remarried a long, long time ago. Heaven knows there've been opportunities and plenty of women who sniffed around him after Mom died. But all he ever cared about was his medical practice and me.

"More than you can imagine," he says finally.

"But...why? You're a doctor. You've been out there, seen the world."

It's one of the finer points of my parents' marriage that I never understood. Why would he come back home, when he had the chance to live abroad, to see more, to be more than just some Romanian doctor lost in a village? He could've been a surgeon, made a great name for himself. I know he'd even gotten a letter of acceptance to John Hopkins, one of the most prestigious hospitals in the USA.

"Why did you come back?" I ask, finally owning up to the one question that's been on my mind since I turned twenty-six.

"Because...this is where I was meant to be." He smiles. "I know you don't understand it, Tassa. Your generation, you live in the world of internet and news that travels faster than the speed of lightning. Everything you do is fast, overboard, and exciting. Me and mine, we are different. And those old wives' tales you are so quick to renounce, we believe in them. *I* believe in them."

I take another sip of soup. "Like the latest bit—that the castle's inhabited by Dracula's lost heirs?"

He starts at the mention. I'd heard it last Friday from an old crone at the pub, and it's been on my mind ever since. Everyone knows Vlad Ţepeş'—Dracula's—story here.

He was the old voivode—the prince—of these parts, at a time when Romania didn't exist and this region was called Wallachia. Its treasures were coveted by every empire known to man. Vlad was the man who single-handedly waged a bloody war against the Ottoman Empire and its sultan to save Wallachia. The man who became so crazed with bloodlust he would impale his victims around his castle— not the one in our area, but the one most tourists label as Dracula's Castle, up in Bran.

But heirs? Everyone knows his kids died, each one suffering a more atrocious death than the next.

"Like that, yes," Dad whispers.

I shake my head. "Foolishness."

His cup clatters on the table a bit too loud. "You can ignore the tales as much as you wish, but do not disrespect them. Some died to carry on telling such tales."

Some died? What the— I bite my tongue, knowing that when he's this riled up, it's better not to add fuel to the fire. But my dad never gets this riled up, period. Even with idiotic patients, even with spoiled kids, he keeps his cool unlike anyone I've ever seen. Better than me, that's for sure.

Seeing him this way... I frown, choosing my words wisely. "What exactly do you mean?" *When in doubt, don't assume, but try to confirm.* I learned that from him, too.

He shakes his head. "Nothing." He takes another sip of his soup, followed by a swig of his red wine. "Why were you staring at the castle, anyway?"

"I told you, I like the way it looks, is all."

No point worrying him further with talk of how I've seen candles and lights there, and I'm pretty sure some of the village kids have taken to partying in there. That won't do anything other than upset him—again.

"The way it looks..." His expression softens. "Of course. I'm sorry your plans to study art in Bucureşti fell through, darling."

I shrug, trying to dismiss the sudden weight on my shoulders. "It's fine."

He reaches over to touch my hand. "No, it's not. I know it's what you dreamt your whole life of doing. And Petru ruined it for you, just as you were preparing to leave." A flash of anger rises in his eyes. "I would have words with that boy—"

"Dad, it's fine," I mutter. "He's long gone."

He's silent a moment. "Be that as it may, I appreciate you helping me out with the practice. You always had more of a head for medicine, you know."

I chuckle, trying to alleviate both of our tension.

Dad gives me a faint smile, then sobers up. "And you don't plan to go there, right? To the castle, I mean. Swear to me you won't."

"I promise." Jeez, what got into him tonight? "Dad, I know you're worried about me, and about what'll happen to me because I'm still single—a perfectly acceptable fact at twenty-six, I might add—but you have to stop making yourself this anxious."

"You're right, of course." He attempts a smile. "You're perfectly right."

He goes back to eating his soup, but his movements are stilted, almost tired. Now I really do wish I had the courage to go up there. To see for myself what the whole mystery is. And maybe check out those lights and where they're coming from... I can only imagine the views from that spot. Still, the stories ingrained in me since I was a child prevent me. I may be reckless, but not that much.

The vampiri feed on kids at night.

The vrykolakas will eat your heart if you go out partying.

Don't bleed, or they'll come for you like the sharks in the water.

Idiocies. Ramblings of old people with nothing better to do than spread rumors and scare every uneducated soul here.

The moment I think that, shame courses through me. It's not fair. Most of our residents are born here, but also educated. They went to some of our best universities in Cluj or Bucureşti or Sibiu, and always came back. Put themselves to work, made something of themselves, and raised families.

It's not a bad legacy to be part of.

But is it bad to want more for myself?

To travel, to see the world and its beauty, to meet other people... Maybe even a man. Maybe not. But just to be out there, try new foods, speak new languages, and learn new things. Sometimes, I feel like I'm stuck in medieval times here, not living in the twenty-first century.

"I'm tired," Dad says, rising from his seat. "Tomorrow's a busy day. I think I'll take an early night."

"Okay. I can clean up here, if you want."

"Please." He heads toward his room and turns to me. "Thank you, Tassa. For being so sweet."

"Of course, Dad."

He's about to head into his room, when a knock sounds on the door. Followed by another. And another. Then fists. One of the bowls drops from my hands, and I shriek at the increasing tempo. No one in this village, no matter what the emergency, would be so rude as to nearly tear down our door off its hinges, especially this late at night.

As if to spite me, a moment later, the door bursts off those same hinges, and a man with a shaved head steps in. He's wearing jeans and a dark maroon coat over his dirty white shirt, and his eyes are narrowed. They glint weirdly in the light.

"Finally. Did I have to come all the way here for what I need?"

What? I— "...Dad?"

Dad moves in front of me, shielding me with his body. "I would have come tomorrow. It's been a few busy days—"

The man smiles coolly. "You had all the time you needed, and then some. Now, we've come to collect."

Another man steps out from behind him, equally bulky and scary. When his eyes land on me and he smirks, I know I'm in trouble.

Chapter 3

Nicolae

Needless to say, Violeta's little snafu left us all feeling out of sorts. It's how I find myself spending the entire day by her bedside, interrupted only by one of my siblings coming on by. Alex to report he wiped out that particular muroni nest. He had a look at Violeta, even went by the greenhouse she's created in a corner of the castle for herself, but could pick up nothing even with his medical knowledge. His frustration at said lack of anything drove him quickly out of the room. It's the angriest I've ever seen him at himself.

Liza then came by to be annoying—but underneath it all, worried. Vlad with theories as to what might have happened... And Mirabela, to sit by and stare. Helpless. Just like me.

"It makes no sense," she says for the fifth time that day. "Violeta's been the strongest of us."

I snort. "Maybe it's that crap grass she's been smoking."

Mira glares at me. "It's her one vice, same as drinking is yours. And you know full well it can't be the cause of all this. None of it makes sense."

I let out a breath, and nod. It's true. If Vi had developed some kind of reaction to the grass—pot, whatever the humans call it—it would've shown up earlier. She's been smoking it for the better part of two years, now. One of us would have seen it, whatever *it* is. But this came out of nowhere.

"We need help."

The words are alien in the air, and I look at Mira in surprise. "Us? Ask for help? Do you forget what happened the last time we did that?"

Lots of bloodshed. Lots of lives lost. And we escaped in the nick of time.

She frowns at me. "It won't be like that. We made mistakes then, we weren't careful. We thought that because centuries had passed, the clans of vampiri would've forgotten their anger toward us. But they didn't, and now we're even more aware of that than normal." Her blue gaze settles on our sister. "But Violeta is too important for us all to lose, and I refuse to allow whatever this is to continue. Humans go to doctors when they're sick. Alexandru is the closest thing we have to one, and he can't even figure out what's wrong. We both know it's because he's not aware of all these human developments. His dislike of them is worse than mine." She purses her lips. "So, we will get one for her."

Thanks to the many centuries I spent at her side, I pick up on her choice of words. "*Get* one? As in, we don't need to seek one?"

Mirabela looks away, fidgeting with the hem of her shirt. "No. There's one in the village."

"And how is it you know that, dear sister?"

She's silent for a long time. Unlike her, really. I've yet to see the day my sister is at a loss for words, meaning she's choosing them wisely.

"Tell me."

She lifts her chin and meets my gaze full-on. Her own is blazing blue, like a stormy night in summer. "Well, how do you think I knew where to find us a new spot to hide, hmm? Everywhere we go, did it not strike you as weird that lately, nothing comes to bother us?"

It had. If I'd bothered to pay attention, which, most of the time I didn't.

"Ah, I forgot. You care about nothing and no one—lucky you."

I frown at her. "Cut the sarcasm, Mira, I'm not in the mood."

"In the mood?" She stands, towering over me, her body trembling.

Instead of focusing on her, my eyes are taking in the room and everything she's doing. Nothing is exploding—not yet, at least. Good thing. Her temper will get us into trouble one of these days.

"That's the thing, Nico. You have time to be *in a mood*. The rest of us don't."

I snort. "Alex and Liza do."

"But they're not the ones whose fault it is we had to run this time."

I scowl. "I wondered how long it would take you to bring it up. You've held your tongue enough, hmm?"

She stands, towering over Violeta's body. Though she keeps her voice low, it's icy and filled with distaste. "Damn right, I have. I thought you'd snap out of it eventually. But it's been two hundred years and still you haven't bothered to deal with your emotions."

"There's nothing to deal with."

"He was your friend."

"My guard."

"Your *friend*. Much as you hate admitting it."

I look away, wanting to shut her up as the memories try to break past the mental cage I shoved them in. *And where I intend they remain. Forever.*

"Silva's death was not your fault," Mira says. "He was meant to protect us. And he did."

"If it hadn't been for my stupid infatuation with that human, he wouldn't have been in the crosshairs. None of us would have. You know that."

My tone is biting enough that she shuts up. At least momentarily. A tidal wave of regret tries to rise inside me, but I push it back down. I've gotten very good at this over the centuries. Even better in the last two.

"Nico..." Mira moves around the bed to stand in front of me. "You have to snap out of it."

"Maybe I would, if you'd stop reminding me."

Her scowl is back, just like that. "You don't make it easy to converse, do you?"

"Because I don't *want to*. Get that through your head. I don't want to hear your opinions about me. I don't want to hear how I should care more. And I certainly don't want to be reminded of Silva's death and how my rage and genocide of an entire vampir clan caused their brethren to come after us. Deal?"

"No. No deal. Elizabeta and Alexandru are younger than us. We should be able to offer them guidance, especially given how they've been acting. They *need us* to keep them in check. Humans have hurt them both and it won't be long before they lose the last bit of humanity they have left. Do you care? Of course not." She scoffs, her face twisted in a disgusted expression. "You, who was chosen first, technically our head of house even though I was the eldest in human years before being turned... You've retreated into nothingness and left me to do all the work." She tosses her hair over her shoulder, and starts braiding it. "So, da, going back to your question, I made decisions without you. One of those is relying on humans. In the last few spots we've lived, I've ensured there is an Order, of sorts, to protect us. Humans have frolicked around us for ages, so it was just a matter of finding the right ones and having the right amount of bribery."

"You... *Humans*?"

I think sometimes Mira hates them more than even Alex and Liza. They might've lost themselves because of human-related evil, but Mirabela lost her entire family to their corruption.

She sneers. "Da, humans. They may only be good for food, but they've also been protecting us. And it's through them that I know there is a doctor in this village. A rather good doctor, one who treats vampiri as well as humans."

I'm reeling from all the information. A glance at Violeta confirms she's still asleep, so I jerk my head toward the door, and we exit her room.

"Who is this doctor? Has he been checked?"

"We don't have time to check," Mira says. "The Order swears by him. Just go fetch him. He alone can help Violeta. Believe me, I'm gagging as I'm saying this at the thought that one of *them* can help one of *us*. That despite our centuries of knowledge, we are helpless in this. But..." She walks past me, then adds over her shoulder, "This isn't up for debate, Nico. His house has a green-painted door, and it's the closest to the woods. Now go get the damned doctor and don't come back without him. Whatever it takes."

The night is darker tonight. I should've gone out as soon as Mira told me to, instead of taking an hour to nurse my ego. For someone who doesn't care and pretends to be indifferent, I'm sure starting to wake up to old feelings.

For a moment, as I walk through the woods on my way down, I wonder why that is. Is it Violeta's unexpected...whatever it is? Or is it the memories of Silva, his friendship, and ultimate demise because of my own doing?

I shake my head and focus on my feet moving to their full capacity—my vampir speed. The forest blurs around me, becoming nothingness, and then I'm on the edge of the village. The night is quiet, and my eyes immediately seek the green-painted door closest to me.

There are two, opposite each other.

A growl escapes my throat. *Typical Mira.*

Shadows become mine. I move with stealth, letting the darkness coat me. We might have lost our shifting abilities a few centuries back, but one thing we haven't lost is our ability to stay coated in darkness. We can't *turn* to shadows, like muroni can, but they still seek us—protecting us, hiding us from peering eyes.

Tonight is no different. All I have to do is lift my hand and they come to me like living things.

It's not magic. Vampiri can't hold nor create magic, given we're undead. But Darkness seems to respond to us as easily as to dark mages, perhaps because it recognizes the blackness of our hearts. It takes time to master this to the extent I have, but then again, I had a teacher. My siblings aren't all as lucky.

My thoughts shift back to Father for a fraction of a second, before I pull them back to the present. *What is this, a day of remembrance or something?*

Once I'm sure I'll remain unseen, I move closer to the two houses.

They may be similar, but something's wrong inside one—I smell blood in the air, thick and fresh. The metal scent raises the hairs at the back of my neck. A human would move cautiously. I step out of the shadows and burst through the door of the blood-tinged house.

Immediately, I am aware of three things. First, the blood is coming from three separate people, and two of them are very much dead.

Second, part of the house is in flames, which should be enough to deter me from advancing since fire can actually cause irreparable damage to us.

And third, a human girl is staggering to one corner, holding the side of her head as if she's been hit. A man is on the ground behind her, a pool of blood underneath him. And a second one is advancing toward her, his focus clear. His hand goes to his pants, ready to unbuckle his belt, even as his other arm reaches for the girl.

He doesn't hear me coming. The scent of her fear, her confusion, permeates the air. His ruthlessness is also there, just underneath. In the steady thump-thump of his heart. The quickening of his heartbeat. A single-minded focus to hurt. To own.

I don't think. A red haze descends on me—the same one I can't always control—and in the next moment I've caught onto his extended hand and ripped it off him. It snaps out of its socket with an ugly ripping sound. The force of my yank also drags him away from her, screeching and shouting in pain.

The girl slumps against the wall, struggling to stay up, and slipping to the ground. Her glazed eyes fall on me—holding onto the bloody, ripped off, extended hand—and then flutter closed. I don't know if she saw me, let alone registered what she saw, nor do I care.

I'm beyond reason, beyond rationalization. Anger fills my every vein, a drug as addictive as the blood I smell around me.

I slam him into the wall. His brown eyes are wide, filled with fear. But there's also something unsettling, something not quite human in them. My eyes shift to his neck—the two puncture wounds there. Normally they would be subtle, or already healed, but these are jagged, almost as if someone tore into him.

The rational part of my brain, somewhat buried by the rage, says to stop. To question him. To find out what he's doing in the house of a doctor, killing him and trying to hurt a—presumably innocent— female.

But that part is too *soft,* too *weak*, in this moment, so I ignore it like I always do when this demon takes over me. In one angry move, I rip out his throat, denying myself the blood despite the hunger rearing its ugly head.

I watch as he slumps, blood gushing everywhere. Eyes fixated on me, then on her. And when he finally drops down, dead for good, I turn back to her.

She's still huddled in a corner, her breath coming out in pants. All I can see is her huddled form, her clothes torn on one side, revealing a bare arm and shoulder.

Eons ago, I used to find the female flesh appealing. Now, it has jaded me as much as everything else. That doesn't mean what nearly happened here doesn't get to me. In an inexplicable way, the fact something was taken from her—or attempted to be taken—without consent, makes me uncomfortable.

The female hasn't moved from her position, and despite the roaring flames, I move to her slowly.

If she saw what I did, the damage I caused, and she awakes, she'll be fearful—probably even scared enough to run off. But I can't leave her here, not until I know what she saw, and see if maybe she can help my sister. If she was living in the doctor's house, maybe she's his daughter?

I glance around quickly, noticing some pictures on the walls. One is of the man on the ground, with the white ponytail now tinged with blood. The person next to him is the same woman huddling away from me now. The resemblance in their features and the age gap tells me enough.

Daughter, then. I was correct.

Indecision wars in me. I could leave her here. Let her die in the flames, as there's no way she'll get to her wits fast enough. I've done what Mira asked and came to seek the doctor, not my fault he's dead.

If you'd come earlier...

I shove the nagging voice again. It's trying to bring back that feeling of guilt.

Although, perhaps if I *had* come earlier, this could have been avoided. Which means I at least owe it to this woman to get her out of the house. But if I do that, I can't let just leave her in village, lest she remember what she saw.

Decisions, decisions.

The crackling of flames burning through wood brings me back from my three-second perusal.

"We must go," I say to her.

Still nothing.

I move closer and gently pull her ripped shirt back over her shoulder. She still doesn't move. Then I kneel in front of her, eye to eye with her. Her eyes flicker open, but the pupils are too enlarged, unfocused—she isn't here with me.

Fuck.

I take a look around. Again, the idea hits me, warring with me. I could leave her here, let the fire consume her. But if the dead man is her father, then perhaps she may be useful yet. And Mira did tell me to fetch a doctor...

I quickly grab a bag and shove some supplies, anything that looks noteworthy. Tinctures in dark amber bottles, notebooks that haven't been consumed by the fire, and a few clothes that carry her scent. In a corner is a doctor's kit, marked by a symbol that hasn't changed much in decades, and I take that, too.

Then I return to her side. "I have to touch you and bring you with me. I'm sorry."

No answer.

I hook the bag's strap over my shoulder, then kneel. The thump-thump of her heart goes from a heady drum to a fainter one—she's fainted. When I pick her up, I'm surprised at how lightweight she feels to me, even with my vampire strength. Why's she hiding herself under these baggy clothes, when the body underneath is all womanly curves?

The question surprises me. If a woman's body has not caught my eye for some time, surely the decision as to why this particular one hides her body should not be on my radar.

I shake my head. Balancing her with one hand, and the supplies with the other, I head out the door. Flames crackle behind me, and I hear the groan of the wood as it protests. By the time I hit the castle, the house will have burned in smoke, unless someone stops the raging fire. I have no vested interest in doing that.

Already, lights are coming on in some houses. Soon, humans will emerge and moan and bemoan over their lost friend. Maybe some will actually mean it. Maybe someone will even come by and save what's left of the house.

Or, maybe, like is more often the case with humans, they'll stand by and watch and take pictures. Remember what was, and regret what could have been.

Whatever the case, it's not my problem.

So I shake my head, grip the woman tighter in my hands, and allow myself the vampir speed I've been blessed with, disappearing into the woods.

Chapter 4

Tassa

I'm dreaming. I must be. There's no other way to explain the sensation of flying, of running away from everything. From the pain in my mind, in my soul—why does it hurt so much? Why does it hurt to breathe?

And then a voice, deep in the darkness, telling me we have to go. But I don't want to listen, I don't want to come back. I'm somewhere in my own mind, protected, at peace, away from the darkness.

So I cower away and refuse to listen, giving in instead to what my body begs, and I pass out.

"Dad, how do you do what you do?"

He looks up from the potion he's mixing, pushing his glasses back on his nose and smiling down at me.

Down? I'm...small again?

I wrinkle my nose at the scent of the dandelions he's crushing. I hate that damn tea, though I can't deny it helps keep my periods regular. But the taste, ugh, the damned taste!

"Do what, my dear?"

"Well, watch people die."

He stops, moves the pot off the stove, and comes to kneel in front of me. His eyes are serious, the laughter gone from his features as he gets level with me.

"What makes you ask that?"

I gulp. If I admit to having followed him, then he'll get mad. But there's no way to back out, and Dad raised me to be honest. In a whisper, I admit, "I followed you to Uncle Stan's house, and saw...how...he died."

Dad bows his head, and I reach out, putting a hand over his shoulder.

It's a memory, I realize. *Not a dream. I must be...ten? Maybe eleven years old?*

I may have been young, but even so, I knew the pain of such a death. He'd been close to my uncle, had enjoyed their nights out, and now he was gone. And so close following my mother's death, too.

Finally, after a long moment, Dad looks up and blinks away his tears. "With a lot of gumption, my dear. Sometimes in life, you have to do the hard things, to live life even when all your loved ones are gone."

"Like with Mommy?"

"Yeah, like with Mommy." He ruffles my hair. "Now come help me."

But as he turns away, this time the door bursts open—not like in the real memory.

It wasn't like that! I shout, or rather open my mouth to shout, but it's to no avail. I'm frozen, watching all over again as Dad gets attacked. A knife to his stomach, and he's dropping to the ground, groaning. Blood pools around him. The knife is shoved again into his chest.

There's a second man, a younger one, and he comes for me. And I know in that moment that he'll hurt me, and I have to stop him, because there's no one around to help me. Because Dad's.... Dad's...

I tear my gaze from the approaching man in my nightmares, only to see Dad on the ground, a vacant look in his eyes. Just like Uncle Stan. Just like Mommy.

No. No. *No!*

"No!" I scream, jumping awake in bed.

It takes a moment for my eyes to adjust to the darkness. My heart is pounding, as I desperately try to.... To what? To breathe. To remember to *breathe.*

Tears choke my throat, snot fills my nose, and breathing is the least of my worries. I bury my head in the bedsheets, trying to stifle my sobs. I'm not home—I don't know where I am, but that question is the least of my worries when...Dad.

Dad.

Dad.

"Dad," I whisper out loud. But he's gone. And it hits me that I'm...alone. For good. No more family. No more relatives. No more anyone. Just me.

Nicolae

"What possessed you to bring a *human* into our home!?"

I pour a large glass of red wine, trying to keep cool in the face of my sister's screeching. We're in the library, a few floors down and it's highly unlikely the human will hear us, but still.

"Mirabela wanted the physician. He's dead."

Liza huffs and puffs behind me. I hear a snort from Alex— unsurprising. If anyone'll be even more against having a human in our castle than Liza, it's him. But their reasons have no business here, not when Violeta needs our cooperation.

"She is useless to us!" Liza screeches.

I turn to face her, just as Vlad says, "You don't know that."

"I know better than all of you!"

Vlad's expression softens, his gaze on her scar. "I know what they did, Liza. We all know, and we'd never let anyone hurt you. But not all humans are alike."

"Like hell, they're not!"

"Watch your tone," I say, firmly enough that Liza shuts her mouth. At least temporarily. I know my younger sister, and silence has never been her forte. "If she hears you, we'll have a problem on our hands faster than you would've thought possible."

"Then let her fucking hear me," Liza hisses. "I don't give a shit about a human's life. They never did about mine. I'd rather snap her neck and you best hope I don't get a chance to."

A muscle clenches in my jaw, and I force myself to relax it. "If you do so, then I'll have done all this for no reason. And we may never know whether she can or can't help Violeta. Do neither of you care for her?"

Alex stares at me. "Funny, coming from you."

I force myself to take a deeper gulp of wine. Out of everyone, he and Liza test my patience more than most. After I deem myself calm enough, I say, "Meaning?"

"You've had your head so far up your ass, it's not like you care much about any of us."

"Yeah," Liza adds. "Why don't you go back to being a shadow, hmm? Out of sight, out of mind."

A sigh escapes me. Of impatience. "This isn't about me, and what I did or didn't do centuries ago. No one's more aware of my shortcomings than I am. This isn't about you, either, or your own mistakes and preconceived notions. This isn't even about Alex being unable to help Violeta despite having a medical background."

He glares at me, taking a step closer. "Maybe if I hadn't been busy killing to keep us safe since you went in Indifferent La-La-Land—"

"Enough," Vlad intervenes. "Can we please stop? I think what Nico's trying to get at is, this has everything to do with Violeta, period."

"*Thank you.*" I level my glare on the other two. "Now if you're done trying to pick a fight with me... Have either of you noticed anything odd about Violeta lately?"

Head shakes all around. At least they've stopped trying to crucify me.

Mirabela walks in then, her expression thunderous. "I said get the doctor, not a pet!"

"She isn't a pet." I grit my teeth. "She's the doctor's daughter."

"That still doesn't make *her* a doctor!" She throws her hands up in the air, stomping away from me. "For fuck's sake, Nico, you had one job."

"And I got there too late." It kills me to admit it, but if I hadn't dallied around here for an hour, I would've been there on time. Probably might've stopped it from happening.

Mirabela focuses her icy glare on me. "You better hope she knows some medicine. Otherwise, I'll have thoughts on how she can earn her keep around here—at least until her veins are empty."

"Not the time, Mirabela." Vlad shakes his head. He, like me, detests talk of using humans. Unlike me, it's because he actually cares.

I slam the glass on the fireplace mantel. "Are you all done? She will help Violeta. Soon as she snaps out of whatever has her mind on hold."

The door opens then, and Violeta walks in. She's only wearing her nightgown and a thick bathrobe over it. Dark circles are prominent in her face, and she looks...smaller. Fragile. The moment she passes the threshold, she sways on her feet. Alex, closest to her, moves in to catch her before she falls.

"I'm fine," Violeta says after a beat and pushes him away. Then she pulls a joint out of the pocket of her robe, and lights it up, arching her eyebrow. The sweet smell permeates the air, even as her gaze travels over each of us. "What's with the dead faces?"

She's pretending there's nothing wrong. How long has she been doing this, to hide it from us? A nagging feeling grips me.

"You're sick," Liza says. "That's what! Fainting in the middle of a nest of muroni... Least you could've done is tell us. What if it's contagious?"

Violeta snorts, and takes another puff. Am I the only one who sees the trembling of her hands? "It's not. If it was, you would've gotten sick a long time ago."

Alarm bells start ringing in my mind. "Vi..."

She shakes her head. "Forget it. What's with the human smell?"

Everyone turns to me, and the subject I've been trying to avoid is now full center again.

"Nico decided to take a pet," Alex says.

I scowl at him. "I did not take a pet." To Violeta, I say, "When you got sick, Mirabela told me of a doctor in the village, one who knows vampiri and their ailments. I went to get him, but he was already dead. His daughter was there, and I saved her from a burning house."

Her eyebrows raise higher. "You? Save a human?"

I roll my eyes. "It's not that surprising."

She takes another puff, then blows smoke in the room. Vlad has already moved to the stained-glass windows and pushed one open, mercifully letting in some cool breeze.

"And, what, you think she can heal me?" Vi smirks.

"We hope so," Mira says. "But you don't seem impressed. What, exactly, is going on with you?"

Vi shakes her head, ignoring the question. "All right, I'll bite. I'll let her treat me, if she can. Where is she?"

"Upstairs, but..." It's my turn to pause. "She's not herself. Trauma of the night."

"I'll go speak to her." Violeta sighs, puts out her joint, and leaves the room.

Tassa

I killed a man.

I killed a man.

I. Killed. A. Man.

The thought won't stop going round and round my head like a stupid carousel. Even as I'm pacing this room.

Where am I, even? Someone saved me from the house. I remember dark blue eyes, the color of an inky sky in summer...And strong hands. I must be at his place. Probably someone from the village, who heard me screaming?

For the first time, a sense of gratitude washes over me—that I'm in a village where people actually care, and not one where they let me die a horrible death.

Death...

I killed a man.

I didn't mean to. But when it became apparent what he was going to do, I had no choice. He'd already killed my dad. No way was I letting him touch me.

All I remember is taking Dad's scalpel and shoving it in his eye. The squelch it made as it went in, his silent cry, and then his body dropping over me. I'd shoved him off, tried to make for Dad, but he was on the floor, not moving, a pool of blood around him...

Dad... Dad. A sob escapes me, then another, and the third gets lodged in my throat. I slide to the ground near the door, and let my sobs wash over me. How could he be gone? He was my last link to this world, my last blood relative.

When I run out of tears, I sniffle and stare into nothingness. The face of the man comes back to me again. He's dead. I shouldn't fear him. But what had he wanted, in the first place? He'd had a wild glint in his eyes, like he'd gone mad.

Grief weighs heavy in my chest, an all-too-familiar weight. I need... I miss... Mom first, my uncle next, my cousins moved out... And now I'm alone.

Alone. Alone. Alone.

An echo in my mind.

One soon drowned out by anger, rising like a slow boil in my veins.

Who did this? And why?

My dad was the nicest man. No one in the village had a grudge against him, or motivation to kill him. So what would have caused a stranger to come after him like that?

Dad took his secrets to the grave. Now it's up to me to uncover them. *Sometimes in life, you have to do the hard things, to live life even when all your loved ones are gone.*

I move to the bed, where there's a bag with some belongings. The man who saved me must've grabbed them—I make a mental note to thank him. Truth is, I can wallow in self-pity and let this grief consume me... or I can actually do something.

I reach for the zipper. Then I stop, my thoughts on my savior.

Perhaps I should be worried I'm in an unknown house. But a glance around has revealed nothing suspicious, and rather than be scared about something idiotic, I choose to focus on what matters. Which is my father's death, and the reason behind it.

Once I know that, I can leave and go report it to the police. They'll take care of finding any other people responsible. Unless the man acted alone...

Decided, I undo the zipper and open it. A fresh wave of thyme and rosemary smells wafts from it. My dad's mixed remedies. Tears spring to my eyes anew—I thought I'd run out of them, but there is no such thing.

I dig in until I find his leather-bound notebook, where he wrote all his appointments. Then I sit in and read. Dad had mentioned going to see the man the next day, meaning there should be some hint of his identity in here.

An hour later, or what feels like an hour, I'm nowhere farther ahead. I've been with Dad to all of the appointments mentioned within. Which means this guy was not after him for his remedies. He wasn't some addict.

Then, what?

A million possibilities run through my mind, each as unlikely as the next. My father was not into drugs, or gambling, or any vices. He rarely even drank, unless it was with me. We have no opioid crisis in our little village, meaning there was no motive to kill him for the few drugs he did have on him.

So what could have possessed this man to show up out of nowhere and take away his life?

Anger rushes through me, sudden and breathtaking.

I'm glad the man is dead. Because if he wasn't, I probably would go hunt him down and kill him, for taking someone so precious from me, without even giving a reason.

But...wait. Wasn't there a second man? I try to think back. The door burst open, one walked through, said, "We've come to collect," and then another... But I don't remember him leaving. I don't remember killing him. I just...

I bite my lip. Maybe there was only one man. And maybe this whole thing was an unlikely random act. Or maybe it wasn't. Either way, I'm still with no answers.

Someone knocks on the door, breaking me out of my thoughts. I get off the bed and turn to it, and a woman steps through. She's wearing a bathrobe over her thin frame. It's the first thing I notice in a woman—a stupid, shallow comparison I can't help myself from making so I can see how I'm lacking next to her. And it always starts with the weight.

Her features are soft, almost cherubic, with a heart-shaped mouth and wide blue eyes. The ugly, purple circles under them take away some of her beauty, and the whiteness of her skin is concerning.

I think back to the man who'd saved me. Could this be his girlfriend—or his wife?

"Hi," she says softly. "My name is Violeta. I'm Nicolae's sister, the man who saved you."

"Oh. Hi. I'm... Nataşa. Everyone calls me Tassa." It's the most I can strum up, my thoughts swarming. Sister. I see no resemblance in their facial structure, other than the blue eyes... But his were dark blue. Weren't they? Then again, not all siblings look alike.

"I hope you don't mind, but he told me about what happened with your father. I'm very sorry."

I wipe at my eyes, nodding, since a lump seems to be permanently lodged in my throat.

"We've only moved here recently, so I didn't know him, but... Feel free to stay here as long as necessary."

I clear my throat. "I have to go to the police. Tell them what happened."

"Of course." Something flickers across her expression. "Nico can take you in the morning, but you should probably rest off the shock."

If anyone needs rest, it's her. The purple bags under her eyes say as much, but it would be rude of me to point it out.

"Thank you." When she turns to leave, I add, "Why was your brother around the area? When... it happened?"

"He was coming to seek your father for a remedy."

I frown. "For himself?"

"No." Violeta smiles. "For me."

Her self-deprecating smile hits me, like she's just humoring him though she knows there's nothing to be done.

My mind automatically lists her symptoms, or what I can see. And then a pang hits me, hard enough to cut off my breathing. Dad would've known...

"Don't worry about it," she says. "I'll be fine. Try and get some rest. Let me know if you need anything, my room is just down the hall."

I nod, vainly attempting to rein in my panic.

The moment she leaves, I let out a gust of air and try to gulp in quick, shallow breaths.

Don't hyperventilate.

Don't.

Nicolae

Violeta exits the room just as I pass it. I tell myself I'd been heading this way anyway, and it's only normal to check on a human I saved. My sister already narrows her gaze on me in a silent question.

"I wanted to see how she was," I say, the words unfamiliar on my tongue.

She watches me quietly for a long moment. Her skin is paler than before, and the way she's standing, with the candlelight on her features highlighting the dark circles under her eyes, makes her seem...tired.

After another beat, she says, "This isn't one of your toys, Nico."

"I resent that."

It's rare she calls me out on my bullshit. Even rarer that she does it in a moment like this, when she's at her weakest.

"Resent it all you want," she says. "We all know you don't take interest in something just for the sake of it. Even less so if it's a human."

I open my mouth to deny it, then stop. It's true. All of it. Unless there's something in it for me, I take no interest in it. Careless, indifferent, ruthless—they've called me all of it. It has been the truth I've lived by since... well. For a long time.

"Just be polite," she says. "She's still reeling from the events, so tread carefully. I know you praise yourself for having forgotten your human emotions, but dig deep for this one, Nico. If you want her to help, that is, and not run away screaming."

She turns to leave, but I stop her. "Vi?"

"Yeah?"

"How are you feeling?"

She graces me with a sad smile. "Like a walking corpse, frate."

I watch as she heads down the hallway, then turn my focus to the door. Hesitate. Debate with myself. She's human, after all. It's been a while since I've been around them, in the sense of conversing. Normally, I just drink my fill of their blood, glamour them to forget, and leave.

Blood...

In the house, during the fight, I hadn't cared for this woman's blood. Now? I can hear her heartbeat, her pulse, almost like a song.

Get over yourself. It's one human.

With a sigh, I reach up and knock.

"Come in."

I step into the room and she turns from the window. Eyes like molten gold and chocolate combined stare back at me. With confusion, desolation, sadness. So damn sad.

I make sure to keep my distance, just in case she's wary of me. "I am not here to hurt you."

She nods, slowly. As if through a fog of memories. I brace myself—if she remembers what I did, this will be over before it begins. Best I be careful.

"You were there..."

I clear my throat. "Da. I was looking for your father."

Something about the way I say it causes a flash of fear to cross her features. "Why?"

I frown, trying to read her body language. Trying to mirror it with mine. Slow breaths. Relaxed muscles. Moving slowly. Painfully slow.

Does she even know what her father did for a living, besides helping out the local humans? *Tread carefully*, Violeta had said. No time like now. But while I must be careful, I have to also figure out what she knows. It would be easy enough to glamour her and get her to tell me what I want. As easy as staring into her eyes and pulling out the thoughts I want. Then making her forget I ever did that. But with how fragile human minds are, I'm more wary of frying her brain given her existing shock.

"I needed his help. My sister, she's sick."

She frowns. "Yes, she told me. I'm sorry to hear it."

Odd. She just lost her father, and she looks like she's on the verge of passing out from exhaustion, yet she finds time to apologize for something that's not even her fault. If that's the way she functions, then I'll be able to get what I want all too easily...

"I'm afraid we don't know what she's sick with, but it seems...serious. Although, I'm sorry. I forgot to introduce myself. I'm Nicolae—Nico." Best I don't give her my last name just yet.

"Nataşa, but everyone calls me Tassa," she murmurs, almost on autopilot.

I don't know what prompts it. The edge in her voice, like she's about to break. The way she's clenching her jaw, like she's barely holding herself together. Or the way she blinks furiously, refusing to cry. But I find myself saying, "Tassa. That's not very Romanian sounding."

For better or worse, my words jerk her gaze in my direction. Their dimness fades for a brief second, replaced by something fiercer. "Yeah, I've heard that all my life. Most people in these parts don't like outsiders, and they use the older Russian diminutive Taşa. My dad travels and he much prefers Tassa because...because..."

As quick as it came, the brief fire is extinguished. She curls into herself, ducking her head and hiding her gaze from me. Just when I'd been so close to determining the exact shade of her eyes... Then, even more surprisingly—or perhaps not, given she's in a room with an undead monster—she glances at the distance between us and hugs herself.

What does that simple gesture mean? Is she afraid?

Luckily for me, Tassa puts me out of my misery. "I... I didn't mean it. To hurt him."

I frown. Hurt who?

"The man... He'd been trying to... That is to say, it was self-defense."

Ah. She's talking about the other man. Now I understand why his bleeding body was at her feet.

"It's all right," I say just as softly. "I'm sorry I didn't get there sooner."

"No. He... you, you came just in time. You saved me from the house. And...the other man?"

She says it like a question. If she doesn't remember, should I hide it from her? Or go along with it?

I nod. "There was a second man, yes."

Her eyes widen. "So, you stopped him. Thank you...for taking me out of there, and stopping him from doing...worse."

"Worse than traumatize you?"

She looks away. "There are worse fates."

"I'm sorry." What is it about this human that's making me apologize and, worse, *mean it*?

"Thank you." She clears her throat. "And I'll go to the police, tomorrow. Your sister said I could sleep here?"

I tilt my head to the side, hoping she'll take it for agreement. She's in a vulnerable place, it's best I don't start disagreeing with her about the cops. At least, not just yet.

"Of course, as long as you need. I'm afraid when I took you out of the house, it was already in flames and..." I trail off, leaving it to her imagination.

She sags against the window, tears filling her eyes. "My father's body."

I've never understood human attachment to the corpses of the dead. Perhaps because I'm part of the walking dead, or jaded by immortality, or both. But seeing how she curves into herself, the pain at losing the last link to her father—that part, I can relate to.

Long ago, I'd lost mine. Not my sperm donor of my living human life, but the man who had given me immortality itself. And that had hurt more than anything, a pain I didn't think I could ever escape. Seeing Tassa, the way grief seems to clutch her in its hands, I'm even more aware of that pain. One I had long since closed off in a forgotten recess of my mind.

"I'm sorry."

That's three times I've apologized now, for something out of my control. Weird. Maybe Violeta's wrong, after all, and I can emulate the emotions. I don't need to *feel* them. The thought shouldn't make me happy, but then again, I've always been very competitive with my siblings.

Tassa shakes herself out of her daze and despite my preconceived notions about humans, I have to admire the way she holds herself up. Even in baggy clothes and her hair a mess, she's still strong. Steady on her own feet. A lesser human would be crushed under the weight of their loss, but this one... She's standing strong, still.

"Thank you. For your kindness, and for saving me." She clears her throat. "And I'd like to help, if I can. With your sister, I mean."

Exactly what I'd hoped for.

"I'm not a doctor like my father, but I did help him with most of his cases."

"I don't want to cause you undue stress, but we are at a complete loss, and anything you could do... We would most appreciate it." She nods, and I can feel the easiness of sleep come on her. "I will let you sleep, for now. There's a shower... bath... down the hall, should you wish to use it. If you need anything else, let me know."

"Thank you, Nico."

I turn and leave the room. The moment the door closes behind me, I hear her muffled sobs. So, not as strong as she gives the impression, then.

I walk away fast, trying to shove those sobs out of my mind. I wasn't responsible for them, not in the full sense of the word. They are not my problem to carry.

Chapter 5

Nicolae

"Do you really think this is a good idea?" Vlad asks me.

I stare at the map of the area, nodding. I've spent the better part of the night thinking back over the fight in the doctor's house, of the man I'd killed, the one Tassa had killed.

And now that we're gathered—Vlad, me, and Alex—in the library, staring at an old map of the surroundings, I ask myself what my motivation is.

Not because I care. Tassa may intrigue me, but at the end of the day she's a means to an end. And that end—saving Violeta—will be better served if I identify whatever-the-fuck it is that caused the attack in the first place. Then she'll at least feel grateful, and talk less about going to the cops and more about saving my sister.

"Da," I mutter to Vlad. "There is no contesting it. The man I killed in the doctor's house was on the verge of turning. The other one was human, which begs the question of how they worked together, but that's a problem for another day. Right now, what I know is the only vampiri in the area are muroni. Which means they must have turned him, and for a purpose."

"Shouldn't you be telling Tassa all this?"

I snort. "You really are an innocent sometimes, Vlad. How can I tell her all of this, and the better question is, why would I? So she can run off?"

"Because she might be able to tell you more details, to confirm your suspicions." He frowns. "I know we need to keep our existence under wraps, but given you've brought her into our home, well... Doesn't it make sense to include her?"

A snort escapes me. "No, it doesn't. She gets no special treatment, and any honesty at this point would be a double-edged sword."

"At least we wouldn't be going on an idiotic quest..."

I arch an eyebrow at his words. "By all means, frate, if you have a better idea...?" I stare at him long and hard, until he looks away and retreats away from the table. "Thank you. Besides, if I probe her mind, I risk her being suspicious or worse, remembering what I did that night. Believe me, it's best I don't. Not until she helps out Violeta, at least."

He's quiet for a longer moment. "What if the ones who turned that human are the same muroni you killed last time? How can you even know it was muroni, and not a vampir clan?"

"Brother, brother." Alex pushes off the wall he was leaning

against, facing us with his bored expression. "Why do we fucking *care?*"

I ignore him and shake my head at Vlad. "No, it wasn't those muroni. This turning was fresh."

It takes less than half a day for our poison to enter the human bloodstream, leading to their transition into a vampir. This was most definitely a fresh turning.

"As for your question of muroni versus vampir, let's just say the bites I saw on his neck were not restrained. Any vampir worth his honor would at least try to hide them. These were...evident." I scan the map again. "Once I figure out where they could potentially hide, we can go and get some answers."

A loud sigh echoes behind us, bringing my attention to the third unwilling member of this little expedition.

"At the risk of sounding repetitive, why does this matter?"

I turn to Alex, knowing he's only here for the bloodshed that will follow. "Because no one fucking hunts on our territory without our permission."

He grins. "Good. For a second, I thought you were going to say some stupid shit about avenging the human's father."

I roll my eyes. "She has a name."

Vlad coughs behind me. "Speaking of..."

I tilt my head to the side, catching the sound of her hesitant footsteps down the hall. A few painfully long minutes—for us—later, she steps in. Her eyes widen when she sees my brothers.

"Behave," I hiss under my breath for Alex, then put on a reassuring smile. "Tassa, meet my two brothers. Vlad, and Alex."

She glances from me to them, and back to me. "None of you look alike."

"We have the same eyes," Vlad points out.

I barely refrain from smacking him. Out of all the things to draw attention to... Our eyes may appear normal at first glance, but the more a human stares into them, the more they're at risk of sensing our true nature *or* being glamoured. Especially with vampiri as old as us. Sometimes we don't actively have to use the power for it to be...used.

Tassa doesn't seem perturbed, though. She glances at me first, then Vlad, then Alex—though she quickly looks away at his scowl.

"Not quite," she says. "The shades of blue are different."

Silence descends at her declaration, then Vlad lets out a startled chuckle. "Very perceptive. Your father must be very proud of you."

"Was."

Sadness permeates her voice. Maybe because I've been around my siblings for so long, and they don't show emotions as easily—or as honestly—but seeing the downward tilt of her lips, the sharp intake of her breath, has the effect of a kick to the chest.

Which, oddly, makes me want to smack Vlad, even though Tassa's reaction wasn't really his fault. And then her next words freeze us both in our tracks.

"Which is why I'm here. Violeta said last night that you could take me to the police station, so I could report what happened."

"That's not necessary," Alex says.

Perhaps the words could have been better delivered, or at the very least not at the same time he's growling and glaring at her like he is. The combination automatically makes Tassa be on her guard.

She stares at him a beat, while I take in the unconscious signs in her body. Humans don't realize it, but they behave differently around us. Same as they would instinctively around lions, but they don't realize why. They may be blind to the psychopaths living in their midst, but vampiri? They may not know exactly what we are, but their instincts are on point, one could say.

I clear my throat, trying to do some damage control. "What Alex means, is I've already gone down and explained the situation. There is no need for you to trouble yourself with it now."

Instead of being reassured, she arches an eyebrow. "You're telling me the cops found a destroyed house, and two bodies, and they have no questions for me?"

"Three bodies," Vlad automatically corrects.

This time, I can't restrain myself and I clap him over the head. He winces and moves away, rubbing the back of his neck and throwing Tassa a sheepish look.

It doesn't fool her, either.

Last night, I didn't tell her the second man was dead. She only assumed I'd taken care of him—how, I don't know, but she didn't seem as shocked as she seems now.

"What do you mean, three bodies? My d-dad, and the guy..." She frowns, trailing off, and I find myself locked in her honeyed gaze as she awaits an answer from me.

"The other man, the one I took care of." I try to keep my tone light, and the glamour out of my eyes, but it's so tempting to just...make things go my way. Get her to change her tune, redirect those questions I see swimming in her gaze, and have her focus on Violeta again.

Tassa's frown deepens. *Shit. Too damn late.*

"But he wasn't..." She's about to say dead, but I can see by the concentration on her features she's trying to remember, and failing.

I can't let her keep pushing, and recall me tearing the man apart.

"Your father was already dead, and when I came in and tried to protect you, he tried to stab me. I protected myself, same as you."

"Oh."

Her features are still twisted with confusion, so I take a step closer, willing myself to sound as reassuring as possible. I need her to trust me, to help Violeta. She may not realize it, but there's no way out of this for her. Not now that I've brought her into our midst.

"The cops didn't need to question you," I continue. "I explained to them you were affected by your father's death, and needed time. They said you can write up a statement and one of us can bring it into the station."

"That's oddly accommodating of them. I've never known them to be nice."

"Humans have mastered the art of deception."

I glare at Alex over my shoulder, and he gives a fake grin back. When I turn back to Tassa, I force a smile. "What all this means, is you can rest in the meantime, maybe have a look at Violeta, and if you need anything at all, we can get it for you. Clothes, food, just name it."

Behind me, Alex mutters something low enough for my ears about not signing up to be a human's servant but I ignore him. I know he's annoyed we're relying on a human instead of him, yet he could at least try to pretend.

Distracted as I am by his mutter, I don't immediately notice the shift in Tassa. It's only the way her heartbeat picks up that warns me something changed. And by the time my gaze meets hers again, this time there's a healthy dose of suspicion in there.

My, but humans really do show everything on their faces.

"Are you saying I can't leave here?" she asks.

Once more, I have to admire her boldness. Faced with three males like us, most females tend to cower. Even vampir ones have, in the past. Perhaps it's the fact she's recently lost so much that gives her this steel, but whatever the case is, I once again feel that odd niggling of...intrigue.

I sigh. "I've said nothing of the like. But you've been through a traumatic experience, and whoever hurt your father could come after you next. Have you thought about that?"

"But...they're dead."

I purse my lips. "I didn't want to worry you, but they didn't seem like they were from around here."

"How would you know? Violeta said you only recently moved here."

Shit. We're going to have to get our stories straight if we're to survive having a human in our midst.

Out loud, I say, "We did, but I've visited many times before, I did my schooling near here. And, I've come to quickly recognize the people who don't belong." The explanation seems to convince her, or maybe it's feeding some suspicions she's been having about her own father's death. Surely she has questions... Instead of lingering on the subject, I ask, "What's the harm in staying here a few days? Lie low. Enjoy a breather."

She hesitates, glancing between us.

"Nico, the clock is ticking!"

I glance over my shoulder at Alex, then sigh. He's already out by the door, Vlad behind him. "I have to go. Promised my brothers we'll go out for a hunt, but we'll be back in the evening. In the end, the choice is entirely yours, of course. Do as you wish."

I turn and leave, hoping my curt tone will come off as hurt, instead of annoyed. Maybe it *would* be best if she leaves. What the hell am I doing trying to get her to stay?

Tassa

What an infuriating man.

I watch as they all disappear into the woods. Going hunting? For what? And they don't even have guns. Plus, while hunting is legal in these parts, it doesn't seem like they need to hunt their own food.

My quick walk down here revealed a rather spacious house. It might be sparsely decorated and in need of refurbishing in some areas, but there are antique items in here that easily cost more than Dad ever made in a year.

So, quite plainly, they don't lack the money to buy food instead of having to hunt it.

Unless they take pleasure in the killing of animals... That thought drives shivers up my spine.

On a whim, I step out the door and outside. I want to see what the house looks like. The first thing I notice is the view. The village, a little below me. Mist moves from the forest to the edges of it, as if embracing it while the sun is rising.

And then I turn around, take it all in... and step backward.

The castle! The one my father warned me against. The one he told me explicitly to stay away from. The one he said, in no uncertain terms, was dangerous.

And here I am.

How the heck didn't I notice? Yes, the grief overwhelmed me, and I've been half-dazed with lack of sleep and nightmares. But the massive space inside now makes sense. No village house would look like this, not when most of the people there are farmers.

How was I blind to this for almost twenty-four hours?

And then another, scarier thought, occurs to me. Could it be these siblings are involved? Not just with what happened, but with my dad's death, too. The idea is ludicrous—or maybe I shouldn't be so quick to dismiss it.

Nico showed up out of nowhere. Coincidence that he came to my house the same night we were attacked? And then there's the two men dying, and how insistent he'd been for me to stay here. Him and Violeta. Not everyone seems happy with my presence here, if I think about his brother Alexandru.

But are they really siblings? They look nothing alike. Alexandru looks downright dangerous, Vlad is a typical nerd, Violeta so far looks normal—albeit sick—and Nico...

I don't want to think about what Nico looks like. About a man's appearance, in general.

So I push my thoughts back to the issue at hand. Am I safe here? Or are they the catalyst to everything that's been happening?

Maybe that's why they don't want me going to the cops.

No sooner does the thought form, there's a cold draft of air behind me, followed by an equally icy voice. "So. You're the stray Nico brought home. At least he didn't pay this time."

I whirl. Where did she come from? Auburn, frizzy locks frame an oval face, with high cheekbones and full lips. Her eyes are the same shade of blue as Nico's—another sister?

If she is, she's as gorgeous as him—except for the scar on her cheek.

She catches my stare on the scar and smiles. "You should see the other guy."

Somehow, the air grows even chillier.

"I, um... I was..."

She rolls her eyes. "Clearly, nothing has changed with your lot."

My lot? Does she mean the villagers? What a snob!

She steps back toward the house, and I follow her in. "What's that supposed to mean? Hey! Don't just ignore me, I—"

She's on me in a split second, and though she's a few inches shorter, somehow her presence feels...more. The glint in her eyes is maddening, verging on an icy blue now. I've never seen eyes that change color so fast, and something akin to a sixth sense tells me to back away—slowly.

When I do, she follows, a smirk on her lips. "Careful. For a second there, it sounded like you're giving orders in *my* house."

"Elizabeta, enough."

She freezes. A dark-haired woman appears a few feet behind her. She holds herself straight, her chin lifted in the air. Another set of equally icy blue eyes settles on me.

Now, my brain is whirring at full power. How many people are in this house, exactly? And how could I have not heard them last night? Better yet, why have I never seen them all in the village? Even if they only just got here...

"Behave yourself," the newcomer says to Elizabeta.

"I am," she snarls over her shoulder.

But the newcomer has already disappeared as fast as she'd appeared. In the blink of an eye it took me to glance at Elizabeta, the other one is gone. What the...

Elizabeta steps back from me, curling her lip. "You're lucky Mirabela's around, and in a good mood."

As if on cue, Violeta steps down the stairs, looking paler than last night. "Liza, we all know your opinions get the best of you, but I hope you're not scaring our guest."

Nope. Not even a little bit. I dig my hands in the pocket of my jeans to hide their trembling. I want nothing more than to get back to the confines of the room that was given to me, or, maybe, just straight out of here.

Something's not right.

"Me?" Elizabeta throws me a warning look, even as she steps backward. And then she stops, tilts her head to the side, as if listening to something. Her glare roots me to the spot. "Who the fuck did you call?"

"Call? I haven't—"

Violeta reaches me, putting her hand on my shoulder quickly. "It's not your fault. The villagers can get a little...unruly. Let us handle it, da? Maybe afterward, I can show you my greenhouse." The smile she gives me doesn't reach her eyes, and is a bit wobbly.

I don't understand what she means. The villagers are a good forty-minute walk downhill, and I haven't heard a single car come up.

Before I can voice any such thoughts, Violeta steps around me and goes to the open door. Elizabeta follows her, hanging back for a few moments. And then...nothing. A few minutes later, I hear grumbles and something that sounds like shouting.

I head to one of the windows just in time to observe a mob—about fifteen people—come up the hill. Judging by their clothing and worn faces, some of them came straight after waking up. Others are stopping here on their way to work. Some faces look familiar, but they're all more my dad's age.

He would have known each of their names and drink prefer-ences. The thought makes my heart deflate, like it no longer has the will to work full throttle.

But what would villagers be doing here? And why does it look like they're out for blood?

I shift closer to the door. Violeta and Elizabeta have stepped outside—to greet them, I presume.

"Can we help you?" Violeta asks.

One man moves forward. "Where is Tassa? We found her father dead. And the creatures who killed him."

Creatures?

"I don't know what you mean," Violeta says.

"We know you're behind this! For years, we kept silent. For years, we kept our kids away. We knew you'd be back eventually. You had to be. But enough is enough. Now we've let you live here—"

"Let us?" Elizabeta moves closer, her voice deadly cold. "*Let us?* Us, the last heirs of Transylvania? Who do you think you are, human?"

What the...

I jerk back from the window, slamming into a small table. The vase atop it falls to the floor, shattering into pieces. I register the noise in a haze, too intrigued by the battle of words outside to care.

Human. She called him human *as if she's...not.*

I clench my fists together, forcing myself closer to the window. That sixth sense inside me? It's roaring now to get the hell away, as far away as I can. But something more draws me in... My dad. Is these people's truth going to be what I need to understand what happened to him?

"Liza, enough," Violeta says. Her voice sounds more fragile, but she faces the villagers firmly. "I understand you're upset, but Tassa was attacked, and not by us. We had nothing to do with the events of last night, other than my brother being in the area—"

"Convenient," another old man says.

"—to seek advice from the doctor," she continues, unfazed. "But he was already dead. Nico killed the man responsible."

"That was no man. It was a vampir!"

I gasp—Elizabeta glances over her shoulder, glaring at me. Gulping, I step outside. The man at the head of the villagers almost sways on his feet in relief. He's the local priest, Marin. Only he hasn't come here dressed in his holy garbs. Instead, he's wearing jeans and a regular shirt, with something poking out of the belt. It takes me a moment to recognize the wooden tip for what it is—a stake.

"Tassa, you're alive."

I advance until I'm almost side by side with Violeta. "Why wouldn't I be?"

Another woman shies away from behind him, reaching out with her hand. It's his wife, I think. I've only ever seen her a few times. Her face has the weathered look of being in the sun for too long, but her dark eyes glint with intelligence. And fear.

"Come with us, please," she says. "This is no place for you."

I shake my head. "I'm tired of people telling me what is and isn't for me. What's going on here? What's the meaning of all this?"

No one says anything.

Then the breeze shifts and someone lunges for me. A man. Flashes of the previous night, of another man reaching for me, assail me. The two images merge together, blending memory and reality.

I strike out.

I don't mean to hurt him, but judging by the grunt as my fist collides with something, I do. I turn around, blindly seeking escape, my heart in my throat, my pulse beating frantically—

"Tassa, wait!"

Marin. The priest. His voice is to my right. I try to move, but it's like my legs are leaden, and when I do, something sharp pricks my hand. The harsh bite of pain has me blinking, snapping out of the nightmare.

A thin hand is wrapped around me, holding me up. I blink—I'm a few inches away from the stake in Marin's hand. It's what pierced my own flesh and caused blood to pour out.

"Tassa—" The woman from earlier moves closer, a frantic look in her eyes. She's holding out a small scarf for my hand.

I take it, in a daze, like all the fight's been knocked out of me. Yet again, I become aware of the arm around my waist, holding me up.

The arm that stopped me from getting staked, it seems.

I wrap the scarf around me and straighten, and the person straightens with me. I hear an odd sound as the arm around me lets go. When I whirl around, I find myself face-to-face with Violeta.

She's the one who saved me?

As if the effort was too much, she sways, and a low sound comes out of her chest, similar to animal's keening whimper.

I move closer, and when she looks up, blood is dripping from her nose... My attention is soon focused on the fangs protruding from under her upper lip. Startlingly white, they look like they could pierce through anything—including flesh.

My flesh.

Vampir. The villager had said it. I'd seen the man, attacking my father. His strength. The wild look in his eyes.

Flashes of movies, TV series, and books pass in a blur in my mind as I try to rationalize the words, and what I'm seeing. In the end, I come up empty.

"Tassa, come!" one of the villagers urges.

Instead of listening, I step closer still.

Elizabeta comes between us. "Best not to tempt her," she sneers. Then she wraps an arm around Violeta's shoulders and heads back inside the house. Over her shoulder, she says, "You *should* go. Save us all the trouble. We'll take care of her ourselves, as we have all this time."

She's right. Probably.

Probably? They're vampiri. *All of them.* I spent an entire night in a castle with six of them, and have come out unharmed on the other end. Next time, I won't be so lucky.

Or, will I?

Should the fact I actually survived the night despite being so clueless work in my favor?

Or how about the fact she saved me, when she could've let me die? Or that I've been bleeding, yet she didn't jump me as she could've?

Nico said Violeta's sick, but he never said from what. Now, seeing her, there's definitely something wrong with her. But not in the human sense... Can I help? Do I even want to?

I stare at the door Elizabeta and Violeta passed through for a long time. Then I turn to the mob. "I'm not leaving here until you tell me what's going on."

I've never been impressionable, nor have I held onto old superstitions of the past. Without a clear explanation, I don't intend to move, not even if it's my own people trying to tell me it's better for me. Dad always appreciated my stubbornness, and I'm not about to change just because he's dead. On the contrary. It's that stubbornness that'll have me finding answers to his death.

Marin, the leader, sighs and gives way to another man. Pepper and salt hair, another well-worn face, and roughly my height, he could be anyone in a crowd. Then he speaks, and his low baritone makes me shiver, though I don't know why. "My name is Victor. Your father and I were good friends."

"Funny. He never mentioned you."

A muscle clenches in his jaw. "We are keepers of the secret."

"Which is?"

He glances around, as if wishing he was anywhere but here, then clears his throat. "That vampiri—and other creatures—exist among us. Those who want to live in peace put their trust in a group of humans in their area, whose goal is to keep them protected. The heirs did that, with us, when we were young."

I take a moment to soak it in. *Vampiri—and other creatures.* Great. Just freaking great. Either he's telling the truth or I've landed in a parallel universe.

"The heirs?" I finally ask.

Victor jerks his head toward the castle. "The six living in there."

"Heirs of what, exactly?" He can't mean heirs of Dracula, for crying out loud. That's a myth.

Victor stares at me a beat, as if unwilling to give me that piece. Then he says, "A bloodline. The most ancient of vampiri."

I shudder. "And how long ago was this, that they recruited you?"

"Forty years, give or take. But they recruited our parents before that. And their parents before that."

I glance back at the castle, then at these people who seem to believe every word out of Victor's mouth. "You're saying they've been here for over a hundred years?" None of them look a day over thirty.

"No," he says. "This particular coven of vampiri—this *family—*

has lived in the area for centuries, longer even. On and off. Every few decades, they move, seeking another shelter, another place to call home."

"Why?"

He lets out an impatient sigh. "We can explain all this back at the village."

I look pointedly at Marin's stake, dripping with my blood, and clench my fist. "No. Explain it *here*. If you're truly a friend of my father's as you said, then you will do me the courtesy of not treating me like a poor virgin maiden in need of saving. I'm neither."

He seems stunned at my bluntness, but for the first time, an inkling of pride runs up my spine. That I can stand up for myself, and not care what all these people think. For too long, I've cared, and tried to belong. While always being so very different. Well, not anymore.

I may not be comfortable in my own skin, I may cripple myself with self-doubt, but I demand honesty and transparency to make my decision. And that's something I won't compromise on.

My eyes survey the villagers, their fearful expressions as they keep glancing between me and the castle. Will they call the cops, if I don't come home? We're a tight-knit community, and my father was just killed... But that's the least of my problems right now.

Clearing my throat, I say, "You were about to tell me why these vampiri leave every few decades."

Victor shares a look with the priest, then nods. "Because they have to continue hiding their presence. So they travel to various strongholds, where a group of a similar Order, like us, protects them. Ensures humans in the area hear rumors of ghosts and supernatural, so they avoid their home. Takes care of them."

"Why would humans take care of vampiri?"

"Because long ago, we were simple-minded and wanted to become immortals of the night." Bitterness coats his tone, making me even more untrustworthy of him. Bitterness, I've learned over the years, gives many men the leisure of acting out on their basest desires. "Vampiri promised us that, and enslaved us to them."

He thrusts his arm toward me and pulls back his shirt, revealing a crest. I move closer. It's like the old Romanian coat of arms, only in black and burgundy ink, with a big D etched in the middle.

Where have I seen this before?

I stare at each of the villagers. People I've had drinks with. People whose houses I've visited. "Okay, so basically your families have been enslaved to these vampiri for ages, and presumably you continue to act out their desires to save your own lives. I can understand that."

He frowns at my cool tone. "You don't seem to understand the danger you're in."

"Because I'm not in danger." I point toward the castle. "These monsters may not be human like us, but they sure didn't bleed me dry last night while I slept and mourned my father. One of them risked his life to save me, and bring me here." I survey all of them, then my eyes land on Victor again. "Even if all you said is true, my father would have helped them. One of them needs said help. And she just saved my life, might I point out. So, I cannot in due conscience leave."

"They don't deserve your help! And if you stay, you could become their next victim."

True. I can't deny the truth of his words, and the evidence was in front of my eyes. I may be sleep-deprived and grief-stricken, but I can't deny what I've seen with Violeta. And somehow, knowing these creatures are real, only fuels my desire to find out what truly happened to my father. Because if anyone will have answers, it's them.

And if Nico's arrival at my house was more than just coincidence, then I shouldn't be running away from here and cowering in fear. Instead, I should use the trust he's put in me to my advantage, and learn all I can while saving his sister—or attempting to.

A stupid plan, extremely reckless, and one I won't have help with. But it's the best I've got, and my entire being rebels at leaving without truly knowing. Dad deserves better. Once I know more, I can go to the cops.

"Thank you for the information, but I will stay."

Marin frowns. "Why?"

"Because I want to know who came after my father, and why. And it sounds like these vampiri, powerful as they are, may have answers."

He shares a look with Victor, who simply shrugs and disappears into the crowd. I don't trust him, not a single bit. But he's not my problem.

"We will keep an eye on you," Marin says, and draws a cross in the air. "May God be with you."

It's not God I need.

Chapter 6

Nicolae

"What's your rush, frate?"

Alex's voice carries on the wind. It's not unusual, for him to taunt me while hunting, but it is unusual to have him nearly risk all our lives by speaking when we could be heard.

Muroni are cave-dwellers, and there are too many caves hidden within this area, old and new. Whenever hikers disappear, it's usually a sloppy muroni job. Luckily the cops in the area are too stupid to put two and two together.

Besides, who would believe the likes of us still existed? We were meant to have died. So many times. And each time we escaped, I think we all lost something very precious to each of us.

"Nicooooo..."

Alex's song on the wind pulls me out of my thoughts and I whirl mid-run. My eyes find him—blurring between the trees—with an innate ability to feel where he is exactly, and I slam against him with all the force I possess. It's the only way he'll get the message and shut up.

Unfortunately, that slams both of us into a tree, which cracks under the pressure and topples over, triggering yet another to fall.

Panting, I turn, and a low growl escapes me. My fangs elongate, and that red haze descends on me. *Must keep it under control.*

"Nico, relax."

Vlad is there, ever the mediator. Does he never get tired of playing peacemaker between us?

I yank myself out of his hold and shove a finger in Alex's face. "You need to watch yourself. This isn't the time for playing games."

"Maybe not, but you haven't answered my question."

"I'm not in a fucking rush! I just want to get to the muroni before they turn anyone else in the area. And this ravine around the bend makes sense as their location. We all agreed, no?"

Alex simply walks over to the discarded tree and takes a seat. "But, see, I'm still trying to understand our interest in this. Muroni know not to move against us. Most of them scamper off into the woods the minute they scent our presence in the area."

"True," Vlad says. "Our lineage is enough to scare any of them away. Or at least make them think twice."

I shake my head. "Has it escaped your notice that these ones haven't run off scared? Maybe we've lost more control than we thought, these last centuries. Maybe it's not just the vampiri clans coming against us. *Maybe* the muroni are trying to form their own armies."

Alex scoffs. "They don't have the brains."

"Then, if not them, who else is turning humans? We can't afford, with Violeta sick, to worry about having to move locations."

At least, that's why I think I'm doing this. Isn't it?

"It could be one of the rival vampir clans," Vlad says softly. "Did you consider that?"

I glance between them, realizing they've been talking about this and not sharing it with me. My jaw clenches. "Could've shared this before we got deep in the woods, no?"

It's never a good idea to take on a rival vampir clan alone. After all, we're supposed to be in hiding from them, meaning we always, *always* eliminate all witnesses. And the last time was too damn close. I might've lost Silva then, but no way I'm going to risk one of us.

"Would you have listened?" Alex lifts a sardonic eyebrow. "It's one of two extremes with you, brother. Either you're in Indifferent La-La-Land, or you get up to your neck in shit and drag us all with you."

"I don't." The denial is immediate, and I regret it the moment it passes my lips. Because he's right. I did drag them with me in shit before... eons and eons ago. First with my human infatuation, then with my rage at losing Silva, and pissing off a powerful clan.

Alex sees the realization dawn on me and chuckles softly. "That's what I thought."

"You know we don't hold that against you," Vlad says.

"Speak for yourself."

Ignoring Alex's mutter, Vlad continues. "The past is the past. If we focused on every time one of us fucked up and got us in shit, we'd never survive living in the same house, let alone being a family."

That last bit is debatable. But I'm no saint, after all. I've contributed plenty to the current dysfunctional element, that bit is clear as day.

"But we also don't want another repeat performance," Alex says.

"Right," I mutter. "Well, you can settle down. It's not like that. The human in this case doesn't have my interest, other than to help heal Violeta. Nothing more." Annoyed with myself and with their questioning, I turn away. "Come help me when you feel like it. Otherwise, stay out of my way."

Leaving their flustered forms behind, I take off. Not the smartest move by far. But if someone with my training, with Țepeș' mentoring, falls prey to attacks, then perhaps I deserve the death that will follow.

At least here, in the woods, I can be myself, never having to constrain myself to what society expects. To what my siblings expect. And though I'm technically not meant to hunt alone—we never do— I find myself doing just that.

Then Vlad is there, somewhere in the trees. I know Alex will follow. He may not fall in line right away, and the years have made him harsher than the rest of us, but deep down, he won't put us in danger.

I think.

Tassa

I don't know where my head is at. Not really. Last night, I lost my father, and a stranger saved me. This morning, I found out that the same Good Samaritan is a vampir, and so are his five siblings.

Vampiri. I'm in a coven of vampiri. Christ.

It was all bravado that I showed the villagers, but when it comes time for me to head back into the castle, I stop past the threshold. The broken vase lies in pieces by my feet as I stare at the villagers vacating the premises.

Vampiri. Ruthless monsters, straight out of nightmares, who need human blood to survive. *The undead.*

And these aren't just any vampiri. According to Victor and the lot of them, they're *ancient* ones. The baddest of the baddest, capable of enslaving generations of humans underneath them.

Out of all the places for me to land in…

Do you seriously believe all that crap and legends? I'd asked Dad this what feels like an eternity ago. And his answer, when I recall it, hits me like a physical blow. *More than you can imagine. Those old wives' tales you are so quick to renounce, we believe in them. I believe in them.*

Dad knew, then. He feared me coming here because he knew the truth behind the façade.

I shake my head. I've lived in these parts all my life and heard the stories. Never thought they were true. Never wondered about their origins. And now…

They're… real. This is *reality.* Not fiction.

More like a straight-up nightmare, is what it is.

And I'm living in it.

My gosh.

I glance around, hesitating some more. Thinking back to losing Dad… to the two men who'd come. What if they weren't human? There was something about the way they'd moved, the glint of madness in their eyes…

And what of the villagers? Are they aware of how much danger they could've been in? Or is it that these vampiri are not as dangerous? And what was that crest on Victor's arm...?

I glance at the vase, realizing where I'd seen it before. The D is *on* the vase, or rather, on one of the broken pieces. I kneel next to it, trying to piece the pieces together and confirm my theory. Sure enough, when they're together, the pieces spell out *Casa Dracului—* House of Dracul.

"What are you doing?"

The soft voice has me whirling around, my heart thumping hard. It's only Violeta—though, remembering her fangs, I know I can't think of her as *only Violeta* anymore.

As if aware of the same thing, she keeps her distance, instead leaning against a wall. Her gaze lowers to the vase. "In my experience, what's broken cannot be fixed."

"Depends on what it is," I add.

Violeta meets my gaze, staring for a long time, then sighs. "I'm sorry."

"Whatever for? The bit where you played sick and lied to me, or where you nearly bit my head off?"

She sighs again. "I wouldn't have bitten your head off. Believe it or not, I have a rather good control of my, um, urges."

It's my turn to lean against the wall, feeling my knees giving way. By some miracle, I manage to remain standing. "Scuze," I mutter. "I don't mean to snap. Especially as you did technically save me. It's just... a lot." I wait a beat before asking, "So it's all real? What those villagers said?"

She nods.

My thoughts shift to Nico, to how nice he's been, to him saving me. "I got played from the beginning, then."

"No." She takes a step forward, but stops when I recoil within myself. "I do need your help, that part wasn't a lie."

"And your brother?"

I should have said brothers. Not trying to single him out. As if I care that he, specifically, lied to me.

But I do. Because he saved me. And I thought that meant he had honor. Obviously not.

Wanting to kick myself, I try to keep my breathing in check.

"Nico is...complicated. But he never meant you harm. And he didn't have anything to do with what happened to your father. None of us did."

I shake my head, still trying to wrap my mind around it. "Why would you need my help? How could you, even? You're immortal."

"Maybe so, but like that vase, my life isn't, umm, well. Something's gone wrong, and I need your help figuring it out. Your father, as the villagers probably said, helped both vampiri and humans. I'm hoping you could, too."

"I never wanted to step into his footsteps, and I want to do that even less now."

Violeta nods, her expression faltering. "I can understand that. I really am sorry to have dragged you into this."

She turns to leave, but I call out. "What's the House of Dracul?"

She freezes and slowly turns to me. "I'm not sure how much I can say. If you leave here and share this with the rest of the humans, we're royally fucked."

"They seem to already know."

"I mean outside of your village...with the world. Our existence has stayed a myth for a reason."

"Fair enough. But what if that's what I need to know so I can decide whether to stay or not?"

She watches me closely for a moment, then nods. "Come have a drink with me? In the library." When I hesitate, her lips tilt in a wry smile. "I promise you're not on the menu. I drink red wine regularly to get some type of energy."

A spark of interest rises within me—the questioning mind Dad always nurtured. "Why? What does it do to you?"

"Mainly tricks the brain into thinking it's blood. For a brief moment, my body acts as if it received fresh blood, and functions as such. It's...useful. For a time."

As she speaks, I follow. The more I talk to her, the less afraid I am. Not because I have a death wish but because she's that good at putting me at ease, and appearing human. Must've taken loads of practice, I imagine.

Once I have a drink in my hand—a glass of red wine, just like her—I'm half-better. Warmer, at least.

Violeta clears her throat. "*We* are House of Dracul," she says softly. "Vampiri have existed for a long, long time, and since they have existed there has always been a royal house. We are it."

I take a stronger gulp. Royals. Yet another surprise to wrap my mind around. How much more can I take? Guess I'll find out.

"We used to be powerful, a long time ago," Violeta continues. "We imposed the will of our sire, kept everyone in line. Ensured humans wouldn't find out about us. Clans of vampiri were subservient to us, knowing they had to follow our rules, else we would hunt them down and eliminate them. But over the centuries, other vampiri—clans of them from various areas—became more vocal about not wanting a royal family to submit to. Our sire didn't agree."

I arch an eyebrow. "Let me guess. Vlad Țepeș?" He's the only

Dracul I know of.

"Da. But he's not the only reason we're royals. Father was an original vampir, and he did choose each and every one of us. But the line he was from was...older. Darker."

"I don't understand. What makes other vampiri submit to you, as monarchs? Were you elected or something? Do they come and swear allegiance every few centuries?"

A bubbling laugh escapes Violeta. She cuts it off sharply when she sees my narrowed gaze.

"I'm not laughing at you," she says. "It's just, elections and democracy aren't a thing in our world. I'll explain."

She settles more comfortably on the couch, her knees brought up to her chest. After handing me a blanket to wrap over myself, she takes a sip of her wine, and continues.

"Father—Țepeș—was the first vampir in these parts but not the first ever. The way he explained it is that whoever created him also created others like him. Some before him, others after him. Those same originals, like him, created their own *royal* families. Families who, like us, would be heads of a particular region of vampiri. We received Romania, first, but then it extended over Europe. Africa and Asia have their own. America, too. And because vampiri live in clans, each clan is subservient to a royal house. But underneath it all, the bloodline all comes from the same original source, and that bloodline is what makes us royalty. It's also what gives us our blue eyes, and...other...abilities."

"And whose bloodline is that?"

Violeta shrugs. "Not sure. Father never spoke of them, and we didn't question him. We were too busy learning about our new existence and, well, then he...died."

I rack my brain for school history. "He was assassinated, right?"

Violeta shakes her head. "No. He escaped that. Most historical accounts say otherwise, but he escaped it. It was the first of many attempts and also what clued him in that he—we—were being hunted. He took us into hiding. Told us to stop trusting the clans. And we have... We've been in hiding ever since, except for the times when we've clashed."

I take a larger gulp of wine as I try to digest the information. "So there are vampiri all over the world? Each clan submitting to a royal family?"

"Well, there *used* to be. Many were killed by hunters; others disappeared into hiding. We do our best to keep track of world events through spies and informants, but these last years, it's become more difficult." A loud sigh escapes her. "The Carpathians and the surrounding areas have become a last hiding place for those left. There are clans left in Yugoslavia—sorry. I mean Serbia, Croatia, Slovenia, Montenegro, and the smaller states that used to make up Yugoslavia. Some of us still exist in France, and far north into Scotland. But for the most part, if any vampiri survive, they're smaller covens. And as for royal bloodlines like ours..." She shrugs. "We have not encountered any of the ones we knew of for the last centuries."

Violeta tilts her head to the side. "So, there you have it. We're a sad bunch of vampiri, hiding in a castle not our own, and now I've gotten sick, which has only added to the pressure on my siblings. I used to be able to hide it and dive into my greenhouse when the waves of pain and dizziness got really bad. I like making little poultices for villagers, you know? To cure whatever ailments they have. I used to make them at our old place... But I digress. That's why Nico brought you here—because of me. He was coming for your father, but when he died...you were my only chance."

I shake my head. "This is...a lot."

"I can imagine."

She drinks some more.

"But you must drink human blood."

"We do. From willing humans. There are many, believe me." She goes to the window and rolls a joint, puffing from it. Her form relaxes. Seeing my gaze, she says, "It helps me relax. Best new human invention."

"Don't know if I'd agree. The effects I've observed on people tend to differ."

Violeta nods, then seems to get lost in the pleasure of her joint. When she moves again, she carries the cloud of sweet smell with her. "Does that ease your mind at all?"

What she's really asking is, will I help?

Before I can answer, she turns around and walks away, leaving me alone. I stare into the fire long and hard.

Dad told me to stay away from this castle. He was adamant about it—scared, even. But he also told me a long time ago to follow my heart. And even though I'm not a doctor, being by his side for so long and seeing him care for his patients, I can't in good conscience walk away.

You can ignore the tales as much as you wish, but do not disrespect them. Some died to carry on telling such tales. Dad meant that advice specifically for the castle. But doesn't it apply to the House of Dracul heirs, too? I can't exactly ignore them.

Violeta saved my life and she needs my help. They may be monsters according to the legends, but they haven't hurt me. So I can either listen to the villagers and leave or stay behind and do what Dad would've. And in so doing, find out everything about their world, and how my father got entangled into it.

Nico's face comes to my mind. My grip on the drink tightens. I'll stay, but I'm sure as hell not going to let him off the hook after the lies he's told to my face. He could've been honest. Granted, I would've thought him crazy and ran away, but who lies to someone after saving them?

Nico Dracul, apparently.

How appropriate. Dracul in Romanian means literally *the devil*, and he looks like one. Acts like one, too. Lies as easily as one.

I chug the rest of the drink and pour myself another one. I won't get drunk, that would be incredibly stupid. But since recklessness seems to suit me, why shouldn't I loosen up a bit?

Nicolae

The hunt did not go well. One could say it was a clusterfuck.

Empty nests—or so we thought. Then some leftover muroni popped out of nowhere, just as some hikers showed up. We had to eliminate them quickly. The muroni, that is. The humans, Vlad made sure they forgot everything, and sent them on their way.

All this failed attempt proved is that there is another nest nearby, and they're organized. And, one could say, smarter than the last one we killed off.

None of this is normal. It's not muroni behavior, and it leaves me...unsettled.

Alex and Vlad took off for some actual food after the hunt, but I declined. Not because I'm not hungry, but because I'm too fucking pissed.

By the time I enter the castle again, my mood is crap. And it's about to turn worse.

Tassa stands there, watching me with fiery eyes. I don't know what the hell *she's* mad about—after I left her, I'd been plenty annoyed at her insistency to go to the cops—but what I do know, is that being around me is the worst thing for her right now.

Hunting sparks my anger, that part of me that I've been repressing for so long. And because I kept my shit so under wraps for so long, now I notice it's hitting me stupidly fast. Hunting is the only time I allow myself to feel, and more than often after the fact I also get trickles of other emotions. So in one moment I feel the rush of anger, followed way too fast by desire. I tone both down as best I can, knowing I need to keep up the indifferent façade.

When I move out of the shadows and Tassa sees the blood on me, her gaze widens, and she takes a step back. But it's not as fearful a reaction as I would've expected, given said blood on me. Instead, after the initial step back, she steels her spine and gives me that damned stubborn tilt of her chin.

"You lied," she accuses.

Lied. Odd word... Did she figure out that we were trying to stop her from going to the cops? Or, worse, is the sight of me with blood on enough to have recalled the memory of that night, when I ripped someone apart in front of her?

Instead of a real answer, I choose an evasive one. "And if I did?"

She purses her lips, shaking her head. "A vampir, really?"

I tense. *How the fuck....?*

Somehow, I didn't expect this. Her knowing what I am explains her reaction to me, but goddamn, it complicates things. Then again, it's not like I could've kept the matter hidden from her in the long term—not if I really wanted her to try and help Violeta.

Vi... It must be my sister who told her. In an effort to get the help she needs. Either that, or Liza and Mira decided to play fucking mind games. Liza's my best bet.

"Who told you?" I shouldn't care, not really, but the question's out before I can stop it. The answer is just as unlikely and surprising.

"Villagers came up from town, seeking me. Had a bit of a show-down with your sisters, and I saw Violeta's...change." I can only im-agine what that means. But there's no fear now on her features, only a deepening frown. "You brought me here under false pretenses and lied to me. Honesty is very important to me, so in the future, if you want to get my help for anything, you'd best keep that in mind. Once, I can forgive. Not more than that."

Honesty. The word stings—that's a concept we outgrew centu-ries ago. Yet here she stands, challenging me with it, expecting it, as if the rules are different for her. And maybe they are. Damn her if she isn't willing to keep pushing, even knowing what I am.

Yet even as I think that, she whirls on her heels and stomps away. I find myself following. When Tassa doesn't slow down, I blur in front of her, making no effort of hiding my fast speed. We'll see how long she lasts, pretending she's not scared shitless of me.

This might just be fun.

Fun. Yet another thing I haven't sampled in a while.

Maybe I should have gone with Vlad and Alex, after all. This...mix of emotions is unlike me. And I don't particularly like it.

I step closer, deliberately ignoring the warning in her gaze. "If honesty's so important to you, Tassa, then why are you still here? What keeps you so close to a monster like me?" I almost hope she'll look away. But she doesn't. Instead, her jaw tightens as she holds my gaze, but she doesn't answer me. So, I change tactics. "What exactly did the villagers want with you?"

Tassa tilts her head to the side. "Not that it's any of your business, but after loads of talk, they said I was best to leave."

I look around, my intent clear. "And yet you're still here."

"Yep."

"Why?" And why do I care?

Her gaze narrows on me. "Because my father was murdered, and you were there."

"I saved you."

"But you know more than you told me."

She stares at me. A spark of interest rises within me, soon morphing into something else. It's hunger, yes, but there's something more. Not the call for blood, but something equally primal, equally dangerous. I feel my restraint slipping, the pull between us strengthening.

Definitely should've gone with them on the hunt. I knew better—lack of blood sustenance makes us all act crazy. This...is not good. At all.

"Perhaps," I mutter, in an effort to gain time. While she stands there staring at me, I step closer, circling her—but at a distance. "Or...perhaps not."

"Don't toy with me."

Oh, but it feels so good to toy... I ignore that part of me.

Why does everything have to come back at once? I can smell her hair and whatever cheap shampoo she uses. I hear the thump, thump of her heart—a steady rhythm. Not afraid. A flush creeps up her neck, barely perceptible, but her scent changes—a note of something sweet and nervous slips through her calm façade, drawing me in closer before I can stop myself.

The predator in me wants a reaction. "Am I?"

"Why are you acting this way?" There's a hitch in her breath now. So, she's not fully unaffected.

Mm, good question. I have to assume she's referring to me turning on my vampire charm, which I didn't realize I was doing. I should be more careful, especially after a hunt. It's what some myths call glamour—though, for me, glamour is when I *intentionally* enthrall a human. This state after a hunt that induces infatuation and easy suggestibility in humans... I suppose it's some type of glamour, too. With our blood, Father's power, it's also more intense. Few are able to resist—although we love the ones who do even more.

Toying with her should be simple, an instinct. But it's the quiet, stubborn fire behind her eyes that keeps me here, wanting just one more reaction, just another hint of the way she refuses to look away, even as her pulse goes crazy.

What if I were to give in to these urges? Scratch the itch, then shove it away. Human females are easily impressionable, and she could be useful... If I don't make the mistake of getting infatuated like last time. Then again, I've taken steps to make sure that'll never happen again. Cool, quick encounters are more my style nowadays.

I could make an exception for her, though. The more I get her to care for us, the better she'll be at healing Violeta.

Or maybe you just want her blood... and her.

I ignore the darkness in my mind. Instead, I allow myself a slow grin. "Because I'd planned to be nice. Oh, so nice. I never intended you to know I was a vampir."

"That makes no sense. How was I supposed to treat your sister?"

I shrug. "Would've found a way. We've gotten quite good at

hiding our presence, you see. But let's just say, the few times we've trusted humans, it hasn't ended well."

"Yet you trust the villagers."

Not because I knew about it. I bite the retort off. No point in showing her just how dysfunctional we are quite so early on.

"To some extent. To whatever extent we ever trust another human being."

"They said..." She trails off. "They said my father helped vampiri and humans alike."

I shrug. "Perhaps he did. What I want to know is, do you have the skills to help my sister?"

Her chin lifts, defiance blazing in her expression, but there's a flicker—barely a heartbeat, just long enough to notice—of something softer. Curiosity? Whatever it is, it's gone when she narrows her eyes. "You know full well I'm not a doctor."

I'm closer now, close enough to smell the wine she must've drunk not that long ago. Did she need some alcohol to add steel to her backbone? Was she afraid to face me without it?

The thought tickles that same interest I'd forgotten about. To face a deep fear rather than run away from it... maybe I shouldn't underestimate her just yet.

"I do," I say simply. "But that's not what I asked."

"I...Maybe. I might have the skills, and I might not. I honestly don't know."

My gaze drops to the base of her throat, and every flutter of her pulse I can see. I'm no saint—for a moment I imagine what it would be like to let the need win. Just once. But I swallow it down, burying the impulse somewhere dark, reminding myself what happens when we lose control. I move away before I do something stupid.

"Wait! Where are you going?"

I chuckle, throwing over my shoulder, "To sleep."

"I thought vampiri never sleep."

"The legends lie. As do we."

Chapter 7

Tassa

To say I sleep restlessly is the understatement of the year. The sheets feel hot and cold against my skin, and the entire night I play and replay Nico's words in my head. *The legends lie. As do we.*

It's more than just those words. It's the way he said them. Cool, aloof, a mix of teasing and serious.

Truth is, I don't know where I stand with these guys. Maybe I fooled myself into thinking I could get answers about my dad's death, when that's not really the case. Whenever I'm around them, I get sucked into their history.

Why it's so alluring to me, I don't know.

Then it hits me.

My entire reaction to this news, my acceptance almost... I've always wanted to travel, to experience life. I may not be doing the former, but with them, here? I finally have a purpose behind putting together tinctures and wiping sweaty brows. Beyond being an assistant.

I'm *someone.*

The idea makes me jerk awake, and I stand, letting my bare feet touch the floorboards. The worn oak glints a little under the light.

A sense of power... That's what this whole thing has given me. Because I have a choice in what I do and who I help. And because these immortal, powerful beings rely on *me.*

Shit. What if I fail?

The self-doubt is always there, quick to latch on me. Too quick.

I shove it away, trying to focus on the facts. But my mind is drawn away from them, and my newfound epiphany, to Nico.

And the way he looked at me last night... At least some of it. At first, when I'd seen the blood on him, I was afraid. Doubly so because of everything I'd learned. But the alcohol had provided a good cushion for my racing heart... Until he got closer. And closer.

How can someone be covered in blood, yet still emanate scents of spices and woods?

And the way his eyes pierced right through me with their intensity... I've never had a man gaze at me like that. Ever. Not even Petru. It makes me all the more aware of my human imperfections.

Absently, I run a hand over my stomach, the not-quite-flat surface, then the love handles that have diminished but are still very much there... I pull my hand away. There's no use confirming what I know.

I get out of bed and head down the hall to the shower. Violeta comes out as I open the door, her body wrapped in a massive fluffy towel and a smaller version for her head.

When she sees me staring, she offers a tentative smile. "There's plenty of warm water. Mira always makes sure plumbing is good enough to last for all of us."

"I..." It takes a moment for my brain to stop short-circuiting and return to normal. "You guys...shower?"

She arches an eyebrow. "How do you think we keep clean?"

"Um..." Good question. Didn't think that through. "But the legends..."

Her smile grows. "The legends lie, as you'll soon find out." Her words are too reminiscent of Nico's, but she doesn't notice my stunned expression. Instead, she continues, "Our bodies may not secrete bodily fluids at the same rate as humans, but we still shower. A lot of it is out of habit—even though we lived in times that were much less modern than these, cleaning up was always a thing. And, well, with all the hunting we do, we'd really stink if we didn't shower."

"Oh, I...see..."

She tilts her head to the side, then winces. Just like that, her easy demeanor is gone, and she sways on her feet. I move to help her, but she holds up a hand and a wobbly smile. Her blue eyes seem so pale.

"It's all right," she says. "Comes and goes."

My earlier epiphany is within reach. I have a chance here, a chance to do good. This is about more than my dad, now, though his loss is still very much in every fiber of my being. That doesn't stop the girl in me who'd studied under her father from immediately kicking into action. "Is it dizziness, or something else?"

"It's...like a wave. Hard to explain."

I frown. "I need to take care of something today, but I'm hoping it'll lead to more answers. Answers that could help you, too."

She nods. "Good luck." And then she's gone down the hall.

I head into the shower and as the hot water beats down my back, I think back to Dad and what he'd say about all this. His loss is an ache within my chest, something not even the hot water can remove. But I've always needed to understand things, and if being around these vampiri helps me do that, then it'll be a less-healthy way of coping with my grief.

Hopefully.

An hour later, I'm browsing the castle in search of Nico. It's massive, and I have no more hope of finding him than a needle in a haystack. Recalling Elizabeta's great hearing the other day, with the villagers, I stop walking and instead just whisper his name.

"Nico?" I feel like an idiot, but if it'll save me time... "Nico. I need to talk to you."

A moment later, there's a gust of wind at my back. I whirl, and he's there. Dressed in jeans and a t-shirt, completely blood-free, he looks...normal.

I gulp. "Thank you."

He inclines his head. "I wouldn't make it a habit, if I were you. We don't particularly like being summoned."

"I wasn't—" I stop myself, because, technically, I was. Instead, I pull within me for that strength that never seems to fail me. "I want to go to the cops."

He purses his lips. "See, I was trying to be tactful the other day. But surely, now that you know what we are, you also know you can't go. And why."

"But you guys have an Order protecting you. Making sure things are swept under the carpet."

"Humans are not trustworthy. Mira may be quick to rely on them, but I hold no such qualms."

Ouch. Good to know where he stands.

"I don't disagree," I whisper. "Most of them are shit. But these ones, the ones meant to enforce the law... They can help."

"You said yourself they're never accommodating."

"I'm willing to try again."

His eyes narrow. "Why? What is it you're seeking?"

"Answers to my dad's death."

"Shouldn't you be trying to fix my sister instead?"

I ignore the bite in his tone. "I'm not here as a servant, I'm here of my own free will. And finding out more about what happened to him *will* help me fix your sister."

He watches me for a long moment. "There's no talking you out of this, is there?"

"No."

A sigh, then, "All right. Let's go."

Nicolae

I should've known the minute she called my name it was going to be for something idiotic. I just never expected it to be this, in particular.

We take great care to stay away from human law enforcement agencies. With the years passing, and the technology advancing, we don't need our faces in their system. Ever.

But if this'll get Violeta the help she needs...

I glance at the human by my side. We're walking to the station, meaning it'll take us the better part of an hour since it's smack in the middle of the village, but she doesn't seem fazed. If anything, her pinched, focused expression tells me she's making plans.

As I should be doing. The moment we get there, I'll have to check the cameras and find out where they keep their footage. Best not to take chances, when you've lived as long as I have. I may be indifferent to a fault, but I won't have my siblings pay for my carelessness.

Tassa surprises me a few moments later with her question. "Did you see or feel anything, that night?"

"When your father died?" She nods, and I shrug. "No. There was no car waiting outside, no...anything." I hesitate, then remember Vlad's words about being honest. A cringe-worthy sacrifice, but when things must... "One of the men, the one who was still standing when I walked in, he had a bite on his neck. He was turning."

She stops walking and stares at me. "Turning?"

"Into a vampir."

"I thought you said legends lie."

"About some things. Not about this."

"But—" She bites her lip, then starts walking again to keep up with me. "So he was turning into a vampir, and all the evidence is gone in the fire?"

"Presumably."

"Was it one of you who turned him?"

I grit my teeth. A fair assumption, but if she knew what we struggle with...

Not like I say any of that. There's no point to it. So I settle for,

"No. We have a strict rule against turning humans. This was a mu-roni's doing."

"What's a muroni?"

"A cave-dwelling vampir. They're the ones you see in movies looking all crazed and bloodthirsty. They're mostly the ones who nearly give our existence away."

She mulls that over for the rest of the walk. It always surprises me how slowly humans go through their lives. They take forever to make decisions, and even longer to think things through. This, de-spite the fact their average life expectancy in the best of cases is a measly eighty years. What odd creatures, truly.

We exit the woods at that point. I made sure the path we took through the woods ended in a different outing, far from her old house. But I see her gaze linger in that direction anyway.

Long ago, I might've known what grief felt like. Might've let myself feel it. But I don't remember enough of it—don't *let* myself remember enough—to actually relate.

Instead, I settle for an awkward, "Not a good idea to go back there just yet. Police station is this way."

"I know where it is," Tassa grumbles.

Moments later, we walk into the old-looking building with paint fading on the outer walls. The linoleum floor inside has seen better days and is caked with mud carried in from outside. There's a stench of cigar smoke, perfume, and sweat that makes my normally non-picky nose revolt.

Tassa doesn't seem bothered in the least. I envy her human senses.

She marches ahead of me to the small desk and asks to speak to an inspector. The moment the old receptionist lady sees who she is, she gets up and runs inside. A man comes out, accompanied by my least favorite type of person—a priest.

I don't need to be close to Tassa to hear what they're saying, but I find myself inching there anyway. If the priest has any nefarious intentions—and most of the ones I've met always did—I'd rather be close by than not.

At least, that's what I tell myself. It can't have anything to do with Tassa's demeanor and the way a part of me feels responsible for her. I shut that bit of myself away a long, long time ago. Now's not the time to revisit it.

"...glad you came out," the cop says as the priest watches on. "Marin here was coming for an update, and he let us know you were recovering at one of his safe houses."

Hmm. The priest is covering for us, but why? Unless he's part of the Order Mira told me about. The way he's avoiding my look could mean that he knows what I am, or not.

"Um, yes," Tassa says, not missing a beat. "Marin was kind enough to help out. I've come, I guess, to see if you found anything when you inspected the ruins."

"Ruins?" The cop turns from Tassa to Marin, and flicks his gaze to me for good measure. "No, the house wasn't in ruins. It was saved. Well, a portion of it. There's some fire damage, but it's livable, I suppose." He makes a face. "We retrieved your father's body and the other two. After a full autopsy, we cremated all three bodies, on the priest's advice."

Tassa sways a little, the only outside sign she gives that the news must have hit her as hard as it did. I watch her closely, the way she straightens her spine and juts her chin forward. This time, I cross the remaining distance and insert myself in the midst of the conversation.

The cop frowns my way. "And you are?"

Marin, the priest, clears his throat. "He's helping out in the safe house and counseling Tassa."

"Ah."

I've known glamoured humans, but it's a bit unreal how easily the cop takes all the information without questioning more. Just like that, he returns his attention on Tassa. "To answer your question, though, we didn't find anything. The two men who attacked seemed to have been unrelated, with no priors, and no links between them. No one saw them come in or out of the village. We're still doing door-to-door with their pictures to see if anyone recognizes them, but it'll be a few more days. Marin here can keep you updated."

Tassa nods. "Thank you, I appreciate it."

Deflated, she turns around and walks out. I watch her leave, knowing she must need a minute to herself. I'll give her that much, even if it's not my usual way.

Sensing eyes on me, I turn to the cop. He doesn't seem to like my attention on him, because he heads back inside.

"A moment, please?" Marin waves me over before I can follow Tassa.

A flicker of annoyance rankles through me. What could he possibly want?

Once we're in a corner away from the receptionist, he lowers his voice. "Tassa is important to this community, as was her father. We may serve the Dracul bloodline, and we have hidden what we know. But if anything happens to her..."

So I was right. He's with the Order.

I smirk at his weak threat. "Don't worry your head, priest. She's safe with us."

"Then why not let her leave?"

He doesn't know about Violeta. None of them seem to. *Good. Then I'll keep it that way.*

"She chose to stay."

"You could make her leave." He moves closer. "You know it's no good for her. It's only a matter of time before one of you snaps."

"Are you seriously suggesting I use glamour to make her leave?" A normal man would've snapped. A normal man might've even taken offense. All I see is his weak, pathetic attempt at getting me to influence Tassa into a decision she has no desire to make—not yet.

"Not like it's anything new for your kind."

"You clearly know nothing of the House of Dracul, in that case."

I leave before the urge to throttle him takes me over. These emotions, the way they come and go especially around this woman... It's beyond frustrating.

When I exit the building, Tassa's nowhere to be seen. I start walking one way, but I hear muffled sobs around the corner, and head that way instead. She's curled into the wall, her forehead resting against the brick. Tears run down her cheeks, falling onto the ground in an uninterrupted stream.

"Tassa."

She doesn't hear me, the sobs getting louder.

I need her to trust me. And for that to happen, I should be caring and empathetic... Isn't that what all humans crave? Understanding?

Biting back a sigh, I move closer and slowly pull her in my arms. She pushes me away, at first, then crumbles against me when I wrap my arms around her waist, holding her close.

Her sobs pick up even more, soaking my shirt.

And while I want to tell myself I'm doing this as a chess move, yet another thing designed to make her trust me, it's not entirely true. It may have started like that. But as the minutes go by, and her sobs slow down, the weight of her in my arms feels...nice.

Her scent is...intriguing.

The sound of her heartbeat is...alluring. Calming.

And the way she feels against me, all woman and curves, allowing me to comfort her...

When's the last time I've felt any of these things?

I'm reminded of the previous night, the surge of desire in parallel to the hunger running through me. Something's happening here, but what?

Unnerved, I grab her shoulders and slowly push her away. She blinks, as if coming out of a trance or very comfortable embrace. A flicker of guilt gnaws at my insides—a surprising apparition, given I've made it a point *not* to care.

"We should head out."

She blinks at my words and her cheeks color. The faint blush, with her messy hair and red nose, should make her look ridiculous. But all I can do is stare into the large pools of her honeyed eyes, filled with unshed tears.

I find myself reaching for her cheek, cupping it, to swipe at a stray tear.

Tassa closes her eyes and then steps away, breaking the moment. But the heat her cheek left in my palm feels scorching, and I pull my hand away, restraining myself from blowing on it.

What is this? And why does it feel so sudden and....encompassing? Like a tangible link that's clicked between us.

I try to reason the feelings out. I'm good at that, I've always been good at that. And it's probably more tied in to her grief, and how it brings up memories of Silva. Of loss. Of Father. Of things I'd rather leave buried.

Da, that must be it.

Tassa tries to wipe away her tears. It doesn't surprise me—she seems the type to hide her feelings for the benefit of others.

I hear the footsteps before a voice resonates behind me, startling her. "Tassa, can we talk?"

I whirl, facing another human. Only this one has a look about him that immediately sets my teeth on edge.

Tassa peeks around my shoulder and sighs. "Victor... What is it?"

"You really should reconsider your current sleeping arrangements."

She clears her throat, sniffling to recover, and steps around me. "And you should reconsider learning someone's boundaries. Just because you were friends with Dad doesn't mean you get to tell me what to do. Not even he did that."

"Foolish girl," he mutters. "So you'll allow a vampir to order you about instead?"

"Watch yourself," I hiss, moving closer. "Perhaps you should reconsider who you piss off in your quest to show off."

"There's no showing off," he growls. "Not with your kind." To Tassa, he adds, "Come with me. I can protect you. It's what your father would've wanted."

She tenses. "Don't pretend to know what he would've wanted."

She scoffs and tries to sidestep him, but he reaches for her hand. And something in me, that same something that'd been admiring her, loosens. Like a chain that's been tightly wound up, and that's suddenly released.

I restrain myself just short of yanking that arm off him. Instead, I grip him by the throat and push him against the wall, trying not to slam him—lest he cracks his skull open and I leave another dead body for the cops to find.

"*Don't* touch her."

"Or, what?" He smirks at me. "Want to kill me? I dare you."

Tassa's by my side, her hand on my shoulder. "Nico, stop. Let's just go."

I've never let another human order me about. But when Tassa says it, I feel the emotion still lingering in her tone, and the way it vibrates through me. I release the human, turn my back on him, and walk away with her.

And it's the hardest thing I've ever done.

I also feel like it'll come back and bite us in the ass soon.

Chapter 8

Tassa

A day passes, followed by another, and another. I spend most of the time in my room, completely undecided as to what to do—and confused as all hells over my last interaction with Nico.

He's gone from aloof to...something. I don't know what it is. Half the time I think he's hungry and wants my blood. The other half, I can almost sense his loneliness.

Adding to all this is the undercurrent of grief I work through every single day. It's exhausting and the only thing that seems to keep me going is channeling Dad so I can help out Violeta.

But the cop's station... Finding out he's gone, truly gone, his body cremated... I understand why Marin did it, of course. It still doesn't excuse the fact I could've been notified, especially as he knew where I was this entire time.

And then Victor. What right does he have to come telling me what to do and where to go? As if he's anything to me other than a stranger.

All of these things go through my mind for not just hours, but days. I lock myself in my room in the castle, reading Dad's notes over and over and over again.

Violeta brings me human food and tries to engage, but I politely kick her out. The entire time I half expect her to push me, and try to get me to talk. Or at least tell her if I'll help. That doesn't happen, though. If anything, by the third day, she has a sort of resigned air about her, like she no longer expects me to help.

And that, of course, brings on the guilt.

Especially when my lunch sandwich comes with a short note written in probably the ugliest handwriting I've ever seen. *If you want to leave, say the word. I'll make sure you get back home safe. – Vi.*

Reassuring as it is to know she's on my side, I also don't want to just...up and leave. Again, back to what my instinct is telling me to do—run as far as I can from these monsters. Then there's the other part. The part that cares too fast and wants to rescue things. And that's the part Violeta speaks to in me.

I may have the power to heal her, and I can't turn my back on that. It would be a disgrace to Dad. And, while obviously the vampiri don't have answers to what happened to him, part of me is starting to think I may be safer here than anywhere else.

Either way, I won't get answers to any of this by keeping myself locked indoors, that's for sure.

Munching on the sandwich, I move to the wide windows of my room and glance outside. Nothing but mist and rain. And then I feel eyes on me and glance below. Something moves in the shadows of the woods. One of them? I shudder, ready to move back. Then I glance below again, and my gaze collides with a dark blue one—Nico, watching me.

Before I get hooked on those eyes, I move backward, nearly dropping my sandwich. I don't want to think what it made me feel, to have him close by a few days ago. That wouldn't do... that's beside the point. I mean, really. As if I have the time to go googly-eyed over him like a teenager. As if I'd ever even consider that again after Petru.

I spend the rest of the afternoon going over my father's note-books, trying to find any tie-in to vampiri or the meetings he would've had. He was old school, and he would've kept a list of not only patients, but ailments and remedies.

Yet there's nothing.

No matter how hard I look, I can't find anything. And it's not like he's around for me to ask him.

I plop back on the bed, groaning and staring at the ceiling. "What should I do, Dad? What would *you* have done?"

There are so many considerations—least of all, my life—that I feel my head spinning. Before long, I fall asleep.

He advances on me like a predator, and I'm his prey. His willing, eager prey. Because I don't move, my back to the wall, the wind

ruffling my nightgown. I don't move at all.

As his eyes hook mine, I find myself unable to blink. All I want is his kiss, his bite... I reach a hand for him but he evades it, instead nipping at my finger. A drop of blood comes to the surface.

He inches ever closer, eyes on me, and slowly licks it.

A shudder runs through me—but it's not one of revulsion. "I..."

"Shh," he says, and erases the last of the distance between us. His lips brush my neck, and my hands find his taut shoulder blades. "Let me take you on the ride of your life."

I come awake with a jolt, panting, an odd type of warmth running through me. My entire body tingles, like I've deprived it of something as essential as breathing.

Running to the washroom, I notice my flushed cheeks, and feel the arousal in my body. What the effing shit? I've never had my body respond like this to a man, let alone in a dream.

But he's *not* a man. Nico's a vampir. The more I focus on that, the better.

Then my expression narrows in the reflection, recalling Nico staring at me from below my window. My fists clench. The annoyance rising within me quickly morphs into slow licks of anger. I warned him. I told him honesty and deception are not how he'll keep me here, helping.

And yet, he's been playing games. Getting into my mind, into my dreams—that's the last straw.

"You picked the wrong girl, Nico Dracul. I'm not falling for some vampir glamour shit."

I stomp down the stairs, forgetting about all my complications and my mind not being able to decide what to do. In that moment, fury like I've only felt a few times in my life fills me. And vampir or not, Nico's about to get the brunt of it.

When I reach the main hallway, I debate on where to go, and head for one of the drawing rooms. Nothing. The kitchen is equally empty. *Figures.*

I move to another room, this time growling under my breath, "Nico! Where the hell are you?"

And for that matter, where is everyone else? I've never gone this long without running into at least one of the Dracul heirs. Then I catch a low murmur of voices and head that way.

It's a pool room. These vampiri are actually playing freaking *pool.*

I shove the door open, and three pairs of eyes turn on me. Potentially the worst idea of my life—also, too late to back out now.

"Can I talk to you?" I say to Nico alone.

"We're in the middle of something," Elizabeta snarls.

Vlad lifts a hand to silence her, watching the exchange between us. Nico takes his sweet-ass time to ping one last ball, then dances on his feet. I try to ignore the fact he's barefooted, dressed all in black, and his muscles strain the fabric of his simple t-shirt. Not to mention the contrast of his white skin against the dark color only sharpens his cheekbones and intensifies the blue of his eyes.

Someone clears their throat. I feel myself flush.

"Alone," I mutter. "I'll wait outside."

I back away before I make an even bigger fool of myself and lean against the wall. Nico comes out a few moments later, an eyebrow arched.

"What is it?"

"Are you playing fucking mind games with me?"

The eyebrow rises higher. "Could you be more specific?"

I take a step closer. Yes, intentionally putting myself in a vampir's reach. A more idiotic human there has never been.

"The damned sexy dreams."

A corner of his mouth lifts. "Sexy dreams?"

And that's when I know he's either fucking with me, or he has no clue what I'm talking about. And if he doesn't...

He grabs my arm and tugs me away, farther out of earshot. We end up in a solarium. Plants line the windows, soaking in the light, surrounded by a wide expanse of glass and the mistiness of the outside.

Is this what Violeta meant about her greenhouse?

The moment we're inside the room, I wrench myself out of his grasp and stomp away to the window. The door shuts behind me, and a shiver racks up my spine. Not the fearful kind.

"Now, tell me all about these sexy dreams of yours."

I whirl on him, scowling. "Don't go getting ideas."

"I'd never dream of it." Judging by the smirk on those lips, I highly doubt he's telling the truth. *The legends lie. As do we.*

I hesitate. If he's humoring me, I shouldn't even mention it, but... "The dream was, um, intense. It was short, like a nap, but it happened after you looked at me, under my window. You said something, in my dream. About wanting to bite me."

The smile falters out of his eyes, if not his expression. "I see."

"What does that mean?"

He shrugs, trying too hard to seem indifferent. "It means whatever you want it to mean, Tassa..." His stare ensnares mine, and my breathing goes up a notch. And two. And three.

Is the beat of my heart alluring to him? And why am I even thinking about this, when what I should be doing is running as far away as I can?

The answer is simple. Because I'm a fool.

Nicolae

Unable to hold my stare, Tassa glances away. She toys with her shirt—another ugly, long, bulky one. And finally, mutters, "I don't think I can do what you ask me to. I think it's best I leave."

Ah. She's finally caught on to her instincts, realizing what's best for her. Part of me wants to admire her. But I also desperately need a fix for my sister. She didn't look well last night, and the last thing I want is more guilt weighing on my conscience.

Tassa's mention of sexy dreams was a nice distraction. And, it may have given me an idea. Or rather, a continuation of our previous encounter. It's not unheard of for humans to develop an attraction to us. The same way as one would find a lion beautiful—before they get killed. But if I can use that to get her to stay...

I take a step closer. "You do, do you?"

"Yes."

"And why is that?" Another step.

She backs away against the window, and the heady thrum of the blood in her veins sings to me. My gaze zeroes in on her throat and her sky-rocketing pulse. I almost miss her words.

"Because I don't want to be another victim, like the villagers seem to think I will be."

"You mean because of your dream?" I chuckle. "I'd never taste your blood. You have my word."

She licks her lips, another tempting distraction.

"B-but..."

That urge is back in me—hotter this time, and even less controllable.

I take my time placing my hands on either side of her head, caging her in, and nuzzle her neck. Right below her ear. My lips brush over the skin. The goosebumps. She shivers, but it's not from fear. I've learned to recognize that in my victims and this is something much, much different. Something sweeter.

"But?" I whisper, pulling away just enough so I can take in her expression.

I want to see the revulsion, to torture myself. To remind myself of the hell I'm in. Of everything I can never have, can never be again. Of everything that pushed me to be the indifferent, callous jerk I am now.

But it's not revulsion I'm met with.

And just as I move in closer, preparing to touch her lips... I taste them, for the briefest of moments—the barest of kisses—nipping at their softness. A second, two, and— She pushes me away. I allow my body to move with the force of her movement, if only to give her the illusion of free will.

"I..." Her eyes are wide, her breathing comes out in pants. And her pulse...

My gaze is drawn to it yet again. *This is dangerous.*

"You swore you never would."

Her dream. Me biting her.

I wouldn't do that again, not after last time. Having a taste of someone I desire—might potentially desire—is madness. It would consume me. And I have a feeling that unlike my last conquest, Tassa would be impossible to forget.

"And according to you, I've already lied."

She shakes her head at the reminder of her words from nights ago, trying to shake my own words off her. "Enough with the mind games, Nico! I want the truth."

"The truth is overrated."

She scowls. "Not to me, it isn't. Did you have anything to do with my father's death, yes or no?"

I lean against the wall opposite her and level my best sardonic gaze on her. "Still on that topic, are we? I thought the trip to the cops would have sorted it."

"You're the one who keeps pushing my buttons."

The fire is back in her gaze. And much as I admire it, it also brings back the weight I'd been trying to shrug off my shoulders. I sigh. "No, I had nothing to do with your father's death."

Silence lengthens between us.

"You won't say more?"

I shrug. "Seems to me you already got the answers you seek."

"No, I haven't. Not even close."

I watch her walk away, trying my best to dismiss those annoying stirs of...feelings. Why does she affect me so?

More annoyed at myself than ever, I head back to the pool game and my siblings. Answering their questions will be a blast.

Later that same day, when night comes, I wander outside, staring at the woods.

What is it with fucking trees? The moon bears down on this particular one, with its large branches and wisdom-filled trunk. Or so would human literature have you believe. Yeah, I've read the bits. What's in a tree, really? Sure, they take years to grow, and cutting one should be akin to cutting a limb. They bring oxygen. Probably why humans are so damn obsessed with saving them.

I take another swig of the bottle of țuică, knowing full well it won't do much. Why am I even here, instead of inside the castle, taking what's been freely offered?

Tassa wants me. I've been around long enough to recognize that. She's taken by my allure, by what I represent, by the unattainable.

She may not want to admit it to herself, but she wants me.

And I want *her*. Crave with an intensity that scares the shit out of me.

I wish nothing more than to deny it and repress the urge, but it's as hopeless as trying to stop Mother Nature in her tracks.

Immortality was supposed to be simple. Easy. It's been anything but. Here I am, filled with...longing. Loneliness. Desire. Conflicting emotions.

I've slept with humans before. She won't be the first, or last.

So why's bile rising in my throat at that last thought?

Have I developed some idiotic attachment because she can save my sister, potentially? Perhaps. Will I do everything I can to get her to save Violeta? Damn fucking straight.

But Tassa's nothing special. She's a human. And this obsession isn't healthy, nor can it continue.

I take another large gulp of the pure alcohol. Fire burns in my belly. The moon shines down on me. The tree looks at me in judgment.

"What the fuck do you want?" I mutter. "So what if I'm here, alone, and drinking my brains out? It's not like it'll matter. Two hours and I'll be back to normal."

Maybe that's the problem.

Who am I kidding? I *know* that's the problem.

Immortality is something only idiotic humans aim for. They strive for it, desire it, and hope with all their stupid, idealistic souls that they can get it. Same as they want to win the lottery or become billionaires. Not once do they realize that it's a waste.

It's akin to watching your skin rot in front of your eyes, watching darkness take away all light, and forgetting how to live.

Yeah, it was fun. The first few years. Now?

I shift my anger to the tree. Disposing of the bottle in a shatter of glass, I stomp toward the tree. Lift one hand, close it in a fist, and punch it. Once, twice, three times. Again, and again...and again, and again. Before long, all I know is the rhythm, the pounding of my knuckles against the rough bark. When I'm done, half the tree has been torn apart, with the other half swaying precariously. Like I sway between humanity and cold indifference. All. The. Fucking. Time.

And Tassa somehow sees in me the potential for honesty and doing the right thing?

A snort escapes me. I move backward. Then lift my leg and kick. With a crack that splits the silence, the tree topples and falls. I watch it tremble, as if it's giving its last breath. Same as humans do. I shouldn't feel anything.

So why do I feel like crying?

"Nico."

Someone's muttering my name, but not even that is enough to wake me up.

"Nico!"

The kick in the shin, that's another story. Groaning, I blink and move to a sitting position, wiping at my face. I glance up—straight into Violeta's face.

"What are you doing out here?"

She laughs. "Me? What about you? Decided to have it out with a tree, of all things?"

I glance around, taking in what she sees. I can't have been out longer than a few hours. The discarded tree is lying only a few feet away, and I laugh.

"You shouldn't take destroying life so callously."

I blink at Violeta. "I'm a vampir, dear sister. How the hell am I supposed to take it, when I live off the blood of others?"

She sighs. Sways toward me. Despite my grogginess, I move and catch her in my arms, supporting her weakened body.

"You shouldn't be out here," I whisper.

"Leave me be. I wanted to see the rising moon. Who knows how many more I will get to witness?"

Something akin to sadness seeps through her voice. It jolts awake all my sense. "What is it, Violeta?"

"Hmm?" She tears her gaze from the skies and frowns at me, as if only then seeing me. "Nothing, brother. Nothing at all."

At a loss, I leave her to it and head back inside. Still, when I reach the oak doors, I turn back. She's staring back at the moon, and even from afar, I can see her tears.

Not for the first time, I wonder how long it's been since I truly opened my eyes to the world around me. Perhaps then her anguish wouldn't be such a surprise.

Tassa

I'm not avoiding Nico. I'm just...not wanting to be around him. Or so I keep telling myself as I go about tidying my room, munching on snacks, and reviewing my father's notes again. No vampiri. No nothing.

I need to go somewhere. Either to talk to someone or find more information that can help Violeta. Ideally, that would be somewhere far away from Nico.

Instead of achieving either thing, I run into Mirabela. She's standing by a window, her attention focused on someone. Mesmerized, I watch her for a moment. The perfectly slender neck, the waves of tumbling dark hair down her back, currently held back in a loose, low braid. She's wearing jeans and a burgundy sweater, showcasing her great figure and long legs. Out of all of them, she looks the oldest in years—human years, that is—and her features have a maturity and beauty that only comes with time.

Maybe in another time, another place, I could feel less inconsequential when next to her. As it is, all I can do is set aside my feelings and take the opportunity to gather information. Her full lips are pursed in annoyance at whatever she's observing. When I inch closer, I find it's none other than Nico and Violeta, outside.

Mirabela turns her cool blue gaze on me, arching a perfect dark eyebrow. "Da? Did you need something?"

Out of all of them, she has the thickest accent. Like she hasn't quite been able to hide it despite the centuries of living. But from what little she spoke to me, she's also the one that sounds most like a human.

"I, um, had a question." Like an idiot, I pause. She rolls her eyes and gestures for me to go on. "My father. Nico said you're the one who knew about his, um, well, the fact he was helping both humans and vampiri."

"I'm still waiting for your question."

Gosh, but she's annoying. The way she even looks at me is like I'm an insect. I shouldn't be surprised. I mean, I did take the time to read up on vampiri while I was holed up in my room. And maybe, just maybe, about ways to protect myself from them. But these guys are nothing like the ones I've read about.

Are they worse? Time alone will tell.

I clear my throat, trying to keep my expression impassive. "How did you know? I mean, did you use his services?"

Mirabela taps her chin, making me wait. She's good at that— pushing my buttons. Maybe not as much as Elizabeta, but still.

"No, I didn't."

"Then..."

She purses her lips, annoyance oozing from her every pore. "Every time we move into a new area, one of us is in charge of security. These last few times, the responsibility fell on my shoulders."

"Like with reaching out to the villagers?"

"Mm. And when I did, one of them mentioned your father. Knew all about his little side business."

I frown. "Oh. So... It's just, I'm trying to figure out how my dad knew vampiri were real. And ended up helping them."

She shrugs. "Don't know. Don't care."

"But I need—"

"I don't care what *you* need, human. The question is, can you help my sister, yes or no?" When I don't answer, she smirks. "You'd best figure it out, else your usefulness to me will dwindle to nothing. This isn't a charity we run here. Sooner or later, your worth will diminish, make no mistake about that."

I don't bother trying to correct her. To point out that my worth is diminished already. What's the use? Someone like her can never understand human insecurities.

Besides, before I can even come up with a proper retort, Mirabela walks away, leaving me alone. So I do the next best thing and stare out the window. Watch Nico as he walks away from Violeta. A moment later, she heads to her greenhouse. Presumably.

Maybe it's time Nico and I had another chat...tomorrow. I don't think I can handle the intensity of his stare again. Not just yet.

The next morning, after a shower, I seek Nico. When I don't find him in the library, I wander the halls. The main floor is empty, and so is the pool room. But as I head toward the courtyard outside, and the extra quarters at the back, I hear something that sounds a lot like metal clanging against metal.

After a brief hesitation, I move down the corridor that way. There's an open door, and like the proverbial cat who got too curious, I move closer.

Vlad and Nico are...sparring. With real swords. I watch them repeatedly lunge toward each other—grinning, parrying and ducking blows. Nico takes a special pleasure in risks. At one point, Vlad's sword slashes dangerously close to Nico's neck, but he dodges at the last second. It doesn't stop the shiver running up my spine at the sight, nor the startled gasp escaping me.

They both turn to me.

I retreat into the hallway, ignoring the fast beat of my heart, and wait. Knowing he'll come for me. Hating how we keep being drawn to each other. But I need *someone* to answer questions, else...

"Looking for me?"

I whirl. He's watching me—how long has he been watching me while I've been lost in my thoughts? His shirt is off, and he's using it to wipe his forehead. That's all it takes to remind me of my fucking dream, and my body turns tingly all over again. I stare at him like a doe caught in the headlights.

"Um, if you're busy, I can come back later."

His eyes narrow on me, and flicker to the pulse at the base of my throat. "Seems pretty important."

I scowl. "You could try not reading my mind."

"A myth, darling. It's your pulse that gives you away. Unless I specifically make you nervous?" His sardonic grin is infuriating. Matter of fact, his entire demeanor today is unsettling. I don't know why. Maybe it's the cooler glint in his eyes, the hardness of his jaw... *Right. Just his jaw, not the rest of the body.*

I look away, desperately trying to avoid gawking at his six-pack, and wave my hand in his general direction. "Put a shirt on, would you? Humans don't have important conversations half-naked."

"But I'm not human." Amusement lingers in his tone, but by the time I look back at him, he's got a shirt on.

Damn, he moves fast.

"I, um, have questions. About vampiri." An arch of an eyebrow is his only response, so I continue. "For... We didn't finish last night. And if I'm to try and help Violeta, I need to know how you guys function."

"Function?"

"Body-wise."

He grins. "You want a lesson in vampir anatomy?"

I roll my eyes. "Yes. If we can both be adults about it."

"Very well." He runs to the door, yells something to Vlad, then is back in front of me—all in the span of a blink. "Follow me to my office."

Chapter 9

Tassa

Office?

We walk down another maze of corridors. Finally enter another room, a smaller version of the big library. Only, this is definitely furnished in male hues. Dark wood, dark sofa, dark...everything. Without the massive windows letting in light, it would be a depressing room. Instead, it's...sexy.

I don't want to admit it. After the way he's blown hot and cold, and the fact I have a big inkling he's toying with me, the last thing I want is to admit his good taste. But, facts are facts. And while Nico Dracul may be a cold-hearted jerk at times, he's not a slob.

My ex was messy and a slob, expecting me to be the dutiful girl-friend who always picked up after him. When I didn't, and actually demanded he do things, he was quick to point out my weight or any other flaws of mine—usually appearance-related—to make himself feel better. Why I stuck with him for two years, I'll never understand.

Shoving thoughts of Petru aside, I take in the full office. It's not immaculate, by any means. There are papers thrown around and books everywhere. But there's an allure to being able to hide in here... An allure that, sadly, I'm associating with the office's occupant.

I turn to the windows, glancing outside, and my breath catches in my throat. I have a full view of the town unfurling below, and the woods looming between us—dark, foreboding...yet, also the woods I grew up around. Where I played as a kid. Seeing them from my new vantage point leaves me with a bittersweet sensation in the pit of my stomach.

"That is some sight."

"Hmm?" Nico glances from his desk, then shrugs. "I suppose so."

"Suppose—" I bite down on my tongue before it goes off on a rant I can't restrain.

He seems to notice it and smirks. "Don't hold back on my account."

"Fine. You know you sound like an entitled rich jerk, right? Not even noticing a sight like this? Just how jaded *have* you become, Nico?"

He gazes at me for a long time—is he debating answering me, or wringing my neck? Could be either, judging by his tight expression.

Finally, he settles in his armchair behind the desk and gestures for me to sit opposite him. I perch on the velvet cushion, trying to ignore how utterly plush it feels against my bottom. Dad and I only ever had hardwood chairs around, and this is luxurious. Despite other areas of this castle that are worn-out and falling apart, Nico clearly takes his office to heart.

"You aren't here to understand my jadedness," Nico says with a hard expression. "You're here for my sister."

The words don't surprise me. At least, not the fact that he's so focused on Violeta. But there's a wariness hidden in those eyes that makes me wonder if I've touched upon something sensitive.

"But I will say this—immortality is not what you humans think it is. At the end of the day, it's centuries, millennia of existence...watching everything we hold dear die. Watching values we believe in become obsolete. Becoming obsolete ourselves." He shrugs. "So, let's leave my jadedness out of the conversation, shall we?"

I nod. His words are callous and he tries to project an indifferent tone. But I'm starting to see through it, the same way I feel he sees through me.

The other day, when he held me, something shifted between us. I've never been more aware of how at odds our existences—our very beings—are, but also how similar, than in this moment.

A moment of pain for him. Of sadness, disappointment, even. I think about his words and what they communicate. No, I can't imagine immortality is easy, at all. And somehow, that makes him even more human in my eyes.

Maybe I did speak out of turn. I've only been seeing the opulence they live in, but never considered what they might have actually lived *through*. Romania has a fairly bloody history, after all.

Gulping, I point to a pen and notepad near him. "Can I borrow those?"

He passes them over and I ignore the jolt of electricity when his hands touch mine. Instead, I settle the pad on my knee and start writing. "All right, first things first. Has Violeta's disease ever happened to another vampir?"

"Not that I know of."

"And what are the symptoms you've noticed in Violeta? I need to know if there's anything I've missed, or anything your vampir senses have picked up on."

His relief that I've switched tactics and subjects is almost palpable. He leans back in his armchair, forehead scrunched up as he thinks hard. "The first was the fainting. Then she was pale, paler than the rest of us. Plus, she has not been drinking blood regularly." A frown. "Do you think that could cause it?"

"It depends. How often do you have to drink it to survive?"

It strikes me, in an odd sort of epiphany, that I'm talking about drinking *human blood* with a vampir. Yet that sixth sense that was telling me to run, previously, seems to have quieted around Nico. Weird. Something to be explored later, when I'm alone, and not under his watchful gaze.

I focus on Nico and his words, jotting down what he's saying. Still, part of me can't stop wondering what Dad would think of all this.

"Depends," Nico says. "Most of our us tend to feed every day. Not killing, not unless we can't control ourselves, but a little at a time. The blood gets used by our system too fast."

I arch an eyebrow. "I'm not asking about most, though. I'm asking about you six, given your...bloodline."

A muscle ticks in his jaw, then he says, "Once every week sustains us. We try not to go past two weeks, maximum. Although, *some* of us feel we need to do it more often."

"Like Alexandru and Elizabeta?"

He smirks. "You picked up on that."

"Yeah, it's hard to miss." I don't tell him I also picked up on their slightly higher-than-average psychopathic tendencies.

"So you've decided to stay, then?" His question surprises me. Before I can even answer, his eyes darken. "Only, last night, you seemed on the edge of leaving."

"Gone now," I mutter. "And I'll be honest with you, it'll be a lengthy process to figure out what's what. I've only helped my dad treat humans, and even then, he was doing most of the work. But I'll do my best."

He nods. "Very well. What is it you wish to know?"

"Let's start with some basics. What happens to one of you if you stop drinking blood? Not drink less, but stop altogether."

"Why? You think that's what caused Violeta's issues?"

I narrow my eyes. "I don't know. *Has* she stopped drinking?"

Nico scowls. His quick reaction, for once not held back, eases my tension. Enough that I give him a half smile.

"This won't work if you answer my every question with a question, you know."

"Point taken." He lifts his hand, gesturing for me to go on.

"You, not drinking blood. What happens if you choose that life?"

"For the vampiri of our caliber? We go to sleep—I suppose in human terms, it would be akin to a coma. Only a fresh batch of blood would awake us. A muroni, however, would find their ability to survive much lessened. Their reflexes would be slowed down, their ability to shift impaired."

"Impaired how?"

"Not able to fully shift. Half-monsters, if you will." He frowns. "But it's not the muroni we're talking about here."

"No, it's not." I tap the pen on the notepad, thinking aloud. "When did the muroni separate from regular vampiri? I'm assuming since you share characteristics, that it used to be all one and the same species—or type—of vampir. But from the little I've gathered, they seem completely different and apart now, no?"

He tilts his head to the side. "You want a history lesson now?"

I roll my eyes. "Just the highlights."

Nico taps the table, and turns his gaze to the windows. "It wasn't so much a when, as a *how*. Father established himself as the ruler in these parts long before I was turned. It was made all the easier because vampiri live in groups—covens, clans, whichever you wish to call them. Easier to subjugate, once he had the leader of each one in hand. Once our rule was established over the rest of the vampiri, we came into contact with various creatures. Father's the one who first caught a muroni."

"Caught?"

"Da. He liked to... understand things. Sometimes this led to bloody experiments. It's how he discovered the limitations of our venom healing."

"Venom...?"

Nico curls his lips and points to one of his fangs, currently retracted. "These elongate when we feed, fight or fuck. But when I run my tongue over the sharp tip..." He illustrates what he means, and I can't tear my gaze away from the movement. Or his lips. An odd burning fills my core, one I try my best to ignore. "The fang cuts into my tongue. My overflowing blood, mixed with my saliva, is a venom that heals wounds. Otherwise, humans would go around with vampir bites on various parts of their bodies, and that's no good."

His gaze zeroes in on my neck, and it's only then I realize I've drawn my hand up to it, as if to protect the vein underneath. I gulp. "Right. And this venom, your sire liked to experiment its limitations?"

"Da. And used muroni to do so."

Charming. I hold back my comment.

"One particular muroni, before Father killed it, warned that we, too, could suffer its fate. Should we choose to give in to darkness." He turns his attention back to me. "Vampiri grow bored easily. A side effect of immortality that no one warns about. Well, that same boredom leads to stupid decisions. Muroni are the result—vampiri who basically give up the remaining of their humanity, giving in to Darkness, and retaining extra powers as a result. *Old* powers."

He flicks his gaze to the windows. "Once it became known that they could shapeshift, when the rest of us could no longer... It became an infestation. Many vampiri chose to give up the remainder of their soul to Darkness for that."

He stops. The pause feels noteworthy, with an odd weight I feel in my bones.

The question escapes me before I can stop it. "Why didn't you? Give in, I mean."

Nico meets my gaze. Harsh, unapologetic, the lines of his face are drawn with an inward tension I can't understand. "Because we, unlike the rest of them, still hold on to hope. For a final resting place, eventually." He nods toward my notebook. "What else did you want to ask me?"

My gaze slips to the books behind him. "Are there any books on the subject?"

"Potentially. Why, *now* you want a proper history lesson?"

"No. You don't sound like you're in the mood for one, and I have a brain. Just give me a book on the subject and I'll read it later."

He gets up from the armchair and turns to his shelves, touching various spines before pulling a worn-looking book out. "This should do the trick." He places it on the table, then resumes his spot.

"Thank you. Next, what about your senses? How do vampir senses differ? And I mean *vampir* senses here, not muroni."

Nico toys with a paper. "Our hearing is much sharper. Sense of taste is gone, however, unless it's blood. Red wine can taste pleasant to us, but that's about it. Touch is...hard to explain. It's enhanced. As is smell. Our eyesight is better."

"Hmm. How much better than a human's?"

He smirks. "Eyesight? Whereas you see the village down there, I could tell you exactly which of the families in there are awake, whether they're fighting, whether they're not."

My eyes widen. "That much?"

"Mm."

I think back to the other night, to all our conversations. "Then your siblings can hear everything?"

"Da."

"But... how do they act like they don't, then?"

The smirk widens. "I said they *can* hear, not that they *do*. We wouldn't survive in the human world if we made a show of these...en-hancements. So, we don't. We learn to block them; it's the first thing every vampir does. We were taught to do it as soon as we were turned, so unless I specifically tune in to that particular sense, I wouldn't hear it. Like a TV channel running in the background, but on mute."

"But why?"

"What do you mean?"

"If you have the ability to see and hear everything, why would you deny it to yourself?"

"Because of our values." He points to the notebook. "Next?"

That's the second time he cuts my questioning short because I'm diving in too deep. An interesting development. I humor him nonetheless by moving down the list. "You said you were taught. By whom?"

"Next."

His hard expression is back once more. I want to probe. Bite my lip to stop myself. Then it comes out anyway. "The ruler of the House of Dracul?"

Violeta had mentioned it, but I need to hear it from him. I can't wrap my mind around the fact one of our national heroes—or villain, by some accounts—could be the monster who turned these six. And I also can't stop the million questions swirling in my mind around that same topic.

A faint flicker of surprise runs through his expression, soon muted. "How did you hear about that?"

"Your vases... and Violeta."

"Ah."

He still says nothing. I force myself to wait patiently, even as he looks away from me and out the window once more. I wonder if it's one of those times he chooses to listen to everything? Then he faces me once more.

"It's not relevant to Violeta's history. Next."

I scowl at him. "You may think it's not relevant, but there could be something there. The history of how you came to be—"

"—is not relevant." He enunciates each word, his gaze growing darker. "*Next.*"

I could keep pushing, or hope that the book he gave me will provide some answers. And if not, there's always the village and the Order. I can find out more there...assuming I can sneak out. On one hand, it's true that it'll give me potential information to help Violeta. On the other hand, it's also true that it'll give me a better understanding of this new world, and why Dad would've gotten involved in it, yet asked me to stay out of it.

With a huff, I glance back down at my notes. "Fine. Touch and smell, you said they're enhanced too, for you guys?"

"Mm. I can smell your shampoo, but also the faint lotion of your skin, and the fact you're near your period."

"What!"

He chuckles. "You asked."

I shift, trying to cross my legs. It's weird and annoying that he knows that. "Does it work same as the eyesight and hearing?" I recall the cop station and how he'd wrinkled his nose.

"You mean, do I choose to block half the smells? Da, of course. Otherwise, I would go crazy."

Part of me wonders if he isn't already crazy. Or if immortality has him so jaded, he's completely forgotten all that made him human...once.

"Has Violeta shown less of any of these? Less...enhancements?"

He thinks for a moment, then shakes his head. "Not that she's told me. Nothing obvious, anyway."

"Damn."

"Why?"

"Well, if it's some kind of infection, assuming you guys can even get them, it would make sense that it shows in her and affects her senses. But if it's not...it could be something else."

"We don't get sick, to answer your implied question. Tuberculosis, the plague, viruses—we are already dead, meaning we don't get them."

It's my turn to stay silent, long enough that he leans forward in his seat. His piercing gaze catches mine. "You're thinking it's something else. Not a virus—not a *human* virus. But something worse?"

Slowly, I nod. "Yeah. I don't know, and that's where the frustration comes from. Without more information on what my dad did, I'm going into this blind. For all I know, he already knew of this disease and had the cure!"

Tears sting my eyes and I break the staring contest, drawing deep breaths to calm myself. It's hard to talk about Dad, harder still not to have him around me. To converse with and get advice from, when he's been there my entire life.

I shouldn't be crying in front of Nico, or losing my shit like this. But the weight of my grief is heavy in my chest. And as he rightly pointed out, I am nearing my period.

Hello, floodgates.

Nicolae

My hearing, the same hearing I told her I could perfectly control, narrows onto the sound of her heartbeat. The quiet grief in her heart permeates my senses and the air. I get up from my seat and walk to the window, attempting to put some distance between us—lest I give in to my craving and take her in my arms.

Being this close was a mistake. I shouldn't have brought her here. Talking about vampir anatomy is one thing, but no matter how sardonic and aloof I try to be, it's like she sees right through me.

More clearly than I'd like, I remember the hitch in her breath as I'd pushed her against the wall that day, the flutter of her pulse at the base of her neck... Mouth-watering. My fangs elongate and I rest my head against the window, letting its coolness calm me down. If only I could also douse my body in the same iciness, that would be perfect.

"Sorry."

Her muffled voice draws my attention. When I turn, her gaze shifts to my fangs, and she gulps. Other than that, her expression doesn't change.

"It's not your fault I don't have access to his stuff. And who knows what survived in the old house." She shakes her head. "Point is, what you've told me here gives me a start. I have a baseline, so even if I know nothing of medicine other than what I've learned from my father, I can try. Are you sure you don't want to get another doctor? An *actual* doctor?"

It's my turn to shake my head. "No. I don't think we have time."

"Even with your renowned vampir speed?"

I roll my eyes. "Even so."

She tilts her head to the side. "Does it use up energy, your ability to blur around at warp speed?"

"No. Not in the way you think. Our powers are not pieces of us that need constant fuel to function. They just...are."

"So using that or glamour wouldn't have gotten Violeta exhausted?"

"No."

"Then why not seek help elsewhere? There's got to be places for people like you, way better places than a village in the middle of nowhere. Is it that you don't have time, or that you're afraid to leave here?"

Her eyes widen at whatever she sees on my face. She could take her pick—anger, frustration, annoyance—because she's hit the truth.

"Why?" She stands, facing me completely. "I mean, you're royalty among your kind and—"

"It's complicated. Too complicated for a human to understand."

"Is it because of the clans Violeta mentioned hunted you? After your sire died?"

I scowl at her. "Let it go."

"No."

I go back behind my desk, using it as a shield. My frustration ratches up another notch. When's the last time I had a human get me to talk this much, and about things I'd rather not? She's pushing about Father, and our powers...

"You know, for someone who keeps pretending he's a monster, you sure act a lot like a human."

My head snaps up, eyes narrowed in warning, but she doesn't stop.

"It's funny, really. Because at first, I could've sworn you're an indifferent jackass—"

"I *am* an indifferent jackass."

"—and then that you didn't care at all for your family," she continues. "Yet that's not true. Just like your whole cool-as-a-cucumber thing doesn't mean anything. I don't think you're as indifferent as you pretend to be, Nico. On the contrary. I think you care. Maybe a little too much. Otherwise, you wouldn't have hung on to a human the way you did to me, knowing full well the chances of me being able to help your sister are pretty slim. And you definitely wouldn't be hiding your family here from whatever danger is out there... If you didn't care, you'd have only looked after yourself." A deep breath. "And if you didn't care, you wouldn't have kissed me."

Her words stir something in me—again. I grow weary of this. For eons, I have felt nothing, cared for nothing, and now she's making me doubt the very way I live my existence. And she *sees* too much. I didn't bring her here for that. I brought her here for Violeta.

This protection, this stupid attachment, it needs to end, and it needs to end now.

"What happened was a mistake," I say, latching on the quickest thing I can attack out of the list she provided.

I see it in her eyes—she knows I mean the barely-there kiss we shared in the solarium. To my surprise, her denial comes as strong as the rest of her words.

"It wasn't."

I turn my back on her, refusing to witness her hurt expression. Refusing to remember the promise I gave her, to never lie. "It was. I am beyond you, and we should not forget that."

Silence, as she takes in my words. My meaning. It's a low blow, made even lower by the fact I've picked up on her insecurities and am now completely using them against her.

In the window—where I'm watching her reflection—I can see that same realization in her eyes. That I am worth more than her. That she is worth less. That we are unequal—because we are, but not in the way she thinks, or in the way I implied. More in the way that her innocence surpasses me and makes me see just how cold the walls I've erected around myself for seclusion are.

I shouldn't care.

Tassa is a human. Brought here for one purpose, and one purpose only. If Mirabela hadn't sent me after her father that night, I wouldn't have run into her. She would have died, probably a rather atrocious death. That thought makes my fists clench, demanding retribution. *Not* the mark of someone who doesn't care.

I'm a fraud. For everything I've said I am, and everything I'm not.

But that's also why she cannot get attached to me, nor I to her. This is no fairy tale.

"You bastard." Tassa comes around my desk, surprising me with her speed, and shoves at me, forcing me to face her again. "You toy with everyone's emotions, don't you?"

I remain silent. What can I say?

She stares at me for a beat longer. That innocence in her, despite everything she's seen, demands the prince, the knight in shining armor. I am neither. I am the monster of her nightmares, and if she's not careful, I'll make her entire life a living nightmare. Not that I can say any of that. So I clench my teeth, pushing down the words, and refusing to speak.

Incensed, tears in her eyes, Tassa storms away and the door to my office slams shut behind her. I let her leave. The sooner I can get back to my indifferent self, the better. And the sooner she cures Violeta, the better it will be for her. She'll be able to return to her emotional, human life. Where she has room to grow. And leave me to my dreary one.

Chapter 10

Tassa

The bastard.

In my anger at Nico, I've gone straight out of the castle and into the woods. The sun is low in the sky—how have I been in Nico's office for almost an entire afternoon? A shiver runs through me. It doesn't help that the air is biting cold. I'm dressed in only jeans and a sweater, so I definitely feel it when the wind picks up.

But it's okay. Because it invigorates me. It also cools my anger and sharpens my thoughts.

At first, it was Nico's words that got to me. Probably because they were so similar to what my ex also said. But then on the short walk to here, I realized it's not so much the words, but the intent behind them.

Nico wasn't trying to be callous—okay, maybe a part of him was. But the more I replay the conversation, the more I realize he said what he did to get me to back off from asking questions. Which, of course, only makes me want to know more about it.

He thinks he can play me like a fiddle, turning my emotions on and off to like him, in order to, what? Hide what happened to my dad? Hide what they know? Or am I looking for problems where there are none, and the only thing he's trying to hide is the Draculs' own bloody history?

My thoughts wander to Violeta, and the information I've gathered so far. The notebook and book in my hand feel heavy—with purpose, with the burden of trying to find a solution to something I'm not remotely qualified for.

Maybe that's why I can't figure it out. Because nothing Nico said sparked a sliver of a clue in my mind...

I try to go back to Dad's teachings. He'd once told me patients can show all kinds of symptoms. And the key to them can lie in some insignificant part of their lives.

For his memory, I owe it to him to save Violeta. Or at least try. And no amount of someone like Nico should dissuade me. Definitely not for some kisses.

I turn to head back, but a noise in the woods stops me. It could be anything. We have all kinds of animals here, even lynxes, but... It almost sounded like breathing. *Human* breathing. Then I remember what Nico said about the muroni, and I hurry back to the castle.

It's only once I close the large oak doors behind me that it dawns on me—I've actually started to think of this place as being *safe*.

Huh. Go figure.

Instead of heading straight to Violeta's bedroom, I walk to the kitchen, drawn there by the smell of cinnamon and chocolate. It's enough to make my stomach grumble. Imagine my surprise when I find Violeta by the stove, happily stirring.

"Are you—*baking*?"

She turns to me, laughing. Her eyes are still tinged with red, and something about her entire demeanor seems deflated, but the smile is genuine. "Vampiri don't bake, silly. And *royals*?" She makes a mock-horrified face. "Heavens forbid!"

A snort escapes me, and I inch nearer, parking my frozen butt on the chair. The book and notepad follow, on the table.

"Out taking a stroll?" she asks over her shoulder.

"Erm..."

Another laugh. "I won't tell, promise. My brother seems to think if you so much as take one peek outside, you'll go running off into the woods."

"Mm, he might not have been that far off. What is it you're making, anyway?"

"Chocolate pudding. Also, hot chocolate." She points to another pot boiling. "Want some?"

"I thought vampiri don't eat human food."

"We don't... Not really. But making the stuff and smelling it is almost as good as actually tasting it."

Taste. Right. Nico had said taste was weird for them. Makes

sense that food wouldn't be appealing, except through scent.

"Want some?"

I waver with the decision. I've held back off sugar for so long, trying to watch my weight and now...bad habits are hard to break. But one night won't kill me, not when it can be such a comfort.

I nod. "Please." A sugar rush is just what I need.

Violeta moves and puts the pudding in a bowl with a spoon, then pours some hot chocolate in a cup, over a cinnamon stick. When she puts the mug in front of me, I inhale deep wafts of cinnamon, vanilla and cocoa.

"Yummm."

She inhales the steam wafting from her own cup, but doesn't drink the liquid within it. "I know. Did you know chocolate didn't enter Europe until around the 16th century? Christopher Columbus discovered cacao beans on a journey to America, whilst intercepting a trade ship. He was so enamored by the taste, he brought them back to Spain in—"

"—1502." I smile. "There are different accounts of it, you know? Some say it was another conquistador... But I don't care. I love chocolate. And I may not be a history buff on everything, but *chocolate*?" I inhale deeply. "Can't get over why people didn't like it back then. It took forever for it to be considered a delicacy!"

Violeta chuckles. "Well, it was pretty damn bitter."

I tilt my head to the side. "Wait... So how did you come to like it? Memory might fail me—I'm only human, don't judge—but it wasn't until the 1800s that it became massively popular because they discovered how to make it sweet."

Violeta beams, transforming her expression into something near-nostalgic. "All true. Thing is, my parents had access to all kinds of new things in their trade. I don't know how, but they got ahold of cocoa beans way before it was in mainland Europe. Everyone else in the house hated it, but Mom used to mix it with hot water for me whenever I had a bad day. She added honey to it because she always said sweetness made everything better...And she was right."

"That's adorable," I whisper. "Hot chocolate before it was hot chocolate... I can't believe your mom technically discovered that before anyone else did."

Violeta shrugs. "She loved experimenting. She just...didn't live long enough to make a name for herself."

I let that go. The pain in her voice is too raw to dive into. Instead, I ask a somewhat easier question. "You mentioned she made this for you on bad days... Did you have many?"

"Enough. I was a sickly child, and grew up into an even sicker adult."

"You seem a bit better today."

It's true. She's less zombie-like, at least for the moment. What kind of virus could have such symptoms—fine one moment, then wrecked the next day? Many theories come to mind for a human, but for a vampir? None.

"I suppose. Spending time in my greenhouse helps every now and again." Violeta stirs her beverage with the cinnamon stick, watching me. "What were you doing outside?"

"Taking a breather."

"Nico being annoying? I wasn't spying, but I saw you head into his office. He never takes anyone there, not even one of us."

And yet he didn't even hesitate with me... Weird.

"How come?"

She shrugs. "We all have our special places."

I tilt my head to the side. "What's yours, then?"

Her smile widens. "My greenhouse. I use the solarium to grow the plants, then I take them to an area at the back of the house. I love the plants I can make grow."

Right. The greenhouse. Thinking of it reminds me of Nico's towering form over me, his lips grazing my neck...the heat in his eyes. I gulp, and try to redirect my thoughts. "What kind of plants?"

"Well, I used to have everything, at our old place. Anything that can be used naturally to make remedies." Her smile wobbles. "I used to help humans, without my siblings knowing. At least, half the time."

I think back to her symptoms...

"And no, before you even go there, I didn't pick this—whatever this disease is—from a human. If that were possible, I would've been ill centuries ago. Besides, I enjoy helping your kind...even when it doesn't always benefit me."

I frown. "Why? That sentiment isn't shared by any of your siblings."

"True. But I have things to make up for." She sets her cup back on the table, her blue eyes turning piercing. "So, why was Nico being annoying?"

Ah, so that evasiveness character trait does run in the family. The more time I spend with them, the more I see the resemblance.

I'm hesitant to actually explain why, but she must see enough from my expression to deduce I'm upset.

Violeta makes a face. "He's not that bad, I promise. Whatever he said to annoy you—"

"It's not about that. It's—never mind. Let's talk about your disease."

She rolls her eyes. "Do we have to?"

"I'm afraid we don't have a choice."

Nicolae

I wish I could say the only reason I'm skulking around at night in my own home is because I need to clear my head. It's not. It's because I'm feeling fucking *guilty*. The word alone annoys me, let alone the actual feeling.

Which brings me to the skulking.

And the fact it's taking me closer to the kitchen, to where I'm most definitely not supposed to be. My nose already picked up something—a faint whiff of chocolate and cinnamon. If I'd had a human stomach, it would gurgle with want. As a child, I loved the stuff.

My steps taper off and I freeze. Where the hell did that thought come from?

Still, I move closer, and then catch another scent. Perplexed, I lean against the wall, trying to figure out the best way to intervene, and failing. Yet, I cannot make myself go away, so instead, I listen.

"And how are you feeling now?" That's Tassa's soft voice.

"Not...that great."

Violeta. How could I not have recognized my sister's scent? I sniff again. Because it's not hers. Not really. Her scent...*changed*.

The realization hits me, but it also roots me to the spot.

Vampiri never change their scent. It remains as it was on the day of their death. For Violeta, it was always fresh, like a valley. How could it now have changed to this sweet vanilla-like one? And why?

"When did the symptoms start?" Tassa asks.

A long pause follows. What's so hard for Violeta to admit? They started in the fight with the muroni, the same day Tassa's father got attacked.

"Two years ago."

This time, it's not only surprise, but that rotten guilt that hits me. Two years? My sister has been in pain and not feeling herself *for two years*, and I never noticed?

I try to think back, desperately looking for clues, but I cannot bring any to memory. Because I was never paying attention. I never cared, for her. Never bothered to pay attention to her whims, her desires, her pain and suffering. Because I was too damn focused on forgetting how to care. Especially after Silva...

It's not just me, I try to reason with myself. Alex, Vlad, Liza, Mira, they all could've noticed it.

But she doesn't speak to them as much as you, a nagging voice at the back of my head points out.

Damnit. It's my problem I missed. Worse, I failed her.

Violeta was there for me after my last hiccup. When I spiraled so far down, that none of them knew how to help me, she was my ray of light. And I haven't been able to be the same for her.

"Why did you wait so long?" Tassa asks.

A wry laugh is my sister's response. "Who would I have told?"

"Your siblings, for one. You seem...close-knit."

"Do we?" Another bitter laugh. "Don't be fooled by appearances. We're worse than a pack of hyenas, at times." A softening of her tone follows. "But I do love them. Even if half of them have forgotten what that feels like."

It's weird, hearing all of this from her mouth. Almost forbidden. Maybe I shouldn't be here, after all. We don't have that much to hide from each other, but we should be entitled to some privacy, even if we live in the same household.

Yet I don't budge.

Tassa clears her throat. "For your symptoms… So far, I'm still in the gathering stage. I want you to know I am committed to saving you, weird as that may sound coming from a human. If my dad were still alive. it would probably be the stuff of a few hours. I don't have his knowledge of the vampiri, so it's going to be a lengthier process. I'm sorry."

It amazes me how sincere she sounds. A human's able to be there for my sister more than me. What does that say about me?

"I didn't think it would be that easy—or possible, to be honest. It's more the rest of them that think there is something you can do."

"And you don't?"

"I've made my peace with death a long time ago. Plus, I have my greenhouse, remember? If there were a natural remedy, I would've found it."

There's some shuffling, and I take that as my cue to enter. Both turn to me in surprise.

Tassa

A few nights should've been enough to come to terms with the fact I'm living with vampiri now, and the way they move so fast. They've given up all pretenses around me now and although that should be freeing, it's also unnerving.

When Nico walks in, making no sound whatsoever, I nearly jump out of my seat. My heartbeat quickens for other reasons, too, like how his blue eyes darken when they land on me.

And then I remember his words, the harshness of his tone, and the way he purposefully hurt me to shove me away. Bitterness coats my tongue, and I turn my attention to my hot chocolate.

Violeta nods at her brother and gets up from the table. Seeing them like this, side by side, with nothing else to distract me, I do notice the signs of her frailty. How her fingertips tremble, and she seems to sway on her feet. Either this is a really bad day, or they're doing shit all for having each other's backs.

Hyenas, indeed.

"Was it me you were looking for?" Violeta asks. After a moment of staring at Nico, she chuckles and says, "Didn't think so."

Without a word to me, she leaves the kitchen. Nico seems to listen to her footsteps fading, head tilted to the side, then he sighs and focuses his full attention on me.

I legitimately *feel* it. Not just in his eyes, but it's as if his entire being is aware of me, making me even more aware of him. It's a torrent of emotions—too much, all at once.

"Are you in a hurry?" he asks.

Yes. "No," is what comes out. And then I want to kick myself.

After his earlier outburst, I shouldn't want to be around him. Ever again. Especially not alone. But my father raised me to be polite, so the best I can do is sit down and purse my lips.

When he says nothing immediately, I take another sip of my hot chocolate. Then another. He's still quiet, yet he misses none of my movements.

Finally, I clear my throat. "I have some research to do, so if this can wait until morning..."

"No, actually, it can't." It's his turn to clear his throat. "I've come to offer my apology. For our earlier conversation."

With a sigh, I settle back into the chair and grab a spoonful of pudding. "No need."

"There is a need. I was rude, and my words hurt you."

"That should be the least of your concerns."

He clicks his tongue. "Woman, will you let me finish?"

I arch an eyebrow at his tone and fold my arms over my chest.

Nico sighs and runs a hand over his face. "I didn't mean it that way."

"Sure, you didn't. Go on, then, explain to me how your version of events is so much truer than mine. Because all women must be crazy, right?"

He narrows his eyes. "That's not—"

"Your expression says otherwise."

"I didn't *mean it* that way, Tassa. Chrissake, let me get a word out, would you?"

"Why should I? You made it clear you're the superior one of us."

"I'm trying to apologize here."

"And doing a shit job of it."

He tosses his hands in the air. "I give up. Apologizing to you is impossible."

"I don't need you to."

"So even when I concede a point, you won't let it go?"

I say nothing, instead watching him. He's been cool and collected and acting all indifferent. It will do him good to squirm for a moment.

In typical Nico fashion, he takes a seat next to me, right in my bubble, and watches me finish my pudding. Then his expression turns envious when I drink the hot chocolate.

"Nico, either talk or stop staring. You're creeping me out."

He yanks his gaze away, instead turning it to the table. "Sorry. It's just, it's been a while. Since I've eaten. And you're reminding parts of my brain of how enjoyable human food is."

I shouldn't indulge him in conversation, but my curious mind can't help it. "Isn't blood the same for you? Different flavors and all?"

He shrugs. "Not really. Blood is blood. Metallic and tasteless for the most part. Sometimes if humans have a specific diet, it'll change the blood's flavor, for lack of a better word."

"Like, if they eat a lot of meat?"

"Or garlic."

I make a face, taking a sip of my hot chocolate. "Doesn't sound too tasty."

"Believe me, it's not."

And just like that, we're back to talking like normal human beings. It makes me wonder how long this'll last for...

As if guessing my thoughts, Nico taps the table. "I do apologize," he says. "For earlier. I was...taken aback by your questions."

"And being a jerk was your coping mechanism?"

He catches my eyes. "Da, something like that."

"Fine. Apology accepted."

With my cup empty, I get up to leave, but he grabs my wrist, holding me captive. "Wait. I... there's more. You're right to want more information on our maker, and I'm willing to give it to you. At least, in as much as it concerns me and Violeta."

"Okay..." I sit back down. "I'm listening."

He doesn't remove his hand from mine, and something about that makes the conversation even more intimate.

"We weren't all human, when we were turned. Țepeș, our father, found us one by one over the centuries. I was the first one he chose, toward the end of the 15th century." A sigh escapes him. "I'm not trying to be obtusely vague, but the years blur together after this long.

Whichever the case, Father chose me after his first wife's death." He pauses for a beat.

"I remember that story," I whisper. "It was a heart-wrenching account of how she committed suicide, refusing to let herself be taken to the Turks...and live without Țepeș."

Nico's silent for a longer moment, then continues, as if acknowledging his creator's sad story would be too much. I don't understand it, but his story is too important to interrupt.

"I already knew Violeta by then," he says. "I'd been living in an orphanage and running away every which way. Violeta's parents had a medieval version of a food truck, selling goods at the local market. I tried to steal from them, and her father would've handed me in to the authorities. Violeta convinced him not to."

He looks at our hands, touching, and removes his. The obvious reluctance in the way he does that makes me think he doesn't really want to.

"I grew up with her family. We were the same age, and I soon came to see her as my sister. But her father gambled, and one night, things got very bad. The people he owed money to threatened to come after his family. I overheard them, and stood watch every night after that for a week. On the seventh night, they came to the house... And I killed every single one of them."

My mouth parts open, and my heart races. Nico gives me a wry look.

"Da, it wasn't pretty. Times were different back then. Lawlessness could overrun towns, and sometimes it was a kill or be killed mentality. I was never a coward. Nonetheless, there were still consequences. The authorities were coming for me... Violeta's dad told me to leave. I was sixteen and had no other prospects. So, I left. For weeks, I wandered from village to village, looking for work. Eventually, I found some in a town not too far away from here."

"You didn't lie, then, when you said you'd lived in the area before."

He inclines his head, then continues. "In that town lived a voivode—a prince of the area. Vlad Țepeș. He was rumored to be... that there was something wrong with him. But when I ran out of options for a job, I sought him out, hoping he would let me clean up his horse stalls. Anything." He leans back in his chair with a deep sigh. "He did... And then he offered me the chance of my life. Or so I thought."

"He turned you, then?"

"Not immediately. He waited years, until I stepped into my thirties. He wanted to test me. To see if it was possible... And then, da, he turned me. A year later, I went back to Violeta and offered her the same chance. Things had gotten worse at home. Both her parents blamed her for being a sickly child and costing them money, instead of blaming themselves for their bad habits. I won't go into the details—Violeta can tell you that—but bottom line is, she was only too happy to jump on the opportunity of a new life."

His fist on the table clenches. "I didn't turn her, though. Father was particular about that. *He* did the turning, once I brought her to him. Something I should never have done. I should've let her live a mortal life, one free of this burden. And then she would be fine."

"I'm sure Violeta doesn't blame you," I whisper. "She doesn't seem to."

"Perhaps." He looks at me, then. "Either way, that's the sordid story. After us, Father found Mirabela, then Alexandru, Elizabeta and Vlad. Mirabela was next in the 16th century. Alexandru and Elizabeta were turned within years of each other, late in the 17th century. And

Vlad is our youngest, really. Early 18th century." A smirk twists his lips. "Each of them came with their own burdens, and none of them are the same as they were centuries ago, but for better or worse, they're my family. And we only have each other left to rely on. Do you understand, now, why I need you to save Violeta?"

His blue eyes meet mine, holding my gaze in an unbreakable hold. How can his siblings say he's indifferent and cold, when all that stare does is warm every part of my body, bringing it to tingling attention? When his intensity awakens my senses, making me wonder if I've ever *lived,* period, before him?

Before my eyes drop to his lips, I swallow past my dry throat and whisper, "I do. And I promise I'll give it my best shot."

The words, which I'd meant placating, ring true to my ears and in my heart. Because they are, I realize in a flash. I've come to care for Violeta because of the kindness she's showed me, and because she doesn't deserve any of this.

I don't quite remember when we ventured to the library. I must've suggested it, or maybe Nico did. Either way, we end up with me on a leather armchair, and him by the fire, both of us flipping through books, searching for clues and mentions of potential afflictions that are similar to Violeta's.

I took the chance to read through the book on muroni history, trying to see if there's anything useful in there. Nothing. Although, it did give me a better understanding of the vampiri clans. I then moved on to some natural remedies books—worn, probably read by Violeta herself many times over.

Still nothing.

After a moment, I toss the one I'd been reading to the side, careful not to crush the spine. Then glance up to find Nico watching me with a peculiar look on his face.

"What's wrong?"

"Nothing."

"You're looking at me weird." I pause. "It's not nothing."

He smirks. "Am I making you uncomfortable?"

"Well, it's not every day you get stared at by a vampir, so, yeah."

He freezes, as if trying to figure out if I'm serious or not, and then I can't stop laughing. The corners of his lips pull upwards. "Touché." A moment later, he points at my book and adds, "Well, I didn't want to make you feel weird. What is it?"

"The book isn't enough. I need..." I think, trying to go through my dad's list. "A trip to my dad's house, to see what else I can find there."

Nico frowns. "You think he treated vampiri with a similar issue?"

"I'm not sure. All I know is what you told me. The guy who killed him wasn't human. And he said he was coming to collect something. *And* he didn't seem all that right in the head. So...it's worth a shot."

Nico shifts in his seat. "What do you remember about that night?"

"Not much." His tight tone makes me frown. "Why? Is there something I should be remembering?"

Nicolae

I can't believe she has no recollection, no nightmares, of me ripping that guy apart, tearing him limb from limb. It's been days since, but the memory seems buried very far at the back of her mind.

Why I feel relief at that, I have no idea, but I crush it as soon as it comes up.

"No, nothing at all." I try for a smile. "What books do you need? I'll go get them."

"No. I want to go. I..." Her breath hitches, but no tears come. "Please. I want to come with you."

It's probably a bad idea, and I'll be getting shit from my siblings, but whatever. I'm not going to let her go by herself, not when we don't know what the threat is. Not when I need her here, helping Violeta.

"Then we will. Tomorrow."

She blinks, as if not expecting my answer.

"What, thought I'd deny you such a sensible request?"

"Weeeell, then that would mean you've kidnapped me. Which you've all been clear is not what's going on here."

"Because it's not."

"Right." She smiles and gets off the couch, nodding at me. "In that case, I'll leave you to your coffin, and get out of your hair."

Bemused, I watch as she slips past me, and heads to the door. Did we just have simple banter? Me, a vampir, with a human like her? What in all hell is this world coming to?

It went from an apology she was quick to accept, to hours of conversation and companionable silence. Not something I'm used to, in the least. Not something I've had—except with Silva.

A pang hits the center of my chest and I lift my hand to rub it absentmindedly.

"Good night," Tassa says at the door, lingering.

I turn toward her. "Good night."

No sooner is she gone, than I hear clapping. "Quite a performance, frate."

"Alexandru." His name escapes me on a sigh and I turn just as he steps through the darkness of the other entrance. "How much did you hear?"

"Oh, the last bit and such. So, you're really going to take her to her dear Dad's home?"

I scowl at him. "Why wouldn't I?"

"Because it'll be in broad daylight. And you're bound to attract attention. Not exactly conspicuous in your perfectly matched outfits, are you?"

"Just because you favor ripped pieces of things you call clothing, does not mean you get to incessantly harp at me for my dress code."

When I turn to walk away, he's in front of me. Gripping my arm in an iron grip, his eyes glittering with red menace. "Watch yourself, frate. She's here to do one job, and one only. Get Violeta better. Then we all know how it'll end. If you want to scratch that itch so bad, how about you go pay for it? It's not like you haven't before. I could even share the name of an escort agency in the area..."

I glare at him, deliberately ignoring the second half of his statement. "We will not kill her."

"And how do you propose we keep her silent on all she has seen? Or do you want to revisit the Nazi experiment times, once again?"

I yank my arm out of his grip, and in so doing succeed in tearing the material. My scowl deepens. "Now you've ruined a perfectly good shirt, and I went to quite some trouble getting it." I look up, meeting his gaze. "Let's get one thing clear. Tassa is under my protection, for the time being. When Violeta feels better, we can decide together—
all of us—what her fate will be. But it will not be death."

His silence is warning enough, but I try not to let it get to me. I must not appear like I'm starting to care for the human. After all, there is a certain decorum to maintain, and if I so much as step out of line, I will become the black sheep of this family.

By the door, I stop. "Did you know about Violeta?"

"Know what?"

"That she's been fighting with this thing for two years."

His stunned silence tells me he did not. And when I turn to him, he doesn't have that extra fraction of a second to school his expression. He may be a jerk when it comes to humans, but with us? He can't deny he cares.

"I didn't know, either," I mutter, and walk out.

HOUSE OF DRACUL

Chapter 11

Tassa

What is the etiquette, I wonder the next morning, as I go about preparing myself? I'm about to be escorted into town by a vampir who doesn't want to leave my side because he thinks there's a threat to me out there. So, how do I dress? Do I wait for him in my room, or go downstairs and find myself something to eat?

Better yet, do I just wait until we're in town, and take care of the feeding situation then?

Midway through brushing my hair, I sense someone watching me. A quick glance around the room reveals nothing, so I let it slide. But already, my normal mood is gone.

It's with tense muscles that I head outside, bypassing the kitchen in favor of waiting until we get to town. Exercise before food, always. Much as I'm trying to encourage myself, by the time I reach the door, I can practically feel my stomach growling. Trying to ignore it won't be easy.

I adjust my dad's satchel on my shoulder. The feel of the worn leather makes my throat clog. A memory of him passing it to me, time and time again, hits me with surprising clarity. *Oh, Dad...*

"Ugh, humans. The smell of tears is overpowering. Go outside at least, would you?"

I startle at the voice and turn, facing Mirabela. She's the one I've had the least interaction with. But if I'd been hoping for a warmer welcome, her cool eyes tell me I'm out of luck.

When I say nothing, she sneers, but she doesn't leave. Thankfully, Nico shows up at that moment.

"Mira."

"Nico."

Whatever goes on between them leads her to huff, then she pivots on her heels and leaves.

Nico faces me, an apologetic smile on his lips. "Sorry I took a while. Are you ready to go?"

"I... Yeah." It's then I notice what he's wearing. "Trying to fit in?"

With his dark jeans, sneakers, t-shirt and a black leather jacket over, he looks almost...human. I can't get over it, no matter how much I try. Half the time I wonder if all the vampir stuff is in my head, and not actually real. Then Nico, or one of his siblings, does something completely un-human and that's a more potent reminder than anything else.

Nico shrugs. "Don't care enough to warrant the effort."

Without further explaining the cryptic statement, he opens the door, and we head out.

"So, you guys have no cars?"

Since we've been walking for the last forty minutes, and we didn't take one to the cop station, it seems only normal that I ask.

Nico makes a half laugh, half strangled sound at the back of his throat. Then he clears it and says, "No. They don't last around us."

"Why not? Need for speed?"

I glance at him only to see him roll his eyes.

"You need to get sparkles and vegetarians out of your head. We're neither, for the simple reason that those types of vampiri don't exist in this very real and fucked up world. And, to answer your question, no, it's not the need for speed. It's our strength. Sooner or later, we get complacent and one foot goes in too deep, one fist clenches too tight..." He purses his lips. "Then accidents lead to questions, and to our blood being stored in human blood banks. No good."

"And why's that a problem?" He arches an eyebrow my way, as if I should realize. A second later, it hits me—for the same reason as his shiftiness at the cop station. "Ah. Because the last thing you need is scientists poking into your background."

"Exactly."

"Has that ever happened?" Curiosity made me ask, but judging by the clenching of his jaw, I probably shouldn't have. "Forget it. I shouldn't pry."

Of course, that begs the question of when and how it happened.

And once more, it reminds me of what he said. I don't think he meant to be as ruthless as he was with his words, with saying I was beneath him. And he apologized. But it's like there's a thin—or thick, depending on how one looks at it—veneer he's set up to keep himself away from the world. And from his own family. Like a fool, I can't help but wonder what caused it.

We walk in silence a little bit, then Nico says, "It happened too many times to count. And none of us wish to relive it."

"Sorry," I mutter under my breath, trying to hide the fact his answer surprises me.

"Wait." He moves in front of me before I have a chance to react—how unnerving is that?—and stares. The sun is barely up right now, and we've gotten much closer to my old home than I thought.

Nico holds his arm up a moment longer, barring my way, before moving. But is it me, or does he seem more tense than usual?

I follow him to the door—my old home—and he unlocks it.

"How did you have a key?" I ask.

"Nicked it the night I rescued you."

I nod. Plausible enough. I really should stop doubting him, even if something tells me he's still hiding part of the story.

Once the door is open, Nico steps aside to let me in. The smell hits me first. Bleach and metal. And charred stuff.

"Someone's cleaned up."

Nico nods. "Most likely the same villagers who came to see you the other time."

"Why? I know what they said when we went to the cop station but..."

He sighs, his demeanor more and more uncomfortable. "It would be in their best interests to keep this covered up, as well. Write it off as an accident to the police, you leaving because of grief, and no one's the wiser."

"Are they getting paid for this?"

"I'm assuming the priest and his Order will take care of it," he says curtly. It's enough to tell me the time for questions has reached an end.

I move around the house, trying to ignore the tears in my eyes and the feeling I'm about to crumble. How many meals did we have at this table? How many times did we read in companionable silence on the worn couch? And how many times...

Get ahold of yourself. He's not coming back. No matter what, I need to get that through my head. It's one thing to have had my dad guiding me my entire life. Now I'm on my own, completely alone, and needing to make decisions for myself.

I glance at Nico. *Good decisions. Not the kind that get me killed.* If Dad were alive, he'd have told me to get the hell away from him and his siblings. So why aren't I making that same choice?

Because you're too soft-hearted. No matter what you tell yourself about finding out more about your father's death, the reality is you've started to care.

I sigh and head toward the remedies area. Nico had grabbed some, but he's obviously no doctor. He missed the most important ones. Not that antibiotics and such could help Violeta, but it's worth a shot.

Then I step into Dad's office, and the library he has there. It seems the villagers got here faster than Nico believed because a lot of the walls are still standing. Aside from half of the living room being burned, the rooms at the back of the house are relatively untouched.

I approach the shelves, reading the spines, pulling some out, rifling through them, and putting them back. Nothing in them tells me Dad was treating vampiri, but then again, he wouldn't have been so obvious.

The thought makes me stop my perusing, and instead I turn to Nico. "Can you help me look for hidden compartments, or something?"

"What makes you think I can find them?"

"You've had more years of experience than me, for one. And two—what, you're too good to get your hands dirty?"

He rolls his eyes again and starts searching. If they're really royals, these guys, they don't act like them. Then I think of Elizabeta. *Well, maybe some of them do. But not all.*

An hour goes by, then two, and still we find nothing. On my second perusal of Dad's library, I find a thinner book hidden between two large ones. The familiar D on the spine makes me pull it out. Sure enough, it's got the House of Dracul crest on it. I place it in my bag, intending to read through it later. I pick up some other meager books I'd found on supernatural subjects and drop on the couch, sighing.

Nico follows me, frowning. "You're not giving up?"

"We've searched every inch of this place!"

He drops on the couch next to me, then just as quickly jumps up with a yelp. Followed by a curse. Only then do I realize he's holding his butt cheek.

When he catches me staring, he mutters, "Something sharp there."

"There's nothing—" I swallow my laugh as my eyes land on a sliver of something poking from the leather seat. His vampir strength, falling onto the couch, must've rattled whatever was hidden within.

With eager hands, while Nico mutters about his injured ass, I tear into the beloved couch and pull out a—

"Is that a *scroll*?" Nico asks.

I nod, staring at the worn parchment. It was the metal holding it together that was poking out. But when did Dad hide it in here? And why?

"I dare say that's enough, no?" Nico says. "Let's go."

I glance at him. He's still holding his butt cheek, a scowl on his face.

"Do you need me to take a look at your, um, injury?"

His scowl deepens. "It will heal."

"On its own?" Despite myself, I'm fascinated. If it wasn't going to turn awkward, I would totally ask him to let me watch as his flesh welds back together. Then I realize that means him taking off his pants, and I can feel my cheeks reddening.

"Da, on its own." Nico seems unfazed, as always.

The moment after, he's out of the house and I have no choice but to run after him.

Nicolae

Why do I find it so hard being in this place with her, when at the castle I'm indifferent? No, not indifferent. That's a lie and even I must own up to it. My indifference to life started taking a walk the moment Tassa popped into my life.

Even now, instead of taking off, I wait for her outside the house. Impatiently. Unwillingly. But...I still wait.

She emerges seconds later. Over the sound of her breathing, and the beating of her heart—something I'm constantly aware of—I catch her stomach gurgling.

"Are you hungry?"

"Um..." She smiles sheepishly. "Yeah, a bit. I didn't eat, figured I'd get something in town."

Not much I can do but acquiesce, otherwise it'll only lead to her reverting back to thoughts of kidnapping and such. So we add the scroll to her bag, and take off.

Morning traffic is full-on moving now, with villagers bustling around, going about their business. For a moment, images of another time interpose themselves in my mind—soon gone, like a breeze that keeps on blowing.

We walk side by side, and whether Tassa sees it or not, I catch the furtive glances people throw us. I'll be a new face in town, someone of interest. And if the other people—the Order—did their job right, most anyone who knew her or her father would believe the priest's story that she was recovering at a safe house.

"Tassa!" An old woman crosses the street, dragging a little boy with her. "Tassa, draga mea!" She crushes Tassa into a hug, muttering sweet nothings and condolences.

I tune them out, having no interest in their bantering. Instead, I scan the area, wondering how long the quiet will last.

Turns out, not that long. In the distance, I catch the eye of a burly old man. His fixed stare sends me on high alert.

With each century passing, each danger averted, my instincts have honed sharper. I don't have to *know* to know. And something about that man instantly sets them off. He knows what I am and he's not happy about it. Order or not, we can't linger.

Without thinking, I lean toward Tassa and whisper in her ear, "We need to go. Hurry up."

My words couldn't have been heard, but the gesture is enough to get the woman to size me properly. Tassa makes her excuses and off we go, before anyone's the wiser, this time heading in the opposite direction.

A merchant stand offers a selection of cold cuts, cheeses and breads. I grab a few of each, toss them in a paper bag, and give money to the vendor. Then I tug on Tassa's hand and walk faster.

For a few moments, I have blissful silence, then she yanks on my hand. "Hey! Slow down, would you? I don't have vampir speed, unlike some."

I turn to her, my eyes scanning the area around us with damn-near paranoia. "Watch your words. Not around here." She blinks, surprised at my tone, and I amend, "Please."

With a nod, we're off again, disappearing into the woods. A glance behind tells me no one's following us—yet.

"Why the rush to leave?"

"Didn't want to cause a scene in the middle of town square. One of the villagers was giving us fixed stares."

"Oh." She nibbles on the food, and says, "Thank you, by the way. For the food. I could've paid."

I roll my eyes. "You humans worry about the silliest things."

"It's not silly."

"I'm not getting into another inane debate with you."

I had plenty with the last one. Her stubbornness is a thing of beauty, but the problem is I've always been a sucker for a woman with intellect. And the more we argue, the more we banter, the more her energy makes me forget I'm not supposed to care.

Tassa mutters something under her breath, then says, "So, you said vegetarian is a no and so are sparkles. What do you mean?"

"About what?"

"Well, you never did explain what you eat. Or, rather, how you find your food."

I glance pointedly at her slice of cheese. "Is this the best time to have this conversation?"

"I have a solid stomach. Plus, whatever you tell me could be useful for Violeta. I'm guessing you all eat the same?"

"Da, for the most part. The only difference is that grass she likes to inhale."

"Pot."

I snort at the correction. "Perhaps that's where her illness is coming from."

"Highly unlikely. I've seen you all drink."

I arch an eyebrow. "Is that a diss? Are you calling us alcoholics?"

"Functioning vampir alcoholics, yeah."

She grins, then takes a big bite of the food, closing her eyes like someone who's truly enjoying every bite. When was the last time I ever enjoyed something with such gusto?

"'s p'rob'ly sum'nin' ahhs."

I arch both eyebrows. "Come again?"

She swallows, a faint tinge of red on her cheeks. "I was saying, it's probably something else."

She chews again. Swallows. Why am I even paying attention to something so mundane?

"So, the food?"

"I didn't think you were serious. But, fine. Have it your way. Just make sure to puke away from me." Throwing my head back, I focus on the sky above. "We choose our hunts carefully. Because vampiri aren't solitary, there's always a few of us in a clan. And with more of us in a single town, it leads to, well, a need for more blood supply. Luckily, we like to share our food, and we don't need to drink an entire human's blood supply to survive. In some towns, humans actually seek us out, wanting to offer their blood. In others, we take what we need, but from the scum of society. With a few occasional lapses in judgment."

"Hmm."

I can't tell what that noise means, so I straighten, observing her once again. She takes another bite of her food.

"The healing, how does it work?" When I only stare back at her, waiting for her to expand, Tassa adds, "Earlier, you said your injury will heal on its own."

"Ah, that." I shift on my seat, oddly flustered at the reminder. *Stupid way to get injured.* "Because of the constant intake of fresh blood, our bodies rejuvenate faster. I'm sure a scientist would have a better explanation, but as far as Alex has been able to say, it's down to the cells. What would normally die in a normal human, and have an end-life cycle... In us, it lives on. Rejuvenates, resets. Whatever you want to call it."

"Wow. Dad would've been all over that theory."

I tilt my head. "You used to debate science with him?"

"Sometimes. Most times, the subject matter went over my head. Except when he talked about natural remedies. For some reason, those always stuck in head." She pauses and takes another bite of the food. "What about healing? What your cells are doing—is that passed on to a regular human?"

"No. It's not contagious, not in the sense you're thinking. But our saliva does have healing properties, like I told you. Alex thinks it's because of the same principle."

"Hmm." She toys with her food a minute, then, "And the blood... You drink it straight from the source?"

"Yes."

"From the throat, the wrist...?"

I nod. "Any main vein." I can't help but tease, "Contrary to popular belief, some women much prefer thigh bites instead of neck."

Tassa snorts, her cheeks pinkening again. "Sure. I'm sure it's such a joy."

My grin widens. "Don't knock it until you try it."

My gaze lingers on her pale skin. I wonder if it's the same lovely shade on her legs... her thighs... or if it's even paler. That brings a very vivid image of my fangs sinking into her milky thighs, which has my body tightening uncomfortably. My smile slips and I tear my gaze away.

Tassa doesn't seem to notice. "Does it ever affect you if the person you drink from is a drug addict?"

"Not past the high in the initial seconds, no. Kind of like what I mentioned with the different diets—it's all a flavor to the blood, in the end."

"What if the person has a disease? Can they pass it on to you?"

"Our bodies run through everything too fast. Your analytical brain cannot comprehend it."

"All right, genius, then how about this—where was Violeta the last few months, or more to the point, the last three years? I need to establish a timeline."

"I can help with that."

We arrive at the castle then, only for Liza to burst outside. Her furious expression is aimed at Tassa at first. Then it switches to me and she cries, "Violeta fainted again!"

Chapter 12

Tassa

Before I can say anything, Nico takes off. One moment he's there, the next he's gone, Elizabeta on his heels. It takes me longer to make my way to Violeta's room. In a way, it also gives me time to ground myself.

This is it. The moment of truth. Whatever will lie behind that door, will be the full version of her symptoms. Not hearsay, but this time I'll be able to see it for myself. And help…or fail at it.

When I enter the room, Violeta is sitting on the bed, paler than normal. Her hair, normally straight, is frizzy. The purple bags under her eyes have deepened, and her lips are dry and cracked.

Elizabeta's far away from the bed, in a corner with Mirabela.

They're whispering too low for me to make out anything they're saying. All I can see are their lips moving.

Without looking at me, Nico says, "You can start."

I move closer, mindful of my heartbeat and breathing. In a room full of vampiri, I can't afford to second-guess myself and act a fool.

Once I'm by Violeta's bed, I reach for her hand. Normally, I'd check for a pulse, but there is none. There is, however, something else. An oddly sickly smell assails my senses. It takes me a moment to recognize it. I've encountered such smells from patients of my fathers, patients who had diabetes. It's the sugar in their blood that makes them smell so sweet, usually in very bad cases.

Can vampiri even get diabetes?

Nico said viruses don't hit them. And I'd thought that meant regular human diseases, too. But if that's not the case, could it be something as simple as this?

But... How would a vampir even go about getting diabetes? It makes no sense.

No. If drugs don't affect them, and neither does alcohol, then there's no way. It's got to be something else.

"How are you feeling?" I ask.

Violeta looks at me, and this time her gaze is not as kind as normal. Some of that vampir indifference has interfered, or perhaps it's always been there. Either that, or they're all wired with the same coping mechanism. Whatever the case may be, I can't allow her change in behavior to affect my care of her.

Forcing my own emotions out of the way, I say, "I know this may seem like a stupid question. But I need you to describe everything you're feeling. What caused you to faint this time?"

She blinks, as if only seeing me for the first time, then starts slow, her voice wobbly. "I haven't fed in a few days. I was planning to go hunt when Liza came by to talk to me. I got a little bit annoyed, and the next thing I know, the room was spinning."

This from the same girl—vampir—who'd made me chocolate pudding and a hot chocolate just the previous night. My mind struggles to grasp the enormity of the change in her. Even her way of speaking is different. Not just wobbly, but *slower*, like words are a struggle.

A door opens and closes behind us. I glance around, no longer seeing Violeta's sisters. In a way, it's a relief.

"Did anything else happen?" I ask.

"No, nothing."

"Are you sure? Did you feel your blood pressure rising at all when you got annoyed?"

Nico chooses that moment to intervene. "Vampiri don't get blood pressure."

"Neither do they get diabetes," I shoot back.

He simply stares at me while Violeta watches in silence. I don't know how to explain it, but something in me says there's more to this. Perhaps my mind absorbed more than I thought, while I was helping out Dad. Perhaps it's just my sixth sense. Whatever it is, there's no way this is simply a random occurrence.

The breadcrumbs pave the way, Dad always said. Time to do exactly that.

Following my gut, I say, "Violeta, can you account for the last three years of your life?"

She turns from me to Nico, and back to me again. Each blink of her eyes is sluggish, like it's taking all her energy to focus. "What do you mean?"

"I mean everything that you did in the last three years. The two you said you were sick, and the one prior to that. Who you saw, where you went, what you ate, anything unusual. Anything unusual *at all*? No matter how small."

She looks at me like I'm crazy.

Nico adds, "Maybe we should let her rest. Come back later."

This from the guy who's been trying to convince me of his indifference. Anyone with two eyes can see how much he cares for her. He may not show it the same way as the rest of them, but it's there. In the way he fixes her pillow, brings an extra blanket, and wipes her forehead with his fingers.

It kills me to interrupt them, but Dad always said you have to fight through the hard times. I've wasted enough days with no answers, and if I don't get some soon, they'll be dealing with even harder times. There's no way this is going away, whatever it is. And with the life they're living? It could threaten their very existence.

"No," I whisper. "This has to be done now. Nico, can you give us a minute, please?"

After a brief moment of hesitation, he leaves us alone. Once he's outside, I turn to Violeta. "I know he can still hear us. But do you think he'll pry, if he's told me he never tunes in to those voices?"

She shakes her head. "He would have left to give us privacy. Why do you ask?"

I take a seat on the bed, reaching for her hand. "Because I feel like you're not telling me everything. I feel like there's something you're hiding. And it may be very important."

She shakes her head again. "I'm not hiding anything."

"Then how do you explain this mysterious illness?"

"Luck of the draw, I suppose."

"Are you sure there's nothing unusual that happened these last years?"

She scoffs. "Unusual? My entire life is unusual. The fact that I've lived this long is unusual. The fact that I have to feed on blood to live is unusual. The fact that I, alone from my siblings, care about humans is unusual. The fact that after so many years lived, I haven't yet given in to the darkest part of me...is also very much unusual." She laughs. "What more do you need?"

To be fair, I hadn't thought of things that way. Nico alluded to much the same. After a while, I would imagine living forever would get very boring unless one had a lot of hobbies. But then again, these guys have money. They have status. They were able to travel. They've been able to do more things than I could ever dream of in my entire life. So, really, how can I feel bad for them?

I shake off the thought. "Just tell me. Help me establish a time-line. No matter how small, no matter how insignificant you think something is, just *tell me*. Let me be the judge of what is important in order to help you out. No one here wants you to die."

She stares at me for the longest time. So long, I fear she won't answer. Then she jerks her head toward my notebook and nods. "All right, Tassa. You win. Let's do it your way."

The moment I step out of Violeta's room and head downstairs to the living area, I'm overrun by vampiri, all shouting questions I can't focus on. It's a mob, rabid not for my blood, but for information. In their own way, they each are worried—probably more worried than they've ever been.

I rub my temples, trying to ignore them all, until snarls echo around me, freezing me in place.

I plaster myself against the entrance wall, having come to recognize the noise. But it's not aimed at me—Alexandru and Nico are head-to-head, their faces inches apart, and their little squabble has also drawn the girls' attention. Only Vlad watches me, impassible, like this is a daily occurrence.

For all I know, it is.

I can't make out what they're saying, as they're speaking in low hisses and an old Romanian dialect that's been lost to my generation. But it's clear by their heated exchange that they're not too happy with each other. The air becomes thick with tension, almost electric, and still, their argument continues. I worry it might escalate into something more physical...

Vlad catches my eye and jerks his head to the side. Without waiting, I follow him. He seems the most stable out of all of them. Something tells me he's also the least likely to rip out my throat, which is more than I can say for Mirabela, Elizabeta and Alexandru.

"How is she?" he asks softly.

I have to strain my ears over the noise in the hallway to hear him, but it's a good distraction. "Weaker." There's no point beating around the bush, so I don't. I focus on the symptoms I've just seen, and what Violeta told me. "She doesn't think she'll survive."

"She's always been a pessimist."

Hmm. Not the side she's shown *me*, that's for sure. And that brings up more questions. How many masks do these guys wear, and how many are too dangerous, yet I don't see them?

I choose to focus on something else. "Maybe, but this isn't the first time she said the words. I'm worried, Vlad."

He frowns. "That she might do something to herself?"

"To escape the pain, yeah."

His jaw clenches. "How much pain is she in, exactly?"

The wall rattles—someone's been slammed against it on the other side. I start, and Vlad moves closer to the window, dragging me with him.

"Ignore them. It's how they get their emotions out."

"Get their—" I gulp. "There's got to be a better way of doing it!"

"Not with us." At my surprised expression, he chuckles. "You think dysfunctional families within humans are bad? I dare you to stick around with us for a year. The things you'll see..." He shakes his head.

No, thanks. Out loud, I add, "Um, shouldn't you go and try to stop them?"

Vlad glances at the hallway, probably tuning in to whatever it is they're saying that I can't understand. He's been the quietest in our interactions so far, but he's definitely not of the humans-are-lesser philosophy, at least from what I've seen and from how he acts with me. The thought is oddly comforting.

"No. They'll stop eventually. I'm more interested in Violeta than their issues. Tell me. Alex said she's been suffering from this for years, now."

I nod. "I've been trying to piece together a timeline of where she's been the last three years, and Violeta just helped me out with it. For the most part, nothing jumped out, but there is one thing... A section in the middle that she didn't want to talk much about."

"Hmm."

"It's around Easter of last year."

"Orthodox or Catholic Easter?"

Good point. They're usually about a month apart.

"Orthodox. Where was Violeta?"

Vlad shifts his weight, glances at the hallway again, then back at me. Almost as if weighing whether it's worth telling me the story. In the end, he must conclude it's better for Violeta's sake, as he sighs. "She had a spat with Liza and left us, for a bit."

"Why?"

"Because Liza killed her friend."

My head snaps up. He says it so...casually. Like his sister killing anyone is nothing new. Then again, judging by what I've seen of Elizabeta, it's probably true.

"But..."

"In all fairness, it was a human male, and he did plan to rob us. But Violeta didn't see it that way. She's always cared for humans and this one was...more, to her. I'm not surprised she doesn't want to talk about it."

A human was stupid enough to try and rob these guys? Wow. No wonder my species is on the verge of extinction. Even I know you don't screw around with an apex predator.

That begs another question, though. If he was stupid enough to rob them, could be he stupid enough to try and hurt them?

"Vlad... Could he have known she was a vampir, maybe fed her something to cause all this?"

"No. He was a complete dimwit."

Well, there goes that lead. If no human fed her some poison, and she can't pick up viruses or diseases, then what the hell am I dealing with?

I deflate, only then there's more crowding behind us and the girls waltz back in, filled with attitude and throwing twin glares my way.

"Are you finally going to earn your keep and help Violeta?"

"Or is all this trouble your idea of fucking with us?"

Neither Mirabela nor Elizabeta seem happy with me, to say the least.

"I'm doing my best."

"Your best isn't enough."

Mirabela's tone irks me. Straightening my spine, I step closer to her. "Can you do better?" When she's silent, pursing her lips, I push on. "Contrary to what you may believe, I *am* doing everything in my power. The rest of you may be heartless monsters, but Violeta's shown kindness to me since I arrived, and I've come to care about her well-being."

"Care." Elizabeta snorts. "How about you fucking do something, then? The clock is ticking, little human."

I turn to her, my gaze as icy as I can make it. "If you have any ideas, by all means. In the meantime, the update I have is this: she needs rest. More so than usual. And the way it's looking, she can't go out in the sun. I've given her a tincture to sleep and boost her immune system. I realize you all think you're above such things, but it may surprise you to know it *actually* eased her into sleep."

In all fairness, that part surprised *me,* considering Nico was adamant that vampiri aren't affected by anything—alcohol, pot, drugs—long-term. But Violeta... If I didn't know better, I'd say she's acting human. Not that I'll tell them that. Instead, I continue, "And while she takes that temporary remedy, I will continue to do research. In the meantime, it's probably best she doesn't drink or eat anything that I don't give the okay for." I level my gaze on all of them, refusing to flinch. "Now if you'll excuse me, I have work to do."

Without waiting for their input, I walk away, passing Nico in the hallway and ignoring him. If they all want to play territorial games, they can do it with each other and leave me out of it.

Nicolae

Rubbing my jaw—fucking Alex and his punches—I move closer to my siblings. I'd only heard the last bit, and am reluctantly impressed by the little human. No one stands up to my crazy sisters easily, least of all someone so fragile.

"Cat got your tongue, Mira?" I tease.

She levels a glare at me, but says nothing.

"Keep your little pet in check," Liza snarls with enough hate for both of them. "The last thing we need is her going rogue and doing shit. Or worse, bringing hell on all our heads."

"*She* isn't the one going rogue, in case you haven't noticed."

Liza rolls her eyes. "Alex is only dishing out what we all think. He has every right to be angry."

"You *would* say that. You'd defend him to the ends of the Earth if you could. Between him and a human, you'll always pick his side."

"Because unlike any of you, he's always watched out for me. And humans don't deserve our respect, let alone my wasted breath." She scowls. "As for Alex, you may want to consider cutting him some slack. He gets his hands dirty, more than either of you ever has. And you've completely cut him off from this process and taken over. When before you didn't even care enough to acknowledge us, instead preferring your whores and your goddamned isolation. If you could get your head out of your ass for one minute, you'd see he has a point."

"He does not. And the more we fight amongst ourselves, the worse Violeta gets."

Vlad adds, "I agree with that last bit."

Funny he doesn't with the first, but I let it go.

"What can we help with?"

I shrug at his question. "Beats me. I'm planning to go help *the human* in the library. If any of you deem yourselves too fancy for such a task, go take a hike and stay out of our way."

Following in Tassa's footsteps, I soon join her. She's already helped herself to a few more books on natural remedies, including some worn ones I recognize from her father's house.

"What do you want me to look for?"

She glances up, tension lines around her eyes, her lips pursed in annoyance. But there's a flicker of gratitude in her amber gaze, even if she doesn't say anything.

"Right now, I'm looking for any mention of skin conditions, and particularly skin conditions as a result of poisoning of the blood."

I nod. "I'll help." It's the least I can do, if it'll move things faster.

"As will we."

I whirl around to face Mirabela and Vlad. Seems at least some of my siblings chose to step over their pride... Unsurprisingly, Liza is conspicuously absent.

I'll take what I can get.

Chapter 13

Tassa

"I found something."

I glance up from my book and rub my eyes. The statement came from Mirabela.

It's a few hours later, and thanks to the Dracul siblings' help, we've managed to go through a lot more material than I would've managed on my own. I even tried Dad's scroll I found at home while they were engrossed in other books, but it's a dead end, filled with a code I can't decipher. I'll have to return to it some other time.

"What is it?" Nico says from the fireplace.

I noticed him taking a break a few moments earlier, around the same time focusing became harder and harder for me.

Mirabela lifts a book, showcasing the worn cover. I frown, not recognizing it. Nico does, though, as does Vlad, if their tense expressions are anything to go by.

"What's wrong?" I ask. "What's in that book?"

Mirabela gives me a distasteful look, but thankfully holds back on any comments. I don't think I could take them politely right now.

"A vampir hunter's memoirs," Vlad answers me.

"Like Van Helsing?" I've seen the movies. Just never expected that part to be real, too.

"Da," Vlad says. "Only, worse. They don't hunt us because they think we're the scum of the earth."

"Well, they do think that," Mirabela adds.

"In part. But the other part is because they want to see what makes us tick. When they catch us, they... test us. Experiment on us."

"But doesn't your Order, or whatever humans you have where you live, protect you?" I ask.

Vlad shakes his head. "They can't, because this isn't a unified threat. Vampiri hunters aren't some society we can keep tabs on. They're lonely, isolated figures. They rarely travel in duos or trios, but sometimes they do, when they know the prize will be good enough."

"And the prize is you." My voice is quiet and I can't help my gaze from flickering to Nico. That's why he'd had that weird reaction when I asked about humans and their interest in vampir blood. Not only are they being hunted by their own, but by humans, too.

"I'm sorry," I whisper.

Nico snaps out of his daze and his blue eyes meet mine. Anger simmers in them, but it's not directed at me. More at whatever he was recalling.

Another thought occurs to me. *Which one of them was taken?* Because for them all to be affected this way whenever their blood is mentioned, one of their own must have been...

Nico tears his gaze from me and points at the book. "That's Silva's. He nicked it from the hunter when we rescued him."

Mirabela lifts her chin in the air, defiant. "I kept it."

She's a lot cooler than him right now, that's for sure. The air seems to thicken with the waves of fury hiding behind Nico's cool façade. Even I can feel them.

Nico takes a step closer to his sister. "Give it to me."

"No." She turns it around, though, pointing to a specific page. "You need to get over that loss, Nico. And *read*."

Loss? What loss?

I bite back the questions, instead waiting until he reads.

When he does, he steps back from the book and just about tosses it back in her lap. "If that's true, if there's one in this area and this is his doing, I'll rip his head off."

"No. The book is clear, and it confirms what we've thought since the beginning. These hunters are nothing more than humans with a grudge against us. And each time one of us is taken captive, it becomes another notch on their belt, another way for them to figure out how to best overpower us, and kill us. We've managed to fight back against the odd loner who found us over the centuries. This will be no different, except for one thing—you'll bring him here. I want to speak to him, and find out how they're passing information from one to the other. It's a bit odd that they all seem to know what works and what doesn't for us vampiri, almost as if they share knowledge in some way. *I want to know how.*" Mirabela points to another page. "You still remember how to find a location via coordinates?"

Nico snarls at her in response.

Unfazed, Mirabela turns to me. "Bring the human along."

"No."

She glares at him. "Why don't you let her decide, hmm?"

I stand, then, tired of being on the sidelines and not fully following the conversation. "What's going on?"

"This book," Mirabela says, "belongs to an old friend of ours. Daniel Silva. He was a vampir like us, one we rescued from one such vampir hunter, and nurtured to health. In exchange, he became our most prized defender." A glance at Nico, then it flicks back to me. "Until he died. But while he lived, Silva made it his mission to hunt vampiri hunters and kill them, before they could enact more atrocities upon our kind. It seems he developed a list of hunters, written at the back of this man's book. He must've been going after the names on that list, one by one, because a lot of them are crossed out. But there are a few names he did not get a chance to cross... One of them being in this area."

I frown. "But what does that have to do with Violeta?"

She rolls her eyes, exasperated. I want to point out that unlike them, I do actually need sleep to function, that it's not a whim, but Vlad speaks before I can.

"If there's a vampir hunter and he knows we're here, he could be the cause of Violeta's illness. They know many ways to make us sick... It used to be with vervain, an herb—"

"I know what it is. The powder or juice of it is said to have purifying properties, and in some vampir legends it's the one thing that's more damning to you all than a stake to the heart and holy water."

Mirabela nods, grudgingly seeming impressed at my knowledge.

"We developed immunity to it over time thanks to Father. Older vampiri have, too, but many newly sired ones are still sensitive. This hunter might've found something worse than vervain, and perhaps he's testing it on Violeta."

I hesitate to point out the obvious but since the hunter subject matter seems to have gotten them all on edge, I doubt they're thinking clearly. "That's a good theory, don't get me wrong. But how would he have gotten it—whatever *it* is—to Violeta?"

Mirabela's eyes flash red, and I take a step back. Maybe this was one of those times I should've kept my mouth shut.

Vlad glances between us then, an apologetic look in his eyes, says, "You did say whatever it is that affected Violeta could've hit her in the last two years. So if he crossed paths with her at any point..."

"Okay, yeah. Good point." I'm thinking of that annoying chunk of time no one seems to know much about. "So, we go find him and ask questions?"

My words seem to have snapped Nico out of whatever dark thoughts he's been in. He moves toward me, his expression fierce. "*We* aren't going anywhere. Vlad and I are."

"Mirabela's right, though. I should be there, so I can see what's in his house. If he's doing this, then he'll have a remedy nearby. You won't be able to identify it before he destroys it, but I can."

I know I've won the battle by the anger flaring in his eyes.

With Nico carrying me, we get to the hunter's cabin within moments. What used to be a refuge for hikers in these parts is now falling apart, its crumbling structure almost blending with the woods, overcome by weeds and vines. The wood, probably saturated by rain and years of neglect, fills the air with a rotting scent.

Nico sets me down near a tree, his body pressing into mine for a sparse moment. I try to brush off my body's traitorous reaction to his closeness, but it lingers. My skin feels overly sensitized, like it's been scrubbed too hard under a much too hot shower. As he pulls away, his eyes lock onto mine and, for a heartbeat, we just stare at each other.

"Stay hidden," he mutters. "I'll come get you when we have him bound."

He and Vlad disappear into the cabin's gloomy interior, leaving behind the chill of the air and quietness of the night. If this is true, if this man is behind Violeta's disease, then we could have her healed within days. Reverse the effects of whatever poison he got coursing through her veins.

Mirabela stayed behind, saying she'd tell Violeta what we found. My hope is it'll be enough to give her some spark of reassurance. I hate to think of the defeated tone of her voice when I last saw her.

A whistle splits the quiet of the night. I snap to and wade my way through the cold. Nico's by the door of the house, and inside, a few lamps offer some much-needed light. The entire cabin is sparsely decorated. A bed, an area that could be a kitchen, and another that's a workshop, just opposite. Weapons of all kinds are laid out on a large, sturdy table. Crossbows, regular bows, guns, knives, even two swords. And stakes. A lot of stakes.

Someone groans and I turn my gaze to the middle of the room. Vlad has a man against the wall. He's holding him by the throat, and the man's hands are flailing as he tries to draw in air.

Gone is the kind Vlad I'd witnessed earlier. Instead, his expression is cool, determined—murderous. "Tell us what we want to know. Did you know we were in the area?"

The hunter is nothing I would've expected. He's smaller than Vlad, and while muscled, I'm having a hard time picturing him killing vampiri. His eyes are bloodshot, his skin is deathly pale, and his clothes are torn. *Maybe this is a case of not judging a book by its cover?*

I snap out of my thoughts as he speaks.

"Many know you are here, heir of Dracul," he croaks. "And many more will soon."

In my ear, Nico whispers, "Look around. See if anything catches your eye. Poisons, remedies, the like."

I do as he asks, but the moment I step around him, the man's eyes widen.

"*You.*"

I freeze, throwing a confused glance around. He's definitely staring at me, though.

"I should've known. Your father was a traitor; it only makes sense that you are one, too."

I take a step closer. Then another. "A traitor? How?" I never would've expected this little expedition to lead to answers about my dad's death, and my heartbeat quickens in anticipation. "Tell me what you know!"

The man chuckles. "He deserved what he got, one of those beasts coming after him. He never should've been saving them in the first place. Not when my poisons were doing their bidding."

Poisons... *That's* what my Dad was healing vampiri from? I glance around the sparse cabin, noticing a few vials filled with blood.

Nico steps around me. "Did you use your poisons on my sister? *Did you!?*"

"You'll never know."

I see the expression in his eyes a second too late. The calmness. The resignation. Then his hand moves with uncanny precision, drawing a small stake out of the back of his jeans. He stabs it in Vlad's thigh, causing him to let go of his throat. The hunter doesn't waste a single second—he lunges at me, a wild glint in his eyes.

I stare in shock as Nico leaps, faster than I've seen him to date, and rips the guy's hand off. The scratch of bone and the tear of limb make me wince. A rivulet of blood flows out of his wounds. I gag, putting my hand to my mouth to avoid vomiting. Still, Nico doesn't stop there. The other arm is next, followed by the head.

And that's when it happens.

Another image superimposes itself over, from another time, another place. At home. With Dad dead. Nico's standing over him like some avenging angel, snarling at the man who'd killed him—and then ripping him apart.

Just as mercilessly.

Just as coldly.

Ruthless. The word whispers in my mind.

How did I get blinded to his true nature, to his ability to hide the monster underneath the layers of clothing? How did I even come to find him...attractive?

Bile rises in my throat all over again as I stare at the monster I've been spending time with.

Nicolae

Tassa's sharp intake behind me makes me even more aware of the blood dripping down my hands. Without a word, I head into the woods, leaving her in the cabin with Vlad.

I can hear a stream gurgling a few meters away and head that way to wash the blood off, as much as possible. And also to collect myself.

What the hell just happened?

I've killed plenty, that's not what bothers me. What bothers me is *why* I did it. Up until now, I've killed to defend myself, sometimes my siblings, and for food. I've even killed in pleasure, over the centuries. And while I could say they deserved it, the truth is, you'd never know.

Now, though... I didn't kill for me, or Vlad. I killed for Tassa.

To *protect* her. A *human*.

A human I shouldn't be caring for, let alone putting above myself and my siblings. Though we've gotten all the information we needed, I could've interrogated the man further. It wouldn't have been a bad idea.

But when he lunged at her, a red haze descended over me. My body tightened with the anticipation of a fight, and I moved before I even thought it through. The primal urge in me to safeguard her against anything was...unreal. *All* I could think of was protecting her, *annihilating* any threat in the process if need be. She reawakened this dormant hero within me, and I'm not sure how to feel about it— and the chaos these unfurling emotions are causing within me.

In all my centuries of existence, no one has ever made me feel so vital...unhinged...so *alive*.

After washing my hands, I wipe them off my jeans and head back to her and Vlad. She's leaning against a tree, a backpack at her feet. They must've collected what they needed from the cabin... Perhaps there will be some answers in that trash.

My gaze shifts to Vlad. He's taken out the stake in his thigh and he seems fine despite the blood drying on his jeans. The wound is probably already healed.

The minute she sees me, Tassa springs to life. "You just killed him!"

"And saved your life in the process. You're welcome."

"Don't give me that shit!" She shoves at me, and Vlad arches an eyebrow in the distance. It's apparent he's not getting involved. "Justify it to yourself all you want, but you didn't have to."

I step closer to her. "I think the words you're looking for are *thank you.*"

She scowls. "Yeah? Like I should be thanking you for ripping my father's murderer apart, too?"

I narrow my eyes. "You said you didn't remember."

"I didn't. Not until now."

Damn it all to hell, I should have realized seeing me fight could bring it all back. Too late now...

"I was also saving your life."

"No. You did it because you enjoyed it, which is the same reason you did it now."

I roll my eyes. "*Enough.*" I refuse to admit how much her lack of gratitude irks me. "Let's get out of here. Vlad?"

He leads the way, making sure to leave a good distance between me and Tassa. Not that it shuts her up. If anything, it only angers her further.

"You didn't have to be so barbaric!"

"Barbaric?" I whirl on her, unable to hold back my tone. "*Barbaric?* Maybe you should live through a few human wars, and we'll see who you're calling barbaric. What I did was a mercy."

"And maybe *you* should relearn the meaning of mercy. It's not what you think it is!"

I cross the distance between us in half a second. "Do you want to keep debating my actions until other hunters show up, or can we get the hell out of here?"

She says nothing, only glares at me for a long moment. Then she spits, "We can leave. I've grabbed what I could find in there, including his notebooks. But there's no way I'm letting you carry me back."

"Fine, then. Vlad can."

Chapter 14

Nicolae

The moment we get back to the castle, Tassa takes off inside, slamming the door after her.

Vlad stares after her for a beat, then meets my gaze. "She has a point, you know. You didn't have to kill him."

"You've got some nerve. Do you honestly think I would've let him live, after the shit he pulled, after the threat he was?"

"Was he really?"

I scoff at him. "You aren't defending him, I hope? His kind have hunted us for centuries. And after Liza—" I pause, feeling myself dangerously out of control at the memory of what our sister went through. "How many times did we escape their clutches?"

"Probably about the same number of times as the count of bodies we left behind."

"Liza and Alex wouldn't agree with your sympathies."

All Vlad does is shake his head. "At least admit you aren't doing it for us. Or even for Liza. But for Silva and his memory."

"This has nothing to do with him."

"Keep telling yourself that."

He walks away before I can retort, leaving me to my dark thoughts. What a fucking mess. I don't know which of his words, Tassa's reaction, or the look in her eyes is gutting me more. And what's more annoying is the fact I'm bothered by *any* of it.

I head inside, to the living room area and the decanter of red wine. Alex is the only one in there, already nursing a glass.

"Rough night?"

"You can say that."

Another voice sounds behind me. "Vlad says you killed the hunter. To save Tassa's life."

I let the decanter slide on the table, avoiding facing my sister.

"Did he, now?"

Mirabela moves closer, her nails digging into my forearm. Some of the red liquid sloshes over the brim of the glass and onto the ground. I glance down—the drops have frozen in midair.

"You should watch your powers, sister." They're getting more and more unruly as she gets older.

"And you should watch your emotions."

"Meaning?"

She lets go of me, eyes narrowing. "Do you remember what happened the last time you cared for a human?"

I turn my attention back to the drink. "That was long ago."

Out of the corner of my eye, I notice Alex hasn't moved. Instead, he's listening intently, letting Mirabela do all the talking.

"Not long enough, not for us," she says. "And it led to Silva's death. To you shutting down. Something you've never acknowledged, let alone dealt with. Don't lie to yourself. And don't do *this* again."

I glare at her. "I'm not. Whatever you think is going on here, I don't care for Tassa that way."

"Keep telling yourself that. But for someone who doesn't care, you're sure protecting her a lot." She lowers her voice. "Watch yourself, Nico. The last thing you want is to repeat history all over again."

She walks off, and Alex chooses that moment to push off the wall. "You really should heed her words."

"I have nothing to say to you."

He laughs. "What, you think because you've been so aloof and uncaring, not getting your hands dirty, that it makes you somehow better than the rest of us? Think again, Nico. You're fooling no one but yourself."

I look up with my most bored expression. "I hear you talking, and all I want to see is you walking away."

His face contorts with anger as he jabs a finger in my direction. "Mark my words. If you put us all in danger with this stupid human of yours, I'll relish tearing her apart, inch by precious fucking inch."

He storms off, and I catch muttered curses in the distance. Wonderful. So my entire family's pissed at me, except for Violeta who's sick, and Liza who's nowhere to be seen.

I don't regret the choice. The hunter was scum and deserved to be torn apart as I did. For every life he took. For every life he ruined.

I think back to Silva and how we'd found him, hundreds of years ago. Chained to the walls of a cave-like basement, bloodied and cut all over, whipped, beaten over and over. He had cuts around his main organs as if someone had opened him up. They weren't healed properly, leaving scars. That generally happens with us if a wound is inflicted in the same place over...and over...and over again.

I shake my head, wiping it of the images. Others replace them. Sparring with Silva, hunting with him. Having a friend. A brother. One who I could talk to freely...even if it was about Țepeș. He was with us a little over a hundred years. And for most of that time, he was my confidant, my friend. A brother in arms I could rely on. He proved that when Liza was taken, and many times after. Until he was killed because of *my* idiocy.

Mirabela's right. I did shut down. I stopped caring, retreated into myself. It's easier not to care, than constantly be assailed by emotions. Especially when you live forever.

I let my head fall back against the chair, my gaze drifting upwards, and stupidly wonder what the hell Tassa's up to now. Is she packing her bags, ready to demand to leave? She'd seemed ready to, in the woods. Scared, too. Like she couldn't get away from me fast enough. If she does ask to leave, I can't allow it. None of us can, least of all Violeta.

But if she'll stay, can I stand to see that repulsed look in her eyes every day? It bothers me way too damn much.

Tassa

The moment I'm in my room, I turn to lock the door—only there's no key. Dammit. Instead, I pull some of the heavier chairs to it and block it. Then back away toward the bed, letting myself fall at its bottom.

What the hell have I gotten myself into?

Before I can even process everything, the handle on my door turns. I freeze. After a beat, someone knocks. Then a soft voice asks, "May I come in?"

Violeta.

Out of all of them, she's the least threatening. She could also be the most dangerous. But I need to talk to someone about it, so why not her?

"One sec."

I move to the door and drag the chairs away. Their scrape is loud—there's no way she won't know what I'm doing. Another moment later, I clear my throat. "Okay, come in."

Violeta steps in. The sun's waning rays hit her pale face, highlighting the dark circles under her eyes. I try not to show my surprise at her appearance, and fail.

She lets out a weak, sad smile. "Not looking any better, am I?"

"I... Sorry. The remedies I gave you?"

She shakes her head. "It's not your fault. They've lessened the pain. Though you probably can't tell by looking at me, I promise you, they have. But, they alone don't have the power to stop what is happening to me."

"I'm sorry. I'll try and find something else."

I move toward the books, but Violeta's there, stopping me. Her eyes search mine.

"What happened?"

"What do you mean?"

"Something happened. You're more wary of me. And you had your door blocked, before I knocked."

I shake my head. "It's not important." *Lies!* My conscience yells at me.

"Tell me."

I don't know what, of her open expression or weak tone, makes me open up. Maybe a combination of both. Maybe because she looks so human, so frail, and so unlike the cutthroat display of aggressivity I've witnessed from Nico.

Chewing on my bottom lip, I say, "Mirabela told you about the hunter?" When she nods, I continue, "We found him. Alone, in a cabin in the woods. He admitted to having poisoned many vampiri, the same ones my father was helping. He said Dad was a traitor. But he didn't want to admit to anything with you. I... I wanted more information." I close my eyes, remembering it all. "He gave us some, though not much. Then, he lunged at me." I swallow past the thickness in my throat. "Nico went after him. He.... He..."

"Killed the man."

I open my eyes. Violeta's angry—it's the first I've seen her like this. But it's not at me. At her brother, more like.

"He says he saved me, but Violeta, the force he showed, the way he dismembered the guy so easily, I—"

She's out the door a moment later, and I don't know if I've done more harm than good. But she needed to know. After all, it's her life that's in jeopardy here. No matter his so-called good intentions, Nico and I both know that guy had more information. And it was Nico's callous actions that prevented us from getting it. By killing the man, he effectively destroyed any leads we could've gotten.

I turn to my bed, dejected. My eyes land on the scroll and Dad's book on the House of Dracul. Almost in a daze, I take a seat and start rifling through the book. The words dance in front of my eyes, not really registering.

All I can think of is—surely, I didn't make a mistake telling Violeta what I have?

Nicolae

I can't stand the oppression of the four walls. So I head outside instead, letting the sun linger on my face. Or what's left of it. Soon, night will come, which means the darkness will blanket the world once more.

Since when have I gone all poetic?

On a sigh, I turn my gaze to the blood-red sunset.

I can lie to my siblings as much as I want, that I had my own motives for saving Tassa, but the truth is, I didn't. It had been a primal instinct, something older than time, something I haven't felt since the last time I got so involved.

And that time, I paid for it dearly.

"How *dare* you!"

Violeta storms out of the castle like a Fury of the old, hands outstretched toward me, practically ready to claw my face. It's only at the last moment that I catch her wrists in mine, stopping her.

"Violeta—"

"No! I trusted you, hoped you would see beyond your own disillusion and stupidity, and this is how you repay me? By killing my *only* chance at getting better?" She yanks her wrists out of my hold, beating my chest with them. "How. Dare. You!?"

"We'd gotten the information out of him—"

"*And there could have been more!*"

I scowl. Who the hell filled her head with—

Tassa. It must be her, no one else. Is she so disgusted then, so repulsed by what she witnessed, that she's ready to turn Violeta against me? Put her through so much pain, clearly making her symptoms worse? There's no way such an outburst is good for her.

Even as she pulls herself out of my grip, I can tell she's weak. Too weak.

"There was not," I tell her, holding her gaze. "Believe me."

She tremble in my arms and collapses against me. Her body feels frail—human. Whatever this disease is, it's eating her inside out, and my inability to help is starting to eat at *me*.

"I'm sorry," I whisper, tucking her against my chest. "If I could do anything, anything at all to take away this pain, I would in a heartbeat. I'm so sorry."

Her sobs tear at me in a way I haven't felt in ages. And damn Tassa for causing this, for messing everything up. Without that primal urge to protect here, would I have killed the man? Why is it that I've gone centuries being closed off, yet in a matter of days, she's become the reason behind my sudden return to wanting to do the right thing?

There's no rhyme or reason to my blaming her, but I sure as hell can't point the finger at the one truly responsible.

Because I'd be looking in a mirror.

Once I put Violeta to bed, I don't waste any time heading to Tassa's chambers. Violeta begged me to be careful, saying Tassa's already spooked enough. And I don't intend to scare her more. Not really. I just want to see what in hell possessed her to rile my sister up this way.

The minute I step through the door, though, all normal sense escapes me. She's inside, all right. Packing. Shoving things into a backpack, with no regard for the mess she's leaving behind.

"What are you doing?"

She jumps at my tone, but quickly looks away. Not enough to hide her tear-bathed face. Or the flash of fear in her eyes. I try to focus on the latter, and not on how the sight of her tears makes me feel. No. Definitely not that.

"I'm waiting for an answer."

"Well, you can take that royal tone and shove it up your ass. How about it, Nico?"

"Your vulgarity might be more poignant if you weren't afraid to look me in the eyes."

She tosses something on the bed and stomps over to me. The fire in her eyes is convincing, but not as much as the venom that spits out of that lovely mouth next. "Read my fucking lips. *Shove. It. Up. Your. Ass.* How's that?"

"Convincing," I mutter.

Only instead of being focused on her tone, I'm too aware of her closeness. Deciding that tempting fate is even more in my benefit than not, I take a step closer. Despite her bravado, I hear her sharp intake of breath. She's debating—fight or flight? What will she choose?

Only instead of listening to her instinct, she tosses her head back and glares at me. "I'm leaving, there's your answer."

"And did you decide this before or after you riled up Violeta so bad, she had another episode of weakness?"

Regret fills her expression, but she doesn't back down. "It wasn't my intention."

"Well, that's what happened. And since I've just wiped away her tears, I'd like to know what the fuck you thought you were doing, telling her I killed her only chance at getting better."

She staggers back. Finally, a normal response. "I didn't say that."

"It was implied."

"Because you did!"

"I didn't!" I scowl, following her every step backward with a forward one of my own. "That man was nothing more than a pawn in someone else's playbook. Maybe the books you got will have answers, maybe not. But he was done talking and no amount of torture would have changed that. If you'd lived as long as I have, you'd know. And had you bothered to talk to me afterward, I would've told you as much."

"There's no excuse for murder in my book."

"Not even when it's done to defend someone's life?"

I know I have her, then, when she doesn't immediately answer me.

"Debatable."

I take another step. "Weak rebuttal. I expected better."

"I—"

She looks at me then, and the last shred of control I had leaves me. I cross the remaining distance between us, and my hand goes to the back of her neck, pulling her closer with a gentle yet unyielding pressure. Our lips collide—two opposing forces, two different worlds, but none of that matters. If I expected her to fight me off, I'm mistaken. Because not only does she kiss me back, but she also bites my bottom lip and yanks me to her, practically devouring the kiss, as much as me.

A groan escapes someone—her, me, I can't tell—and then I'm maneuvering us across the room, clearing a path around the furniture until I've got her pinned to the door. My hands frame her face, thumbs tracing the contours of her cheeks as I continue savoring her lips, nibbling and teasing. The sweet torture of her carotid pulse underneath my fingertips is almost too much to bear. It could be filling my mouth, tasting so sweet...

But I've done that before. I drank from a human I was interested in, and it led to the death of my dear friend. It's not something I can risk again. No matter how much I want to.

I could have gone on kissing her forever. Feeling the softness of her body against mine, hearing her pulse skyrocket with every sweep of my tongue against hers, or her breath hitch. But the thought of the past is enough to clear my mind like a cold shower. I push myself away before I do anything stupid.

Tassa stares at me, just as shocked as I am at what happened.

And then she ducks under my arm, and returns to the bed, avoiding looking at me. "You should leave."

"I should."

And yet I don't move. My body is tight with tension, desire, and so much more it hasn't felt in ages. Because I haven't allowed it to. What am I supposed to do, just remove myself from this?

No. Not that easily.

I turn to her, running a hand over my face. "Don't antagonize Violeta again, please."

"It wasn't my intention."

"Nonetheless."

A beat, two, three passes. Tassa doesn't say anything else. Without another option, I walk toward the door, pausing one last time with my hand on the doorknob. "For the record, that man *was* going to hurt you. And I did save your life. Not that I expect you to understand."

The door closing behind me echoes the sound of my own disappointment.

Tassa

After he's gone, I spend a good few minutes frozen on the bed, trying to hide my shaking hands. Not from fear—there was no fear involved when he'd kissed me. Only desire, so powerful and overwhelming, like I've never felt in my entire life.

Then again, said life has been much shorter than his own, so I shouldn't expect to understand anything of this magnitude. But what had I been thinking, allowing it to prolong? If Nico hadn't stopped, it would've gone much, much further.

Further than I cared for.

Or, did I?

He's a vampire. A monster. They all are, regardless of how they portray themselves.

Dad didn't think so... He helped them out. Many of them, according to his notes.

I finally move off the bed, intending to continue packing. My reasoning was simple, before. I couldn't stay in a house with a murderer. But could I really call him one, when he's so obviously convinced he saved my life? When I know that he did, in fact? I may not agree with his methods, but it doesn't take away from the truth of the matter. And at least his methods deliver a quick ending. My words, meanwhile...

I close my eyes, disappointed in myself. The thought I hurt Violeta, caused her agony by somehow implying the hunter had had more to offer—when Nico's probably right, and he never did—

bothers me. It's easier to focus on that than it is to replay every second of that earth-shattering kiss.

Stepping out of my room, I make my way to hers. A quick rasp on the door, and she yells from within to enter. When I do, I find her in a bath, covered by bubbles and the scent of jasmine. A scent slightly overpowered by the joint in her hand.

"I didn't mean to interrupt."

"You didn't." Her voice is soft, defeated once more.

I move closer, kneeling by the bathtub. Reaching for the loofah, I run it under the water, then over her back, watching her expression. She's quiet, so damn quiet and forlorn, I don't like it. Something inside me breaks.

"I'm sorry, Violeta. I didn't realize how my words would affect you."

"You only spoke the truth." Her eyes are glassy as she takes another puff of the joint. "Not your fault."

"Nico has a point, though."

"He came to see you?"

I nod. "Yes. Angry, and with reason. I swear to you, we will find a solution to this. I took notebooks from the man's place and a bunch of vials that looked like antidotes. If there's anything useful in them, I will find it. And you will not die."

Powerful words, and a powerful promise. I only hope I can deliver on it.

Violeta nods, but I have a feeling she's doing it more to placate me. I wash her back once more and whisper, "Just hang in there. Have hope."

"Hope deserted me a while ago. I just didn't expect the will to live would, too."

I bite my lip. Instead of going back to my room, I continue washing her, then help her get bundled up in a soft robe and watch over her as she falls asleep. I can only hope I'll have the physical strength to stop her if she tries anything to harm herself.

It's my fault she's in more pain than before. And I tell myself, then and there, that I can't leave. Not until I fulfill my promise to Violeta and give her the cure that's eluding us. Not until she's better, safer. It's what Dad would've wanted.

And if that means I have to deal with her draconian brother, so be it. It's a risk I'll have to take. Even if it's one I'd rather not... So long as I can avoid his kisses, I should be fine. One can hope.

But how much control do I really have over my life, and my choices, when I'm in a house full of vampiri?

Chapter 15

Tassa

The woods are quiet around me, what with the approaching dawn. Maybe it wasn't such a great idea that I left the castle on my own—again. I could've asked Nico to accompany me, I could've even asked Violeta. Instead, I chose to go out alone, despite the fact it's been explained to me time and time again that I should be careful where I go and who I go without.

But who can blame me, really?

I needed to clear my head after the incident with Nico. Even more so after seeing Violeta in another low. Not to mention Nico's fury and disappointment in me. I shouldn't care about his opinion, yet it's as painful as a knife to my ribs.

Why? Why do I care so much?

Without an answer, I redirect my thoughts to Violeta. It's maddening, not being able to help her. I shouldn't feel this crippling disappointment in myself. Medicine was never a field I aspired to be in. But helping people? That, I've always done without fail. Being unable to do so in this case is infuriating.

We've followed the clues. And they've led us nowhere.

I'm starting to wonder if there's something more to Violeta's illness. Something beyond the realm of scientific explanation. Could the answer lie in the blood? Could it have something to do with Violeta's previous engagement with the human Elizabeta killed? From the way Vlad spoke, I can only deduce the man had been a boyfriend, lover, or maybe even fiancé.

Yet it makes no sense. Even if I don't go by folklore, by our myths and legends, the truth is there for everyone to see. It would not be the first time vampiri cavorted with humans. But for them to get sick as a result? Impossible.

So what the hell am I missing?

Something moves in the woods, causing me to stop walking. I look around, but there's nothing to see—nothing's coming up to me. I'm reminded of the other time when I'd been near the woods, and the same thing happened. A shiver runs up my spine.

Maybe I should've waited until the sun was fully up. *Get over yourself. If anyone was following you, there are way more interesting people to stalk, like the six vampiri in the castle.*

My pep talk does nothing to ease my worries. But I do need air, and a moment away from the castle, that much can't be denied.

And, at the end of the day, I have to keep in mind my reason for being here. To clear my head. To erase the memory of Nico's lips, the feel of them against my own. I have no business falling for a vampir. I have no business *lusting* after a vampir.

And then there are all the questions without answers. While my mind has been focused on healing Violeta, I also can't deny the other part of me. That wants justice. Yet I'll never get it. Or perhaps justice is Nico having killed the man who hurt my dad? Me taking another life?

None of this answers the main questions. Who killed Dad? Why was that person turned? Was it a targeted attack? Does any of it have to do with the town people so intent on me leaving the castle? Why would a vampir hunter in the middle of the woods not only know of my dad but also despise him?

When another breeze rustles the leaves, I start moving, more determined now. I ignore the shiver still firmly nested in my spine, telling me that something's wrong, that I'm being followed. If the hunter believed my dad to be doing something treason-worthy, then the villagers would know more.

And out of all of them, one in particular has been boasting of being Dad's friend. Let's see what he has to say.

My knock sounds too loud in the overall quiet street. Good manners say I should've waited until at least breakfast time, but needs must. The walk here only steeled my determination to seek answers. And if the vampiri can't give them to me, at least not fully, this part I must find out for myself.

Within moments, someone shuffles inside, and the door opens. His eyes are wide when they land on me, but he moves aside to let me in.

I have a moment's hesitation, wondering just how safe this is. After all, the last time I'd seen Victor was at the police station. And not only was he a little forceful, but Nico also made the situation worse.

Stop chickening out. You want answers, and this man could have them. I straighten my spine and head inside.

The interior is a blend of traditional charm and modern comfort, similar to our old house. Whitewashed walls, cedarwood shelves loaded with colorful ceramics and large windows. There's an odd flowery scent in the air, something I wouldn't have associated with Victor.

Hands in his pockets, Victor clears his throat. He doesn't seem like he was sleeping at all. On the contrary, he's fully dressed and his eyes are bright—alert. In contrast, I feel rumpled.

"What do you want?" he asks.

"What do I..." I push my shoulders back and cross my arms over my chest. "How about you lay off the attitude, Victor? I saw you for the first time at the castle. Before then, I've never even seen you around these parts. And in our last encounter at the police station, you seemed mighty determined to get me away from Nico. So, let's start with some real answers. Why the sudden interest to get me away from the heirs?"

He looks away. "You know why. We'd found your father dead, and you were gone. We thought they were responsible."

"Hmm. Try again."

"It's the truth!"

"I believe it's some truth, but not all." Instead of leaving, like he obviously wants me to, judging by his body language, I find a seat and plop down. "I have all day."

He sighs, shuffling his feet. "What have those creatures told you?"

I snort. "You're afraid of breaking vampire confidentiality? Please. They told me what I need to know—what they are, why they're here."

He nods, seemingly more at ease. "Then why are you *here*? You chose to stay with them."

"Da, because I want to know what happened to my father. But I'm starting to think the answers lie within this town, not outside of it."

He sighs. "He was a good man, your dad."

"I know. But funny you should say that." I tap the table with my fingers, before realizing it's a habit I picked up from Nico. I stop, lying my palm flat on the wooden surface. "Last night, I went with two of the heirs into the woods. Where a certain vampire hunter was hiding. And he seemed to be very adamant on the fact Dad was a traitor." I level my gaze on Victor. "Care to explain that?"

"What were you doing on such a dangerous—"

"Spare me, Victor. I may be many things, but I'm not dumb. I don't believe you were Dad's friend. Matter of fact, I don't think you even knew him at all. Am I right?"

He scowls at me. "Perhaps you should leave."

"Not until you give me some answers. Real ones, this time. What was Dad involved in? Why did he die?"

He arches an eyebrow. "Sure you'd like to know?"

"Yes."

"All right. But your vampir buddies won't thank you for it." He takes a seat opposite me, his expression blank. "Your father was recruited into our Order at a young age, same as I was. As he grew up, he had many chances to leave, to make a life for himself out of these golden shackles. Time and time again. But he returned here. When your mother died, he swore he would never let you become part of the Order. That your existence wouldn't be threatened by the vampiri. So he made us swear to protect you, should anything happen."

That sounds like Dad, all right. "Is there more?"

"Da. Your father ran experiments on vampiri."

"Experiments?"

"He wanted to figure out how to kill them. Even the oldest of them. So, he worked in tandem with vampiri hunters to ensure they were found and staked."

Bile rises in my throat. "What?"

His expression hardens. "Maybe you should let sleeping dogs lie, girlie. Get out of here, far away, while you still can."

"Don't you get it? I'm too involved in this to leave. So you might as well tell me what I need to know. That way, at least I won't be taken unawares."

He sighs again. "All I know is, the last few years, your dad stopped with the experiments. Had a change of heart or something, I don't know. Instead, he tried to help the vampiri."

"Help them how?"

"He became known as the healer of the clans. Like I said, *I don't know* the specifics. But it was too late, either way. He came to us one night, real crazed. Afraid. Said someone was after him. Someone had figured out he was helping vampiri."

"Someone like who?"

"He didn't say."

How convenient. I keep my comments to myself.

"But he did say if ever something was to happen to him, to go to the castle."

I frown. "As in, that they'd be guilty?"

"He never specified."

Dad did tend to keep his cards close to his chest, it's how he's always been. But something tells me I should take Victor's words with a pinch of salt, and not jump to conclusions. After all, much as his words fill in the blanks I've desperately tried to fill in these last days, they also raise darker questions. And paint an unfamiliar picture of the man I thought I knew.

Could my father really have committed such atrocities? *Experiments*? I know he was afraid of the heirs. But to break the very vow he'd made of helping others... My entire being rebels against the idea.

"So his words, they could be taken to mean 'go to the castle' for help. Or they could also be aiming the spotlight on the vampiri, implying they're the guilty parties?"

"I suppose so."

He doesn't seem too happy that I'm inclined to trust vampiri. I shake my head. "Is there anything else that you remember?"

"No. Not from that night. But a few nights later, I saw him returning at dawn, and he looked exhausted. Like he'd spent the whole night working on something."

"And where did he return from?"

"The old mines."

A shiver runs up my spine. Those mines—smaller than the more famous Rosia Montana mines, but no less bountiful for their gold—

and ancient tunnels have been silent for centuries, ever since the gold ran out. But growing up in these parts, more than one kid got hurt when they decided to bravely—and mistakenly—try and venture within their depths. Some never returned.

What would Dad have been doing there? It's not much to go on, but it's better than nothing.

"Thank you for your time."

I stand to leave, but he does, too. Steps just enough to make me pause, not quite blocking my way, but not really freeing it, either.

"Be careful with the vampiri."

This again. "I am."

"They're good at acting like humans, but they are not."

I'm surprised by the vehemence in his tone. "For someone who's meant to protect their identity, you sure hate them."

He has the grace to look bashful, for about two seconds. Then his fierce expression returns. But he says nothing else, only watches me.

On a sigh, I leave the house, not realizing how relieved I am at having escaped it. I guess part of me still doesn't trust him. *Maybe I should listen to that gut feeling more.*

Unwilling yet to return to the castle and at a loss about my own failures healing Violeta, I wander the streets some more.

Have I truly learned anything? Not really. Besides what my dad may have done. But the mines... That gives me something to check on. If Dad was running experiments, he would have kept meticulous records. And if they're not at our home, they have to be somewhere, dammit. If I can find them...maybe, just maybe, there's an answer to Violeta's ailment in them.

A glance at the sky reassures me the sun is still high, meaning any creatures that could potentially be harmful to me—like, say, muroni—will be out of commission. Another part warns me that going into a dark, damp space, away from sunlight, doesn't really hold with that reasoning. I ignore it.

I won't lose anything by trying.

Nicolae

I hesitate outside Tassa's room. I shouldn't be here—not again. Haven't I learned my lesson, after last night? But it's like I can't help myself.

She doesn't understand why I killed that hunter. There's nothing I can do to explain it, but I miss the companionship I've gotten used to over the last few days. I can't understand the urge myself. It's been growing in me, getting more and more intense. And the kiss the other night, the way she'd felt in my arms—

Da, I'm still annoyed with her for riling Violeta up. But I also know she went to see her, to apologize.

Hesitantly, I knock. Once, twice. No answer. No sound from within, either. When I listen closely, I can't even hear her heartbeat.

Recalling the packing she'd been doing the night before, I turn the knob and open the room. To my relief, the bag is still on her bed, clothes thrown about. Meaning she hasn't left—not yet, at least.

Unless she decided to leave without these.

Before my mind has caught up, I'm already taking the stairs two by two and bursting into the living room. Mirabela and Violeta are sitting in opposite armchairs by the window, reading.

"Have either of you seen Tassa?"

A long pause, then, "She's gone," Violeta says softly.

"What do you mean, she's gone?"

"Gone." Mirabela looks up from her nails. "As in, away from here. Why do you appear so crazed, brother?"

Do I? I don't feel crazed. I don't feel any different, period.

"I'm not crazed."

Violeta looks up from her book. "Beg to differ."

Choosing to ignore that, I follow it up with another statement. "Her clothes are still here, though."

Violeta frowns. "Why wouldn't they be?"

"You said she's gone."

"Yeah... As in, for a walk. Or something. To clear her head, I guess." A glint of amusement shines in her eyes, at odds with her overall exhausted expression. "I saw her leave this morning when I was out for a smoke."

Relief hits my chest so hard, for a moment I sway. Then I catch myself—too late to hide from Mirabela's perceptive gaze. Too late to hide from my own self. But I'll deal with those feelings later.

"What direction did she go in?" I ask Violeta.

"The village."

Of course, the fucking village.

Doesn't take a genius to realize why. She's been asking me about her dad, about who could've killed him. After last night and what she'd seen, she's bound to have gone seek out the Order. She needs to know, to put it to rest, and I haven't been able to explain it to her satisfaction.

Of course she'd seek answers from her own kin. It's only human instinct—we flock to those we are more alike with.

Without another word to my sisters, I take off.

Why do you appear so crazed, brother?

Mirabela has an annoying way of saying things that stick in my head. Like that.

No, this is not craziness running through me. It's something I haven't felt in a long, long time—fear. Pure, unadulterated fear.

Like the fear I felt when I couldn't find Silva. Like the dread in my stomach as I searched everywhere for him on our property, knowing he'd never leave his post or me without checking in first. Like the deep-seated knowledge that I'd lost him, the one friend I'd ever trusted with my life, even before I found his decapitated body.

I take a deep breath, one I still don't need. That's not the case here. For one, Tassa is more careful. And yes, she may be a human living a very fragile human existence, but...

Where the hell would you go, Tassa? When this entire town is on the verge of losing their shit?

I stop at the base of the hill, sniffing the air, but I'm no wolf. I can only catch her scent if she's close, or if I've drank from her. Since that's not the case...

I blur by at full vampir speed, rushing through the trees, then stopping again, trying to think. Where would she have gone, exactly?

Her father.

I'd thought before she left because of her father, but I didn't bother trying to determine why, exactly. Now I wager a guess. Learning about everything I'd done that night, and remembering the extent of my bloodthirsty nature, must've put into question my role as a savior.

I stop moving. So why am I even chasing her? Aside from making a fool of myself, this isn't the best way to spend my time. Or to show Mirabela that I'm not interested in the human. Yet the minute I'd heard she was gone, I'd taken off. Pushed by some innate need to find her, and make sure she's safe. Could that kiss have addled my brain?

No. I've had better. It's the curse of living for so long, there's nothing you haven't experienced.

But it did rock something in me. The innocence in her body, the rightness of how she'd felt against me...

Too late to turn back now.

I might as well find her.

Tassa

I wipe a hand over my forehead. *At least I'm getting in a proper workout.* Though going up and down the stairs at the castle is good movement, I've missed a good cardio session. And this hike to the mines, through unruly terrain and sharp slopes, has properly exhausted me.

Too bad I didn't have the foresight to bring some water.

A gurgling stream babbles nearby, but I won't chance it. Learned enough from Dad about acid mine drainage and heavy metal pollution. Our town's efforts to preserve the environment haven't erased the risks entirely, especially with the recent construction boom in the neighboring town.

Shifting from foot to foot, I watch the entrance of the mines. The noon sun casts an eerie glow, and the weathered and crumbling façade of the entrance seems to absorb all the light. The air is thick—

with my anxiety, with the supernatural, with the ghosts of the past? I have no idea. Maybe a mix of all.

Is it really smart, to come here on my own? Probably not. But it's too late to back out now.

Despite my reservations, I take a deep breath and step forward. Again, a twig snaps somewhere, pausing me in my steps, then I continue. Once, coincidence. Twice, maybe not. A third time? Concerning.

I glance around. Have the vampiri followed me? Maybe they're waiting for me to enter so they can officially kill me.

A wry chuckle escapes me. No, not likely. Unless it's Elizabeta or Alexandru.

Shaking my head, I continue toward the mine's entrance. The rusting gates, screwed tight into the stone wall, creak as I push them open. As soon as I'm out of sight of the forest, I bend down and grab the first sharp rock I find, and tuck it into the sleeve of my sweater.

I never said I was stupid—just reckless.

The quiet inside the mines is unnerving. I must've been inside for, what, half an hour already? And walked at least half a kilometer. But there's nothing around except the old railroad, and debris. Near the entrance, there had been litter—teenagers from the village, I'm guessing—but nothing since. As if no one has ventured this deep in ages.

"Probably true," I mutter to myself. "No one else is stupid enough. This cave could collapse at any moment."

Not only that, but who's to say the hidden depths aren't hiding some creatures just waiting to snack on my blood? Nico had mentioned that muroni live in caves... No number of sharp rocks will save me from them. Then again, no number of sharp rocks can save me from him, either.

Our conversation last night pops in my head. Soon set aside by what Victor told me. If the vampiri find out about Dad's alleged activities, will they hate me as they did that hunter? They never would've sought out my dad if they'd known...

If it's true. A part of me still hopes it isn't.

Shaking my head, I continue onward. But I trip over uneven ground and go down like a rock, at the same time as a chunk of rock from the ceiling falls toward me. I roll out of the way, narrowly avoiding the electric line. It must've been precariously set or something. But the sudden burst of sparks brings a little light—and helps me see something I wouldn't have otherwise.

Slowly, I get up and make a wide berth around the power line, still staring. At my father's writing, scratched into a boulder. It's not much. Just a few letters. *Pentru M.M.* "For M.M." Maria Mureș was my mother.

Hands trembling, I creep behind it and search under. Wedged between the base and the ground I find a notebook... Similar to the one I've been rifling through nonstop. I reach for it with a trembling hand. Tears sting my eyes—leave it to Dad to keep himself so organized, but also to be so wary.

Sure enough, when I open the notebook, it's filled with more notes about his patients. Only this time, it's not the human ones...but the vampiri.

"Holy shit."

Nicolae

I've been in the village and back but found no sign of her. Hands ruffling through my hair, I'm pacing the length of the forest, wearing down the grass, annoyed at this nagging feeling inside me. It almost feels like I've neglected these feelings for so long, now they're coming back with a vengeance.

"Where the fuck could she be?" I mutter. I'm half tempted to head back to the castle and order a full-scale search, but my siblings will only think I've lost it.

And maybe I have. Why care so much about a puny human?

Because she can help my sister, that's why. Or, at least, that's what I tell myself.

I keep pacing, trying to think where she could've gone. Then a twig snaps, and I turn—and Tassa's there, as surprised to see me as I am her.

She's filled with soot and dirt from head to toe, and I smell blood, from a gash on her hand she doesn't seem to notice. She's clutching something else in her un-bloodied hand, but I'm too relieved to see her to wonder about it.

Gone is the hesitation about these feelings. The annoyance at her callous behavior last night. The knowledge we're from two different worlds. I rush to her, grasping her by the shoulders. "What the hell were you thinking, leaving like that?"

Her wide eyes settle on me, taking in my expression. I don't know what I'm projecting, but if I had a heart, it would be somewhere in my throat. As it is, I swallow, and grip her tighter.

"You're hurting me." She glares at me. "And I didn't know I had to ask your permission to leave."

I'm taken aback by the vehemence in her tone. My walls go right back up, and I let go of her, taking a step back. "And yet, you do. I vouch for you in this family."

"Funny. I thought Violeta did."

She walks ahead of me, head held high. And much as I want to wring that pretty neck, I also can't deny the relief coursing through my veins.

What is this woman doing to me?

"Are you going to tell me where you were?" I ask after a few moments of trekking in silence. Since she refuses to let me carry her, we're stuck walking the woods together. For close to an hour. Alone.

It took me this long to sort through my feelings, or rather, to push them to the back of my mind so that I can focus on what's important. And that's how my gaze is now zeroed in on the notebook in her hand. What could it be?

"None of your business."

I'm in front of her the moment after, stopping her progression. This close, I catch the faint whiff of her perfume, and the dark circles under her eyes. Good thing to know I'm not the only one affected by everything. Then again, maybe I'm being egotistical, thinking her sleep issues revolve around me.

"Well?"

She taps her foot, then finally hands over the notebook, her free hand on her hip. "I went to the village. Initially, I just wanted to clear my head, see if I missed anything about Violeta's condition. Away from all of you and your distractions."

A wry smile twists my lips. I know just what distractions she's talking about.

A faint blush creeps up her neck and she looks away. "It didn't work. So I went to Victor's house—remember him, from the police station? He was also part of the mob who came to the castle."

I frown. "That could've been dangerous."

"Yeah, funny you mention that. They don't seem to love you much, do they? For people who are meant to protect you, I mean." She rolls her eyes. "Anyway, I didn't ask him about Violeta, before you imply I did. I'm not stupid. I asked instead about my dad and if Victor knew anything. He said something about how Dad had been acting scared a few days before his death, and that he'd seen him coming from the direction of the old mines."

I take in her sooty appearance, and groan. "Let me guess. You decided to go there by yourself."

"Yep. And it paid off."

"Uh huh. What about the blood I smell on you?"

She shows me her palm, and the graze. "Inconsequential. But look in the notebook."

My gaze lingers on the blood a moment too long. She realizes what she's doing and snags her hand away from my face, but I have a knee-jerk reaction and grip her wrist in my hand.

"You're wary of me."

"I'd be a fool not to, after what I remember from the night my dad died."

That stings. I don't know why, and I don't want to analyze it, but I want to fix it.

So instead of letting go of her hand and the caked blood gathered there, I lift it closer to my mouth. The movement has Tassa stepping toward me, her lips parting.

"Nico—"

I close my eyes, inhaling the scent of her blood. Listening to her heartbeat picking up. Then open them, snatching her gaze into mine. My eyes never let go of hers as I slowly bring my mouth to her palm, placing a kiss right where the blood is. Tassa inhales sharply. And then my tongue comes out, licking the blood away from her scratch.

I'd expected the usual taste—different for my siblings, perhaps, but for me, it's always been a faint mix of the coppery blood tinge with a hint of the human's fragrance. But this particular scent, it's like the best of ports. Sweet, and rich, full of an aroma that calls out to me. One I could get drunk on. And, oddly, one I want to savor, not drain until there's none left.

My entire attention continues being on her palm until I've licked every drop. Then, with a final sweep of my tongue, the venom I carry does its healing. The two flaps of skin draw closer, glue themselves back together, and the cut vanishes under my eyes.

I lick my lips, the fragrant taste of her blood still resonating on my tongue. Tassa's eyes widen in shock, her gaze locked on mine. I release her hand, my own fingers trembling slightly. I don't know what that was, but the rich, velvety smoothness of her blood surpasses anything I've ever drunk. I've never tasted something so... rich. Not even when I'd been previously infatuated with a human.

It's as if the very essence of her awakened a long-dormant craving inside me. I'm shaken to my core, my carefully constructed walls shaking in their foundation—*and all because of a human.*

In an effort to hide my reaction, I turn my gaze to the notebook. "May I?" She hesitates, then hands it over. Flipping through it, I notice a few things. First off, the dates. Second off, the locations. Everything is a distance away from here, but...

"How would your father have been able to travel so much? And why, to heal humans?" I look her up and down. "No offense, but it doesn't make sense. Everything in your house was as battered as my castle, and you're wearing old clothes. He clearly wasn't earning what human doctors do. Which makes no sense for how he'd have had the money to travel so much."

"He wouldn't have."

Tassa doesn't seem fazed or insulted by my comment. Instead, she looks at me as if waiting for me to connect the dots. When I simply arch an eyebrow, she grabs the notebook out of my hand. Her fingers graze mine, and the touch feels like fire. For a fleeting moment, I'm consumed by a maddening urge to grab her and kiss that assured smirk off her lips, to redirect her excitement and make sure her heart races for *me* alone, and nothing else.

But I restrain myself—barely—summoning every ounce of self-control I've honed over the centuries to suppress the primal impulse. My grip on said control is tenuous at best, but I force myself to refocus on her words, to prioritize reason. Surely, I can do that, given I've been doing it for centuries already?

"This is a similar notebook to the one he'd had about humans. Only it contains his notes about *vampir* medical visits."

Ah, fuck.

When twigs snap around us, I decide it's time to head back to the safety of the castle once more.

Chapter 16

Tassa

Once Nico's done dragging me back to the castle, we head into the library, this time armed with Dad's notebook. It's filled with notes about times he's seen vampiri—one would think immortals don't get sick, but one would be, apparently, wrong.

Though on the outside I pretend this is my sole focus, I can't deny I'm still shaken by what happened in the woods. I was stunned when Nico licked my wound, and even more stunned that he healed it. But nowhere more stunned than at the sharp licks of desire I'd felt as he tasted my blood.

After the revelations yesterday, I'm insane to even think like this.

Surely. But I can't deny that when my eyes travel to him, my heart kicks up a notch every now and again.

To draw my attention from that, I focus on Dad's scroll and the notebook from the mines. And the House of Dracul book I dragged from my room to here. Out of all three items, what's interesting are the dates listed in the notebook. From my recollection, these were times he'd told me he was at some conference or another. And Nico has a point about the money. While we've never been dirt-poor, we lived comfortably. But definitely not comfortably enough to account for expenses to Serbia, Hungary, and Bulgaria. Or France. Or Scotland, for that matter.

My best guess is he got paid very well for it, which also begs the question of where the money is?

Focusing on Dad's writing keeps my attention elsewhere. Away from the vampir next to me, the same one who'd kissed me senseless last night, and who sought me out today like a crazed man. If I didn't know better, I'd think he was afraid of me leaving—him.

But, of course, that's idiotic thinking. The exact kind of thinking that'll end in a broken heart and not much else, so fuck it. I tear my gaze from the way the sun falls on him, giving his features even more of that aristocratic shadow.

Nico pulls out a map and says, "Give me the locations for the last six months. Let's start there."

One by one, we map out where my father had offered his services, then stare at the map in confusion. He'd not only gone all over Romania and its surrounding countries, but all over Austria, Germany, the French Alps, and more.

"Were vampiri moving him?" I ask. "Is there some kind of word-of-mouth newspaper or something where they could have contracted his services?"

He shrugs. "Not that I know of. Then again, me and my siblings have kept away from the rest of our kin."

Right. Because of their feud with the clans. Or rather, the clans' feud with the heirs.

Nico leans over the table, and the movement stretches his shirt around the shoulders, outlining his lean biceps as he presses his weight into the wood. At the same time, his hunched posture draws the back of the material up, exposing the muscle of his lower back. My mouth dries.

"What worries me," he says, snapping me out of my daze, "is that a lot of these locations are so remote. How was your father so sure he wouldn't become food?"

"My question exactly." I shake my head. "Even if they promised him safety, I can't imagine what went through his head." A thought occurs to me. "Do vampiri usually rely on human doctors?"

"No. Too many chances of things going wrong. In most cases, they'll take a doctor and turn them to a vampir, then use him on standby. But to a have a human doctor on retainer is akin to exposing our world. Which is not smart." His teeth grind. "And something the House of Dracul has always explicitly banned."

My eyes roam over his features, the annoyance in his expression. It bothers him, more than I thought, that their influence has dwindled so much over the clans of vampiri.

Not your problem, Tassa. Focus on the task at hand. I tuck a lock of hair behind my ear and say, "Either way, I'll go over the notes in detail, see if anything comes up in the ailments. Anything that might match Violeta's symptoms."

"I'll help."

It's now or never. I've been biting my tongue, but it only makes me a hypocrite if I don't tell him.

I clear my throat. "Before you make that commitment... There's something else I have to tell you."

My tone must alert him to the seriousness of the issue, as he tenses. His gaze sharpens on my features and he narrows his eyes on me. Dark blue meets my light brown.

"I'm listening."

"When I went to visit Victor, he said something. Something I have trouble believing, but it ties in to what the hunter said. And it finally gave me the answers I've been seeking, though it left many questions in its wake."

He sighs. "Will I have to glamour it out of you?"

"Not funny."

He ignores my mutter, instead leaning his hip on the table.

At a loss, I blurt it out. "My father was helping experiment on vampiri."

It's like all the air is sucked out of the room. Nico straightens again, his gaze even sharper. "Repeat that."

I gulp. "Victor said that my dad was experimenting on vampiri, that it's how he was known to them in the first place. But that something happened and he changed, started to help them instead."

Nico lets out a sharp exhale at my revelation, and one of his fists clenches on the table. He must be applying pressure, because the wood creaks underneath. The air in the room feels drawn, like his anger at my revelation is about to explode.

Then he releases his fist and rolls his shoulders. Just like that, the tightness is gone, and I can breathe easy once more.

Nico frowns at me. "Did you notice anything different in your father's behavior?"

"No, but—"

"Then Victor could be lying."

"Yes, but—"

"You can't believe everything he or anyone else would say. You knew your father best. Was he a bad man?"

His words drive a jolt of something in my chest. Gratitude. It's gratitude because he's reminding me of everything my dad stood for. And Victor's words can't take that away.

"No. Never."

"Then he wasn't." He turns his focus to the map. "That still doesn't explain any of this. But his notebook just might. And if—*big if*—he was doing what you fear he might have been, his notes will have clues to that effect. Let's do this, da?"

When I don't answer right away, he glances up at me. I don't know how to express what his utter belief in me means. Or his trust in my father, though he never met him. It's baffling.

But it's also reassuring. That maybe he does have a soul. And maybe he's not exactly the monster I've been picturing in my head.

I nod. "Yeah, let's do it."

Three hours later, we've sped read through the entire last year of notes and found all kinds of things. But...

"Nothing like Violeta's illness," Nico says, disappointment filling his tone. "And nothing about him doing experiments, either. These notes really seem to indicate he was seeing vampiri as regular patients."

"I know. But that doesn't mean there's nothing in here. I'll keep going backward, covering the last two years, and let you know as soon as I find something."

Nico sighs and pushes off the couch, ruffling his hair. There are no comforting words I can offer, nor can I focus too hard on that... If I'm to save Violeta before she gets worse, my entire attention needs to be on her.

As Nico gets into a pacing-drinking-pacing routine, I keep poring over the notes, jotting things down in my own notebook. Little by little, a pattern emerges. Some vampiri report issues with skin ailments, weaknesses, lack of desire for blood. Dad's notes next to each incident are even more concerning. *NNC.* The legend indicates the acronym stands for *non-natural causes.*

Was Dad referring to the hunter? But, no. I'd seen the man's poisons, even brought some back here. They're entirely natural—plant-based, judging from the smells. So was Dad alluding to another, more dangerous threat? Something that could be tied to Violeta's symptoms?

"Hmm?"

I wave my hand toward Nico, implying he should keep at what he's doing. I then drag the House of Dracul book closer and open it to the first page. We might've found our first clue, but I'm not about to give anyone blind hope until I'm sure.

"There's an entry here..."

I look up when Nico doesn't come rushing over, only to find him asleep by the fireplace. I glance back at the notebook, at the words dancing on paper that could be yet another clue, but my eyes betray me by flickering to him, over and over again.

I could blame it on the crackling of the fire. I could even blame it on the fact that I'm starting to feel sleepy myself. But that's not the case, not really.

The truth is seeing Nico the way I am, it makes him seem even more human. Which is a dangerous allure, a thought I shouldn't even entertain. He's a vampir. A ruthless, ancient one. I've seen him dismember people as easily as I can tear a paper into pieces. He's definitely not someone to get involved with. Of course he knows how to kiss, he's been kissing women for centuries. But that doesn't mean anything.

As if to spite my thoughts, the library opens, and in comes Elizabeta.

"Nataşa, *Nataşa*..." She stares at me, then at Nico, a sneer on her lips. "Fallen asleep halfway?"

"Yes," I say, trying to keep my answers short and concise. I clearly remember our last interaction and I'm not ready to have a repeat performance. Not with her.

Alas, it doesn't seem like she's ready to give up. She walks inside the library, pretends to rifle through some books, all the while making her way behind me.

"And how goes the research?"

"Good enough," I say.

What is she doing here? To say I'm afraid of her is an under-statement. Out of all of them, she quite easily might be the most psychotic one—even worse than Alex. And her hate for me is clear.

She walks some more, looking around. Despite myself, I can't help staring at her. Without the scar on her cheek, she would be the picture of perfection. In a way, she still is. A harsher perfection.

She walks like a cat, checking everything around her. I feel her eyes on me and I try to ignore her, returning my attention to the notebook instead. But it's hard. Will she lunge at me? Is Nico pretending to be asleep? Or is she simply toying with me like a cat with a mouse?

"Was there something you wanted?" I finally ask.

She chuckles. There's nothing warm about it, and it sends shivers up my spine.

"Nothing much," she says. "My brother sure seems to spend a lot of time with you."

Ah. So that's what this is about.

I close the notebook and stare at her. This is the first time she's actually tried to have a conversation with me, rather than sneer at me or just plain shout at me. Should I trust it? Is it an olive branch?

Something about the tone of her voice and the glint in her eyes tells me it's none of those things. On the contrary. It's just more mind games. And after Victor's earlier lies, I really can't be bothered.

When she sees I'm not about to answer, something changes in her expression. Her eyes grow more opaque, and I feel a tingle run up my spine. I hurry to glance away, knowing she's trying to use glamour on me.

I clear my throat and—keeping my gaze firmly away from her—speak in the coldest voice I can. "You have no right to use that power on me."

"I have every right," she says. "Every right given to me by my birth, by my immortality, and my *everything else* you can never understand. Do you honestly think there could ever be something between you and my brother?"

"I never said anything like that." I toss the notebook away on the couch and stand, no longer willing to be subservient to her. "And whatever is going on or not going on between me and your brother, you have no right to intervene."

"Again, with that no right business." She snorts. "You forget who I am and whose house you are in."

"Funny. I thought this house belongs to all of you. Or is it that you're above all your other siblings?"

I see the change in her the moment I say the words—she's about to strike me. I hurry to get the rest of my words out before she does. "I'm trying to save your sister. And you're interrupting what could be a breakthrough right now. Would you mind leaving the library?"

The look in her eyes is no longer amicable. She prowls toward me, drawing closer with every inch. "You dare ask me to leave a room in *my* castle?"

I open my mouth to speak, but Nico moves at that moment. Elizabeta doesn't turn to him, just tilts her head in his direction. She must've already known he was awake, way before I did.

"We're making progress," he says lazily. "Why don't you leave us, Liza, and find someone else to bother?"

Though there's a drawl in his tone, it's combined with a steely undertone that leaves no room for argument. With one last sneer at me, Elizabeta listens and leaves.

I take a deep breath and let it out on a shudder. "Thank you."

He nods, rubbing the back of his neck. "I'm sorry I didn't intervene earlier. I keep hoping she might be less..." He shakes his head. "I know she seems psychotic, but there's a reason for it."

I let out a nervous chuckle. "I'm sure there is."

A muscle in his jaw ticks. A beat later, he says, "Long ago, the hunters experimented on her. That's as much as I can tell you—it's not my history to share—but if I were you, I wouldn't mention your doubts about your father around her."

"I... Christ, I'm so sorry, Nico." That explains his reaction, earlier. He has close knowledge of the experiments.

He's already moving back to the wine. "It was a long time ago. Just let it go."

Nicolae

After Liza's idiotic appearance and bear-poking, Tassa can't focus. Probably also my fault for mentioning Liza's past. I don't know what possessed me to do that.

I suggest she get some sleep and that we continue the work later. It's not just her who needs rest. While I don't sleep, per se, my mind demands a quiet place to assess everything that's happened, to determine whether I'm slowly losing my mind or starting to care for a human—both impossibilities, at this stage.

After Tassa's safely inside her room, I head to mine. My thoughts are running rampant, unable to focus on anything. This hell...is a new kind, even for me. And with each passing day, I'm hating it more and more.

When night comes, I toss and turn in bed. Hunger burns inside me, but for once it's more than just for blood. It's for *her*. When I finally sleep, my dreams only reflect the unattainable...

The door opens on a soft whoosh. It takes me no time to get accustomed to the darkness. She's curled up under the bedsheets, covers drawn to under her chin, the most peaceful expression on her face.

I move closer, both wanting and yearning and craving to touch her. My feet make no sound, and then I'm at the foot of the bed, and moving closer. By the nightstand, I slowly drop to my knees. The entire time, my eyes have not stopped staring at her.

She makes a soft sound in her sleep, halfway between a moan and a groan, and my body tightens. Desire rushes through me with a force I am unaccustomed to. I should have stayed quiet—but I can't. A hiss escapes me.

Tassa's eyes flutter open at the sound. She blinks once, twice, slowly coming out of the daze of sleep. I wait for that telltale sign, the moment she'll scream when she realizes I'm there. But she doesn't.

She shifts on the bed, drawing closer to me, and reaches a pale hand from beneath the bedsheets. Strokes my chin, my cheek, my forehead. I hold still under her ministrations, but my control is close to snapping. I tremble under her touch, and she stops her movements.

"Why aren't you what you're supposed to be?"

I have to swallow, thickly, before I can form words. "Meaning?"

"You should be ruthless. You claim to be. Selfish, psychopathic, the lot. I can see it in some of your siblings, those traits. Their humanity is gone. But you... No matter how you wish to, you can't escape your humanity, Nico. It's there, bright as the light of day."

Her words shake me. I try to cover it with a denial. "It is not. It has long been gone."

"You say that, yet what I see is different. I see—"

I move, then. I can't bear to hear any more, not when her words have already had such an effect on me. In one movement, I'm towering over her bed. My face hovering above hers. My breath mingling with hers.

"Be afraid of me. I am no pet."

She chuckles. "No. One would have to be crazy to try and domesticate you." Then that damned hand reaches for me again, this time touching the bare skin of my chest. "You aren't alone in these desires, Nico. Much as I want to fight them... You're not alone."

She pushes closer to me, her lips pecking mine. Once. Twice. The third time, I bury my hand in her hair, clutching her locks, tugging. Baring her neck to me.

"You want to play, little human?"

"More than anything else."

I don't know which of us moves first, or faster. But before long, her limbs are intertwined with mine, and my body's aching for more—more closeness, more pressure, more friction, more of her. I yearn to bury myself in her, to forget about my centuries of hate, and allow the purity of her light to imbue every essence of my being.

Wipe away my sins, Tassa.

Make me whole.

Love me...and never leave me.

I don't say any of that—not out loud, anyway. Instead, inch by inch, I kiss her skin, moving clothes out of the way, baring as much as I can. There is no human hesitation, no lingering doubt of insecurity in her. Not like when she's awake.

Does this mean we're both dreaming the same thing? Does it even matter?

I wrap my tongue around her tight nipple, drawing it into my mouth. Tassa arches into me, silently seeking something more. I keep licking, teasing, nipping—my fangs elongate, and I let them trail down her skin, light as feathers. She shivers under me, writhing until the sheets are tangled around her.

I settle between her thighs, move the nightgown up, up and up...and taste her sweet honey, until she cries and comes all over me. And then I do it again. The entire time, I'm aware of the heady thrum of her pulse, the beat of her heart, the rattling of her rib cage as she draws in breaths that get ever shorter.

When I'm done with my delightful torture, I thrust into her. And finally learn the meaning of eternal damnation.

Needless to say, I get no rest at all, let alone peace of mind. Morning finds me in the main living area, sipping on a dark red wine this time. It doesn't take long for Vlad and Alex to join me, yapping about something or other.

I'm not ashamed to say I tune out within moments. There's more in my head that I have to disentangle if I'm to be around Tassa again. These dreams are no good—at all. To her, or to me.

"Have you heard a single word I've said?"

I glance from my glass. Alex's eyes are narrowed on me, like a cat playing with his food.

"No." There's no point in lying when he's this focused. He'll see right through me anyway.

"Where were you, just then?" he asks.

"None of your business."

"It is when you're not paying attention to something of this magnitude." He moves closer, his expression pinched. "Are you fucking her?"

"Don't be crude."

"Don't be stupid."

"Enough!" Vlad stops us. His voice is usually quiet, but when he wants to, he can be the bear in the room. "I'm done with your childish behavior, both of you. Violeta needs us. Nothing else should matter."

"Precisely. And if our brother is busy screwing the doctor who can help her—"

"I'm not, and she's not a doctor."

Vlad looks at me, then nods. "So be it. Alex, you heard the man. Let's move on, da?"

He shrugs and backs off, much too easily. "Fine. Perhaps it might interest you to know the rumors, then."

"What rumors?"

"Of a new pack of vârcolaci in the area."

That does pique my curiosity. Vârcolaci are werewolves, but the Romanian kind—a gene passed down from generation to generation. Unlike the more popular Western stories, they don't shift under a full moon. Rather, they can take on a wolf's mantle—his body—at any time. They have the canine body, the canines, and the strength most humans associate with werewolves from movies or shows. But their bite can't turn someone into a werewolf unless their blood drips in their wounds. Neither can silver bullets kill them, only a stake through the heart will do.

Kinda like us. On that bit, legends are true.

"That's impossible," I say. "There haven't been any for a while in these parts." Our presence tends to scare them off, like most other apex predators. Another suspicion rises in me. "Where did you even hear these rumors? You better not have tried relinking with other vampiri in the area, Alex."

"Relax, frate. I heard it from a muroni I'd killed. Just because you've stopped cleaning house since your non-doctor showed up, doesn't mean I have to." Alex laughs. "Seems our quiet time is over, then."

Something about his tone and stance makes me wary. "What do you propose?"

"Let us welcome them to the area. Flex our muscles. A little show of strength never did anyone wrong."

It's my turn to frown. "Have you lost your mind, or watched too many human renditions of us? Wolves are not our enemies."

"These ones might be."

Why is he angling for a fight? There's got to be more to this for him, but I don't have the time to piece together Alex's motivations. For once, my brother will simply have to grow up and not give in to his impulses. "We put it to a vote or do nothing at all. End of story."

The fire in his blue eyes, so similar to mine, tells me this is far from over.

Chapter 17

Nicolae

That night, I'm busy wandering the halls again with no particular purpose in mind. Just an inexplicable restlessness, a need to fidget that doesn't translate well when confined to the four walls of my room. I've lost track of the countless cracks I counted in an effort to still my mind, to no avail.

My feet lead me to the library and I'm somewhat not surprised to find Tassa there again, poring over books and books. Seeing her like this, so focused, so driven, all to help my sister... It ignites something in me. A sense of pride, of ownership almost. Which is idiotic, to say the least.

I stop the thoughts in their tracks. I've been avoiding her since that last dream. Not trusting my baser impulses to behave just yet. None of that makes me walk away. On the contrary, I linger around.

"In search of a magical cure?"

She glances up at me. Her eyes are red-rimmed, and she has dark circles under them.

"How long have you been at this?"

"Hmm?" She seems distracted. "A while."

"When was the last time you ate?"

She snorts. "Some point earlier today. Your sister tried to chop my head off."

I don't have to ask which sister. "I'll have a word with Liza soon."

"Don't. Please. I have enough to do, and the drama that will result from your talk will only distract me."

Despite her words, I can tell the issue with Liza is bothering her. Who wouldn't it bother? A vampir psychotic redhead who's got it in for her, any human would cower away at that. Anyone with any sense would run away. But not Tassa. For some reason, her desire to help Violeta outweighs her fear of Liza. Yet another contradiction that makes her much too interesting to me.

I glance at her out of the corner of my eye, trying and failing to hold back my admiration. I can't remember the last time I've been so engrossed in a human. The one before didn't compare. The one whose name I can't conjure, who was at fault for Silva. But this human, this siren in disguise, with her intelligence and her sass and her ability to stand up to my crazy psychotic siblings, has truly drawn my admiration.

I don't tell her any of this. Why would I? After all, she's here to do a job, and one job only. And that is to help Violeta. Nothing else, not even the crazy insane urge I have to kiss her again, can take precedence over that.

"Regardless, I'll speak with Liza. She can't keep cornering you like that, especially when you're trying to help Violeta. If nothing else, she should give you a break."

"You would think so."

She dismisses me and goes back to the books, but I'm not so easy to get rid of. I don't even bother justifying this urge to help her. I'm too tired, and too wrung out. Who would've thought emotions are so...exhausting?

I head to the kitchen and pile something that seems edible enough—an apple, some nuts, some cheese—on a plate, then return to the library and place the plate on the table. "Eat."

Tassa glares at me. "You can be bossy, you know that?"

I recall the dream, the way she'd writhed under my touch, and my body tightens, unbidden. I try not to show my thoughts. "You have no idea."

A beat later, she finally listens and digs into the food. After the first bite, she practically inhales the rest. I'll have to keep an eye on her eating habits or teach my siblings to feed the human if they want Violeta safe. There are many ways she could die around us, but starvation should not be one of them.

Once she's inhaled the last bite, I push a glass of water her way.

"Have you found anything?" I repeat.

She swallows. "You really want to know?"

"Da."

Tassa hesitates, her eyes searching mine. Then she sighs, reaching for her father's notebook. "Fine, look at this."

She goes to turn the notebook so I can read, but I stop her and point. "Herbology?" I'd only just noticed the cover of the other book next to her.

"Yeah, I was refreshing my plant knowledge. You guys used to be sensitive to vervain, right? Don't act so surprised—it's in my dad's accounts. And you'll be interested to know you were wrong. It seems he wasn't the only human playing doctor to the vampiri."

My eyebrows arch way up. "There are more?"

"Yes, but don't ask me where, because he won't say. Could also be his information is outdated." A flash of pain crosses her expression. "Was, I mean. Anyway. The fact you developed immunity against this herb got me thinking—it shows evolution. What if you then developed a weakness to something else?"

I perch on the arm of the sofa, leaning toward her even as I'm trying to rein in my anger. "The pot she's smoking."

Tassa lets out a chuckle, as surprising to her as it is to me, judging by the slight pinkening in her cheeks. "You really have to let that go. No, it's not the herb Violeta's been inhaling. It's the ones she's playing around with."

"You mean... the greenhouse?"

Tassa nods, pursing her lips. "Yeah. I saw her a few days ago, when she was better. And before that, she mentioned making these natural remedies for the villagers, many of whom suffer from various ailments in their old age. Dad used to help them. One of the ways he did so was with herbal poultices, using ingredients like ginger, fenugreek, feverfew, gingko balboa... In sum, the same plants growing in Violeta's greenhouse. They're all natural blood coagulants."

"But your father's patients weren't dying from what he was making them take."

"No, because Dad was giving it to them in small doses. As is

Violeta. But *she* is touching those potent herbs, undiluted, day in and day out."

I shake my head. "Humans are around herbs twenty-four-seven and they don't get sick from handling them. Look at the apothecary in the village."

Tassa leans closer, her eyes wide with excitement. "True. But those humans never had issues with herbs prior... Whereas, you guys did. With vervain."

"You're saying we've developed some kind of allergy to it?" It's plausible, but...I run my thumb over my jawline. "Then how do you explain Vlad and I aren't having a reaction?"

She shrugs. "You didn't come into contact with it as much."

I mull it over, then nod. "That's... really interesting, Tassa. Fantastic find."

"It's not much. Not like I solved it or anything. But it's a start."

I barely hold back my frown. Why must she be so hard on herself? "I beg to differ. This is more potential answers than we've had to date." I angle my body toward hers, peeking over her shoulder at the words she scribbled in the notebook. "So, what's our next step?"

Tassa

I try to ignore the way Nico's leaning over me. The way he smells, the way he feels so close to me, especially after our kiss. The last time we'd been this close, I'd had my entire being all wrapped up around him.

Shoving those images away from my head, I focus on what I've written down and explain it as best as I can. When I'm done, he grins. And it's more devastating than anything else.

"This is amazing," he says. "So if she did develop some kind of allergy, it could manifest with the thickening of the blood she drinks from humans. Therefore thickening the very thing that gives her life, in her veins. And if you feed her the thinning herbs instead, it'll fix her up. That simple? And she just has to stay away from them in the future."

I want to join in his exuberance, but I can't. Not just yet. "Yes. But that's not all of it. We still need to find out *why* it happened. Otherwise, I'm only treating symptoms, and not the root cause. Also, Nico..." I look up at him. "We can't tell anyone else yet."

"Why not?"

Because I might be wrong. Because it's too easy. Because I still feel like I'm missing something. Because none of this explains Dad's notes about non-natural causes.

I don't say any of that. I haven't been able to decipher Dad's code in his scroll, and until I do, there's no point. Instead, I settle for, "Because, first we need to test this out. If it doesn't pan out, then no harm to Violeta, but at least she won't be worried about it. Can you imagine how destroyed she'd be if we give her hope, only to wrench it away?"

He purses his lips, considering my words. Clearly, it's been a while since he considered anyone else's feelings but his own.

"And how would we test it out?"

I think for a moment. Glance back at my notes. My brain is swarming, but not just with theories. It's also overwhelmed to be so close to him. I hate myself for my heartbeat picking up, but at the same time, cannot help it. I'm only human. I'm only female.

"I'll think on it and let you know." I point a finger at his chest. "But in the meantime, *don't tell anyone*, especially not Violeta."

"Fine," he says. And there goes that devastating grin again. "Care for a drink? To celebrate a potential solution."

"Sure."

One drink turns into two. Then three. Then Nico breaks open a bottle of fine port he's been saving—according to him. By the time we're halfway through it, our excitement over my find has dwindled, but is no less intense.

I catch Nico looking at me. I've been staring at the fire, lost in thought. Mainly about Dad's notes. But the weight of his gaze is impossible to ignore.

When I turn to him, his eyes lock onto mine with a fierceness that makes my skin prickle. He has the oddest expression, as if whatever he's thinking about is both entrancing and daunting. *Conflicted* is the best I can come up with, yet even that word pales in comparison to the flames flickering in his irises, reflected from the fire.

"What is it?"

He shakes his head. It almost sounds like he's grinding his teeth, mulling over something. He takes another sip from his drink and then says, "You were honest with me so it's only fair I tell you something. Something I know you've been wondering about." He blows out a breath. "Centuries ago, when we first had to go into hiding, we heard rumors of experiments. At first, we didn't want to get involved. Our safety overtook our desire to help. But Liza's always been stubborn and given her own history, she convinced us to risk it."

He stares into his drink for a long moment, the fire's light flickering across his cheekbones. My heart tugs weirdly, sensing that what he's about to share won't be a happy memory.

"We tracked down a pair of hunters. We disposed of them and

went into their basement... That's when I saw Silva for the first time. He was bloody, and he'd been cut into—I'll spare you the atrocities. We rescued him, took him in, and offered him a chance to regroup with us. He realized who we were, of course. He and Liza grew close over the next few years."

Nico meets my gaze then, and his voice drops a few octaves. Filled with pain. "Not as much as we did. He became a new brother to me, one who didn't judge and had my back unconditionally. But I didn't have his." He drains his glass and gets up, agitated, to refill it. This is the first time I've seen his hand shake.

"There was a human, in the area we were living in. I can't even remember her name, you know? That's the stupid part. But I was infatuated with her. My siblings warned me. But I didn't listen...nor did I stop to check myself." He turns to face me again. "See, we were living in enemy vampir territory, then. The kind of people who don't take kindly to one of us hunting—even if it was a royal—and feeding on *their* food. Which is exactly what I did."

My heartbeat picks up again. He'd liked a human, once. Enough to put his entire family in jeopardy.

His gaze lowers again to the wine glass, as if it has all the answers. "I didn't know why, but her blood tasted addictive. I couldn't stop myself and I accidentally killed her."

My sharp indrawn breath draws his eyes on me again. A wry smile twists his mouth.

"Ironically, it wasn't until I licked your blood in the woods that I realized why that is. It seems when we develop an attraction to a human, their blood is more appealing than all others. But hers doesn't even come close to the taste of you, Tassa. Your blood is...*so* much sweeter." He closes his eyes, as if reminiscing.

I gulp. Fear should be consuming me right now, but all I can focus on is the pain in his voice. The tight grip on his glass.

"What happened with Silva?" I ask.

Nico clenches his jaw. "He died. Killed. After I... After the other vampiri discovered the woman's body, they traced us down. Hunted us down, more like. Silva protected us, made sure we could escape. He was decapitated in the process." He looks away, but not before I catch the tears brimming in his eyes.

This death, more than anything else in his centuries of existed, shattered him. I don't have to be a psychologist to figure that out. And he still carries the guilt with him, after all this time... My heart squeezes painfully at the realization. How did I ever think this man was a monster, when he's so *human* in this moment?

Setting my glass on the table, I get up and walk over to him. Then I do something I probably shouldn't, given everything he just revealed. I turn him—he lets me—and hug him.

At first, he's tense in my arms, then he relaxes and his entire body shudders against mine as he buries his head in my neck. We stay like that for long, calming moments, until Nico pulls away.

"Want a refill?"

I nod, knowing it's his way of coping.

Over the next few hours, I don't know how many drinks we have. All I know is the room starts potentially spinning around me, when I've never been a lightweight. Nico himself actually seems affected by the alcohol. Unsurprising, given how much he ingested. Can vampiri even get drunk? When he laughs, I realize I've asked the question out loud and I can feel myself blush.

"Yes, we can," he chuckles. "Just not in the same way as humans. With humans, you tend to get goofy and lightheaded and get massive hangovers the next morning. Our senses and organs aren't alive like yours, so it's more of a buzz. It doesn't last long, but for the duration, we lose our inhibitions."

"Lose your inhibitions? What does that look like?"

His gaze meets mine. He'd been reaching for another glass, but now he pauses, focused on me. I can feel myself warming, and not just from the alcohol.

"It looks like this." Without missing a beat, he moves in, and his lips are on mine, his hands grip me, and all I can think of is to continue the kiss, to give into it, for my entire body to melt into his.

We can't do this. Part of me knows it. But the other part is so damn done with holding back, with being a good girl, with doing the sensible thing, with not giving in to my impulses. Nico has an eternity ahead of him. I don't. Losing Dad showed me that, and also revealed how little I've truly allowed myself to *live*. I want to experience everything that I want, before it's too late.

For Nico, too late probably doesn't exist. For me, it's a reality I have to get accustomed to. I only have one lifetime and I might as well make the most of it. So instead of putting distance between us, I reach for his neck, tangle my hands in his hair, and pull myself even closer still.

He groans, and then one hand goes to my hips, and he presses his hardness against me. I moan in his mouth and he catches the sound with his lips. The way his tongue sweeps over mine, pushes for dominance, it feels like he's devouring my very soul. And while I should be running away, especially when I can feel his fangs with the tip of my tongue, I don't. Instead, a feverish urge runs through me to have skin upon skin, to have him inside me, to get what only he can provide.

Part of me wonders after centuries if there's even anything that will surprise him. Questions like *can you still orgasm after so long* run through my head. And what about sexual diseases? Do vampiri even get those?

But I push those away and try to focus on the pleasure in the moment. No matter how much my head wants to ruin it. No matter how much my adult doubts want to ruin it. No matter how much or how many things should be standing between us.

Nico picks me up at one point and we must be moving to the couch because he's on top of me or I'm on top of him. I don't care, but what matters is he's touching me and my shirt is half off and his hands are on my skin, kneading my breasts. The coolness of his skin against the heated temperature of mine provides a sharp contrast. One I've never felt before. Obviously.

I pull back, realizing that I'm on top of him, feeling his hardness between my thighs, and I look at him. Stare deep into his eyes. He reaches out with one hand. Touches my lips, caressing them, running his thumb over the bottom lip. I pull it into my mouth, sucking on it gently, biting on it. I don't know what possesses me to do that. I never have before.

A hiss escapes him. His eyes darken. "What you do to me..."

I smile, though it feels a bit wobbly. "What do I do to you?"

"You drive me to distraction." The way he caresses my cheek, and the rest of my body drives *me* to distraction, but I don't say that. He doesn't need me to make his head any bigger than it already is.

I lean over him, ready to kiss him again, but something changes. I'm not sure what exactly makes me realize it, whether it's the way he turns his head to the side or how he grips my hips. The tightening of his hands on me is my only warning before he shoves me off the couch and covers me with his body.

The minute after, something explodes—a deafening noise. It takes me a moment to realize it's one of the windows of the library. Painted glass flies everywhere.

Nico growls in my ear. "Stay here," he says, and then he's gone.

Shaking, I scramble to my feet and curl up in a ball, but he's already at the window, staring outside.

"What is it?" I ask.

"I don't know." His expression is dark, with no trace of the pleasure from before remaining. He opens his mouth to say something, but the door to the library is thrown open in that moment.

His siblings walk in. Not all of them, thankfully, but enough. Elizabeta is among them, as are Alexandru and Vlad.

"What the hell just happened?" Alexandru shouts.

"Do you think I know?" Nico says.

I'm incredibly aware of my half-nakedness as I scramble for my clothes, but it's already too late. I sense Alex's eyes on me—or, more to the point, his glare.

"I see you're getting busy with the human," he says.

"None of your business," Nico retorts.

"Guys," Vlad says, "maybe it's best that we focus on what actually happened here. Are we in danger?"

Nico shakes his head. "I don't know."

"Then maybe it's time someone here does something useful and finds out," Alexandru says and leaves.

Nico comes to my side and wraps an arm around my shoulders. "Are you all right?"

I stare at him and wonder. I would not have expected him to be touching me in front of his siblings, let alone demonstrate such affection. When I try to move away, his arm around my shoulders is like an iron hold. What the hell does this even mean?

"Yeah."

Never mind the fact that we just got interrupted in our hot and heavy session. Never mind the fact that his siblings walked in on us. Never mind the fact that it's not like I have the perfect body. None of that matters at that moment, because weirdly he's holding me and he's still showing me affection. Recognizing me as an equal...*worthy*.

His expression softens, his eyes never leaving mine, and I swear I see in that gaze an apology at the interruption. The Good Samaritan who turned monster who turned friend, then monster again, and now...lover? Ha. How fucking insane.

Alexandru bursts back into the room then and says, "You have to come see this. Including the human."

He disappears again but, this time, we follow.

Chapter 18

Nicolae

I want nothing more than to grab Tassa and drag her to my room, finish off what we started. It takes all the self-control I lost earlier not to do exactly that. Still, I can't keep away. As we follow Vlad out of the library, trailing after Alex, I inch closer to her.

"Are you all right?"

"Yes, I already told you."

I frown, then shrug off her tone. She must be scared. I can't blame her. First, her father is killed, and now her own life is in danger. Because I have no doubts about what just happened. Whoever attacked, whatever it was, it has nothing to do with our family, and all to do with hers—maybe even what she found in those mines. The timing is too coincidental.

Vampiri clans are not only stealthier when they wish our death, but they also come in huge numbers. As for muroni, they wouldn't bother with mind games. That leaves the wolves Alex mentioned, but their appearance in these parts is inconsequential as far as I'm concerned.

"Alex, what..." Vlad trails off. It's enough to get Tassa to tense more, and I tug her by the sleeve of her sweater until she's behind me.

Not that it saves her from seeing what I'm seeing.

"A dead cock? Really?"

Alex throws me a glare. "Have a closer look."

Despite my disgust, I listen, heading closer and staring at the mass of black and gold feathers, red beard, and extremely dead eyes. Only one thing is missing.

"No blood," Vlad says.

"Yes, I see that!" I snap at him.

Tassa's already moved past me, kneeling next to the dead rooster, as if trying to revive it.

"Tassa, it's dead, there's no point—"

"There's something in its beak," she says.

We all step closer. It's a testament to how far she's come, that she doesn't even flinch at being so cooped up, surrounded by our three bulks. Instead, she opens the beak gently and pulls out a piece of paper. It's definitely paper, not parchment, which alone tells me we're not dealing with any of our old enemies.

Still, I feel Vlad's eyes on me and glance up. He quickly averts his gaze.

"What does it say?" I whisper.

"What do you think it says?" Alex snorts. "It's a warning."

"Would you shut it?"

"He's right," Tassa says, surprising us all. Well, all except Alex. She shows me the note.

Death lives in those walls and death will find them, too.

"What the hell does it mean?"

Alex scowls. "How stupid are you, brother? Death. As in, us. The exsanguinated cock. Do I have to draw you a fucking map?" He sniffs the air. "I bet you it's the wolves."

"Wolves?" Tassa asks.

Alex starts pacing, not paying her attention, so I quickly say, "A new wolf pack has set up in the mountains, not far from here. Were-wolves. Vârcolaci. Alex thinks they're going to try to assert their dominance over this territory. I disagree, and we haven't yet had time to put it to a vote."

"Because you're too busy trying to fuck your human pet!"

I whirl on him, barely aware of my restraint snapping. My fist finds his jaw and sends him flying into the closest tree. It cracks, toppling backward, Alex following it. He's up the moment after, taking the same tree and tossing it my way—and Tassa's.

"Vlad!"

Thank fuck for my brother's speedy response. He moves with keen accuracy, grabbing Tassa and whisking her away from the fight.

Not that it stops Alex. After the tree cracks open on my head, he tackles me, and our dance of death begins. Only, this time, I'm not intending to hold back. Seems I've been indifferent for far too long, to allow him such callous behavior. Maybe it's time someone taught him a lesson.

Alex decks me in the jaw before I can move. He's swift, fast, rapidly hitting me.

I get up off the ground, wiping at the blood I feel trickling down my shin. Only he could match me like this, drawing blood while barely exerting much effort. Then again, he's had more experience than me with hunting and fighting for his life—I've got no one to blame but myself for not being in tip-top shape.

I spit a glob of blood, grinning at him. "That the best you have, frate?"

Before he can reply, a strident voice rings out. "Fools!"

Mirabela's there, stopping us both without a single movement. I sense her power immobilize me and glare at her, to no effect. Her eyes are red slits, flickering between the two of us. "Do you not see the little human's run off already? What in hell's name do you think you're fighting over?"

My eyes are already seeking Tassa out, but Mirabela's right. "Mira..." Whether it's the plea in my tone or just her inability to maintain her power for longer than a few intense seconds, I sense the hold of her power loosen over us. Instantly, I start heading toward the house.

But as usual, Alex has got to have the last word. "Fuck you both for being blind to what's right under your noses. I'm going to fix this my own way."

Then he takes off.

I toss over my shoulder, "You'd best go after him before he causes issues with the wolves." The last thing we need is more attention on us, and something tells me baiting the wolves would ensure we get exactly that. And not in a good way.

A whoosh of air indicates Mirabela's gone, thus freeing me to finally go after the one I want.

Tassa

I can't stand watching them fighting. Not only because seeing their ruthlessness toward each other scares me, but also because part of it is due to me.

Nico told me just hours earlier what that kind of infatuation caused him to lose control before... I saw the pain on his features, heard it in his voice. That kind of emotion scares me more than seeing an entire tree being thrown at him like it's a regular stick.

You're too busy trying to fuck your human pet!

Alex's words were harsh, but perhaps truer than I'd like to believe. Nico might be infatuated with me, but it's my blood he wants. Once he has that...

I run a hand through my hair, clutching the long locks with trembling fingers. What did I think, that Nico was starting to fall for me? That he cared for me, all of a sudden? Ridiculous. No matter how much my treacherous heart wants to hope, I can't afford to.

I've been in a relationship before. And Petru broke my heart. My confidence. My everything. Then he left. And he was a human, someone who didn't have at his disposal all the tools Nico does. He was lucky, is all.

Nico's a vampir. Not just any vampir—a freaking royal of his kind. And eventually, whatever's going on with that, he'll take his rightful place in this world.

What's *my* role in such a life? After I heal Violeta, my use here will be gone. There is no place left for me...other than as his human pet or something. And I'll never allow myself to be that. My pride's all I have left.

It's a jarring realization, what awaits me. It spoils the fairy tale of whatever I'd been googly-eyed enough to believe. And it's made even worse by the fact I do like Nico. Too bad I forgot for a moment exactly why I can't have him. Joke's on me.

Even as I rush back inside the castle, Vlad comes after me. "Tassa, wait!"

I wipe the tears I didn't even know I had and face him. "What do you want?"

He stares at me, at a loss. I know what he's thinking. He saw me in Nico's lap. Probably something along the lines of, *What the hell is the human doing with my brother?*

"If you're about to give me a lecture about what you witnessed between me and Nico, save your breath."

"I wasn't going to." He shuffles his feet. "Just wanted to see how you're coping. If you're all right."

"Why wouldn't I be?"

"Because we keep fighting each other around you, without taking into account how this is affecting your psyche. We act as if you're not human. As if you're one of us—used to all this. I don't know what it's doing to your mind, but it can't be good."

As if you're one of us. I hold back a cringe. I know he didn't mean it that way, but all it does is reinforce my own thoughts. "Don't worry about me. I've gotten used to it."

"That's what I'm worried about." He moves closer. "You may not realize how much all of this is changing you, but it is." He pauses. "My brother has his appeal, I can understand. Just be sure this is what you want."

"Nothing is changing me."

"Don't be so sure."

"What's that supposed to mean?"

When all he does is stare at me, I shake my head. I don't want to engage in this particular conversation, not right now. And not just because they all saw me half-naked.

I'm used to hiding my emotions and right now they're spilling out of me faster than I can grab them. I turn to leave, intending to check on Violeta.

Vlad calls after me one more time. "If you ever need me, someone impartial to talk to, I'm here."

As if I'm stupid enough to fall for that. The only vampir I trust is Nico, and even that should be debatable. The fact it isn't... I'm not ready to accept that, either.

I walk away and get to Violeta's room. Only, Elizabeta is exiting it. I stop in my steps, unsure. She must've had the same thought I did and came to check on her after we'd all gone outside. There's no one else here. Will she take the chance and hurt me as she plainly wants to?

Elizabeta closes the door and pauses. Without looking at me she says, "You know, it's funny." She turns slowly, meeting my gaze with a smile that creeps me out. "Humans are the only creatures in the animal kingdom born confused."

She takes a step closer. And another. I tell myself not to move. To not give an inch of space to this crazy bitch.

"Do you know why?"

"N-no." I hate that my voice is shaking, but for fuck's sake, she can be intimidating.

"Because they constantly seek a purpose, their place in the world. And they never realize that place was already chosen for them." Laughing under her breath, she leaves, and I let out the breath I'd been holding. She hit the nail on the head, with that one. I obviously still don't know my place.

After I'm sure she's gone, I head to Violeta's room. At least I can't be bothered here for a bit, maybe enough to pull myself together. I feel raw, exposed. Like I'm close to falling off the edge of a cliff.

The minute I step inside, I realize Violeta's asleep. I'm even more grateful for the quiet—a peace I need as badly as I need my next breath.

So much has happened, in so little time. What am I doing, screwing around with a vampir? Why can't I get rid of this itch, just go to a bar in town, and hook up with a human?

The answer, when it comes, has me groaning softly. Because I like Nico's mind. I like his soul. Even if he supposedly doesn't have one.

But Nico isn't mine. And he never will be. And it's not my place to save his soul. It's not his place to play my knight.

I take a seat in the armchair and curl up, watching over Violeta.

"Tassa." A soft voice says my name, growing increasingly impatient. "Tassa!"

I wake up with start.

Violeta's peering at me. "What are you doing here?"

The way she's watching me. The softness in her eyes. I can't stand it. Tears fill my eyes and before I know it, I'm bawling my heart out, and I don't even know why.

By the time I come to, Violeta's moved off the bed and has me in a hug. "Hush. What happened?"

"N-nothing."

"It's obvious something has, else you wouldn't be this upset."

Hesitation fills me. I should be comforting her, taking care of *her*. In the end, though, my emotions are too much. So, I tell her. About losing control and nearly sleeping with Nico and the attack and everything else. Violeta listens. Just listens. I never would've pegged a vampir for being such a great listener. Or for being such a good hugger.

When I'm done, she pulls back. "I don't know what my brother is playing at. But is he what you want?"

Her bluntness startles me. Maybe it's because she's sick or has lived this long, who knows? But Violeta's gaze isn't mean, just curious. Expectant. Waiting for me to make up my mind.

If only it were that easy. My thoughts are a maze, my heart and mind at odds. How can I have become so utterly consumed by Nico in such a short time? Every time I'm around him, nothing else matters—except our connection. The way he sees me. The way he engages my mind. My senses. My emotions. It defies logic, yet here I am, drowning against the turbulent tsunami of my emotions.

Is it possible to fall for someone this fast, this deep? It's terrifying—almost unnatural.

No. No *almost* about it. It *is*. It's also exhilarating.

Of course, he chooses that moment to walk in.

I turn my head away from Violeta and wipe my eyes. She stands off the bed, walks to him, whispers something, and heads out of the room.

It's an illusion of privacy, but one I'm thankful for, nonetheless. Although it does put me in a precarious position, with my mind still unmade up. I'd come here to find safety. What does it say about Nico's understanding of me that he's been able to find me so quickly, and so precisely?

To his credit, Nico just stands there, a few feet away, watching me. Whatever Violeta told him has rooted him to the spot.

"What's going on?" he finally asks.

"Nothing."

"Your coldness says otherwise."

"It's nothing."

To think he's calling me cold? I must really have dropped the ball in trying to school my expression. I try again, wanting to offer a reassuring half-smile, but the muscles of my face won't listen. Not when all I want to do is cry.

"Nothing?" He's next to me in a flash, his hands on my shoulders, forcing me to face him.

I hate looking in his eyes. Seeing the glimmer of something dim out into nothing. It only makes the heavy weight in my stomach that much worse. He sees too much, more than I want him to. Feels too much, in the way I try to angle my body away, instead of leaning into the safety of his arms.

"Tell me again how it's nothing," Nico murmurs.

I can't. I want to. Everything in me forces me to. But I *can't*. Doing so would be akin to cutting off one of my limbs. Or better yet, yanking my heart out of my chest and stomping on it until it's as flat as our renowned Romanian schnitzels.

The dilemma I was struggling with, the question Violeta asked me before he walked in, it's now resolved. In my mind, at least. And the answer is very clear.

We're of different worlds, of different minds. And this will only end in heartache for me. I'm nothing for him. In the grand scheme of things, he'll still be a vampir, and I'll still be a human. He'll still think lying to protect is all right, and I'll still believe honesty is our best bet.

There is no compromise. There is no hope. There. Is. No. Future.

Nico moves one hand to my neck, then up to my chin, forcing my gaze to meet his. "Talk to me, Tassa."

I gulp past the lump in my throat. "Whatever that was in the library, it can't happen. We both know that."

"Do we?"

His eyes glitter. His mouth hardens. I'd kissed that mouth, felt it on my skin, and the memory is enough to make my body sway toward him. He notices it, I know he does. Because I feel that same sway in him, that inability to keep away. Magnets. We're magnets and right now, our polarized poles are about to go haywire.

I nod. "We do."

His hand on my shoulder tightens. His jaw clenches. Something flashes in his expression. Annoyance? Hurt?

"And when did you make that decision?"

I steel my spine and force the words out. Words I know I can't take back. "It was already made. We, this, it's not happening."

He lets go of me then and staggers back. "Meaning?"

"Meaning I'm done playing games. And I need you to leave, so I can focus on Violeta."

He stares at me for a beat. Followed by another. Then his indifferent expression—the one I'd gotten used to, the one he'd given me in the first days—switches on. I hate seeing it. "I see. I expected more."

I laugh. Bitterly. "More? Like what, me plastered at your feet and worshipping you?"

"No, that's not—"

"I have a job to do, Nico. *You* asked me to stay here. For *Violeta*. So let me focus on her. Because the more you try to seduce me, the more it blurs the line and screws with my mind, reducing my ability to help her. This isn't a game."

"And you think it is, to me? What kind of a man do you take me for?"

I narrow my eyes on him. "You're *not* a man. That's the whole point. You're a vampir—self-serving, uncouth, and ruthless. I refuse to be whatever it is you *think* you want, when there's a serious problem I'm trying to solve here."

His stunned silence fills the room. I force myself to turn my back on him and redirect my attention on anything but his ramrod, statuetill self. The tinctures by the windowsill. The torn sleeve of my shirt. Anything. But. Him. Despite the tears burning my eyes. Or the sobs raging in my chest. I need to convince him I mean this. That there's nothing here.

And after a beat, it seems to work. Finally.

A whoosh of air passes behind me, and by the time I glance back, he's gone.

"And he left, just like that?"

"Yep."

I try to sound as nonchalant as possible while recounting the facts to Violeta. Though I pretend to be engrossed in setting up my dad's tools to draw blood, my mind is really on Nico—more specifically, the hurt flashing over his features at my words. And therein lies the problem.

He's taking up way too much space in my mind and, if I'm truly honest, my heart. Which is beyond dangerous. He and I are worlds apart, no matter how much we may be starting to wish that weren't the case. But it is. And I've always been a realist. It's that realism that warns me Violeta's illness is beyond my ability to fix. That even if I were to send the blood I'm drawing to a human lab to test, anonymously, it still wouldn't show much—no more than it will when I take it up to my room and run it through the variety of tests Dad's notebook laid out.

It's that same realism that tells me I *want* this. I *need* this. The space, the distance, the lack of anything between Nico and me. I can't do what I have to do if things get complicated. Deep down, I know that I'll never be able to detach myself if things progress much further between Nico and me. The only chance I have to protect my heart is by convincing Violeta—and Nico, and myself—that I don't want this connection between us. It's the only way I know, and it has to work.

Even if it feels like I just ripped my heart out and fed it to, well, wolves.

"I don't believe it."

"Why not?"

"My brother is many things, but he doesn't quit easily."

I snort. "You may be mistaken. He's been a quitter since I've met him."

She sighs. "I know it seems like he's this disillusioned immortal, but I swear there's more to him."

"Violeta. Please, stop."

She lifts her hand. "Hear me out, please. Eons ago, when Nico was a new vampire, he still had his human habits. To care for people. He was chosen because of his empathy, which ended up working against him."

I tell myself I don't want to hear it. It'll only humanize him more. But despite myself, I'm drawn into the story. "How so?"

"I...can't tell you the whole story. But ask him to talk about Silva, and about how he died. Then you might understand how the two of you are not as different as you think."

I soften my voice. "He already did. He told me about Silva and everything that happened. And I understand his guilt, I understand...everything. But it doesn't change things. We *are* different, Violeta. He's immortal. I'm not."

"You weren't thinking about that over the last days. I've seen this connection develop. There's more to it, and you shouldn't—"

"I understand you want that to be true," I say softly. "But what do I have to contribute to any of this?"

She watches me, a faint smile on her lips. "Will you allow me to finish?"

"Sure."

"Once he was turned, Nico came back for me. He told me about this other life, and Țepeș turned me. You know that. At first, I hated him for it, and Nico. Then I grew to like it—a little too much. He held me in rein, and helped me control the hunger so I didn't turn into another Bloody Countess. But in the end, it was his own control that snapped. And the consequences of that destroyed him. For centuries, he refused to come out of his shell. Until you."

I shake my head. "We all know I'm here to help you, Violeta. Not to cater to his needs or feelings."

"That may be so, but can you deny there's something between you?"

"No. Denying that would be like trying to convince you the Earth is flat. But I can't pursue it."

"Why not?"

"I don't belong with you. With any of you. Today made it even more clear."

"Because of that warning? Or him fighting with Alex? Because that last bit isn't all about you, you know."

"It's more than that. It's all of it. I can't explain it."

Violeta's quiet for a long moment, looking away from me. In a whisper, she says, "And if he's starting to develop feelings for you?"

The thought alone makes my pulse race. "Even if he is, what's the point?"

She frowns, meeting my gaze again. "Did Liza get to you?"

"Maybe. It doesn't matter. How many more ways can I say it? I'm *human*. There's no future here for me. Whatever else there is, won't mean shit to me without a future."

She watches me closely. "You want the happily ever after."

"I do. And talking about that, in this context, is ludicrous."

She sighs and hands out her arm, letting me draw blood. "What then?"

"I'll ignore the attack and leave it up to your brothers. They can figure out who's behind the cryptic warning. Meanwhile, we're going to try this new remedy."

She nods. "I trust you."

I get up and pack my shit. When my hand is on the doorknob, she says, "Give him a chance. Please."

But no matter her pleading, I've made up my mind. And it's not in Nico's favor.

Chapter 19

Nicolae

Leaving Tassa in Violeta's room didn't do anything for my peace of mind. On the contrary, it only made it worse. A thousand times worse.

This isn't a game.

You're not a man. That's the whole point. You're a vampir—self-serving, uncouth, and ruthless.

I refuse to be whatever it is you think you want.

Everything she said plays on a loop in my mind. I'd wanted so badly to change her mind, but words failed me. And being in bed isn't soothing my thoughts. My gaze shifts to my hands. The same hands that had held Tassa, caressed her skin. I'd been so close—to be inside her heat, to hear her moans, to finally know what it's like to have her come apart under me. And now, that possibility has vanished like dew at sunup.

I shouldn't fucking care about her rejection. But how many times have I told myself the exact same thing, over the last few days? And how many times have I been proven otherwise?

"She's a fucking human. Get over it."

My body's too tightly wound, my mind unable to let it go. I never thought I'd find someone more stubborn than me. Yet, lo and behold... How am I supposed to fix this? Can I even fix it? And why is there a dark pit in my gut right now, warning me I can't let this go, that I can't let her go?

My thoughts go back to Silva. To that human whose face has blurred over the centuries. Silva's has not. His is as clear as day in my head, and if he were here, he'd tell me to get a fucking move on. To go after what I want. What makes me happy. And Tassa... She's not just the light to my darkness. She's kindle to my flame, teaching me to burn bright again.

I rub at my chest, at the phantom pain settling there. If I still had a beating heart, it would be hurting more. None of that matters.

I stand up in bed, running a hand through my hair in sheer frustration. *Fucking hell.*

The half-moon is high up in the sky by the time I decide to leave the confines of the castle. It shouldn't surprise me that none of my siblings are out... at least, all but one.

"Nico."

I stop in my tracks, but don't turn to face her.

"Don't do it."

"Don't do what?"

"You *know* what. You've had countless useless sexual encounters, and you always do it when you're too close to feeling something. You and Liza have that in common. Don't do it again. Not when you have a chance at something real."

I laugh, facing her. "Something *real*? Tassa made it clear she wants nothing of the sort. Besides, she's human, Vi. There's nothing real there." Is it wishful thinking, or does she actually seem less pale? Could it be some of what Tassa's doing is working?

"There is, if you'd allow it. If you'd care. Allow yourself to care."

"I do care! And she won't let me. I may not be perfect at it, but I was trying before all this. And it all evaporated like mist in front of my face. So tell me, what's the point of caring, when all it does is fuck you over even more?"

Violeta's expression softens, and pity fills her eyes. "Oh, Nico... Why must you make things so difficult?" She takes a step closer to me, cupping my cheek. "Since Silva's death, you've shut yourself off. Willed yourself from emotions, from us, from the world. After all these centuries, don't you realize these emotions are bombarding you because of how long you tried to keep them away?" She shakes her head at me. "Have you told her, how you feel?"

"I have. It didn't matter." Technically, I didn't tell her, as much as show her, but if I say as much to Violeta, it'll just spur her on.

"Then *tell her again*. Humans are peculiar, Tassa more so than most. She carries baggage that prevents her from hearing you. So, try again."

"What, and grovel? You know full well my stance on that, dear sister."

"Just because we're royals of blood doesn't mean we need to act above everyone else."

"Tell that to Mira and Liza. They outdo us all."

Ignoring the condemnation in her eyes, I pull away from her touch. Allow vampir speed to take over and run like hell, blurring into the woods. From her words, from the possibility she put in my mind, from everything else.

I run and run and run... until I'm back in a goddamn circle right where I started.

In the olden times, it would've been called a brothel. She would've been called a whore. Nowadays, these fine young women don't fit the stigma of society anymore. Instead, they're fresh-eyed and classy, much like the name of the agency that dishes them out. I choose the place. They send the girl. For me, it means a seamless encounter, something to scratch an itch and get back to my life. I'm not a regular by any means, but Violeta is right in that it's my way of escaping whenever things get tough.

I push off the wall of the church where I'm meeting her and wave at the woman walking my way. She must be a year or two younger than Tassa, not that she looks it with all the makeup caked on her face. Still, she's sexy in a tight-fitting black dress number and high heels. Sultry. A sway of her hips, a widening of her eyes, a parting of her lips tells me she finds me just as attractive.

Then she glances behind me, at the old church, and arches an eyebrow. "Kinky."

I allow a rumble of laughter to escape me. "You've seen nothing yet." I hold out my hand and because she sees the perfect face, the confidence in me, she takes it. I have no qualms about deceiving her. Not when she's oh so willing.

We walk, at first. Chat about inconsequential things for a few moments, just enough to break the ice. Then I find us a quiet corner, on a bench in the shadows, and sit. She sits next to me, hiking up her skirt as she does.

"So..."

The over-trailed word tells me enough. I reach a hand into my coat and pull out a wad of cash, tightly rolled. Her eyes widen, this time with a little fear. "What exactly do you expect, for that amount?"

"Your best package, darling." I lean back, arching an eyebrow. "Make me forget. If you're up for the challenge, that is."

She grins, a wicked gleam entering her eyes, just as I'd hoped it would. She has no qualms, this one. She's quite ready to take me to town.

In one smooth move, she's closer, and her lips are on mine. They taste like cherry-flavored lipstick, sticky and sweet all at once. As we duel for dominance, I let her take over, take charge, because I need that illusion.

The illusion of normalcy.

The illusion of maintaining control, of pulling the strings, even when I'm not.

Because my own illusion has shattered wildly.

I try to ignore the thought, to push it out of my mind. Her hands move in my coat, tracing my chest, moving lower, to the bulge in my pants. She licks her lips and traces the zipper, stroking me over the material.

A rush of pleasure runs through me. I cup the back of her neck and pull her closer, nibbling on the sensitive skin of her collarbone. My fangs elongate. Eager. So fucking eager. It would be so easy to lose myself in this...

And for what?

The thought hits me hard enough to make me gasp. She thinks it's because of her hand stroking my semi, but it's got nothing to do with it. If anything, the lack of reaction her touch provokes is telling.

I could take her blood. Take her body. Take her everything, right here and now. And she would enjoy it, because she's willing and I'm a great lover.

But what the fuck do I get out of it, other than scratching an itch? And when has that become so...fucking...tedious?

Fuck's sake, Violeta was right.

With a groan of disgust at myself, I push the woman off me and stand up. Run a hand over my face, rake my fingers through my hair. I can't get Tassa's features out of my mind. Her responsiveness to my touch, her kisses. The way her every touch made me *feel*. Invincible. Grounded. Aroused.

I wipe the cherry-flavored lipstick off my mouth, as if trying to erase this entire encounter.

"What's wrong?" The woman leans in closer, dropping her voice to a conspiratorial whisper. "Do you want to try the church? I've never done it in a church. If you're afraid of someone walking in on us out here, I know it's empty and abandoned."

Empty and abandoned.

The hilarity hits me—and only me, I can tell by the confused look in her eyes when I burst out laughing. Empty and abandoned—exactly like this encounter. Exactly like her. Exactly like me.

We would be a great match, for the night at least. We would be suited for each other, for the needs our bodies have. And then, come daylight, we'd still be as empty and abandoned as ever before.

"Thanks, but not tonight."

She stares at me in confusion. "But I thought—"

"It's fine. Keep the money."

I walk away and the moment I've turned the corner, I go full speed, eager to leave her presence. To leave those eyes.

What the hell was I thinking and, more to the point, why didn't it work?

I know the answer, deep down. Because I've changed. These meaningless encounters no longer hold my attention. And not because Tassa has some magical vagina I can't wait to get into. But because there's something more, there. With her. Something I haven't felt in a while.

A connection.

She got me talking about Silva. She got me talking about my previous life. And all without ever prying. I...trust her. As easily as I do my siblings. To some extent, maybe more, because she's not jaded and she has no hidden agenda.

I think about her soft curves in my arms, how the feel of her body against mine had not only roused my body but my...soul. If I even still have one, she's the siren song sent to bring me salvation.

Fucking hell, she's brought out the romantic in me, too. If that's not enough proof of this connection between us, I don't know what is. But I'll be damned if I give up so easily.

Tassa

After the conversation with Nico, and Violeta, it became even more apparent that I need to leave here. But I can't just take off without helping Violeta first... And fast, before I lose my heart for good.

So I go back to my room and pore over Dad's notebooks—for the human patients and the vampiri—as well as the scroll we found in my old home. And this time... This time, the code makes sense. It took me a moment to see it, but only because I was looking for something so *hard*. When, in fact, Dad wrote the key to the scroll's code within the pages of the House of Dracul book. The last bits of the picture emerge from the notebook I found in the mines.

Finally. I could cry that I didn't see it before!

I grab a fresh piece of paper and start working on it, decoding it little by little. Every number corresponds to a letter. That first section done, it gives way to new words. But they're random words, making no sense... and then it hits me. Anagrams. I start reorienting them, playing with them, grateful for the distraction.

An hour later, I have the decoded version in front of me. And it's...a recipe. A remedy recipe for a vampir, to help out with any rare poison. There's a note at the bottom that says the recipe is meant for poisons of unnatural causes. In brackets, Dad added two words—*dark magic.*

I lean back against my bedpost. Was that what he meant the entire time with his NNC note? "Non natural causes" meant black magic?

I tap my pen on the notebook, staring at the list of ingredients and biting my lip. If someone's out there truly poisoning the heirs, it's not my problem. I can tell the vampiri everything I found out, but it's up to them to fix this. In the meantime...this recipe could be the answer to Violeta's illness.

Excited, I get off the bed and start preparing everything together. Luckily, I have most of the ingredients—some of them come straight from the hunter Nico killed. And one of them... I stare at the label on the vial and double-check my notes, my decryption of Dad's code.

If this is true... If this works... What the hell does it mean?

For long moments, I hesitate, holding the vial in my hand. Finally, I flip the top off and pour its contents into the rest of the recipe mix.

A few hours later, I head to Violeta's room. I can hear the shower running on my way there, and sure enough, she's not there. I leave the vial on her nightstand along with a note.

Hopefully, it works. *Hopefully*.

After dropping off Violeta's remedy, I couldn't sleep. I tossed and turned all night long. Despite my potential success at finding a solution for her, all I could think of was Nico. His expression when I told him off. I must've made the right decision for me, given all the heartache he could cause me. But then why do I feel so shitty?

A cold shower before the sun rises helps me get my head back on straight. Sadly, it's nowhere as good as if he'd been there with me.

Stop it, I tell myself.

I need to get over this obsession. This itch can be scratched in other ways. And besides, if that remedy works, I won't need to check on Violeta, which means less time spent around Nico, and more time spent away from him.

Is that really what I want, though?

I'll miss his laugh. And the banter. And the way he can hold a conversation like no other man I've met in these parts, yet without sounding conceited or pompous despite his confidence.

But there will be others.

Once I'm truly done with Nico and his people, I'll be able to leave this area and remember what it's like to be normal. Human. And *normal.* Away from weird incidences. But I'll also always carry with me the sense of accomplishment, of having done something, of having influenced the world a little bit in my own way.

Speaking of... As I exit the bathroom, I see a single rose by the windowsill. I'd left the window open before heading for my shower.

For a moment, my heartbeat increases, thinking it must've been Nico who left it. Then I notice the note, and something tells me he wouldn't be leaving me love letters.

I reach for it shakily and open it. It's the same message as before, with the rooster. *Death lives in those walls and death will find them, too.*

Someone is watching me, but who?

Trying to ignore the trembling of my hands, I get dressed and finish the packing I'd started last night. I want to be ready when the time comes to leave, so I don't get sidetracked. At least, that's what I tell myself.

Yet despite my best efforts, my thoughts keep swirling back to Nico. I get why I'm drawn to his darkness, his rough edges, the arrogance of his immortality...and also the shattered pieces of his soul. But I'm deluding myself if I think I can be the one to mend them. Time and time again, I helped Dad with all his cases—easy and hard alike. I saw the despair creep on him in the instances when he couldn't do much more but convince family members to head into the larger city hospitals. Those were the cases that stayed with him the longest. And I knew, especially in those moments, that a path in medicine wasn't meant for me.

It's the same with Nico. The truth is, I'm powerless to fix him. And even if I weren't, I'm not the one he needs. I'm just a temporary distraction from his demons. The sooner I accept that, the better. As I've been reminded many, many times before, I don't belong here. Perhaps it's time I start believing it.

I pick up the note, tuck it into my jeans pocket, and continue packing, trying to fill the hollow in my chest with the mundane task.

Nicolae

I don't know how long I spend wandering around, but I end up in the woods. Near the spot I'd found Tassa, after she'd taken off and gone to the mines.

Weirdly, it's a memory of Silva that brought me here. Him mentioning how in every event there's a hidden pattern—which had me thinking about the dead rooster and the presence I'd felt in the woods when I'd last been here with Tassa.

And, without her distracting me, I become aware of other, fainter scents. Older. But human, nonetheless. I move in a perimeter around the area, searching for something I can't quite pinpoint, until I find it.

On the ground is a crucifix. A wooden one. I stare at it in wonder. There is no moss over it, nor rain. It has been here since Tassa was last, meaning we were not alone. Someone was spying on us. Someone who knows what I am. Could this have anything to do with the attack at the castle? If it's the same people, they followed us back to the castle. Meaning they're not afraid of the danger my siblings and I represent.

I'm not okay with that, or any of it. If I put Tassa in danger...

Feet as heavy as lead, I head back to the castle. My mind is again consumed by feelings—the same feelings I've desperately been trying to suppress. The ones I've denied for so long.

Is Violeta right? Have centuries of repression finally taken their toll, unleashing a torrent of emotions I can no longer contain? Can I somehow stem the tide and restore the numbness I'd been so comfortable with, or has the damn been irreparably breached?

The more I think about it, the more I fear now that the floodgates have opened, there's no turning back. I may be arrogant, I may be a dick, but even I am in tune with myself enough that after all these centuries of existence, I can safely say I have changed.

What originally made me shut down, is no longer as intense because I've acknowledged it. Speaking about Silva with Tassa, even if I didn't go over how guilty I felt over his death, was cathartic. I hadn't allowed myself to fully think about him in so long, that I deprived myself of his memory. Now, I can remember the good times with fondness, as he deserves.

That same hurt was even more healed by Tassa's presence, by seeing the way she, time and time again, stood up against my siblings. By seeing them stand by each other, even when all they want to do is tear each other apart.

By feeling my own need to protect Violeta, to make sure nothing happens to her. Something about her illness has rallied all of us, as messed up and dysfunctional as we are. We will *always* be messed up and dysfunctional. You cannot survive immortality without losing yourself along the way.

But does that mean we cannot redeem ourselves?

Perhaps we've done many wrongs in the past. But it's not too late.

And as for feelings, well. I may just have to accept finally, once and for all, that they're back with a vengeance. And sooner or later I'll need to learn how to deal with them and communicate effectively.

I'll start with Violeta. Then, maybe, Tassa. If she'll hear me, still. If she'll give me a chance, after all the crap she's seen. After what I almost did, yet again. Something tells me she actually values monogamy.

But I'll never know unless I ask. So I force myself to put one foot in front of the other and move faster and faster until I'm home once more. In front of the castle, I hesitate. For once, I'll be entering while aware of the new me. Of my new *feelings*. What kind of chaos will all this cause now?

Time to figure it out.

Chapter 20

Tassa

Unable to rest, and with all my stuff packed, I head out of my room and to Violeta's. Might as well do something productive and see if she's feeling any better. Assuming she took the vial I left her, that is.

The moment I step into her room, I know something's wrong. She's not where she should be. I run around, checking every nook and cranny, but Violeta's disappeared.

I remember everything she said, before—feeling like there was no cure for this, that there wasn't a point in living like this. Did she take off? Did she do something stupid? And if she did, how in hell am I supposed to tell her siblings...

They'll eat me alive. Literally.

Nonetheless, I rush out of the room—and run straight into Vlad. He steadies me with his hands on my shoulders, at the same time taking in my probably panicked expression.

"What is it?" When I say nothing, he glances over my shoulder, noticing the empty room. "Violeta."

He whooshes past me and, in a few seconds, comes to the same conclusion. "I'll help you find her."

I shake my head. "She said if things get worse, she will leave."

"Why didn't you tell us?"

I scowl at him. "I get you all are used to getting your way, but there is such a thing as doctor-patient confidentiality."

"And yet you're not a doctor."

"We can keep arguing, or you can help me find her."

"Fine."

We check every room on her floor, without luck. And then, as we're passing the wide windows of the library, I glance outside and catch sight of short, dark hair.

"Violeta!"

I rush outside the moment after, Vlad on my heels.

"You scared us," he says. "What are you doing out here? Won't the sun weaken you?"

She turns to us then, her smile bright, her complexion...normal. A gasp escapes me, and even Vlad seems rattled.

"Violeta..." I step closer. "You..."

She grins. "I'm better."

"You...how?" Vlad asks.

"The remedy Tassa left me."

I frown, recalling my hesitation for mixing that recipe. *As a last resort, for anything that is fatal, add a vial of muroni blood. Mix it into the rest for exactly five minutes, then have the patient drink it every few days. Stronger doses at first, which can taper off after a week or so.*

It's mind-boggling, to say the least. Muroni blood—the worst of the vampiri, the scourge of this earth according to some—and it provided the healing Violeta's been needing all along? *How?*

I gulp past the knot in my throat. "It really helped?"

Violeta nods, eyes glinting and no longer dulled by her ailment. "It did. I've even got my vampir speed back."

I can't share in her enthusiasm. I thought Dad was crazy. How did he even come across this remedy? To use another vampir's blood, especially one of *those monsters*...the implications are mind-boggling, to say the least.

More to the point, how in hell am I supposed to tell her what her remedy contained?

Vlad's head is turned toward the castle, tilted at an angle. "Nico's back," he says. "Violeta, let's go let everyone know. They'll be so relieved."

"And Tassa needs to share the secret recipe." Violeta grins.

I clear my throat. Yep. I'm so screwed.

Nicolae

And just like that, we're back to fighting.

The moment I stepped through the castle, the noise attracted me, and now I'm leaning against a wall and wondering what in hell was I smoking hours earlier, thinking about what we've overcome together as siblings.

Instead, I stare morosely at Liza and Alex arguing with Mirabela about the werewolves. Or, as Alex calls them, vrykolakas. Seems my dear brother couldn't listen to what we'd agreed and *stay put*. No, instead he had to go do reconnaissance on them, and ended up getting a tad too close.

Sighing, I down the rest of my drink and push off the wall. "The harm is done, Mira."

Everyone falls silent. Mirabela arches an eyebrow. She may be as bad as the other two, but sometimes her age works in her favor and she reins in her emotions. Unlike our hot-headed younger siblings.

"Whether the wolves saw Alex or not, they'll know he's been there. If they're any good, they'll trace him back to us, and then we're really in trouble."

Alex scowls. "Are you not listening? We're the ones in trouble. These aren't any wolves. They're not even pure vârcolaci! They're vrykolakas, as damned and strong as the rest of us. *Undead* fucking werewolves who live off human hearts! That's who we want in our backyard? We might as well put a neon beacon leading humans straight to our existence."

I narrow my eyes on him. "The fact they're undead doesn't mean they're automatically a problem. On the contrary. It should be yet another reason to learn to use them to our advantage, not make enemies of them!"

"Who died and made you king?"

I roll my eyes. "And since when have you started acting like a petty human?"

The wall shudders against my spine as Alex slams me against it, and a few frames fall to the ground, shattering. His blazing eyes stare into mine, a dangerous red glint in them. His grip tightens on my throat.

I smile despite it. "It's a good thing I don't need air, frate."

We glare at each other a moment longer, and longer still. His muscles bunch under his shirt, as if he's truly debating tearing my head off. It wouldn't be the first time. Over the years we've all been together, we've had more feuds than I can count.

We just never had a human live in the castle at the same time.

"Alex, enough. We have company."

I smirk, and he lets go of me. It's only then I glance over, meeting Tassa's gaze. It's darting between me and the rest of my siblings, clearly wondering what she stumbled upon—again. I try to smile reassuringly, when all I want is to take her the hell away from this horde of maniacs. Problem is, she won't even let me.

One way or another, I need to convince her that we're not a doomed case, and there is something salvageable about me. But now's not the time. Out loud, I ask, "Did you need anything?"

Despite the scene she just witnessed, her voice is even as she speaks. She must be getting more used to us. "Erm, I have some news."

Then she moves out of the way, and in walks Vlad, trailed by Violeta. Only, this is my sister at her best—a way I haven't seen her since she first fainted. While Mira, Liza and even Alex surround her, my eyes dart to Tassa.

How did she do it? Something about her demeanor clues me in there's more to this, and potentially a rather more complex reason than I'd initially thought.

"Thank you," I say to her, drawing her a little aside. "I don't know how you did it, but—"

"That's what I'm here for," she says. "I'll make another batch of the remedy, then return to the village."

It's like she knocked the breath out of me. The same breath I just told Alex I didn't need. "What do you mean?"

"I've done the job you tasked me with."

I take a step closer, mindful of Mirabela watching us. "You know it's become more than that."

She shakes her head. "No, it hasn't. Nico—"

"There are still dangers," I rush on. "Those people, whoever they are, behind the message with that rooster. They were watching us in the woods, by the mines. I'm pretty sure they followed us here afterward." Her expression is less surprised than I would've thought. "You knew?"

She nods, glancing away. "Da, I figured as much. And it's not a problem, Nico. Or I should say, not *your* problem. Once I leave here, they'll probably leave me alone. It seems their issue is with me being in a nest of vampiri."

"And if they don't leave you alone?"

A wry smile is all I get.

Mirabela chooses that moment to approach us. She taps my shoulder. "How did your little side business go? Back to old habits, I take it?" When I don't answer, she grins slyly. "No shame in it, brother. Liza may be the most promiscuous one of us, but we all have needs we need to fulfill."

My gaze shoots to Tassa, but she's already moved away from me, and is clearing her throat to gather everyone's attention. "I need to tell you all something."

If I had a heart, it would thud painfully against my chest. As I don't, all I can do is watch in silence, ready for anything that might get out of control. *Damn Mira and her wandering mouth!*

Part of me knows she did it on purpose. She heard what Tassa was saying and gave her a little push, probably thinking she was doing me a favor. She couldn't have been more wrong.

"As you can see, Violeta is feeling better," Tassa says.

"Much," my sister says. And it's good to see her this way, I can't deny it.

"The problem is the reason why." Tassa pulls out a notebook I recognize as her father's. "As you all know, my father treated both humans and vampiri. Well. Nico and I found a scroll a few days back, buried in the remnants of my home, but I wasn't able to decode it until last night. It held ingredients for a recipe, something that was meant to heal any non-natural vampir ailments."

"What do you mean by non-natural?" Vlad asks.

"Dark magic... or so Dad's notes said. He also had things scribbled about the intricacies of bloodlines and lineages. A lot of stuff that didn't make sense, at least until I matched it with a book he had on the House of Dracul. He spoke of vârcolaci and vrykolakas—"

"Ha!" Alex smirks, baring his teeth. "See, even the old fool knew the trouble."

I glare at him. "Shut the fuck up and let her talk."

Tassa waits for a beat, then continues. "The mixture I prepared and left for Violeta to consume contained muroni blood, mixed with human, and some herbs."

A stunned silence descends on us. While Liza cusses under her breath, and Mirabela shushes Alex, I tune them out to zero in on Tassa's explanation.

"It seems my dad knew what he spoke of. He must have encountered this recipe during his travels, but there is no record of where or from who. Then again, I don't have all of his medical journals. This one only covered the most recent years."

I shake my head. "Muroni blood? I don't..." Glancing at Violeta, I add, "And you feel all right?"

She nods, seemingly conflicted. "I do. I... I don't know why, but I do."

I jerk my gaze to Tassa, pleading silently for her to explain. Her expression tells me she's as much at a loss as me.

"The only thing I can think of," she finally whispers, "is that it ties into the rejuvenation you explained to me. If your body—a regular vampir—is able to rejuvenate properly, but you're not able to do some things... And the muroni can... Maybe their own rejuvenation is different. Stronger. And that's why this recipe mix works."

Violeta's eyes widen and she gulps. "Does that mean I have to hunt them, now, to survive?"

Alex shrugs. "Good thing we have an entire supply nearby, then."

Tassa says, "Seems so. I'll leave for now..."

"Finally," Liza mutters.

I scowl at my sister, but Tassa's still talking. "...as there is no reason with Violeta's stable condition for me to stay. As I said to Nico earlier, I'll make another batch of the remedy. My dad's notes say to take it daily to begin, then after two weeks you can ration it to once every week. You can come find me in the village to mix more—or you can mix it yourselves, if you prefer. The recipe is pretty straightforward." To Violeta, she adds, "I'd like to do one last checkup, if that's okay."

Violeta nods and follows her out the door. Before fully disappearing, she ducks her head back in and says, "Don't go destroying the house while I'm gone!"

I want nothing more than to follow them both, to corner Tassa and expel whatever doubts she has after Mira's words. But the room erupts in chaos and, once more, I'm prevented from going after what I want.

It takes a while to calm down and get over the shock of Violeta's miraculous recovery—and the reason behind it.

"In the end, we will kill whatever she needs," Mirabela says. "We've stuck by each other across the centuries. Now is not the time to get squeamish."

"Who said anything about squeamish?" Liza grins. "I love a good muroni hunt. They always fight back more than humans."

I sigh, pinching the bridge of my nose. "Back to the other problem at hand...and the wolves."

"Did I hear that right?" Vlad asks. "Alex ran into them?"

"Da, and according to him, they're not the usual vârcolaci we would expect in these parts."

"There's no *according to*, frate," Alex fires back. "They're not, period. Vârcolaci have a different scent and, aside from a few, the majority are vrykolakas."

Vlad arches an inquisitive eyebrow my way. "I thought vrykolakas were extinct."

"They aren't. Though priests did their best... Last I know of the story, a descendant of our father was excommunicated down the line. He had the vârcolac gene in him—the shapeshifter one we've lost the ability to use—and when he died, excommunicated, he underwent a change. That change resulted in him being the first vrykolakas, or undead werewolf." I rub my chin. "A few packs still exist. My understanding is they differ in strength and feeding habits from the regular vârcolaci, since they feed off living, beating hearts, to keep themselves alive." Turning my attention to Alex, I add, "What else did you find, exactly?"

He scowls. "I told you. They're not just in passing or visiting, they're setting up camp. Houses and shit. And mating."

"Mating?"

"Yeah. I smelled some human female around."

"Only one?"

"Does it matter?"

"It does, if she's their Luna." Their she-leader, as it were.

"Fucked if I know. If you're so interested, why don't you go over there yourself?"

My gaze moves to the door Tassa left through. What *interests me* is to go after her, to explain myself. But perhaps a breathing moment is just what she needs. Besides, I won't be gone long. And this is another chance to stick to my new promise—being there for my siblings, too.

Smirking, I say, "I think I just might. Vlad, care to come with?"

"I will," Mirabela surprises me by saying. "Vlad can stay here and make sure these two don't kill your precious human, instead."

Good point.

Rather than show my uneasiness at her statement, I nod. "No time like today."

Chapter 21

Nicolae

The woods are quiet. Oddly so, given the village we passed was bustling with activity, and it's still daytime. The farther we go, the quieter it gets. And I'm weirdly aware of Mirabela's gaze on me.

"What is it?" I ask after a few moments.

"You're starting to care for the human."

She was never one to mince words, my sister.

"What makes you say that?"

"Your body language changes the minute she walks into the room."

I chuckle under my breath. "Maybe it's because I want to fuck her, and none of you will let me."

"No, I think it's bigger than that."

Her actual pensive tone has me turn to face her. "Is that why you had to blabber on about my old habits?" Her only answer is a shrug. "For your information, I didn't do anything. So your comments were off base, regardless of what you think you saw."

A chuckle escapes her. "I saw nothing. I merely guessed, because even I can smell the cheap perfume surrounding you. And I knew your little pet would take offense."

"What are you getting at, Mirabela?"

"You can play around all you want, but I can see through it. Remember, I've always been able to see through all of your bullshit, the lot of you. And you're falling for her."

The distaste in her tone is apparent, though I try to keep my emotions in check. And my facial expression.

"I'm waiting for the punch line. Why is this your business?"

"Why?" Her upper lip curls. "You'll bring doom onto the rest of us. When you feed off her and kill her, that's another disappearance we'll have to explain to the townsfolk. Perhaps one too many. Already, it's bad enough that with the new technology, they could film us."

I roll my eyes. "Mirabela, the townsfolk know despite everything that we protect them. It's always been that way, regardless of where we lived. They won't do anything to jeopardize it. Don't you trust your precious Order?"

"Don't be such a fool! We are outsiders, at the end of the day. Monsters that haunt their nightmares. There is nothing they won't do, if they smell weakness."

"I grow tired of this conversation."

When I try to move, she's there to grab my arm, yanking me backward with a force that surprises me.

"If you allow yourself to feel for her, you're giving her power over you, and over us. And how long do you think it will last? Human marriages fall apart in less than a decade nowadays."

I yank myself out of her grasp. "We're here to find the wolves, not discuss my personal business. Back the fuck off, Mirabela."

She laughs, and says, "My, and I thought you were the one, out of all of us, who would remain unchanged. Uncaring about everything and everyone. How wrong I was. Interesting."

I ignore her and blur through the woods.

The history between wolves and vampiri is a hell of a lot more complicated than humans would have you think. No, it's not that we hate each other, nor that we are mortal enemies. But we are alpha predators, and realistically, having both in a region? In general, it's pretty bad news for humans. For us? It could be a good development, depending on how we play it.

As we move through the forest, I know Mirabela will have my back. Despite her words and the anger I still feel coming off her in waves, she's the type to be loyal. She may want to gut me... but she'll be loyal while doing it.

The one that worries me is Alex. He's too unpredictable and has become more and more volatile. If the wolves sense him and track him back to us—and he is bound to return here, knowing him—that will be bad news. The last thing we need is a pack of vrykolakas to hunt us down *on top* of our own vampiri subjects.

So it's cautiously that we approach. Perched on the cliff's edge, we gaze at the valley below us, with its crystal-clear stream. Bustling encampments catch my attention. Wolves—both in human and animal form—of all ages hurry about, some tending to makeshift shelters, others gathering firewood and stacking up supplies. Even across the distance, I can sense their trepidation, their excitement. The air's alive with the sounds of conversations, laughter, and construction.

They really are settling down here.

"Alex was right," Mirabela says, her voice low.

I nod thoughtfully, taking in the scene. With my heightened vampir senses, I focus on the details, my vision sharpening to the intricate workings of their village—the fibers of the roofs, the glint of sun on the stream's surface and, more telling of all, the subtle movements of the wolves. That's when I see it. "Almost."

"What do you mean?" she asks.

"He was *almost* right. Look closer. Does this look like a rogue pack, to you?"

She does as I bid her, and I hear her sharp inhale. Despite the very telling signs of the vrykolakas, these aren't frothy creatures foaming at the mouth. On the contrary. They're listening to an alpha, and he looks about as human as wolves can get.

And then I catch another scent on the wind. "Is that...?"

Mirabela takes a step closer, having sensed it as well. "A *human*." Alex wasn't wrong about *that*.

Awe fills her voice, and not for nothing. Vrykolakas live off the hearts of humans. And yet here is one such human—a redhead, from what I can see—who is not only alive and in their midst, but when I peer closer, she's petting two of the wolves shadowing her every step.

Fucking *petting them* like they're domesticated dogs instead of rabid creatures.

And the way they surround the redhead? Like she's theirs to protect.

"The wolf mated a human," I breathe. "Incredible."

"Don't go getting ideas."

I glare at her. Is it so hard for her to view humans as something other than prey? What am I saying... Of course, they're prey. Until recently, even I thought of them as little more than idiotic. Then Tassa came and changed my mind. *I wonder if that's what happened here.*

"One thing is clear," I add. "We cannot go in there uninvited."

"And what do you propose? That we let Alex blunder about, causing even more issues?"

"No. We'll send an invitation."

By the time we leave, I'm not feeling any better about these wolves in town. Something tells me it's only the beginning.

Tassa

I can feel Violeta's eyes on me as we head back to her room. Halfway to the hall, she takes a right into the library, and I follow there instead. My tools are laid out.

Violeta heads in front of the fireplace and sits on the couch, then extends her hand. I go through the process of taking some of her blood, the entire time ignoring her gaze on me.

I try to shake off Mirabela's words, but they linger, festering like rot on wood. Or an open wound. Nico, with someone else. The thought alone makes bile rise up my throat and my stomach churn.

He'd hinted at his old habits, and I'm not an idiot. He's lived centuries, obviously there have been others. And there will be others long after me. But we'd been so close to...

Angrily, I shove the memory of our almost-moment aside. It's tainted now by the realization I'm just another face in a history of conquests, for him. Like I should've known I would be.

"Don't."

I look up. "What?"

"Don't think of what Mira said."

"Hard not to." What's the point of denying it, when it must be written all over my face? Violeta and I have been through enough together so far. No point in me being coy.

"Nico is past that."

"Doesn't sound like he is." I pull the syringe and drop some blood in a vial, then add a few drops of Dad's mix, watching as the blood turns dark. *Crap. So Dad was right about this, too.*

Violeta must sense something in my mood, because her gaze shifts to the vial as well. "What does it mean?"

"The drops I added are from a mix Dad was using, also mentioned in the scroll recipe. It's used to detect these non-natural causes. It seems to confirm there's something in your body that shouldn't be there."

"So it has nothing to do with the greenhouse and herbs I was playing with?"

"No, nothing at all. But it also means I don't know what's causing it, either. Dad seemed to think dark magic was at work, but..." I shrug. "You'd know more than me."

I expect Violeta to be sad but when I turn to her, she smiles. "But I have a remedy now. So long as I take that mix, I'll be okay?"

I nod. I don't know for how long, but I don't want to leave her with more depressive thoughts. Let her have her hope; I'll make sure to document everything for her siblings to know, and they're bound to find her a better doctor.

As I pack my tools, Violeta touches my hand. "Thank you. For being so perseverant."

I smile. "My pleasure."

She bites her lip then says, "Do you think... That is, can you be as perseverant with Nico?"

I shake my head. "Let it go, Violeta."

She's in my face before I can leave, scanning my expression. "You *like* him."

I look away. "It doesn't matter."

"Why not?"

"Because of everything that can come between us."

I leave then, allowing the dark thoughts to assail my mind. Maybe it's not the best use of my time. Rather than head back to the entrance, I move down to the kitchen. And then Alexandru shows up out of nowhere.

I pause in my steps. He's the last person I want to be near.

"How is Violeta?"

The fact his tone is so calm, almost...polite...is enough to get me on my guard.

"Better."

He glances over my shoulder, then back at me. "Liar." It's not a shout, not a whisper, but a statement. A cold, icy statement that grips me and makes me take a step back.

I'm afraid of Alexandru, yes. Him and Elizabeta. And while I've been able to stand up to her, I cannot with him. Why is that? Because he's a man? Because he's taller, stronger, immortal?

Maybe all of the above.

All I know is, I'm listening to the damned instinct in the pit of my stomach telling me to keep a distance between us and get away as fast as I can. So I gulp and say, "Sorry, what?"

He inches closer. "Do you know what I used to be, before I was turned into a vampir?"

I shake my head. Alexandru, in a sharing mood?

Another glance at the library, as if he knows Violeta is in there. "A doctor." He meets my stunned gaze with a faint, cool smile on his lips. "Surprised, human? You should be. I was in the business of helping humans. Not killing them. Ironic."

I gulp. "Why..." He takes another step. My back is to the wall. I lift my chin. "Why not heal Violeta yourself, then?"

He scratches his chin. "Medicine was not as advanced back then as now. A lot of it was *leacuri*—natural remedies, like these poultices my dear sister loves to give humans. And while I've observed medical advancements from afar, I don't have the keen medical-oriented mind I used to. One could say I've grown, hmm, *detached*. Yes, I quite like that word." Another smile, even icier. "But what I am not, is stupid. So what is it you're hiding?"

"Doctor-patient—"

"Confidentiality." His voice drops. "Don't fuck with me, human. What's going on with Violeta? She's my sister, I have a right to know."

I try to avoid his eyes, but it's too late. He grabs my chin and forces me to look at him. The glamour starts, washing over me like a cool, icy shower. In a monotone voice, I hear myself declaring, "The blood. The muroni treatment is working, but it's not a cure."

"Why does she look so much better?"

"Because it's giving her body the sustenance she needs, temporarily."

"And when it expires?"

"She will regress."

A muscle ticks in his jaw. "Then your job isn't over, is it?"

I yank my chin out of his grip, and sidestep him. Take in a deep breath. I've never been glamoured before, and I still feel the effects, like my mind is bathed in fuzziness. Forcing myself to shake it off, I face him again, with a good distance between us. It won't make a difference, if he uses his supernatural speed, but at least it gives me the illusion that I have some measure of control.

"You can't keep me here forever."

He laughs. "I don't have to." He gestures to the library. "You've grown attached, as humans are prone to do. I simply intend to use that to my advantage."

"What advantage?"

He grins and leans against the wall. In the light of the dawning sun, he looks so much like a blond version of Nico, it's almost weird given they're not blood siblings.

"I have gotten used to my siblings, human. And I will not make do without them. *Any* of them. So, you and I are about to go hunt for some muroni blood. And then you're going to use that to run more tests until you find out what this dark magic is and why it's affecting Violeta as it is." His eyes flash. "And let me be extremely clear—you're not going anywhere until you figure it out."

I glance around, hoping someone will emerge to help. No one comes. Nico must be gone, Mirabela with him—not that she would help. Violeta must have fallen asleep, or else she'd be here. So, who's left?

"I could scream for Vlad."

He smiles, as if he knows a secret I don't. And he probably does. With his senses, he can make out my heartbeat, my pulse, the fact that while it's rapid, it's also got the steady thrum of a decision made. When he calls my bluff, I'm not even surprised.

"You could. But we both know you've already made up your mind."

Screw these royals' arrogance.

I knew it was a bad idea from the start. I mean, leaving the castle with one of the vampiri who hates me the most, it's not exactly my brightest moment. But he's right about one thing—I've gotten to care for Violeta, and I do want to make sure she'll be okay.

Alexandru is walking ahead of me, leading the way to somewhere. Not that he actually explained anything—let alone gave me a plan to follow.

"What, precisely, will I be required to do?"

He shrugs. "Collect the muroni blood."

"After you kill them, I assume?"

"Yes, and before I dispose of the body." He glances over a shoulder. "Muroni cannot just be killed, they have to be torn apart, limb by limb, and destroyed until nothing but ashes is left of them."

"Ah."

He grins, a wicked glint in his eyes. This is the first time he's spoken to me in so long, and I can't help but wonder what else is behind it.

"And taking me to this nest is risk-free?"

"Nothing is risk-free these days, human. But don't worry. I'll protect you."

Nothing about that statement reassures me. I peek between the trees, wishing—stupidly—for Nico, but it's useless.

Within another half hour, we reach a valley. Alexandru hops around as easily as an elf, while I make my way more cautiously. To his credit, he waits for me, even if impatiently.

"Finally," he mutters when I reach him, then takes off again.

Another hiking bout, more cursing under my breath, and we reach a cave. Alexandru lifts a hand, gesturing for me to wait. And then he goes inside. I may not have been the smartest thus far, but I'm definitely not following him in there.

Instead, I move to the side of the cave and use a large tree trunk to hide myself. My darker clothing should help, too. In Dad's satchel, I reach for one of the wooden stakes I'd shoved in there. Might as well be safe.

A moment passes. And another. And yet another.

How long does it take to kill a muroni? I shouldn't be making assumptions, but given how sure Alexandru had seemed of himself... But what if he's in danger? What if there were more of them? I shouldn't be fucking caring about his psychotic ass, but he's Violeta's brother, and Nico's.

"Alexandru!" I hiss. Surely my whisper will carry to his vampir ears...

And then I realize my mistake. There's a whoosh of air behind me, a sharp inhale, and someone chuckles under their breath. Someone who's definitely not Alexandru. "*Carne proaspătă...*"

Fresh meat. Oh, fuck.

I whirl around, but the muroni knocks the stake out of my hands. He reaches for my hair, grasping a handful. In full self-defense mode, I kick my knee out between his legs. He may be a vampir, but his anatomy is still that of a man.

He hisses and lets go of me, leaning against the tree for a moment. Long enough for me to crawl away. *Where the fuck is the stake!?*

And then he's there again, his sharp nails raking my back. I scream. Blood pours out of the wounds. Dimly, I think about what remedies Dad would use to close the wounds. Then I realize it doesn't matter, because this thing is going to kill me anyway.

My hand closes on the stake and with the last of my energy, I roll to my back just as he covers me with his body. The stake goes up into his heart. A stunned gasp escapes him—and then Alexandru is there, ripping him off me, cursing under his breath. I don't hear the words, but then he's rummaging in my satchel.

He doesn't find what he's looking for and drops the search with another curse. Then he's lifting my head and putting something to my lips. I smell metal, but taste cherries, before darkness pulls me under.

Chapter 22

Nicolae

We make it back to the castle shortly after the reconnaissance mission. And leaving Mirabela behind, I seek out Tassa. Seeing the wolf with his mate had my insides roiling with something akin to urgency. I want to talk to her, and get through to her. Find out what obstacles I need to overcome to get her to believe in us.

Her room is clean—too clean. And then I notice she's packed her bags already. For real, this time. Does this mean I've run out of time to convince her to stay?

Violeta bursts in then, her eyes wild. "Have you seen Tassa?"

"What? No. Why?"

"She was taking my blood and I fell asleep. Now I can't find her anywhere, and Alex is also gone."

I clench my fists. If my brother hurt her...

I storm down the stairs, following her scent. It's mingled with his, and they've gone out into the woods. Where the hell would he take her?

And then something else carries on the wind. The smell of blood—Tassa's blood.

With a low growl, I tear through the woods, Violeta on my heels. We almost collide with Alex, and the body he's carrying in his arms— Tassa.

"You son of a bitch!" I growl and move to strike him.

He holds her up as a shield. "She's alive."

Filled with fierce protectiveness, I can't stand to see his hands on her. I nearly rip her out of his grip, feeling her shirt, wet with her blood, as it touches my fingertips. She's pale, deathly pale, but there's a pulse underneath there.

"Where is she hurt?" I ask with all the decency I can muster.

"The back. Muroni got her when I was in the cave."

"Why the fuck would you bring her in the woods?"

"To get more sustenance for Violeta."

"It wasn't urgent."

"It is." He throws an apologetic look at our sister. "Your *doctor* didn't tell you all. The muroni blood will keep Violeta safe, but only temporarily. She needs to run more tests to find out the full picture. I wasn't about to let her leave when there's still work to be done."

"Bull*shit*."

"It's true. Ask her when she wakes up, she'll admit as much."

Is that what Tassa had wanted to tell me, earlier? When we were interrupted?

Violeta blinks, once, and then she shoves Alex into a tree. It cracks with the force of the blow, but he does nothing to retaliate. "She did tell me that, idiot! If you'd have bothered to ask me, I would've said as much. She hasn't hidden a single thing about anything during this process! And even if she had, that doesn't give you the right to put her in danger."

"It wasn't intended."

None of us say anything, knowing full well the last thing he gives a shit about is her life. The life of a human. I stare back at Tassa and rush into the castle, leaving a trail of her blood everywhere, my heart somewhere in my stomach. Dread grips it, and it grips me, as well.

Am I losing her?

I've settled Tassa on the bed and removed her duffel bag off it. But I don't know what to do. Feed her my blood? If it were up to me, I would turn her immortal now and spend the rest of eternity apologizing for it. But I can't even do that since we lost our ability to sire new vampiri.

Violeta steps in, Alex behind her.

I let out a purely animalistic growl. "I want him out."

She shakes her head. "He's the only one of us with a medical background, remember?"

"Then he can tell you what to do, but he's not touching her."

Violeta sighs, and nods. She sets Alex's satchel to the side. From it roll a few vials filled with blood.

I glance at Alex. "Let me guess. Muroni blood?"

"Yes. And I disposed of their bodies after, don't worry."

"While she was bleeding on the ground?"

The idea makes me murderously raging. Alex is smart enough not to answer. Then he turns to Violeta. "Roll her over to her stomach—the wounds are on her back. You have to cut off her shirt, and apply some salve or something. Ideally, it should be deeply cleaned first."

The tone of his voice—so detached, so clinical—is more than I can stand.

"Out. Both of you. I'll take care of it."

Before they can argue, I point to the door, and they reluctantly leave. Alex says, "Just so you know, I gave her some of my blood. If only to stave off infection."

My fists clench so hard, I draw blood. "Get. Out."

When he's gone, I turn back to Tassa. Something squeezes in my chest. Something like fear. When has that ever affected my ability to breathe, though? It's irrational when I don't even need to breathe.

"Get over yourself," I mutter.

And then I move to her and do exactly as Alex said. I roll her to her stomach, making sure her head is as comfortable as possible, then bring a cloth with warm water and some disinfectant I pull out of her duffel bag. Inch by inch, I spray her back, then clean it in depth and wipe it dry. I would much prefer taking her with me under the shower and letting the water do a thorough cleaning, but I don't know how she'd feel about that.

Not true. I do know. She'd be horrified. Because she doesn't want my hands on her.

With every stroke of the cloth, more of the blood clears her skin. The smell of it doesn't bother me as much as it did originally, though its sweetness is alluring as all sin. If Alex gave her some of his blood, it should at the very least help her heal faster.

The thought strikes me that she could've died. Humans are insanely fragile. What would I have done then? Without the ability to tell her that I'm sorry, that I made a mistake, to explain myself, to lay out everything I feel... Would I have gone back to being indifferent?

I'd like to think I wouldn't have, but I don't know for sure.

A groan escapes Tassa, drawing me out of my thoughts. I stop with the cloth on one of the deeper gashes, and lean over her. "Tassa, can you hear me?"

Another low sound escapes her. I stop in my movements.

"You're back at the castle. It's me, Nico."

She blinks, and her eyes find mine. The pain in them tears me apart. I don't want to see that in her. What I want is to kill Alex for allowing this to happen to her.

But this isn't about me.

"How are you feeling?"

"In pain." Another slow blink. "My back..."

"A muroni scratched your back. Deeply. Alex said he gave you some of his blood to stop the infection. I'm cleaning it now." I hesitate to voice the rest of it but I have to. "I'm not sure I'm getting it all... It would be easier if we take a shower. Will you allow me to be in there with you?" When all I get back is a blank stare, I bite the bullet and add, "I didn't touch her, Tassa. I know you heard Mira's words, but she was fucking around. With both of us. Yes, I went to meet someone, because it's what I do when everything falls apart. And when you pushed me away... It *hurt*, dammit. But I didn't do anything. You have to believe me."

She closes her eyes and for a moment I think she might've fallen asleep. Did she hear me at all? Did anything register?

But then she opens them again. Her voice is a low, barely there whisper. "Okay. Help...me."

Relief spreads through me. I'll worry about getting her to understand the truth later. Right now, I need to clean her back.

I move slowly and, as gently as possible, I help her up. She sways toward me, the sides of her cut shirt falling off her shoulder.

"We can walk there, or if you can, you can wrap your legs around my waist. Clinging to my neck or me picking you up will only stretch the skin of your back...It's the easiest way I can think of. And I'll do the rest."

She hesitates. I wish I could read her mind, to know whether that hesitation is from the pain, or from not wanting to bear my touch. In the end, Tassa nods.

I bend at the knees and rest my hands on her hips, then pick her up gently, trying not to jostle her. "Now, darling. Wrap your legs around my waist." She does as I ask her to, and with my hands still on her hips, it's enough leverage to hold her.

I want nothing more than to pull her against my chest, and protect her from everything else that would come her way. But this small inkling of trust she's given me, I can't fuck it up.

I grab one of the smaller kits—from her father's house—packed with creams and things, and step by step, being as careful as I can be, I move us out of her room and into the bathroom down the hallway. At the last moment, I decide to take us to the next floor—where my room is. At least we'll have more privacy.

Once there, I drop the satchel by my bed, and head to the bathroom, kicking it open with my foot. The old wooden frame groans at the force used, and I wince as Tassa startles in my arms.

"You can unwrap your legs now."

She does as I ask, and once she's standing, I remove the rest of her clothing as carefully as I can. Kneeling in front of her, I peel off her jeans, and decide at the last moment to keep her underwear. Even if a part of me, a darker part, wants nothing more than to see them disappear so I can feast on her as I have in my dreams.

I clear my throat and stand once more. There's one more piece of clothing—her bra. And much as I want her to be comfortable around me, not removing it will pose a barrier to me cleaning her back.

"Tassa..."

She closes her eyes, her tone tired and resigned. "It's fine."

I remove her bra with what I'd like to say is a deft flick of my wrist. But I'm so nervous, and my hands are shaking so, that it ends up being a fumble. Finally, the bra falls off her shoulders, and I help her in the steaming shower.

"This will hurt," I say, "at least for a moment." I hesitate to say more, but I can't hide anything from her. "If I... My blood. It could alleviate some of the pain." She glances at me, questions in her eyes, but in too much pain to voice them. "It won't turn you, we can't do that anymore. Even with Alex's blood in you, there's no risk. It'll just be enough to keep you from the pain you'll feel otherwise. And it will add to staving off the infection, and aid your healing." Another hesitation. "Let me help you, please."

She gulps, and finally nods. I move my wrist to my mouth and let my fangs protrude enough to cut into it. Then I offer it to her. Burgundy droplets fall to the bottom of the tub. Tassa glances at them, then my wrist. Closing her eyes, she sways toward me and puts her mouth to my wrist.

The feel of her lips is enough to make me groan, but I stifle it the best I can. I've had humans drink from me before, but this is a sweet torture I didn't know was possible. I feel myself growing impossibly hard, and I'm thankful for the dark jeans I'm wearing, and the fact she's in too much pain to notice anything else.

After a few more seconds, I gently tug my wrist off. Too much, and she'll grow sluggish. Too many times, and she could get addicted.

With my thumb, I wipe a droplet from her mouth and slowly turn her around. Then I take the shower head and say, "Brace yourself against the wall."

Tassa does as I say. When the hot water hits her back, a whimper of pain escapes her. I clean her gently, thoroughly, but also as fast as I can to minimize the agony. When I'm done, I turn the shower off and tenderly help her out, keeping my eyes fixed on her face instead of her body. *She's vulnerable here, don't fuck this up.* All I can do is bundle her up in a towel, dry her off as lightly as I can, then give her a bathrobe to put on in reverse—the back of it covering her front, with the flaps on her back—so I can easily open it at the back once we're on the bed.

I crouch under her and reach under the material, tugging her wet underwear off. When I get back up, she says, "Thank you."

I nod, and steer her into the room, helping her lie back down on her stomach. I bring up the covers to just above her ass, then undo the belt and push the robe open until it bares her back to me. The wounds are clean, but gaping open. I want to find the muroni who did this and rip them apart, finger by finger, toe by toe, but I know I can't. Because Alex already killed them.

At least he did something right.

Tassa breaks me out of my daze and points to the satchel. "There's a...small container. Ointment. Green lid."

I find it in seconds and start spreading it on her back gently.

"Your cold hands feel good," she whispers. "And you were right. The blood did help...thank you."

"I'm glad."

She glances at my free hand, the one I'm using to support my weight as I lean over her. I don't realize why until she speaks.

"Alex, he— You didn't fight him again, did you?"

"No." I expel a breath. "I wanted to tear his throat out when he came back with you, and you were so hurt. But I was more preoccupied with helping you."

"It wasn't his fault."

"He brought you into the woods and left you without protection."

"I went...for Violeta."

My movements on her back stop. "So it's true, then? About the treatment being temporary?"

She nods. "I'm sorry."

A sigh escapes me, and I resume my massage. No new blood pours out of the wounds, which I take to mean my blood is working— and her ointment is probably helping, too. With some luck, by tomorrow, they'll have started healing in earnest.

"It's okay. I'm just... It's good you're alive, is all."

She turns to look at me, something I cannot decipher in that gaze. And then she falls asleep, dozing off within minutes of me finishing off the massage.

I lie beside her, wanting to make sure she'll be okay. And to cover her, once the ointment soaks in the skin. But as I lie there, watching her sleep, it hits me. The realization that's been eluding me for so long.

This has always been about more than sex, more than scratching an itch. On some level, a deeper level than I've ever understood—a primal level that transcends reason and defies explanation—Tassa has awakened a fierce protectiveness within me. From the moment I saw her in her father's home, to every fleeting moment since, this unyielding instinct simmered, waiting to erupt. It's as if my very essence has been reshaped, my defenses shattered, and my soul laid bare before her.

The truth is, I've been helpless against the pull of *her*, captive to its unrelenting force. And now, I have to face the deepest truth of all—I'm irreparably hers, bound by a love that can't be tamed.

I can't explain it any more than I can stop it. But...it's there. Indomitable. Unmistakable. Immovable. And it's high time I stop lying to myself.

Chapter 23

Tassa

I don't know what wakes me up. Maybe it's the sudden silence in the room, or whatever it was. Either way, the moment I wake up, I'm aware of not being alone in bed. Actually, I'm not even in *my* bed. And Nico is next to me, looking oddly...young. Relaxed. Carefree.

Asleep, he's as innocent as an angel.

Of course, that thought is followed by flashes of his brutality. Of everything I've witnessed in my short time here. Da, perhaps he is an angel. A vengeful one, at that. Other images replace his brutality—I remember his soft touch, his caring. For someone who's jaded by immortality, he sure has good bed manners.

Don't give in to it.

This feeling in my chest, this need to draw closer to him, to stop fighting... I can't. My heart can only stand so much. And already it's on the verge of breaking, what with Mirabela's comments yesterday.

I didn't touch her, Tassa.

Yes, I went to meet someone, because it's what I do when everything falls apart.

When you pushed me away... It hurt, dammit. But I didn't do anything.

Nico's words run on a loop in my head, fighting against Mira's. And though I try to remind myself of why I need to stay away, to keep the distance between us, I can feel my resolve weakening by the minute. Adding to it is a warmth in the pit of my stomach, a slow lick of desire that's making me want so much more. To want *him*. Fully. Before I leave, before I never see him again, before he has another lapse and actually goes seeking out another human for his needs.

No, that last thought is petty. It's not why I want Nico. I want him for *him*. For the way he reaches for me, even when his own walls try to rise higher. For the way he cares, worrying over me—to the point of fighting his only family for me. For the way he makes me feel—like I'm the only one in his eyes, even when the notion is ridiculous.

Is it so bad, to desire something forbidden for myself, for even a moment? Even if it doesn't last forever?

I'm aware of the ache in my back, though it's lessened now. I get off the bed and head to the bathroom. In the mirror, I glance at my back. The gashes I expected to see are closed, only faint red lines visible. The vampir blood at work, I suppose?

My gaze travels over my body in the mirror. These last few

weeks, Nico's attention has made me realize something. And no, it's not my uncommon beauty—this isn't a romance novel. I have flaws, yes. And I will forever be more critical of my body than I should be. But…it doesn't mean I can't accept it, and enjoy my body as it is. Good days, bad days, they're part of being a woman. I'd be stupid to think otherwise.

I let my fingers trail up my thigh, then my hip, and over my waist. I *should* be proud of everything I've put myself through. And I should remember, before it's too late, to thank Nico for the fact his attention has reminded me of the good parts I love about myself.

I pull the bathrobe flaps back together and I'm in the midst of tying the belt when I turn—and that second is all it takes. Nico's there, in the entrance, watching me with an expression I can't decipher.

"Does it hurt?"

I shake my head. All I remember is the pain. Woods. Then his arms. The shower. The taste of his blood, sparking things inside me that I wanted to ignore—unlike with Alex's. But I can't. Because that hunger's been unleashed, and I'm done, so damn tired of fighting.

"No." I move closer, too close. Decided. Unwilling to stop, not this time. Not when I've come so close to death, and after all… I'm human. Weak to the desires of my flesh. Desires that have grown more rampant than ever. With an ache that's intensified since I drank his blood.

As if seeing this, he steps away from me, causing me to chuckle. "Afraid, Nico?"

"Of course not." He frowns when I undo the bathrobe sash once more and let the whole thing drop at my feet, revealing my naked body to his sight. "What are you doing?"

"Something I've been wanting for too long."

I reach for him, fully aware of my nudity, of the fact he can push me away. He doesn't. He allows me closer, allows my lips to brush his, and his hands fall to my hips. He allows the one, small, tiny kiss—enough for the blaze to reignite—and *then* he pushes me away.

"Tassa, this isn't you. It's the vampire blood. Humans react to it differently."

"How so?"

"Addiction. Hallucinations. A, uh, spark of desire."

"My desire has nothing to do with me drinking your blood. If that were the case, I'd be hot for Alex."

The words have their desired effect. His eyes darken. "Don't say that."

"Why not? I'm just following your logic."

He runs a hand through his dark hair, tugging on it. Steps away. Shakes his head. "You can't know that. You have too much in your system."

I smile, inching closer still. "I may not have your vampire metabolism, but I have common sense. This is all me."

He shakes his head. Clearly, I'm going to have to work at it.

"None of this means I believe in a happily ever after. I have no illusions, Nico. You're immortal, I have maybe fifty years left to live. Less, if I stay by your side, given the dangers. You'll want others, as proven by your actions yesterday. And I almost just died, which only emphasizes my mortality. But despite all this... I want to know what it's like, Nico. I want to have everything. No regrets. Just for a moment."

He stares at me for so long, I think he'll never make up his mind. But then he does.

"I'll give you a hell of a lot more than one moment, Tassa. I'd give you forever, if only you'd let me."

He doesn't give me a chance to reply—not that I'd know what to say, stunned as I am by his declaration. In the next breath, he's pressing me against the sink, trapping me with his body, and kissing me like our lives depend on it. His tongue snakes around mine, playing with it, teasing me.

His hand goes between my legs, forcing me to spread them, and I moan when his fingers find my heated core. Thank fuck his kiss swallows the sound.

Am I aware we're in a castle with five other vampiri who can probably listen in, if they so choose? Yeah. Absolutely. Do I care? Not at all.

Not in that moment.

It's not about the bad boy. It's not about the vampir lore. It's about him, and me, and the fact we've been dancing around this for too damn long. And that I've lost too much time. And that I don't know how long, really, I've got left to live.

Adrenaline does funny things to a human's mind. The difference is, instead of wondering about what-ifs, I choose to see for myself.

So I give in to the kiss, palms resting against his bare chest, and I don't let him go slow. He tries—oh, he tries. Teasing me with soft nips around my neck, sucking on my nipples, driving me to insanity, and leaving me on the edge of the cliff. The remaining ache in my back is gone, dulled by the desire curling in the pit of my stomach.

And still, Nico teases, toying with his fingers around my clit, until I'm panting, and I can't wait any longer. I edge my butt up on the sink, and pull him closer, shoving his sweatpants and boxers down his legs. Then I hook my legs around his hips.

"Tassa, I—"

I don't let him finish. Instead, I arch just so, and the tip of his cock slips into me. He groans, never finishing his thought. I throw my head back, enjoying the feel of him as he slides deeper inside me, and the sensations he's giving rise to.

Panting. Out of breath. I'm murmuring his name, or something else, I don't know. I've lost all sense of self. Not because he's a vampir and that makes his lovemaking supernatural. But because he's a man, and he sure knows his way around a woman's body.

"Fuck."

The low sound has me open my eyes, watching his thrusts, the way his thighs clench, the way his eyes blaze. It's the hottest thing I've ever witnessed, seeing the tension in his features as he tries to hold himself in check.

Until I pull him even closer, and whisper in his ear, "Harder. No gloves with this human."

When he *finally* lets loose, I do, too.

Nicolae

She's everything I'd wanted, and more. Even as I'm thrusting deep inside her, admiring her body, making sure this is as good for her as it is for me, I'm keenly aware of that little epiphany. I have never had the connection I just did with Tassa. Ever.

And that's a long time, for someone as familiar with immortality as I am.

Maybe that's why I both avoided and sought her out. Maybe that's why I'm trying to draw this moment out, when all she wants is to get it out of her system. But I won't allow her to. This, us, isn't something to be done and over with.

Not for me. It hasn't been, since that second kiss that broke me.

Tore at my insides, ruined me to the point I could barely function. Since the dreams started, all I've wanted is her touch on me. All I've dreamt of is being connected with her like this, of having her look at me with fire rather than cool analysis in her eyes.

And while the desire is there, and seeing her so shaken by my touch feeds my ego, I also need something else. Something more. Something to feed my *soul*.

So once she comes again, I pick her off the sink, letting her toes touch the floor, and pull out of her. Hands on her hips, I flip her around, press on her shoulder blades so she bends just so—being careful to avoid the red lines of her scars—and thrust back inside her.

She gasps, her gaze meeting mine in the mirror, and a wicked smile stretches her lips. I take my time kissing the scars on her back, enjoying every other gasp and whimper I elicit from her, every moan when I bite low on a particularly sensitive spot.

My fangs elongate, that hunger to bite her driving me closer to oblivion.

"You can do it, you know," she says, staring at our reflection in the mirror.

I glance up, not bothering to hide the fact the fangs are protruding past my lips. "Bite you?" When she nods, I add, "Do you know what you're asking for?"

"It's just a love bite, no?"

I shake my head. "Better I demonstrate."

I bring her wrist up to my mouth, and snag her gaze in the mirror. "Watch." When my mouth draws closer to her pulse, it flutters wildly. As if part of her knows the danger. And around my cock, she tightens impossibly more, making me groan and drop my forehead to her back.

It takes me a long moment to rein in my senses. A long moment where I push inside her just so, relishing another moan. My body tightens, my release so fucking close...

I lift my head. "Do you get it, now? How it can become addictive?"

She shakes her head. She's toying with me, the little minx, but I'm not about to let her win this. So I slow my thrusts inside her, and instead tease her with my fangs on her wrist, then my lips, alternating.

At first, she only gasps. But when I keep slowing down my thrusts, focusing her attention on what I'm doing to her wrist, the gasps turn into pants, into mewls of protest, and finally into wriggling.

"Okay, okay. Point taken!" she shouts, yanking her wrist out of my grip, and pushing against me at the same time.

Laughing, I surrender to her whim and give her what she wants. What we both want.

Thrusting harder, faster, deeper inside her, until her moans become a garble of incoherent sounds, and my own growls fill the small space. Until she's so tight around me, convulsing and shaking in my arms, that I can't hold back and come inside her, spurt after spurt of my essence filling her. It won't get her pregnant, since my sperm is dead. But fuck if it doesn't feed some primal urge inside me—some caveman instinct yelling that I've claimed her, and she's *mine*.

When we're done, I allow myself to wrap my arms around her, my chest to her back. Feeling her heartbeat slow to a gentle rhythm, I'm met with a sense of belonging I've never known. This quiet intimacy, this tender connection, is a revelation. It's as if I've finally found the missing piece of my eternal existence.

I'd once coveted immortality, only to find it a hollow prize. But now, I'd willingly surrender it all to grant her this gift, to bind her to me for all eternity. The irony is not lost on me—I'd sought forever, only to discover that forever means nothing without her by my side.

This quiet intimacy, this intense connection...is worth it. Whatever the price is. I'll gladly pay it, for an eternity with *her*.

Tassa

I could say that one time was enough to get it out of our systems, but it would be a lie. After the bathroom, Nico took me back to the bedroom. And then the shower. After that third time, I needed another nap. Not least because I was sore, and I was starting to feel my back aching once more.

So it's from that nap I wake, hours later, to find myself entangled in his arms and something hard poking my lower back. I smile to myself. So even vampiri get morning wood—who would've thought?

In more of a mischievous mood than I should be, given what the consequences of this little lapse in judgment will be, I rub my butt against him. Once, twice. Then Nico's arm tightens around me.

When that only spurs me on, his hand slides to my hip, gripping it. "What are you doing, inima mea?" he murmurs in my neck.

My heartbeat flutters at the endearment—*my heart*—but I try not to read too much into it. "I thought that was obvious."

"What's obvious is you're insatiable."

A chuckle escapes me, and then I move my butt from side to side, then up and down. He growls, his arm tensing around my waist, its iron grip enough to cut off my breath. I only let out a chuckle.

"If loving's what you want..." He trails off, then releases me, allowing the hand that was on my hip to dive between my legs. "Fuck. You're already soaked and ready, aren't you?"

I moan when he rubs my clit, then his fingers slip inside me. I'm still sensitive from the previous rounds, but my gosh, does it feel good. Nico has this way of moving, be it with his cock or with fingers, and then pausing to gauge my reaction. It's infuriating.

When I'm close to coming, he stops, and shifts behind me just so. In one smooth thrust, he's inside me, and my strangled groan echoes in the room.

It's his turn to chuckle against my neck. "What? I thought that's what you were aiming for."

"I...was..." I pant. "Just...surprised."

I can feel him grinning, and then he thrusts again. And again. Before long, I'm lost to his touch, to the rising wave in me, to the detonation of stars behind my closed eyelids.

Even as my whimpers subside, Nico pulls out of me and rolls me to my back. His gaze roams over my features, searching. His eyes are dark blue, intense, filled with something so beyond a quick fuck, I don't want to look deeper.

"What is it?" I ask.

"You. This. I didn't expect it, is all."

I lift a hand to his cheek. "Neither did I. But it's been brimming, no?"

He nods. For a moment, I fear he'll say more. That he'll ask for more. No matter how great this is, it can't last, and we both know it. I just want to enjoy it.

Nico must read some of that on my face, because he doesn't say any more. Instead, he just kisses me until my toes curl and my body aches for him once more.

Sometime later, he leaves to take a shower. I wait a moment, two, until the water starts running. And then I get up, grab the bathrobe, and tiptoe out the door, heading to my room.

Do I feel guilty, knowing I'm leaving without even an explanation? Yes. But by the time he realizes I'm gone, Violeta will find the note I'll leave for her. She'll understand, and maybe even stop him from doing something stupid.

Besides, at the end of the day, I'm still just a human. And this was still just to get it out of my system, out of both our systems, so we can continue with our lives.

So I exit the castle and, once I'm far enough, I turn to look at it once more. The towers reaching for the sky, the gothic architecture, the calling of the wild all around it. I will forever remember it like this—to the day I die. No regrets.

Then I turn to leave, only to be smacked over the head. Darkness pulls me in its depths as I fall to the ground, unconscious.

Chapter 24

Nicolae

When I emerge out of the shower, Tassa's not in the room. At first, I don't think anything of it. She could've easily gone back to her room for a shower.

Or she could have joined me.

I take my time getting dressed, tug on a shirt, and head out bare footed. Something doesn't sit right with me. After what we've just shared, her taking off like that feels...unlike her.

On the way to her room, Alex intercepts me. He takes one whiff of the air and his disgusted grimace tells me everything I need to know. Despite the shower, he must smell Tassa on me—and me on her, then.

"Keep your comments to yourself," I mutter before he can say anything.

"Who and what you decide to fuck is entirely your business," he says. "But maybe next time you can do it on your own time."

"What's that supposed to mean?"

He drops something at my feet. I glance at it quickly, then more closely. "Is that—"

"A wolf head, yeah."

My teeth grind together as I stare at the blood dripping from the furry head, tainting our carpet. "Tell me you didn't fucking attack the wolves, Alex."

Panic rears its ugly head in my chest. Long ago, I was similarly incensed and thought I had it right. And I unwittingly put all of us in danger. If Alex did the same—

"Do I seem stupid to you?" He snorts. "No. I didn't. But I did find this on the edge of our territory. Someone's trying to make it look like we did."

I frown. "For what purpose, to start a war?"

"Apparently."

"But that would require them to know the wolves came into town."

"Mhmm." When I say nothing else, he rolls his eyes. "Can you be any denser? The humans in town. The villagers who came up here for your precious human. Fucking hell, man, did she screw your brains out too?"

"Matter of fact, she did, not that it's any of your business," I growl. "Either stop speaking in riddles, or fuck off."

He picks up the wolf head and says, "Join us in the library, and I'll tell everyone at the same time."

"Fine. In a minute."

He glances toward Tassa's room, then back at me, and shakes his head in disdain. Then he leaves.

I couldn't care less about Alex's disapproval. But I'm increasingly rattled, now. And despite our presence so close to her room and our rather loud exchange, Tassa didn't come out to see what the fuss was about.

I wait until Alex is down the hall, before continuing onward. Even before I open the door, I know she's gone. Somehow, at the back of my mind, I think I felt it the minute she had disappeared from my room.

"Dammit."

Her duffel bag is gone, as are her father's notebooks and the scroll. The only thing left is a faint trace of her scent.

"Nico!"

I exit the room, to find Violeta running toward me, a letter in her hand, the scroll in the other. "Tassa, she's gone!"

I take the letter. It's impersonal, apologizing that she had to leave, but she had a life to get back to. Offering a list of ingredients for the remedy and instructions for how to mix it. Attached to the letter is the scroll with the original recipe, translated from some code.

"Dammit."

"What did you do?" she asks.

I shake my head. "Nothing."

"Clearly, you did something."

This time, I flat out scowl. "We made an adult decision to fuck. One that seems to have everyone obsessed around here. But it has nothing to do with any of you."

"Nico..." She's on the verge of crying, red tears brimming in her eyes.

"I'll find her," I say. "I promise."

Alex yells then, "Are you two coming or what!"

Sighing, I head to the library. I'll give Tassa her head start, let her think she's slipping away. But she's not leaving—not like this. Not after everything. I can't let her walk out of my life and pretend none of it matters. Not when I've spent lifetimes—both human and vampir—searching for something I didn't even know I needed. For her. For *this*.

"What does Alex want?" Violeta says.

"Trouble with the wolves."

Her footsteps echo behind me, and I don't know which of us is more forlorn at Tassa's disappearance. Dammit to hell, when I get my hands on her again, I'm going to cuff her to the bed and make her listen. Time and time again. Until she actually hears my words and registers them, not pretends that she does until she can take off.

Tassa

The dampness of the place wakes me, seeping into my body and causing me to shiver. And then I wish I wasn't awake. A throbbing headache pains me enough to groan out loud. A moment later, I realize it's the worst thing I could've done. I've just given a sign that I'm awake to whoever the hell took me.

I pant, letting out heavy breaths while trying to ignore the pain and also figure out if there's anyone else with me in the area.

A quick peek around says no one is. At least not yet.

So who could have taken me? Humans? Vampiri? Muroni? One of the royals' enemies? The list seems endless, the longer I run it through my mind.

Gingerly, I reach for the back of my head. My hand comes back bloody, making me wince. "If it's vampiri who took me, I'm so fucked."

Despite the ache in my head, I try to stand, crawling almost to a standpoint. They didn't tie me. More fools them...or so I think.

My vision blurs and, before long, I pass out again.

"Is she awake?"

She is now.

Should I bother trying to play dead though or... Tempting as it might be, I'm more concerned with who took me. So I groan and slowly stand, turning to face my two kidnappers.

The one who'd spoken, I don't recognize him. But the other—

"You!" I yell at Victor, my dad's supposed friend. "Why?"

He shrugs. His expression isn't paternal anymore. "Someone has to stand up to them."

"I don't understand." My gaze flicks back to the other man. I've never seen him in the village... Who, exactly, is he?

"No, you wouldn't," Victor says. "Let me tell you a story."

I lean against the cool wall, letting its dampness and grounding effect seep through my clothes, and hopefully alleviate some of my pain. Oddly, it works.

Does Nico know I'm gone? Does he think I've left him, as I intended, until this happened? If he does believe that, he won't be looking for me. None of them will. And everyone from the village knows I'm gone... These men could kill me now and no one would be any wiser.

I gulp, trying to push those thoughts away. It's up to me to escape this mess.

"I'll humor you," I say. *For a time, at least.*

Victor sits cross-legged on the floor and hands me a water bottle. Could it be drugged? Yes. Do I care? Not when I need it like I need my next breath. So I uncork it—semi-reassured by the plastic ring being untouched—and drink deeply.

Meanwhile, Victor speaks. "You already know the history of our Order and how vampiri cajoled us into helping them. What you don't know is how many of us have lost family members to vampiri, in general."

"Vampiri, or muroni?"

"They're one and the same."

I scowl. "And that's where we differ in our assessment. I've seen both, and they're nowhere close in nature."

The man behind Victor snorts and steps out of the cell I'm in. In the faint light, I catch sight of a white beard and goatee, trimmed neatly, before he turns his back to me. His footsteps echo outside, but not for long. He must be a hired gun, then.

Or a hunter, my mind whispers.

"Think what you will," Victor says, "but both types are ruled by bloodlust. Muroni may be the wilder of the two, but are the others any better?"

I think back to Nico and his siblings. To how oddly human they've seemed to me, and even despite their illustrious need for fighting, how they have each other's backs. And then I think of the muroni that had tried to kill me. Alexandru saving me, though he could have easily let me die.

"You're wrong."

The man outside slams his palms against the metal bars. His face is contorted in anger. "Listen to the story and stop protecting those bloodsuckers."

I force myself to meet his glare. "And who the hell are you, telling me what to do?"

Victor looks over his shoulder. "Settle down, Liviu. I will handle this." To me, he adds, "Not that it's any of your business, but he's a hunter—of a sort. I've brought him on board, given your friends killed our other ally."

"Other..."

Even as my mind puts the pieces together, the other man—Liviu—snorts. "I can't believe that hunter didn't kill you when he had the chance. He got taken out way too early by that princely heir. Tell me, female, did you ever bother to see past your rosy-colored view of the world and what you've read in romance novels to understand that you are *nothing* to that monster, other than prey? And food?"

His words register, but they don't penetrate. They ricochet off me similar to bullets off a bulletproof car. Instead, I'm still stuck on the first bit of what he said. My eyes widen, the last piece finally slotting into place. "He was working for you, then."

Victor says nothing. I think back to everything he said about my dad. Dad's notes then pop up in my head, as clear as if I had them in front of me: *Some vampiri report issues with skin ailments, weaknesses, lack of desire for blood. Linked to non-natural causes— NNC. The recipe is meant for poisons of unnatural causes (dark magic).*

"It was never my dad doing the experiments, was it?" I whisper. "It was you all along. When he was talking about black magic, about *non-natural causes* of death..."

He smirks. "Very well. You do have your father's brain, after all. Da, your father was not part of it. He did find out, because he was helping vampiri. And he noticed a pattern. We had to change our tactics, but even so, he wouldn't let it go."

Angry tears fill my eyes. "You killed him."

"No, we are no monsters. We only sent his way some...new blood."

I think back to that night, to the men, and those wild glints in their eyes. Nico telling me they were mid-turning.

"You turned them," I accuse. "You took humans, turned them, and made them do your bidding. But, how?"

Victor shrugs. "Captive monsters have their uses."

I think back to Elizabeta's story, what Nico shared of Silva's, and my heart contorts. Whatever vampiri they're keeping prisoners, they're using them for their own means. And Nico and his siblings have no idea.

I meet his flat gaze, barely holding back the urge to spit in his face. "You're the only monster here, Victor."

"No. We have a reason for our vengeance."

Wonderful. I'm with a bunch of lunatics. And worst of all? I still don't know what he wants with me. I'll have time later to mourn everything I've learned and let anger rule me. Right now, I have to be smart. So to give the illusion that I'm listening, I incline my head and nod.

Thinking he's got my attention, Victor continues. "I lost my wife, one fateful night. When these new vampiri came into town, I wanted to believe they would be different, while knowing they would not be. Nothing has changed. And then they took you."

"They didn't take me. They *saved* me."

"You're wasting your time, Victor," Liviu hisses. "The vampiri will be here soon, with or without her cries to lead them. I've made sure the wolf head was sent to them. As for this one, clearly, she's already brainwashed by their glamour."

"Brainwashed?" It's my turn to send him a withering glare. "You call being brainwashed the fact I have my own ideas? Well, I got news for you, buddy. In this little scenario, you guys are the villains."

The man raises a hand as if to strike me, his features a mask of rage. The room seems to darken with it, and a pit opens in my stomach—he's no regular human, this one.

At the last moment, Victor steps in his path, as if to stop him from launching himself at me. "Leave her." To me, he says, "Think what you will. But we know the truth. They cannot sire new vampiri, which is why they try to get the humans to protect them. That is why they hide here, instead of proclaiming to the entire vampir race that the royals, the heirs of the House of Dracul, are still alive and well. Because they know they are weak. And we will make sure to weaken them, for good."

I swallow past the lump in my throat. "What do you mean? And why did you take *me*? I have nothing to do with all of this."

Victor snorts. "Maybe you didn't before. But with your stubborn need to be there with them, you have put yourself smack in the middle of this war. And as Nicolae's consort, he will come for you."

"His...what?"

The hunter outside snarls. "His whore."

"Or mate," Victor shrugs. "Whatever you prefer. You're his *pereche*, his pair. And he will come. So, sit tight."

He gets up, and me with him. "Wait, I'm not done!"

Victor arches an eyebrow my way, as if amused. "Haven't you

realized? You have no power here. Now sit prettily and be the perfect bait." To the hunter, he says, "Liviu, prepare the others."

Oh no. If Nico does come, he's walking straight into a trap.

They're already leaving. I slam my hands on the bars, but it's to no use. They've told me all they will—purposefully not giving anything away about whatever's ailing Violeta.

Could *they* be behind Violeta's disease? If they are, this means they're going to do the same to the rest of the Dracul line. To eradicate them.

I need to get out of here.

Nicolae

My mind sways in and out of the conversation, like a bad radio. I can't help my thoughts going to Tassa, time and time again. Where did she go?

"Nico?"

I snap to. Violeta's staring at me, as are Vlad, Alex and Mirabela. Liza's scowling, as per usual.

"What?"

"Alex's idea," Vlad supplies. "He wants us to surround the wolves and warn them off."

I shake my head. "We already established someone is trying to drive a wedge between us. What we need to do is be upfront with them, and talk it out. Explain we had nothing to do with this."

Alex snorts. "And you think that'll magically be enough?"

"Haven't you noticed our dear brother has become more and more enthused about the diplomatic approach since that human bitch landed in our lives?"

Something about Liza's tone rankles me.

"Liza, did you do or say something to Tassa?" I move on her, even as she backs away. "Tell me the truth. Did you fucking say anything to her?"

She glances at all of us, then her cool gaze meets mine. She smirks, an icy glint in her eyes. "And what if I did?"

Chapter 25

Nicolae

I love my sisters in equal measure but the only thing I want to do right now is rip Liza's head off. If she contributed to Tassa leaving... After Alex's stunt the other day, I don't think I can take much more of their meddling.

Liza likes her games, so I do my very best to stay cool. If I reveal exactly how much Tassa means to me, it won't lead to anywhere good. What I need to do instead is figure out Liza's game and then play it better than her. Fast.

"What exactly did you do?"

"Nothing any of the others wouldn't do." Something about the sly look in her eyes and her smile tells me she did way worse than I could have figured out.

"I'll ask you again. What did you *do*?"

Instead of Liza answering, Alex decides to step in. "How about we fix the wolf situation first? We can discuss your little pet after."

I glance at Vlad and Mirabela for their help, but for once, they are silent. It's Violeta who comes to my aid.

"No. *Before* the wolves, we're going to figure out what happened to the human who did everything in her power, including risking her life, to fix me."

"We've all tried to fix you—"

"Yeah, but did any of you succeed?" Violeta says. "Because last I remember, I was nearly dead. Without Tassa's help, without her perseverance, without her ability to see beside the monsters that we all are, I never would have gotten a chance at a second life. And a second immortality, for that matter."

Alex mutters under his breath. "You mean a temporary new immortality."

Liza and Mirabela seem surprised. Guess Alex hasn't shared this little nugget with them yet. Surprising, really.

I pinch the bridge of my nose, trying to hold back the headache threatening.

"Alex, why do you always have to start trouble?" Vlad says.

"Because that's what he does best. But Violeta is right." I level my gaze on each of them in turn. No matter how different my siblings are, I know they will help me when I need it. "Tassa has done everything in her power to help us. To help Violeta. And none of us want to lose our sister, da? Well, Tassa's got more work to do to uncover the root cause of Violeta's ailment, therefore she's not done helping us. So how about for once we work together and save this one tiny human?"

Alex simply shrugs, pouring himself a drink. Mirabela leans against the wall, arching an eyebrow, as if encouraging me to go on. I'm surprised at her reaction. Did something happen that I don't know about, making her more lenient toward Tassa? I'll table that for another day.

Vlad nods, adding to the list of voices in favor of saving Tassa. Only Liza refuses to speak.

I move closer to her, reaching for her shoulder. She tries to pull away, but I firmly grasp it, forcing her to meet my gaze. "I need you to do this one thing for me, Liza." My words meet a resolute silence.

Once upon a time, I used to know everything going through her mind. But all the centuries of immortality, and especially these last two, have disconnected me. Not just from her but from all of them. Violeta was right. I *have* been closed off. "Is that what this is about?"

"What's what about?"

The defiant tone she uses only tells me that I might've struck a nerve. A very important nerve. Perhaps even the one that will give me the answers I seek.

"Have you been so jealous of Tassa because she grasped my attention, and for centuries prior, none of you could do the same?"

An odd silence follows my words. I look around at each of my siblings. Some of them meet my gaze full on, others don't. I wonder just how much I've missed in the centuries of so-called indifference, of rebellion, of realistically having a non-stop self-pity party over Silva's death.

"Well?"

"You think too highly of yourself, brother," Alex cuts in. Yet despite his contempt-filled tone, he's staring intently into his glass, refusing to meet my gaze full on.

My eyes roam over Mira, Vlad, and Liza again. My touch on her shoulder tightens. "Liza, I am sorry if your feelings were hurt throughout the centuries. I had things to work through, things that I know you understand. You were close to Silva, too. It just took me a longer while to figure them out. Originally, I thought it was better not to face them, to hide away from them. To block out everything and everyone. Surely you understand that?"

She stares at me. Is that a hint of tears in her eyes? Before I can tell for sure, she yanks herself out of my grip and puts some distance between us.

"Shut your trap up already, Nico. This has nothing to do with you. I'm not some weak human who needs attention from her big brother nonstop. If you want to know what I did with Tassa, why don't you go and ask the humans in town? The same ones who came after her so dearly?"

The humans in town... My gaze flicks to Alex. He'd also mentioned them derisively. "Are you talking about the Order that's supposed to protect us?"

She snorts, sharing a glance with Mirabela. "Sure. *Protect us.*"

"What am I missing?" My gaze sweeps the room, even as I try to rein in my impatience. My siblings love their riddles sometimes but I don't want to waste time trying to untangle their meaning.

It's Mirabela who speaks again. "It turns out the humans from this 'Order' are as far away from protectors as possible."

"What do you mean? You chose them."

"Da, because I was at a loss and needed a quick fix. They came from families that had helped out before. But while you were busy cavorting with the human, we went to check on these humans that were supposedly protecting us. And we found out that not only are they very anti-protecting us, they're also more inclined toward destroying us."

Liza whips out a letter from her back pocket and waves it in the air. "At least if this letter we intercepted is any indication."

I'm in front of her in a flash, taking it and reading it. I shouldn't waste time with such things but at the same time, how the fuck did we miss this, any of it? And what does it have to do with Tassa?

The truth is there, black on white. Those humans are definitely not here to protect us. On the contrary. This letter is addressed to the leader of a clan down south. And it mentions other letters, to other vampiri clans... Clans that would sooner see us dead. In Romania, Hungary, Serbia...

I glance up at Liza. "They were contacting our enemies. Offering our location."

"Yes."

"But why?"

"Because," Liza says, "they intend to destroy us—the vampiri that is. Starting with our lineage. Obviously they knew we had someone in our midst who was weak. And they decided this was the perfect time to come here, to get close without us being suspicious. And they got their confirmation when they saw Violeta." Her gaze narrows on our sister. "Especially when she tried to save Tassa and got weakened."

I crumble the letter in my fist, tossing it to the ground. "Please tell me none of these letters actually reached who they were supposed to."

"Do you think I'm stupid?" Liza scowls.

"Of course not," Mirabela says. "We intercepted every one of them, and destroyed them."

My mind is whirring, connecting the remaining dots as my attention turns to Liza. "So you knew about this. And you knew the humans were on our backs, and that they had shown interest in Tassa before... Is that what happened, then? You gave Tassa up to the humans, in exchange for them leaving us alone?"

Liza laughs. I want to slap the mirth off her face, but she stops of her own accord. "No, the humans only wanted to know of her movements. I told them that sooner or later she would leave; she doesn't belong here. That led them to watch her a little bit closer than they had already been. That's all. Anything else that happened, including her leaving, is entirely your fault, Nico."

"Fine. I'll take full accountability for that. But this isn't over."

I think back to the meeting with the cop, the priest, and Victor. How Victor lied to Tassa about her father—because I have no doubt he did. The question is, did Tassa leave of her own accord or was she taken? I'd originally presumed she left on her own but if she didn't—

I need to know. Now.

As I turn to leave, Alex speaks again. "Now that we've gotten the human pet problem out of the way... What the fuck are we doing about the wolves?"

"Nothing until I get back here." I face each one of them in turn. "I am still the oldest, am I not?"

The heaviest silence by far settles on them. A beat goes by, then another. Liza folds her arms over her chest and stomps away to the fire. Alex rolls his eyes and takes a drink.

Mirabela and Vlad come up to me. "We're not letting you do this alone," he says.

Violeta joins them. "Me either. I want to help."

"No. You stay here, I won't have you in danger after you've only now started feeling better." My gaze lands on the other two. "As for you two... Keep up."

Tassa

We know they are weak. And we will make sure to weaken them, for good. I can't get those words out of my head.

To think, all along, Alexandru had these grand notions of who their enemy was. Meanwhile, Victor was right under their noses, in my town. Pretending to be my father's friend. But only working to undermine him. I need to find out if they did have more to do with Violeta. If they're the cause of the black magic my dad talked about, and if that's what's driving her illness.

How wrong I was, thinking Nico and his siblings were the monsters, a few weeks back... And here I am, trying to find a way to save them. Because no matter their supernatural assets, the Draculs are walking blind in this.

I think of Nico. Of his hands on me. Of last night. And I try to imagine him afflicted by the same illness as Violeta—because these men will not stop in their quest to hurt the Draculs, that much is obvious. An ache begins deep in my chest, cutting off my breath within seconds. It's worse than being punched to the solar plexus, and infinitely worse than any panic attack I've ever had.

Focus, Tassa. Your dad would want you to. Focus on doing something—anything. As small as it may be. You can't fall apart now. There'll be plenty of time for it after. I try to push the sensation away, forcing a short breath in, and a second, and a third. The tightness remains, but my mind clears somewhat—enough so I can focus on my next steps.

I need more information, but that doesn't mean I should allow myself to remain in this position of weakness. *Come on, come on. What do I see in my immediate surroundings?* They've got me in some sort of a cellar. But I know this town inside out; there's got to be a way out.

I look around and my gaze falls on the metal bars. They're thick metal, but also a bit rusted. There's no way I can break through. And yet, some crazy part of me tells me to try.

I touch the back of my skull, only now noticing the headache that has been plaguing me since I woke up is no longer there. And when I pull my hand away, it comes up empty of any fresh blood.

How is this possible? I'm human. I shouldn't be able to heal this fast. And yet...

With a startling realization, I remember Nico feeding me his vampir blood. Coupled with Alex's... *I must still have enough of it in my system that it's speeding up my healing.* The same way it helped with the gashes on my back, which I no longer feel.

And if it helped with healing, what else could it help with? I think back to whenever Nico fought with Alex, the trees he could break so easily, the way the walls shook... Vampir strength is a force of nature. Could it be I can wield some of it, temporarily, and break myself out of here?

It's insane to even consider it. But there's only one way to find out.

Step by step, I move closer to the bars. The rational part of my brain, the same part that was able to connect the dots, tells me this is crazy. But I ignore it. Instead, I grip the bars with my feeble human hands and pull. There's no magical fireworks, no crazy sounds. Just a...snap.

I stare at the broken bars in shock, then at my hands, mouth agape. Some alternate part of my brain, fixated on survival, takes over. I move, leaving one bar on the floor and keeping the other as a weapon.

Stepping out of the cellar, I pause, listening for any weird noises. Nothing immediately comes to my ears. Not at first. But then I catch a faint hum. Like electricity. Or a car? As if someone would come for me...

I steel myself for whatever comes next and push on. I hope I won't run into anyone, but at least I'll be prepared to kick their asses if I do.

Through the dark corridor, I move, and it's only as I do so that I realize where I am. In the old mines... Where Dad left his notebook.

I glance back behind me. The cell I was in is hidden, lost amid all the darkness. Could it be this is where they'd been conducting experiments? The experiments Dad was trying to stop?

It has to be. Because if anyone else in the village knew what they were doing, they would have to answer to more than just me. There may not be much police around these parts, but there sure is justice.

More noises reach my ears. Muted. What could be causing all that ruckus out there?

"What the hell are you doing here?"

The voice comes from behind me—how many entrances are in this place? I whirl, but I'm too slow. Victor shoves the bar out of his face and punches me. I gasp, bending over, and drop the bar. Guess vampir blood doesn't last forever.

He moves on me, grabbing me by the hair and slamming me

against the wall. Then his hands are around my neck, squeezing, a wild glint in his eyes.

"All you had to do was stay put and play the bait. You couldn't even do that right, could you? Well, this is the end of the road for you, pretty Tassa. You're a traitor just like your father and I will enjoy killing you. Watching the life drain right out of you will become my newest pleasure."

Chapter 26

Nicolae

After leaving my non-cooperative siblings behind, I rush out of the castle. On the road to the village, I pick up Tassa's scent, and another. A male one I know only too well.

"Victor," I hiss.

Vlad stops by my side. "That confirms it—she was taken."

I nod and rush into the woods at full speed. The trees pass me by fast. I move unseen, because my entire focus is on Tassa. Is she still alive? Did they hurt her?

If they've touched even a hair on her head, I will rip them apart limb by limb. I may do it anyway.

To think of the betrayal... Yes, Tassa left. But it was Liza's irresponsible actions that led to her being captured. Can I forgive my sister for being so lost in her own pettiness that she would willingly cause hurt to the woman I love?

I stop dead in my tracks. Vlad hits me from behind. Mirabela only narrowly avoids us. And as much as I'm aware of this, I'm also aware of the increasing sensation in my stomach. An unfamiliar feeling.

The woman I *love*?

Sure, I've concluded that I have feelings for her, that Tassa means something to me. But...*love*?

"What the hell just happened?" Mira asks.

Vlad gets up slowly, dusts himself off, and stares at me.

"I... Sorry." I don't know what to say. It's not like I can admit to them the little epiphany I just had. Can I?

It turns out, I don't even have to. Vlad says, "Whatever it is that you've realized, now is not the time for it, unless you want to lose your human. Isn't that what we're here for, to save her?"

"You're right."

We start moving again, and the trees are blurring past us. But while I move automatically, I still try to come to terms with my realization—and struggle. After two centuries of shutting down and refusing to feel something, I've now fallen in love...in a matter of a few weeks?

It's mind-boggling. And exhilarating. And probably the scariest fucking thing I've ever done.

We stop at the edge of the mines. Tassa's scent led me here. It makes sense that this is where they would have taken her, but it also doesn't bode well. A secluded place, it leaves room to do anything they'd wish to.

"These mines are old," Mirabela says. "What are the chances we're walking into an ambush?"

"High. But I'm going anyway."

She shifts from foot to foot. "And if one of the letters did succeed, reaching its destination? And we get caught here? What then? It'll be history repeating itself all over again. Only instead of losing Silva, you'll lose one of us."

I stare at her. "What do you mean? I thought you said you intercepted all of them."

"The ones we found out about, yes. We learned of them from a human we glamoured into telling us. But we may have missed some."

I clench my fists. "You should have warned me."

"For that matter," Vlad says, "they should have warned all of us, but they didn't. As always." He touches my shoulder, lowering his voice. "We both know Liza, Mira and Alex will always do what they feel is best. No matter how psychotic and how many bad situations it leads to. Haven't you figured that out yet?"

It's the first time I've heard Vlad say so much at once, hinting at his own issues with our siblings. And, oddly, again the idea pops in my head that I missed out on a lot while trying not to care. There will be a lot of atonement after this—and not just from me.

I shake my head. "You can both leave. If this is an ambush, if there's even a slight chance, I'd rather take that chance on my own."

"No way. I'm with you to the end," Vlad says softly.

Mira scowls. "Are you insane? We're not letting you go in alone."

"Well, I'm not leaving Tassa, either. I'd rather die with her than live without her."

I don't think Mira expected the vehemence in my words, as her eyes widen. She stares at me for a long moment, then nods. "Fine. I can see there's no talking you out of this. So, what's the plan exactly?"

I glance around, trying to identify the sounds. I can hear human heartbeats inside, more than one. But less than a dozen. Where the hell are the rest of them?

"You go for the humans, and I will find Tassa."

Mirabela arches an eyebrow. "Simple enough. And what happens when everything goes wrong?"

"We'll cross that bridge when we get to it."

Without another word to her, I head inside, pausing right at the edge of the cave.

It would be stupid to call out her name. Incredibly stupid. So I don't. Instead, I tiptoe inside, aware of the crunch of the gravel under my boots. The mustiness of the air. Or something else. A scent I'm only too familiar with. Fear.

I close my eyes, inhaling deep. What is it? Why is it right at the edge of my consciousness, but I can't—

The heat comes out of nowhere and I feel the sting of silver on my skin. Then, Vlad calls out a warning. "Watch out!"

In the darkness, my eyes adjust. It's not a human I'm facing, but a muroni. What the hell is one of them doing here?

I don't bother to think. Instead, I attack. In one fell swoop, I've ripped off its head, followed by its limbs, and tossed them into a corner. Then I continue to move onward, my mind whirring.

The muroni was slow, almost as if it was still learning about its powers. And though I didn't bother checking, I bet I would've found fresh wounds on its neck.

This explains it—the nests of muroni we've been hunting, always replaced by more. The humans they were turning. Someone was trying to see how well we operate, and whether we're still at peak capacity. They were making *more* of them. This is probably where the two who attacked Tassa and her father came from.

This entire time, they've watched us, hunted us, baited us, and we didn't even realize it.

Vlad shows up at my side. Blood drips off his arms. He must've killed his own attacker, too. "This doesn't feel right. They feel like a distraction."

"I know. Where's Mira?"

"Disposing of the bodies."

Of course. Bet she'll enjoy that.

I turn my senses outward once more. Trying to find any scent of Tassa... And then, farther in the distance, I catch her scent—her blood.

I'm vaguely aware of Vlad having my back. He's intercepting humans, muroni, anything in our path, even as I go through them at vampir speed. What was their plan, anyway? To use Tassa as bait? It wouldn't have worked.

Humans have never been able to stand against us. Not since the beginning of time, and not now. With all their weapons, with all their new technologies, they are still inferior. Because we have learned something they have not. We have learned to go with our gut instinct, to trust in that voice deep inside of us, to push past the limitations of our bodies, something humans cannot and *will not* do. They're too afraid to do that.

Another human pops in my way, with a stake in each hand. I assess him in a matter of seconds. He raises one stake toward my heart—I remove it with a flick of my wrist. To his eyes, I must look like a blur of movement. His wide gaze clashes with mine. I feel it the moment he realizes that he is doomed.

I take one step closer, grabbing a fistful of his hair and pulling his head to the side, baring his neck. My fangs tears into his flesh, enjoying the taste of fleeting blood for a moment. And then I cast him aside, not even bothering to finish him off.

I blur in a red haze, aware only of the noises around me. Vlad and Mirabela, somewhere behind me. Groans of pain. Flesh being torn apart. Bones broken. They're having a little too much fun, but that realization is compartmentalized as soon as it arises. Instead, my entire being is focused on finding Tassa.

My eyes move through the darkness until, finally, my gaze lands on her—and the man holding her by the throat, slowly choking her. A hiss escapes me, followed by a low growl.

He spares me a glance, and I'm not surprised to see it's Victor. I should've killed him when I had the chance. "If you try anything, I will snap her neck before you can snap mine."

I focus my attention on Tassa. "Everything will be okay."

She stays silent, but her hand moves—swift, deliberate. The man grunts, a wet sound follows, and the metallic tang of blood fills the air.

He drops to his knees, clutching his side as crimson pours between his fingers. Tassa crawls away from him, staggering toward me. In her hand is a stake—she must've taken it off him.

I wrap my arms around her, inhaling her sweet scent. Amid all the chaos, she alone matters. This human who stole my heart without even trying to. "You never needed saving, did you?"

Tassa

Nico's here. I don't even know where he showed up from, only that he's here, I'm in his arms, and I'm alive.

Blood drips off my fingers and from the stake I used to kill Victor. I'd felt it poking me from Victor's pocket and remembered he had one even at the castle the first time I met him. But I didn't mean to kill him. The whole thing feels like a bad nightmare. I'd acted on pure It was survival instinct, nothing else.

"I guess it's a good thing cops in this town are easily subdued, huh? Otherwise, I'd have a murder charge in my future." It doesn't even strike me as odd, saying that. This is the world I've stepped into, for better or worse.

Nico pushes me away from him, caressing my cheek. "I would never let anything happen to you. You have to know that."

I do. True to his word, Nico whisks me out of the mines, and back into the safety of the woods. We move too fast for me to notice the surroundings, but I do see fire. Whoever came with him must be burning bodies.

When Nico stops moving, I say, "There was another man. Besides Victor. A vampir hunter, Liviu. Or maybe he wasn't a hunter—I'm not sure. Victor said he was somebody *like* a hunter."

Nico frowns. "I didn't come across him."

"He's been... they were working together, experimenting on vampiri. Dad found out, he tried to go against Victor, and they turned new humans—using the results from the experiments—into vampiri, to kill him. So his death couldn't be traced to them."

Nico's hold on me only tightens, pulling me against his chest again. "I'm so sorry."

Rather than surrender to the very alluring safety net of his arms, I press my palms against his chest, forcing a little distance. "But there's more, Nico. Before I left, I tested Violeta. Dad was right. Her illness isn't natural. The symptoms are only masking something else, something that, for some reason, the muroni blood helps—for now."

"Shh. It's all right, really. Tassa, you did what you had to, to survive. No one blames you, least of all me." Nico sighs. "As for Violeta, we'll keep searching. At least her condition is not as dire as it was before, and more information is bound to follow. I'll search all corners of the globe if I must."

When I say nothing, he adds, "Tassa..." I already know what he's going to say before he does. It doesn't make the words any easier to hear, especially when he speaks them in that raw, vulnerable tone. "Why did you leave?"

The one word hanging—unspoken—in the air is, *me*.

"I had to. It was time for me to go."

Vlad and Mirabela emerge into the woods then, wiping their mouths of the blood of their enemies. I should feel something, given a bunch of humans just got killed so I could be saved. But since those same humans were more monstrous than these guys... I find it hard to dig out an ounce of remorse.

"These lunatics wanted to eradicate all of you. I was trying to come warn you, when I escaped."

"How nice of you." Mirabela rolls her eyes.

I try not to let her brittle tone get to me. After all, she's entitled to not like me. The humans probably wouldn't know as much as they do about them if it wasn't for me. But I also have to let go of that sentiment.

"I..."

"Are you okay?" Vlad asks pointing to my neck. "There's a lot of bruising."

I suck in a deep breath, realizing that I am alive, unharmed...that I survived. Again.

More than that, I have my freedom. My duty to Violeta is done, and I can return to my life, knowing that I did something. That I've at least had the joy of knowing Nico's hands on me, too. And I have the memories of our time to hold on to. *No regrets.*

"Thank you for coming to save me. I really appreciate that, more than I can say." I pull away from Nico's arms, trying to ignore the pang in my chest. "I can tell you what it is they said, it might help out."

None of them say anything.

"Victor said that over the years, a lot of them had lost some family member or another to vampiri in the region. He didn't say it was specifically you guys, but he did imply that it was vampiri who have a higher standing. That's what led them to be against you, rather than protect you. Once they knew you were back in the region, they tried sending out letters to the other clans around."

"Yes, we know that," Mirabela says. "We intercepted some of them."

"What you might not know—or maybe it will only confirm your suspicions—is that they also tried to screw things up with the wolves taking residence here. Victor didn't admit as much, but the other human, the hunter, said he had made sure the wolf head was delivered to you." As I relate the events, part of me feels detached, untethered.

I take in my surroundings, followed by a deep breath, and continue, "Whatever the case may be, you may want to contact the wolves as soon as possible. And as for Violeta's illness... Much as I want to give them credit, I don't believe they had anything to do with it. Something else is going on. Something the muroni blood is staving off, but barely. Unfortunately, it's not something I can help with any longer, but I'm sure that same as with my dad, you can find another doctor nearby. But..."

I hesitate. What's the point of telling them Victor's final dying words, the words he whispered to me with his last breath? *His curse will be your own. He won't live enough to enjoy you.* Senseless words, deprived of meaning. A lunatic's last bait, one I don't plan to take.

"But nothing," I finish off. "Only, it feels like the balance around this area is changing and you should be careful."

"I'm sure we can manage as much," Mirabela says with a smirk. And then she turns and leaves, just like that.

I watch her disappear into the woods, knowing that I'll never see her again. An odd sense of sadness grips me. I would have learned much from her if circumstances were different. Not that I will ever get the chance.

Vlad steps toward me. "Thank you for helping my sister. I will not forget what you did."

And then he, too, is gone.

Which leaves just me and Nico.

I stare at him, remembering the feel of his hands on my skin, the prickling of electricity he causes. The flame of yearning usually within me tries to poke its head at his proximity, but I quickly douse it, and shove away the emotions. I'll have to be strong and collected if this is to work. "I know you don't understand why I have to leave, but I do. This has no future. You and I...*we* have no future."

He stares at me for the longest time, and for a moment I think he might just fight me for it. But he doesn't. All he says is, "Will you allow me one last kiss?"

I tilt my head back, meet his intense gave, and give him my silent permission. His lips brush mine softly. It's a consuming kiss, a mix of all the sweet ones and desire-filled ones we've had. But it's also more, like he's reaching into my very soul to squeeze my heart, and leave his imprint on it.

I can't hold back my reaction. I reach for his shirt and curl my fingers into the fabric, holding him to me. For a breath, two, I kiss him in earnest, knowing it's the last one I'll have from him. Enjoying the last strokes of his tongue against mine, the way my toes curl at the sensations he elicits in me. Sensations I'm getting ready to say goodbye to.

And then Nico steps away, much stronger than me, and nods my way once more. In the shadows of the trees, I can't make out the expression on his face, but his tone is heavy with meaning. "Take care of yourself, Tassa."

A breath later, the woods swallow him like he's a figment of my imagination, and not the real-life prince I could've had.

Chapter 27

Nicolae

My siblings are way ahead of me by the time I get my feet moving. But though I let the woods engulf me, I don't disappear. Not just yet. Instead, I watch over Tassa, silently following her until she makes her way back into the main section of the village.

Once I see her there, surrounded by other humans that are—one hopes—lesser lunatics than the ones I've just finished off killing, I turn back toward the darkness of the woods, and of my own soul, and head back home.

No sooner do I get back to the castle, that Mirabela and Vlad intercept me at the entrance.

"What is it?"

"The wolves."

A moment later, Alex steps out of the house, a defiant look in his eyes. "I don't think they want to hear from me, dear brother. The wolf head seems to have steered them to the wrong conclusion. Perhaps you can be more persuading."

Ah, for fuck's sake. I hold back a groan—barely. All I want is to bury my mind in the strongest bottle of țuică I can find, *not* play diplomat.

"Why me? Vlad is better at small talk. Or Mira."

Too late. Already, my ears pick up the sound of leaves rustling, of paws on the ground. And by the time I turn toward the trees, a dark wolf emerges from their midst. He's larger than a regular wolf, and his fur is dark, except for a white line running from the top of his head all over his back. His intelligent eyes, a pale gray color, have blue irises.

I step toward him, accepting my fate, insofar as I ever have. Holding my hands up, I crouch low. "We are not your enemies."

He stands back, glancing over his shoulder, and then the red-head I'd seen earlier, during the recon mission with Mirabela, also exits the woods. Other wolves—vrykolakas, judging by their larger bulk and feral gazes—follow her, their gazes glued to her.

She really is their Luna. Wolf packs of their kind have an alpha male and alpha female, ruling on equal footing. The thing is, I've never seen a *human* Luna. Guess there's a first time for everything.

I straighten to my full height and feel my siblings' attention on us. It's useless to pretend we are anything but what we are. "Welcome to our corner of the land."

The redhead stares at me, at my siblings, then lets her hand trail over the wolf's back. "Thank you. I'm Lucrezia, and this is my mate, Dominic. We come in peace."

"As do we."

A slight narrowing of the eyes is the only indication she doesn't believe me. "We did not realize others were in the area."

"Nor we."

"Until one of ours was killed."

A sigh escapes me. "We had nothing to do with it. A rogue pack of humans in the area is trying to stir trouble."

"Don't fucking defend us to her!" Alex shouts, stepping toward me.

Growls rise from the vrykolakas, but before anyone can do anything, a spark of lightning shoots right at his feet. We all freeze, trying to determine where it came from.

And then I notice the woman, and the glaze of lightning in her eyes, the faint smile on her lips.

"Rogue humans or not," she says, "it might do us well to sit down and talk. We can arrange a meeting, on neutral territory if you wish to discuss terms of sharing the land. But... we *are* here to stay."

I nod. Meeting them on neutral territory should be interesting. "Very well. We will await your invitation."

"Thank you...voivode."

And then she turns and leaves, the wolves following her. If I don't know any better, I'd think the glint in the eyes of her mate is one of amusement at my reaction.

Voivode. She knows of our lineage. That our sire—our father, for all intents and purposes—Vlad Țepeș was the prince, the voivode, of Wallachia, and of these lands. *How in hell...*

I turn back to my siblings and usher them inside the castle before they do something stupid. The meeting, if nothing else, served to distract my thoughts from Tassa, and her words that cut at my non-existent heart.

Tassa

I'm back home. The villagers must've worked hard to clear the debris, because most of it is livable. Half of the walls in the living room are burned and I'll need to repaint them, but the structure itself held. All the burned furniture has already been tossed out. So while I came back to less furniture than before...it's *livable*.

Yet nothing feels the same.

I don't know why I thought it would. These last few days, weeks, have been a rollercoaster of emotions. My mind has been bended in ways I couldn't fathom before all this. It's only normal seeing the leftovers of our life doesn't feel like home.

The first thing I do is shower, then get in bed. It's cold, and lonely, and I'd better get used to it, but at least it's also safe.

After everything I've seen—never mind the fact I just killed a man—I shouldn't be able to sleep. But I crash like I've been without sleep for ages, and wake up with a start a few hours later.

It's pitch dark outside. I know, because I go in the backyard and look at the stars. At the sky. Wondering if Nico is out hunting. Or Violeta. Or any of them.

And then I go back inside the house, lock all the doors and windows, and make myself a cup of tea. As I sip on the chamomile beverage Dad always said would help me sleep—with a touch of valerian tincture—I let my thoughts wander.

There's no point thinking of what could have been. But surely I'm allowed, even for a moment, to just... be. Be happy that I'm alive. Being faced with my own mortality, has given me a thirst to live. To be everything I wish to be. To travel everywhere I want to travel. And, more than that... To actually live. Stop holding back. Jump. Seize the day.

But not with Nico.

Why *not* with Nico?

Dad always used to solve problems this way. *Why not, why not, why not...*

The mantra rolls over and over in my head. *He's a vampir. He'll forever crave your blood. Put you at risk.* And yet, he's also protected me.

He's a royal. He has enemies. And yet, I've proven I can stand my ground.

There is no happy ending when he can live for centuries, and you can't. That one, I have no answer to.

So I sip my tea some more, and eventually fall asleep. And in my dreams, at least, I'm free to think as I wish, to kiss him, to embrace him, to allow his caresses to drive me crazy. In my sleep, I live another reality... but when I wake up the next day, I'm still stuck in the same loophole.

And it's as I'm cleaning the house that I realize the truth—I need to get out of here. Either I stay with Nico, and allow him to show me the world as he knows it, or I leave, and make my own way. There is no in-between where I get to have both.

Like it or not, I have to decide, and stop lingering in ifs and buts. This life will not be lived unless I live it.

In an effort to escape my ruminations, and also to feed myself, I leave the house and go into the village. It's been a while since I've been around regular humans, with nothing to do with the supernatural. Every face I see, I cannot help but think of the lunatics who took me. I always expected a level of safety with these folks. That turned out to be not the case at all, and it's screwed some with my sense of trust.

As I move through one of the market stalls looking for fresh vegetables, I become aware of a few weird glances being thrown my way. Dad always raised me not to care about other people's opinions. It makes sense that in my absence I would've become something of an eccentric tourist attraction, for lack of a better phrase. But by the time I have surveyed enough stalls and I'm ready to make some purchases, the looks start getting on my nerves.

I move to a cheese vendor and ask him for a couple of slices of smoked cheese and some cașcaval—his best ripened cheese. Instead of going and getting it for me, he stares at me. Something is his gaze makes me uncomfortable. It's not exactly hate, but it's weird. Most of the vendors in this market have seen me at some point or another. So why are they acting all of a sudden like I'm the enemy?

I open my mouth and bluntly ask, "Are you not going to serve me?"

Instead of answering me, he simply turns to another client. I back away in shock, but force myself to keep a neutral expression.

There are a few other vendors down the line so I move on to the next one. The guy there is younger than the last. He serves me happily, while others keep sending glares my way. Once I have the purchase from him, I switch gears to vegetables. And I'm greeted with my second experience, very similar to the first.

By the time I move on to the meats, it's more of the same story. Disheartened, I turn away with just my cheese purchase and prepare to leave. That's when I see an older lady waiting for me at the edge of the market.

Her expression isn't hateful, but it's not welcoming, either. It's almost a little *too* neutral. The weathered face of someone who has lived many experiences. In a flash, I recognize her—she's the local priest's wife.

I approach her, but she tilts her head to the side and motions for me to follow her around the edge of the park pagoda. Given my latest adventures with the humans, I hesitate for a brief moment, but then trail behind her.

"Planning to treat me with disdain as well?" I ask, once she comes to a stop.

"Why do you think they treat you this way?"

"Perhaps for the same reason Victor and his people kidnapped me and were ready to kill me. Before I killed him." I'm not about to pretend the people who died last night were good souls. "Or perhaps because they love to judge, despite not knowing the full story."

She nods, as if taking in my words. "I understand your anger. Victor and the others were not right in their actions."

I scowl. "So you know, then, what they did. And that they tried to kill me?"

She gives me a little shrug. "It is not right, like I said. But we must defend our own."

"And aren't I one of you?"

"Not anymore. Not since you gave in. Since you became theirs. You must at the very least understand where they were coming from, having lost so many members of their families to the vampiri in the region."

"But it was not because of the vampiri in the castle." I've been about to say *my* vampiri but that is definitely not a possession I can admit to.

"No, it was not. However, at the end of the day, monsters are monsters. Aren't they?"

"The only monsters I have run into lately were Victor and his cronies."

She stares at me for a moment longer than necessary then reaches into her bag. She pulls out And a weird looking stone, something I've seen before, but can't quite put my finger on.

"Something tells me you have already made up your mind. But if that is the case, you cannot fault the rest of us for not seeing you the same way anymore."

"My father treated almost everyone in this village at some point or another."

"He also treated vampiri."

This is news to me. Not that Dad treated vampiri, that part I already knew. But the fact that the village also knew... Victor didn't mention that. I thought only the Order people were aware of everything. Yet her words imply *everyone*, Order or not, knows. Which, admittedly, explains the stares earlier.

"So you knew, too. And Marin? Did everyone know?"

She glances around, seemingly upset at my rising voice.

"You chose to stick to your old superstitions and judgmental minds instead of helping one of your own. Unbelievable!"

She glares at me. "What were we supposed to do? Help him out, when Victor and his cohorts would have had our necks next?"

"He's gone now. How do you justify your behavior to me, then?"

She says nothing.

I scoff. "Yeah, I thought so." I move to leave, but she grabs my arm.

"We cannot go against forces much bigger than ourselves."

"Forces like what?"

Her only answer is a shake of the head.

I frown, a niggling at the back of my mind. "Do you know anything about vampiri being sick?"

Her gaze goes to the castle and back to me. "It is a curse. One you will need protection from now, too."

It's not the answer I had expected. Not after all this time, after everything I'd hoped to find. But I guess it's the only answer I will get.

His curse will be your own. He won't live enough to enjoy you. Victor's words echo in my ears.

I steel my mind against the anguish trying to drag me under. "According to you, it's a curse. But for all I know, you're lying, just like Victor did."

"You can believe what you will. You are truly your father's daughter. But in order for you to live a happy life, there is a choice you must make. And because of the allegiance you have already shown the vampiri, that choice may end up taking you far, far away from here. If you still wish to live among the humans, that is."

With her part said, she leaves, but not before dropping the

necklace in my palm. "For protection."

I glance at it. It's a stone. A swirl of browns and coals and honey colors. The Tiger's eye stone, meant for protection.

Protection from what?

More shaken than I want to admit, I make my way back to the house. And only once I'm inside do I let the tears come. Tears for my old life. Tears for my future. Tears for the decision I must now make.

Chapter 28

Nicolae

We're all still in shock the next day, following the wolves' introduction. When I head into the library, Violeta is there, reading a book. It takes me a moment to recognize it. It's the same one Tassa was reading.

I clear my throat and she glances up. Something on my face must have hinted at my thoughts, because she closes the book slowly and gives me her undivided attention.

"How are you feeling?"

She shrugs, leaning her head against the sofa. "Better. What Tassa did helped. I may not be to my fullest, but at least I'm not so close to dying anymore." Her chews on her bottom lip. "Why did she leave, Nico?"

"What do you mean?" I'm purposefully avoiding her question, and we both know it. But I'm not about to get into the ins and outs of my romantic life with my sister, even if she was very close to Tassa.

"I know full well something happened between you two. That she has feelings for you. So why are you two being so stubborn?"

"Shouldn't we worry about next steps for you instead? Because your story didn't have the fix we'd all hoped for. That concoction Tassa prepared is only temporary, and the disease underneath it is still kicking. Knowing you, you're not planning to let things slide. But taking off and hunting for answers on your own isn't the way, Vi."

Violeta seems stunned that I figured it out. It wasn't that hard. Before all this happened, I used to gauge her intentions quite easily. Now that I'm back to *feelings*, it's all coming back to me.

She places the book on the small table by the sofa and stands to face me. "What I do with my life..."

"Is no business of mine. Da, I know. Then how is mine your business?"

She smiles. "It's my business because you have a chance to actually be happy and you're throwing it away."

"The chance is already gone. Tassa made it clear. There is no happily ever after for us. And she's right. She's a human. I'm a vampir. Not exactly a match made in heaven."

"Are you really that stupid, Nico?"

I don't know how much I appreciate my sister calling me stupid. But at the end of the day, is there a chance that she's right? Obviously.

"You know, Father would have given anything for one more day with his first wife—his consort. The fact you so easily give up on yours is an insult to his memory."

That odd hurt in my chest returns. A consort is precious to us all—a being who is our better half. A *pereche*—a pair to the soul. It's a term I've done my best to forget, the same as I've tried to forget love and the idea of ever loving anyone. Now both are present in my mind, and no matter what I do, I can't get them out.

Before I can say anything, Vlad chooses that moment to walk in. "She's right, you know."

Wonderful, now there are two of them against me. "What's next, Alex and Liza joining in?"

"Funny," Violeta says. "If I didn't know any better, I would say that you're afraid of what they might think."

"That's not it at all. I've never cared what people think."

"Is that so? Then how do you explain the fact that you were so quick to pull away from what life has to offer? Out of the six of us, you were the first one to dig yourself into a life of indifference, Nico."

"I didn't choose to think myself into indifference. Things happened, and it was the best way forward for me." Why am I defending myself to my siblings, when I have done nothing wrong?

Or...have I?

The reality is, they may have a point. When things became hard, I was quick to retreat into a life of indifference, rather than care too hard. It resulted in me being completely alienated from my siblings, although we lived in the same castle and we were around each other.

But even though we were around each other, we have never been so alone. When I come to think of it, me with my indifference, Liza and Alex with their psychotic behavior, Mirabela with her so-called coldness, Violeta staring death in the face, and Vlad... Vlad just being there, trying to keep the peace.

I shake my head. "What a life, huh?"

Violeta smiles. "It's a rather good one, if you don't spend it regretting important choices."

"And what's your advice, then? That I should just go and force her to listen to me, to be with me?"

"Not force," Vlad says. "But you have a chance, after living a completely disillusioned life, to now be... Well, maybe happy is too optimistic for the likes of us. Just don't turn your back on it."

I find myself outside Tassa's house, staring. I've been here for over an hour. How many times did I walk up and down the street? Has she seen me? Probably not. The lights are off, except for a slight flicker that makes me think of candles.

She's either asleep, or in deep thought. I should go. Come back another day. Or maybe write her a letter.

Letters are for three hundred years ago, idiot.

Finally, I knock on the door. It takes a moment, then two, and Tassa opens it. Her eyes widen when they land on me.

"What are you doing here?"

Before I can answer, she pulls me inside, then shuts the door behind her with a definitive slam.

I frown, facing her. "Why the secrecy?"

"No secrecy."

"I beg to differ."

"Differ all you want, but there's no secrecy. What do you want?"

I glance at the door she's plastered to, trying to put together what she's not saying. Then it dawns on me. The only reason she wouldn't want people to see me...

"Have they been giving you a hard time?"

She shakes her head. But the way she averts her eyes tells me more than enough.

Anger rises within me and I try to push past her, my hand on the doorknob. Tassa places her fingers on mine, trying to detract me from opening the door.

"There's nothing you can do," she says. "Small town superstitions."

I meet her gaze, aware of how close we are. "It isn't superstition if it's the truth, though."

She nods, her eyes never once leaving mine. "True."

My hand goes slack around the knob, fingers seeking hers instead. "Tassa, I'm sorry—"

She pulls away, walking a few paces before facing me once more. The steel in her spine speaks of her determination. "It's fine."

"It's not fine. If you helping me and my siblings has resulted in issues in this town for you, it's not fine."

She shrugs. "It won't be a problem for long. I'm leaving." She clears her throat. "I have the ticket, and everything."

My eyes are already roaming the living room, falling on a packed bag. And another, smaller, satchel right next to it.

"Where?" The single word is wooden on my tongue.

"Western Europe. Spain first, maybe France in a bit. I need...to be away."

I nod. Something in me falters. And then I remember Violeta, and how close she came to her life ending. And how it may be my fate, in a hundred years—or tomorrow. It takes everything in me, but I push the nausea aside, and take a few steps closer. Not close enough to touch, but enough to inhale her scent deeply.

"I understand. Truly, I do." On autopilot, I turn to the door, closing my eyes. "But I can't let you leave without saying something." And then I whirl back to her, cross the last few steps, cup her cheeks, and kiss her.

The embrace starts off soft—I'd meant it cajoling. But like always with Tassa, that need inside me takes over. Demanding closeness, connection, wanting to give her all of me, so I can have all of her. Before long, we're glued to each other, my body aching to take hers to the brink of all pleasures.

I force myself to pull back. To look into her eyes, trying to find the words. "I can't ask you to stay—I won't rob you of the chance at another life. But I beg you not to dismiss us, this thing between us, so easily. If it were just physical, we both know it wouldn't last—wouldn't be enough. But these last few weeks, we've had a merging of minds, of *souls*. You can't deny it, Tassa. Tell me you feel it, too."

Her eyes flutter closed. When her head gives a small inclination, I sigh. I'll take what I can get.

"Then remember me, and remember how you infused color into my life, into my bleak existence. Your light burst its brightness into the gray darkness of my existence. And I don't know if I can go on without you, inima mea."

Tassa

Inima mea. My heart. He called me his heart.

I watch him walk out of the house, and out of my life—if I let him. Can I? Will I let our story stop here, and never know what could have been?

The lady's words from earlier ring in my mind. A choice. I have to make a choice.

But it's a choice I'd already made, giving myself to Nico. A choice I repeated when, in my imprisonment, I thought only of him and warning him. A choice I stood by even when speaking to her, not regretting anything—not taking my back my time with him, apologizing for it, even when it could have meant acceptance for me. A choice I...

Dad always said you work through the hardest things. *Sometimes in life you have to do the hard things, to live life even when all your loved ones are gone.* And now, when the darkness has passed, and I'm offered a chance at more, I just...back off? Cower away?

I glance at my reflection in the mirror, and I see a person I barely recognize. That glint in my eyes yearns for life, for adventure, for *passion*. The blush on my cheeks gives me a color that's been absent since I left Nico's castle. I stand taller, speak more confidently, and it's been ages since I so much as berated my own body. I've *accepted* myself, because life is too short to live otherwise. So why can't I go one step further?

My dad didn't raise me to be a coward, and I won't start being one now. The paths laid out before me are crystal-clear: follow my heart, live life to the fullest with an immortal by my side, or dismiss my experience with Nico as nothing but a dream—something I'm not worthy of—and continue down the passive path of my human life.

Who are you trying to fool, Tassa? This choice, you made it ages ago. The first time you laid eyes on him.

I run out of the house, heading onto the path I'd taken with Nico a few times. And I run and run and run. The cold air whips at my cheeks, the branches scratch at my sweater, but I still run. I'm nowhere as fast as his vampire speed, but I know, deep down, I need to catch up to him. So I keep running until the woods surround me and all that's left is the breath in my lungs. Coming out in little puffs of air.

And then Nico's there, popping out of the woods, stopping my run with his hands on my shoulders. "Are you okay? What happened?"

I step back, bend over, panting. "I—" Stupid, idiotic lungs.

I take in a deep breath, and end up nearly coughing them out. Through it all, Nico watches me with a concerned, albeit guarded, expression.

Finally, I straighten up. "I don't want to love you—but I've fallen. And I don't want to leave you. I'm also under no illusions about my mortality. But for the time being, for the years I have now... I want to see where this can go, Nico. I'd be a coward to run—"

He's already kissing me, stealing the air from my lungs all over again. Only this time, I welcome it. I hang onto him, kissing him just as hard, my toes curling in my boots.

When he pulls back enough for my lips to move, I finish my sentence with a pitiful, "—away."

He growls, nips at my lips again. "You're not going anywhere. Other than my bed, *now*."

I laugh as he picks me up, already heading toward the castle.

"But I insist on living in the village."

He frowns. "After the way they're treating you? I don't think so. I want you by my side at night."

"Then you'll have to come see me, won't you?" I let my hand caress his cheek, and ruffle his hair. "I'll win them all back, taking over Dad's business. And in between, I'll travel."

"Then I'll go with you."

A smile stretches my lips. "Maybe we'll start with scouring the four corners of the world for that magical cure for Violeta, hmm?"

Nico looks down at me, his blue eyes shining, full of love and gratitude.

He may be a monster to everyone else. He may be descended from a bloody legacy. But to me, he's just my prince...my everything.

Epilogue

On the edge of the woods, the dark wolf watched the castle and all its inhabitants. He hadn't intended to land his pack in the middle of vampir territory, even less so *royal* territory. But it had so happened, and now that he'd met them, something told him their fates were intertwined.

He moved away, running back through the woods, clearing the overwhelming scents filling his nostrils. For the time being, he would keep his distance—but he would speak to his betas to increase patrols around their camp. Whoever was trying to stir shit up between the wolves and vampiri was probably not done yet.

Moments later, he emerged from the woods into another area. His own little haven of peace. Still in wolf form, he putted about, glancing left and right. Mud filled the area, mainly from the new houses his vrykolakas were building. They were old-school huts at the moment, but they did the trick.

He stopped outside of his own. Light shimmered all over his form, and soon he was a naked, male man once more. He ran a hand through his blond hair and shook the chill of the air off him, before entering his hut.

It was sparse, as they'd only taken the bare minimum from their last place, but it was home. His blue gaze zeroed in on the redhead in bed, her mass of thick red curls spread over the pillows.

Tiptoeing, he moved to a corner and wiped his feet with a wet cloth, then slid into bed with her. She turned to him in her sleep, her soft breath fanning over his chest. Something in him seized with love. His hands found her waist, pulling her closer still against him, and he buried his nose in the crook of her neck.

"Luz, wake up."

She groaned in his arms, then he felt her stirring as she stretched against him. She blinked, slowly, and her eyes took him in sleepily. He couldn't resist stealing a kiss before she'd even properly woken.

"You sure have a way of waking me." She chuckled against his lips.

"Mm. I just got back from the vampiri's castle."

Luz pulled away. "Dominic—"

His index was on her lips before she could lecture him. "I was careful."

"I don't like the look of them. They seem...unhinged." She sighed, making a face. "Probably are. Tytus warned us they would be."

"But he didn't actually say why this would be a good spot to set up our new home, did he?"

Luz shook her head. "No. Only that because of what was coming, this would be best."

Dominic shrugged. "It's weird, don't you think? Twenty years go by, our son is grown, and now this... A complete change of scenery, moving to an entirely remote area, and all to land in hot waters with vampir royalty?"

Luz moved closer to him, her lips finding his chest. "For now, let's just focus on keeping a distance. Until we know more."

"Your words are my command, draga mea."

He rolled her on her back, hovering over her for a breath to take in her features. Time had only made her more beautiful, and he was as besotted as he'd been in that mechanic's shop, when he'd offered to be her pretend boyfriend. *Best decision of my life.*

He kissed down her neck, and lower, and lower. Years had gone by, and still he couldn't tire of the taste of her, nor of having her in his life.

No vampir will take this away from me. I'll kill them all if it comes down to it, to protect what's mine.

Will Violeta's illness eat her from the inside out? Or will a chance encounter with a rogue soldier help her find the answers she seeks? Find out in the next Lost Royals of Transylvania installment, Cracked Casualty.
The Draculs' story continues...

Curious about Dominic and Lucrezia? Find out their back story in *First to Fall*, book 1 in a completed paranormal romance series with sexy werewolves, feisty females, and inspirations from various mythologies and folklore.

And if you enjoyed Nico and Tassa's story, please consider leaving a review at your choice of retailer. Even a line or two makes a huge difference to an indie author!

Rogues Extended Universe—Reading Order

Moonlight Rogues

Flaming Rogues

Immortal Rogues

Lost Royals of Transylvania

Vârcolac Legacy (coming 2022)

Love my books?
Want to get your hands on them and review them
first, before anyone else?
Sign up for my ARC team now
And you'll get to read and review everything first....

Including the next *Lost Royals of Transylvania*
novel!
Vampires, sibling rivalries and mysteries continue.

ABOUT THE AUTHOR

Alexa Whitewolf is a fiction writer, newspaper columnist of daily issues and author of the critically acclaimed **Moonlight Rogues** shifter series.

Alexa has been a lifelong writer and first began creating other worlds and characters at the ripe age of 12. Growing up in the Transylvania region surrounded by epic mountains and a never-ending stream of legends and stories was bound to create an overactive imagination. This shines through Ms. Whitewolf's writing by creating worlds filled with unique folklore, life wisdom and plenty of furry creatures.

An avid traveler, Alexa writes under a penname and spends her days between an office job and writing in Canada's capital, when she's not flying somewhere with lush landscapes and plenty of hiking trails.

Her series focus on strong heroines, kind yet sexy men, fights of good and evil and the never-ending learning curve of humanity's strong—and weak—points. Romanian folklore is intertwined with her writing, more notably in her shifter romance series, the Moonlight Rogues. Her other series draw on world mythology, such as the Avalon myth and Arthurian legend (**The Avalon Chronicles**) and Ancient Egypt (**The Sage's Legacy**).

You can follow her blog at www.alexawhitewolfauthor.com or on social media. Her column in Observatorul also tackles various issues, including health, technology, and a writer's life.

If you want up to date releases, make sure you sign up for her newsletter. For new releases notifications, you can also follow her on:

ALSO BY THE AUTHOR

Rogues Extended Universe

Moonlight Rogues series

Moonlight Rogues: Origins

First to Fall

Second to Surrender

Third to Tumble

Last to Love

Exclusive inside look inside the series

Flaming Rogues series

Fanning the Flames

Igniting the Ice

Exclusive inside look inside the series

Immortal Rogues series

Secret Shadows

Archer's Arrow

Dead Dilemma

Fickle Fate

Exclusive inside look inside the series

Lost Royals of Transylvania series

Immortal Illusion

Cracked Casualty

Deadly Deceit

Sinful Salvation

Angry Addiction
Primal Protection
Exclusive inside look inside the series

Demoni Sancti Extended Universe

Standalone
Blazing Ashes

Demoni Sancti series
Fallen
Broken
Unshackled
Risen
Ascended
Exclusive inside look inside the series

The Avalon Chronicles series
Avalon Dreams
Avalon Wishes
Avalon Nightmares
Atrox
Exclusive inside look inside the series

The Sage's Legacy – YA series
The Dragon Medallion
The Dragon Manuscript
Relics of the Underworld
Exclusive inside look inside the series

Standalone novels
Blood Ties, Love Binds
Unconditional Love
Exclusive inside look inside the novels